OUTCAST

KJ

2023

Cover: Em Schreiber

I wanted to write something different this time. Again. It seems to be a habit. My last book, The Forever and The Now, is beautifully weighty, so I thought I'd have a go at a light romantic fantasy. I haven't ever written a fantasy, so I wasn't aware of the rules. Apparently, one should world-build before writing the story. There should be a plan in place. Fantasy books have certain criteria. I was informed, at the fifty-thousand word mark, that fantasy books and pantser authors don't play well together. So, of course, I continued on my merry way, writing by the seat of my pants, world-building as I went along, Googling the criteria for fantasy novels two-thirds of the way through the manuscript, and generally writing how I normally write. It was chaotic and hectic and fun.

Because I'm me, I didn't make this story completely candy floss. There are some serious themes, such as refugees, caring for the environment, being cast out from your home and then finding one that fits.

However, the vessel that holds the story of Sev and Ori has a playful nature, so I hope you enjoy the fun banter, the scenes which might produce a chuckle, the words which I hope produce images in your mind, and the romance.

Outcast didn't just appear. There were indispensable people involved. People who have so many skills, and so much knowledge.

Such as my wife, Roanne, who is the best trampoline to bounce ideas off. So many times she was minding her own business on the couch when I'd plonk myself next to her, and ramble on with a thought I'd had about Ori or Sev or something to do with a major plot point. And she'd happily engage in the 'but what if', and 'hmm I'm not sure', and the 'yep that'd work.' She's the best alpha.

Such as Sarah V who knows a lot about Egypt, which is handy because I don't know anything. Those sections where Sev references Egypt and technology, and sounds fabulously intellectual? All Sarah. Thank goodness.

Such as Ange who built me a website using Internet magic and fairy dust. I have neither of those, but Ange does, and after many Zoom chats with screen sharing and conversations that went a lot like, "Ange, can I just do this thingy?" "No, KJ you can't", and "But what about this click bit, Ange?", "It'll blow up the site, KJ", and "I like purple, Ange, so can I—", "No." she made me shiny on the Internet.

Such as Em Schreiber who is a magical unicorn, and the creator of Outcast's exquisite cover. Em is also a language interpreter because early on I shared a folder with her that was filled with pictures of random sword-wielding women stomping about in realms, and followed it up with an email consisting of six dot points where I poorly explained the story. Em speaks KJ. I'm so grateful.

Such as Chloe, Conny, Laura, Jess, Heather, Sel, Cheyenne, Angela, Maggie, and Neen. Outcast was looked over, critiqued, and analysed by this amazing team of volunteer readers who understand that beta reading is not skimming through a book because it's free. Nope. Betas provide detailed feedback. They tell an author what works and what doesn't with detailed justifications. My beta team knows that I am every author; a fragile flower, so each beta reader in my team, without knowing what the other betas had written, waved pom poms while delivering coaching advice, then slapped me on the back with a, "Go get 'em", and sent me onto the field. Betas are priceless.

Such as Maggie who proofread Outcast. She is a miracle worker because I sent her a manuscript covered in comma confetti; a veritable Mardi Gras, then received a crisp, clean, tidy story because Maggie had hoovered around the sentence structure and found all the extraneous punctuation.

Such as the readers who have ever picked up one of my books. Thank you for trying out my writing style. It's unusual, and not for everyone, but you stayed for the entire story, and I'm eternally grateful.

Giord (Gee-ord)

Bianuwruh (Bee-an-a-roo)

Joskado Yol (Joss-car-do Yoll)

Irmirn Solduz (Er-mern Soll-duz)

Ralwi Solduz (Ral-wee Soll-duz)

Proneuth (Pro-nee-ooth)

ORI'S MAP

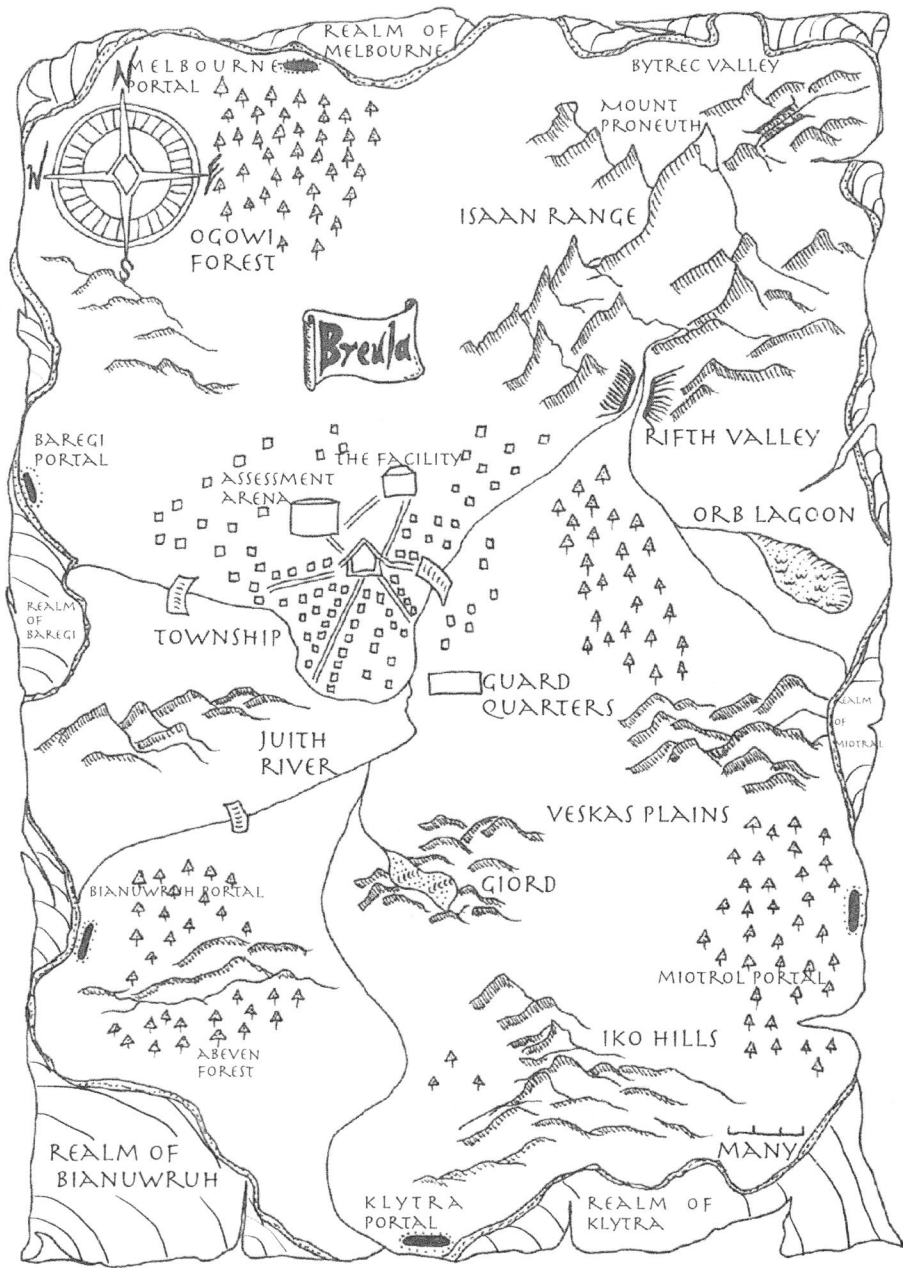

For anyone who has ever felt
Cast out
Dismissed
Excluded
A darkness that nibbles at your soul
A dimming of your light
Tugging at your threads
And you become a
Small
Person
But
Your spark
Fights, Follows, Finds
That place where the best of the small becomes the mighty of the
large
Because, because
Small, mighty elements in your soul
Which fight for, then follow, the light in your heart
Will find their way home

My Roanne
We found our mighty elements
We found our way home

Rhiannon Clarke is having a week. A week in which her identity is stolen, she is pursued by underworld thugs, then, at the back of a laundromat, she falls through a portal into another realm.

While making every effort to return to Melbourne, Rhiannon is renamed Sevich, must win a sword fight to gain her freedom, discovers she can manipulate elements, and falls for Orilaevar Reysandoral, the sexy warrior princess of Breula; the realm at the end of the spin cycle.

It's a lot.

As her feelings start to grow, Sev must decide if returning to Melbourne is really what she wants. Will her increasing elemental powers and relationship with Ori divide the realm, or will Sev stay to save Breula from a danger it has never encountered before?

A romantic realm-hopping story about finding your home when all the elements come together.

PS; One should always consult a map or two when entering a new realm.

Pronunciation Guide

Breula (Bree-oola)

Orilaevar Reysandoral (Oree-lay-var Ray-san-door-ral)

Sevich (Seh-vich)

Privana Trissandoral (Priv-arna Triss-an-door-al)

King Rodlamar Reytoris (Rod-la-mar Ray-tor-iss)

Queen Sermeh Reytoris (Sir-meh Ray-tor-iss)

Councillor Buwrec Robrong (Boo-reck Roe-brong)

Councillor Dasoskach Vaern (Dass-oss-catch Vay-ern)

Jino Kirmiz (Jee-no Ker-miz)

Askal Kirmiz (As-kal Ker-miz)

Tuarn (Too-arn)

Denjern Sohe (Den-jern So-heh)

Nusaed Taah (Noo-sayd Tar)

Likovu and Tonn Finjuk (Lee-koe-voo) (Tonn Fin-jook)

Ukih (yoo-key)

Kotrol (Cot-trol)

Juith (Joo-ith)

Sev's Map

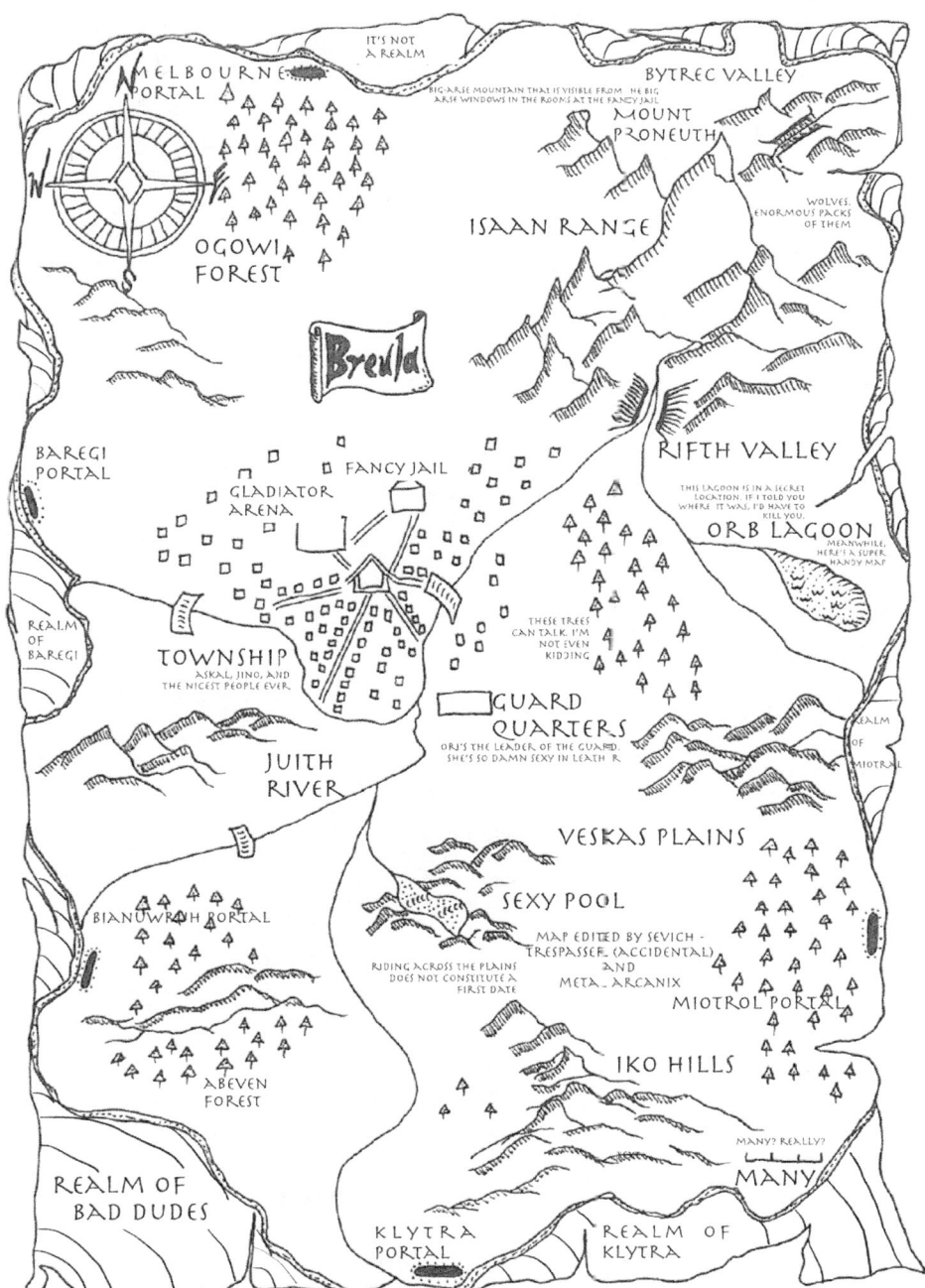

MELBOURNE PORTAL

IT'S NOT A REALM

BYTREC VALLEY

BIG-ARSE MOUNTAIN THAT IS VISIBLE FROM THE BIG ARSE WINDOWS IN THE ROOMS AT THE FANCY JAIL

MOUNT PRONEUTH

OGOWI FOREST

ISAAN RANGE

WOLVES. ENORMOUS PACKS OF THEM

Breula

BAREGI PORTAL

FANCY JAIL

GLADIATOR ARENA

RIFTH VALLEY

THIS LAGOON IS IN A SECRET LOCATION. IF I TOLD YOU WHERE IT WAS, I'D HAVE TO KILL YOU.

ORB LAGOON

MEANWHILE, HERE'S A SUPER HANDY MAP

REALM OF BAREGI

TOWNSHIP

ASKAL, JINO, AND THE NICEST PEOPLE EVER.

THESE TREES CAN TALK. I'M NOT EVEN KIDDING

REALM OF MIOTROL

GUARD QUARTERS

ORJ'S THE LEADER OF THE GUARD. SHE'S SO DAMN SEXY IN LEATHER

JUITH RIVER

VESKAS PLAINS

BIANUWRAH PORTAL

SEXY POOL

MAP EDITED BY SEVICH - TRESPASSER (ACCIDENTAL) AND META_ARCANIX

RIDING ACROSS THE PLAINS DOES NOT CONSTITUTE A FIRST DATE

MIOTROL PORTAL

IKO HILLS

ABEVEN FOREST

MANY? REALLY?

MANY

REALM OF BAD DUDES

KLYTRA PORTAL

REALM OF KLYTRA

Chapter One

"Two hundred? That's a bit steep!"

It was the sneer that did it.

"Look, mate," Rhiannon replied with the fake politeness reserved for certain customers. "I spent days sourcing the metal, then shaping and joining and welding each feather to create that." She waved her hand at her favourite ironwork in her market stall collection. "Sixty centimetre piece of art and if you add up my time and materials, then two hundred is probably under what I should be charging."

She ran her hand through her hair, knowing the choppy ends would have turned into echidna spikes, and sighed. Explaining to the cheapskate tyre-kicker why an artist's prices were justified when those cheapskates had no interest in hearing the explanation was always pointless. All it did was make her sad. And frustrated. And pissed off, which, at that moment, was an emotion she had to rein in because there were potential buyers hovering.

Launching into a tirade at the bloke in the rugby shirt and the denim pants that hung below his waist, where they cradled his genitals like a bag of potatoes, would not be great for her Saturday sales figures.

"Well, it's too much for me," the bloke huffed, and shuffled sideways in that manner people have at markets as if they were really interested in the next stall but after three steps disappear into the crowd flowing through the centre of the row.

Rhiannon clenched her teeth. It completely sucked that her love for her craft—the envisioning, the creating, the finished piece that wore its metal cloak with pride—didn't translate into dollars that would easily pay the studio's rent, pay for her equipment, or the petrol that her car drank as she trawled through junk yards and metal refuse bays searching for the bits and pieces that begged to be moulded into beauty. Dollars that would easily pay for her contribution to the flat with its threadbare carpet and cupboard doors in the kitchen that didn't quite line up with their frames.

Nope. Didn't pay enough at all.

Her flatmate, Alex, had brought up the only solution again just last week. He mentioned it at least once a month. Worded differently, but the same message.

"You could put your stuff in a gallery, you know. It's good enough, Rhi."

"I know it is."

It wasn't a boast. Her art truly was worthy of a gallery. The metal seemed to tingle under her fingertips as she worked and when each piece was finished, it warmed her palms as if it was telling her how pleased it was with what she had created.

"You know it's good but I know you won't, though," Alex sighed, his expression collecting his riotous black eyebrows, because he was resigned to Rhiannon's illogical thinking. He continued to spoon vegetarian lasagne onto their plates. Rhiannon loved it when it was Alex's turn to cook dinner, which was nearly every night, except when he was feeling sick and then they both had toasted cheese sandwiches. Her culinary skills only travelled so far.

"Yep," Rhiannon muttered defensively, scooping up her plate and walking to the table.

Alex, head tilted so his long black hair fell sideways, spoke around a mouthful. "Rhiannon Clarke! Galleries. Commissions."

Rhiannon grumbled. Using her full name meant that he'd reached the end of his patience for this section of the argument.

"You know why I don't do either of those things. I don't trust gallery owners or rich wankers who commission. They're all likely to rip people off. Either they take a huge cut or they don't pay."

"Yeah, yeah, but you only just make the rent on this place, and I know how much that studio costs." Alex threw Rhiannon a concerned look. He was always concerned.

Rhiannon continued working in the studio she rented in the artisan's workshops; her metal-smithing space next to a glassblower on her left and another metal craftsman on the right. Each studio was divided by solid brick walls purely for insulation from heat and noise.

Although Karen, the glassblower, was probably getting tired after six months of Rhiannon smacking her hammer against her favourite tool: the anvil. It was just so medieval and every time she heated metal, shaped it, moulded it, she felt as strong as the iron or steel that she bent to her will.

***

"Not that I actually bend it to my will,' Rhiannon muttered the following Sunday, rolling her eyes at the fanciful notion. She placed the final sword in the rack behind her, away from the people poking and prodding who could potentially test the sword's capabilities and that was a lot of paperwork. She attached the council permit to her table stating that she had every right to display and sell weapons that shouldn't be tested.

The buff blonde, her hair tied back in a ponytail, who sold candles in the stall across from hers looked up at the same moment as Rhiannon and smiled. And right on cue, Rhiannon's skin broke out in goosebumps. The one month crush she'd had on Tahlia was becoming ridiculous. Yes, Rhiannon had found out her name. Yes, she now knew how many millilitres of lavender oil a soy candle needed. But asking Tahlia out? Nope.

Maybe I could threaten her with a sword.

The whole crush business was inexplicable. Her heart had been broken the last time she'd had any sort of relationship. Diana, also blonde and buff, had ripped out that vital organ and stomped all over it when she'd unexpectedly left for a new life in Perth. Any sort of date with Tahlia was bound to result in another visit to the relationship accident and emergency department.

She stared at her ridiculous crush for another minute or so until a small voice brought her attention back.

"How much is the tiger, please?" A young girl, maybe ten, stared up with wide brown eyes, then dropped her gaze to the little silver tiger that crouched on the white cloth ready to pounce and take on all comers. "I have ten dollars and Mum said I could spend it on whatever I want."

Rhiannon tilted her head in the vague direction of the stream of weekend shoppers.

"Where's your mum, kiddo?"

The girl lifted her chin to the left.

"At the candle stall on the other side."

Understandable.

"The tiger is really pretty." A small finger pointed to the animal's head. "She's fierce."

"It's a she?" Rhiannon surreptitiously slid the sixty dollar price tag away from the tiger and tucked it into her pocket.

A quick nod.

Suddenly, there was a flurry of floral scarf, and perfume.

"Julia, sweetie, I didn't know where you were." The mother, her breath hitching in that manner of I'm-puffing-because-of-parental-terror, looked about the stall, taking in Rhiannon, silver animals, jewellery, large pieces of iron art. And swords. Her eyes widened, and she snaked her arm about her daughter's shoulders.

"Mum, I like the tiger." The girl's face wore a Labrador puppy expression.

The woman smiled tightly at Rhiannon, then leaned down. "You don't have enough money, sweetie."

"She does, though." Rhiannon said softly so only the girl and her mother could hear and not the hordes who'd suddenly be up for a bargain.

The mother blinked and Rhiannon nodded. "The tiger's ten dollars."

The girl wriggled out of her mother's embrace, dug into her pocket and pulled out a ten dollar note. She thrust it forward in triumph. "I've got ten dollars," she repeated.

"That's awesome. Would you like to buy it?" Rhiannon raised her eyebrows in question.

A serious nod followed, and the note was proudly presented, the tiger carefully wrapped in tissue paper, then placed into a small bag and passed over to Julia who clutched her purchase and beamed. Rhiannon looked up and found herself on the end of a long look from the mother.

"That's silver. Are you sure about the price?" A head tilt was added to the long look.

"Absolutely. I love it when my art goes to people who love it as well."

The smiles, wide and grateful, filled the faces of the mother and daughter as they backed away from the stall and disappeared into the crowd. A breath, filled with happiness, left her lungs.

"That was nice of you."

The compliment made Rhiannon turn. A man, tall, pear-shaped, clad in dress pants and a collared shirt tucked his hands into his pockets. His smile, half the wattage of Julia and her mum but no less genuine, reached his blue eyes. "My name's Chris Johnson. I have a storage unit full of metal pieces, iron, you name it, and seeing your work here, I know you're the right person to sell it to."

Rhiannon fizzed with happiness. A whole storage unit? That'd save her a month of trawling through junk yards, particularly if Chris's price was good.

"That'd be fantastic," she enthused, satisfied with her gut feeling that he seemed authentic. Her radar for fake hadn't pinged. "I won't be able to take all of it, though, because my storage is limited in my studio."

Chris shrugged, his hands coming out of the pockets with the movement.

"That's fine. Would you like to see what I've got?"

He pulled out his phone, tapped the screen, then placed it on the table. As he scrolled through photos of wonderful, contorted, rust-laden base metals like iron, corrugated sheeting, reinforcing rods, Rhiannon's imagination kicked into overdrive. Already she could see the finished products; the flattened iron curved into wall art, the spikes of iron twisted and folded together as they were forged into steel, the intricate animal pieces. So many possibilities, which filled her brain and pushed aside any potential cautionary warnings.

She looked up.

"Where is your storage unit located?"

"Northgate." Chris flicked the screen, closing the app.

Rhiannon calculated the distance, the haul of metal, and the general space in her hatchback. It'd be a couple of trips.

"That's doable. How much would you like and do you want a deposit or anything?" She tapped her fingers together as her radar gave a tiny ping. "And, if you don't mind, can I see your driver's license and your email or phone number?"

Chris smiled. "Of course. That's wise."

He slid the laminated license and a cardboard business card from the back of the phone, and passed them over. All aboveboard. Excellent. Rhiannon's gut feeling wasn't wrong after all so she ignored the ping. She delivered a sigh of relief and handed back the license, pocketing the business card.

"So, price? Deposit?"

"Well, I'm a huge fan of your work and I know you're here every weekend and Thursday nights, so how about fifteen-hundred for the lot and two-hundred deposit?" He scribbled the bank details on the back of another business card.

Rhiannon nodded slowly, calculating the price—cheap—the amount of metal she'd seen in the photos—extensive—and the deposit—small—then leaned over to pluck one of her business cards from the little stack she always had on hand for would-be customers.

"That's really good of you, Chris. I can send that through to you now," she said. Saving a massive amount of money on material for her craft was such a temptation. One that she took, as she reached into her pocket, and pulled out her phone, laying it flat on the table. Her fingers automatically tapped in the four digit passcode to the banking app even while an enormous metallic crash came from behind her. She whipped around, and took in the awful sight of her sword collection scattered on the ground.

"Jesus!"

Grabbing each by the blades—the bluntness another concession to the council's bylaws—she quickly fitted the swords into their individual runners. The weapons were difficult to dislodge so the person must have made a good effort.

Scowling, Rhiannon hefted the final blade and turned back to Chris, who was in the process of replacing his phone, looking for all the world as if he was about to leave.

"Sorry, Chris. Had to grab those straight away. They're too valuable to leave strewn about like matchsticks." She stared at the Celtic blade in her hand, lifted it, and twisted her wrist so the point gently impaled the cloth, like Excalibur appearing out of a dining table. Chris's eyes went round, and Rhiannon laughed.

"It's all good. It's blunt. Well, blunt-ish. But, this." She pointed to the tiny scratch on the intricate Celtic Shield knot she'd created on the pommel only last week. "Is why I jumped out of our conversation mid-sentence." She growled. "That's going to require some burnishing and time."

Chris nodded. "Sorry about that. People can be careless." He tsked, and a small smile, which could have been sympathetic, but seemed disingenuous compared with the others given earlier. *Strange.* "So, look. How about you text me with some times for next week and I'll let you know when I'm available?"

Rhiannon frowned. "But the deposit?"

"It's all good. Let's leave it until tomorrow, hey? I've got the info I need." He smiled toothily. "You'll want to come out and have a look at the stuff before you decide. Anyway, you've got your hands full. You never know." He chuckled. "Maybe I'll be buying some back off you as an amazing piece of wall art." He tapped the tabletop, then pointed at the sword. "Again, sorry. Talk to you later, Rhiannon."

Chris melted into the crowd and Rhiannon blinked. That was a weird but awesome interaction. Glancing down, she realised her phone was still face up on the table, the black screen hopefully hiding the details of her account and other important information. Thank God no-one saw her enter her passcode.

"Dipshit," she muttered, annoyed at her lapse in security. She laid the sword down, swiped the screen and sure enough, the app was still open. It frustrated her how her bank set their automatic log out time at what felt like seven-hundred hours.

God, she hated technology. It was why she loved the rawness of her craft. Technology breathed through it but in the original sense, as in technology was the art of problem-solving to create beauty.

Just like the Ancient Egyptians. People dismissed that civilisation as primitive. Hardly. They were the most advanced society to have ever existed. Shoving the phone into her pocket, she quickly replaced the blade and slapped a smile on her face for the customers winding their way home on a late Sunday afternoon.

***

"What pieces did you sell today?" Alex peered over his water glass. He needed to know at the end of each market day because he said it nourished his inner artist which was being stifled by the felt walls of his booth at the call centre.

Rhiannon smiled. "The emu and the big twisted leaf garden art and the little silver crouching tiger."

Alex beamed

"Oh! They're all so beautiful, but I love that tiger. It looked alive. It's almost as if you moulded that metal like it was clay. I adore your ability with that element." Then his eyes widened and he blinked rapidly. "Uh…uh." He coughed. "Bit of broccoli," he rasped and thumped his chest.

Rhiannon stared at him. It was another moment in quite a few moments lately where he looked like he'd freaked himself out as if he'd said something he shouldn't have. After a beat, she shrugged, then gulped down a half-chewed carrot.

"And I scored a storage shed full of scrap metal for fifteen hundred." Rhiannon pointed her fork as cutlery punctuation.

"Seriously? That's amazing?"

"Yep. Chris, um." She reached around and dug into her backpack which was hanging heavily on the back of the chair. "Johnson," she finished, dropping the business card on the table. "He's a collector and needs to unload some of his metal so he sought me out. Reckons I'm the real deal which is nice, and wanted to sell to me specifically."

"That's fantastic." Alex lifted his water glass in a toast, and drank heavily.

"I know. I couldn't believe it actually. Thought it too good to be true and you know how I'm overly suspicious." She glared at Alex's attempt at hiding his smile. "But he seemed pretty honest, I guess. I checked his license."

Alex raised an eyebrow. "After all these years, I still find your need to distrust people, and then your peculiarity to go ahead and trust those same people a complete paradox."

Rhiannon waved him away with another piece of carrot speared by the fork.

"I had a sword spill, though. There's a tiny mark on the pommel of the cloidem which sucks." Alex hissed in sympathy. "I didn't see who did it. Probably a teenager wanting to reenact a scene from *Outlander*."

***

It was early evening on Monday when Rhiannon shook off her heavy gloves and slapped them onto the workbench, shaking her arms a little to relieve the tightness. The hand she wiped across her brow would leave a black smudge. It always did.

She took a moment to gaze proudly about her creative space; the blackened tools, the heat from the furnace, the soldering irons, the welding gear, and the tiny curls of metal from the grinding and drilling machines.

Getting caught up in work was a common occurrence so when Rhiannon turned the key to the flat and breathed deeply, she smiled at the thought of her productive day. Two beautiful half-finished pieces of wall art and a couple of silver animals to add to her stock. One of the pieces, a carefully polished mouse, had practically wriggled in her hand as if it were excited to investigate the back of the small bar fridge in the workshop where all the scraps of food lived.

The sense that the metal in her hands felt alive was happening more and more lately. It was a completely fanciful notion and

Rhiannon put it down to the fact that she was simply thrilled every time it hit her that she was doing what she loved even if it didn't pay much.

She shrugged off her backpack, letting the straps slide down her arms so the heavy bag rolled onto the couch. Carrying around some of her gear seemed ludicrous but it saved having to replace it if it was stolen. The two cobalt drill sets at a hundred dollars each, two hand flat files at two hundred each, and a cold chisel at another hundred meant that she was lugging around seven hundred dollars each day.

Which was fine because she wasn't leaving it in the studio. Everything else was either bolted to the floor, locked away in cabinets that were also bolted to the floor, or too bloody heavy to lift and knick off with in a hurry.

After a decent shower to scrub off the day's grime, Rhiannon wandered into the kitchen to hunt-and-gather dinner. Alex was out on a date, which she knew both thrilled him and made him want to vomit with nerves.

"Rhi, I have the body of a melted candle," he'd said the previous day. "The most exercise I get is staring aggressively at my daily call list. How does this woman want to go out with me?" He whipped out his phone. "I'm texting her to cancel."

"Alex, you're a catch. You're funny, and sensitive, and you pay attention to people. You're a beacon of warmth. People are attracted to you, so any man or woman would be lucky to go out with you." Rhiannon took his phone and held it out of reach. She was taller than him; handy for blackmail and the top cupboards in the kitchen. "Promise me you won't back out."

Alex glared. "Fine. I won't back out. I'll back in, like Sia, so my date won't see my face and decide to run."

So, tonight's dinner was two minute noodles, which was healthy because of the little packet of dried vegetables. Suddenly, mid-stir, Rhiannon remembered the deposit to Chris.

"Oh, gees. He's probably wondering what the hell happened."

Twisting the fork in the noodles to stop it from falling out of the bowl, she walked over to her backpack and pulled out the phone from the little zippered compartment. Opening the banking app, she tapped in her passcode and waited the half-second until her banking details shimmered into view.

And blinked.

"What the hell?"

Instead of the little bit of day-to-day money and the in-case-of-emergencies five-thousand dollars, there was a large zero. Rhiannon tapped back and forth, hoping that the number was an error. But the amount didn't change. There was nothing in the account and a sharp drop on the expenditure graph showed that the money had been removed Sunday night.

Rhiannon's hands began to shake.

"Oh God. What's happened?"

That money was her fall back. Her just-in-case. Like just in case a metal shard buried itself in her arm. Like just in case the anvil fell over and crushed her foot. Like just in—

"Okay. Okay. Right. God. Okay." Rhiannon paced. Three steps, then spun back, clutching her phone to her chest. Then she stopped, logged in to the account again, hoping to confirm that the absence of funds had been a mistake.

"Oh, shit. Come on." The zero seemed to be enlarging every time she looked at it. She skipped a screen and found the bank's twenty-four hour number.

"Right. Okay." Putting the phone on speaker, Rhiannon restarted her pacing, pausing to sit on the couch before leaping up and circuiting the room. The bank's automated system required pressing numbers after each prompt but eventually Rhiannon was waiting in the correct queue for account issues. She paced and waited and paced and finally put the phone on the kitchen bench. Then attempted to eat her starch and preservatives in a cup. The food barely touched her lips before she was dropping it back into the container.

"Come on. Come on," she whispered, staring intently at the phone as if willing someone to answer it. A feeling of dread settled in her stomach.

"Your call has timed out. Thank you for calling East Melbourne Bank. Your local bank where we care for our community."

"No. No, no, no." Rhiannon clutched the phone and redialed the number, domino-ing through the prompts, and tried again. Tears welled in her eyes. How could a bank, even a little bank like East Melbourne, lose money? Who loses money? Where did it go? Was there an electronic holding bay where lost money waited before it was collected by its rightful owner? Again, technology racing ahead of the people inventing it.

She could feel her panic attack rising like a tsunami.

"Your call has timed out. Thank you for calling East Melbourne Bank. Your local bank—"

Rhiannon stabbed at the end call button, redialled, skimmed through the numbers, and tried again. And again. And again. And eventually gave up after two hours, resigned to the fact that her bank didn't really have a twenty-four hour hotline at all.

Tossing her dinner in the bin, she logged on to Alex's computer, thankful for his generosity with sharing the device, and found the bank's website. A quick search found an online form for customer issues.

"Okay. Well, yes. This is an issue. A huge issue." She typed as her muttering sped up. "This is an issue. A five thousand dollar issue. A big issue, okay? Huge. Just…"

Pressing the send button, she sat back in the chair, spun the ring encircling her thumb—a present to herself last year—and stared at the wall above the screen for ages. Eventually, a sense of detachment settled in her mind. There was nothing else to do tonight. She'd deal with the all that money currently running free in the financial pastures tomorrow.

***

It was a fitful sleep. More a horizontal resting of eyelids, but it provided enough energy for Rhiannon to be first in line at the bank, practically sprinting towards the teller behind the glass.

"Yes, I know you're a small local bank with hardly any branches and that's why I chose you but surely you can find out what happened?"

Rhiannon's hands grasped the wood and vinyl ledge on her side of the partition, as she rocked side to side in time with the anxiety beating in her heart.

"I see you've lodged an online form." Pauline, the name badge announced, was much too calm as far as Rhiannon was concerned. She should be running around in circles with her arms flailing in the air.

"Yes. Last night. When I found that zero in my account. The zero that you're seeing on your screen right now." Panic was bubbling.

"May I see your license, please?"

Thankful that she drove a car, Rhiannon passed the laminated rectangle through the little gap.

"You're the account holder."

Rhiannon resisted the urge to liquify herself, pour into Pauline's cubicle and strangle her. Of course she was the bloody account holder.

"Yes."

Pauline looked confused. "We phoned you this morning, just before opening, as we do for all account holders when a large sum of money is withdrawn. You confirmed that you'd withdrawn the amount indicated."

Rhiannon inhaled too quickly. "But I didn't. You didn't. I…" More quick breathing. "Can I get it back?"

"But you have possession of the funds. I don't—"

"But I don't!" Rhiannon could literally feel the weight of the gazes from the people she'd out-sprinted to win the Panicked Bank Customer Olympics.

"Well, I can open a case for you to investigate the transfer of the money, if you like." Pauline looked askance at Rhiannon. Clearly Pauline believed that Rhiannon had hidden the money but forgotten she'd done so, then the dozen cats she owned, like some weird cat lady, had pulled the rug over the loose floorbcards to hide it because the cats belonged to the cat mafia and her five thousand was hush money. She pinched the skin between her eyebrows.

"Yes. Please do that."

Pauline tapped some keys and frowned at the screen. "The investigation may take up to forty-eight hours, particularly as it shows that you are currently in possession of the funds."

Rhiannon clenched her fists under the counter. "Oh my God. Okay. Fine."

Pauline squinted at the screen, tapped more keys, the printer beside her whirred, and a pre-filled-in form was squeezed through the portal. She pointed to the signature line, still looking at Rhiannon like she'd lost her mind.

After shoving the paperwork back through, a thought occurred to Rhiannon. "Can you tell me why the money was withdrawn? Like, is there a—did I give a reference or a description or something?" It felt so bizarre to ask about something she'd done but not done.

Pauline beamed. This was obviously a question that seemed logical. "Yes, of course. It's a compulsory section on the form. You said you were changing banks." She nodded encouragingly. "Which bank did you decide to go with?"

Rhiannon's heart sank. "I didn't. I don't know." She felt like Jason Bourne withdrawing money from a Swiss account and any moment a crack team of commandos would come flying through the window. "Can I block my account?"

Pauline's face reverted to wide-eyed confusion. "You want to block your own account?"

"Yeah. I mean, there's nothing in it. Or maybe I could close it? Can I set up a new one?" Oh God, she'd have to change every direct debit. This was beyond imaginable.

With her new account in hand, also containing the princely sum of zero dollars, Rhiannon wandered out of the bank into the bright sunlight where thousands of people were going about their business.

"This is truly awful," she said, and a passing teenager nodded wisely.

***

Realising that working on her art would solve two problems; making money and taking her mind off awful things, Rhiannon continued crafting the large Crusades sword which would become the centrepiece of her stall in a few weeks.

Her mind tickled at her heart as she realised that she couldn't tell Alex what had happened, despite Alex being her greatest confidante. He already carried the majority of the financial load in the household. If he found out that the bank had lost her money for however long it decided to lose it, he would be incredibly disappointed, and disappointing Alex was just too much to contemplate. Even if it wasn't her fault. She'd just have to work harder on her pieces and maybe, just maybe, accept a commission or two. Even if there was a risk of a customer shirking on their payment. And meanwhile the bank would find her money.

No, she couldn't tell Alex. She'd work it out then tell him when the whole thing was sorted, and then they'd share a drink and laugh as if the entire episode was a sitcom. Or a movie. And in the past.

So, Tuesday rolled into Wednesday which rolled into Thursday with no word from the bank. Finally, late Thursday afternoon, she hauled out the last of her pieces from the back of her car, which she'd backed up to its spot behind her stall.

"All good sales. All good sales," she intoned.

And there were, luckily. Some of the larger pieces. A lot of the small figurines and three of the swords. It was probably one of the best Thursday market evenings she'd had for a very long time. Finally, the last few customers made their way back to the carpark and Rhiannon began to return her small animals into their individual slots in the carry case.

Suddenly, a strong hand wrapped itself around her wrist, and her head shot up. A face created by angles and a pair of ice blue eyes stared through her, then after a quick glance to her right, she found another man, standing with his back to the table as if looking for customers to subtly frighten away. She jerked her hand, wriggling her entire arm to escape his hold. Yet despite strength honed from years of wielding heavy tools, she couldn't pull away. The man leaned closer, his sour breath washing over her face, and she leaned back, but not far because her hand was secured to the table top by his flesh handcuff.

"Don't pull, girly. You'll only make life hard for yourself. You need those fingers for your art here, don't you?" The menace in the whisper sent shivers down her spine. "You'll get the money to us by tomorrow afternoon, you hear? You don't want to visit Madison out of hours, do you?"

The abundance of rhetorical questions was staggering. The pain in her wrist, the white noise of fear, the incomprehensible words that the man was saying filled her mind.

"Wh-what's the Madison?" Rhiannon asked shakily. She wasn't very good with scary blokes who whispered menacingly.

The man tightened his grip. "You being smart, hey? Fine. I'll humour you. Madison the person. The Madison who runs the poker comp in the city. The Madison who you owe five K to because she gave you that marker on Sunday night. The Madison who expects her loan paid tomorrow. Got it, Rhiannon? Tomorrow. Otherwise you might not be around any more, right? Just a blip on the radar, okay? And no one would know." The threat hung in the air.

"But I—ow," she hissed as the man dug his thumb into a particularly sensitive area of her wrist. Her forearm felt like it was on fire. It felt like her eyeballs were shaking.

"Before midday, then it's all good, right? Everybody's friends again." He released his hold and Rhiannon felt the blood flow into her fingers. Her arm hung limply even if the rest of her was rigid with terror. The man straightened to his full height of much-taller-than-should-be-allowed, and maintained eye-contact until Rhiannon blinked, which he took for acquiescence, then he nodded and ambled away, his buddy following close behind.

Rhiannon massaged her wrist and looked around. Surely someone saw that. The men. The whispered menacing conversation. The possibility of her death. But no. Most of the stalls had packed up for the night and the remaining stall holders were down the other end of her row. Her hands shook.

"Oh, god. Shit shitting shit. What the hell?"

Apparently, a person had withdrawn her money and used it to play poker in an illegal establishment run by a person named Madison who employed tall, scary men to frighten the life out of people whose identity had been stolen.

Because that's what had clearly happened.

"Oh, Jesus."

Suddenly, all the art work was too heavy to carry, but she heaved, paused, and cried a little, and manoeuvred, paused, and cried a little more, then got behind the wheel, and drove to her studio while watching for cars travelling too close with their headlights on in I'm-stalking-you mode.

Then heaved and manoeuvred and cried a little more and drove home watching for insistent glue-like vehicles, then hid from Alex in her room. Because this was something else Rhiannon couldn't tell Alex. He'd try to protect her like he always did whenever he thought something was threatening her. But he'd be in danger as well. She needed to solve this herself. Somehow.

Then, like a bomb going off in her mind, she realised that this was something she couldn't tell the police either. She ran the potential conversation through her mind.

"Yes, I'd like to report identity theft."

"Whose identity?

"Mine, you dipshit—officer."

"How do you know your identity has been stolen?"

"Well, I—a person, stole money from me and played poker illegally and now I—they owe money to a person called Madison."

"Who is Madison?"

"Now that is the question of the hour, Officer Dipshit."

She rocked back and forth on the bed, then grabbed her phone and looked up illegal gambling and Madison in a combined search. Nothing. Of course.

"How do I pay this person even if I did have the money?" she mumbled.

It was insane. Again, the *Bourne Identity* whipped through her mind and while being the wrong gender, with not nearly as neat hair, and not as many muscles or fluency in fourteen languages, she felt like the main character in that film. Which kind of sucked. She preferred to watch movies, not star in them.

After another night of horizontal eyelid resting, and delaying her breakfast to ensure that Alex had left for work, Rhiannon grabbed her backpack with its little collection of expensive tools and stared at the couch as if it held the answers she needed.

"I'll do it. Police. Right. It'll be fine. I'll be fine. No, I won't. The police suck. They won't take me seriously because I'm a flaky artist who sells at a flaky market and has a flaky story. God, I'm basically puff-pastry. Jesus." She grit her teeth, then finally shrugged on the bag, locked the front door, and trudged down the steps. The police station was only two kilometres away so no need to waste petrol and money for a parking meter. If she had the money, anyway.

Turning her head to check for traffic, Rhiannon crossed the street, noticing a small white van crawling along about a hundred metres away. Dismissing it as simply a courier looking for the correct address, she ducked into a side street to shorten the distance to the police station, and hustled along the footpath.

It was a handy short cut as it travelled straight to the main road, and it wasn't busy despite the various small businesses dotted along its length. Kebab shop. Alterations. Corner store despite the lack of corners. It was fairly quiet, which meant that Rhiannon heard the vehicle's engine before it was close. She whipped her head around, and spotted the same white van.

"Oh, shit."

She knew, without a shadow of a doubt, that the driver and the passenger were her visitors from last night. Tailing her was going to achieve…what? Scare her into paying the five thousand dollars that she hadn't borrowed and didn't possess? The scaring part was working. Were they going to kidnap her and do God knows what so she would eventually pay up the non-existent money?

"I'm in a movie. This is can't be real. Christ!" Her backpack jostled as she picked up speed, power-walking to reach the main street more quickly. Surely she'd be able to get to the police station before anything awful happened.

She snuck a look over her shoulder and saw the horrifying sight of the second man leaping from the van and hurrying towards her.

"Shit. Shit."

Rhiannon ran.

Pumping her legs, backpack smacking heavily against her, she figured she could throw off the guy with a back door escape through one of the nearby shops, which seemed very apt considering this was a movie. The director would be yelling "cut" any time soon.

The laundromat, suddenly upon her, was convenient and seemed like a perfect place to outwit a maniac bad guy sent by an underground crime boss to kidnap and disappear her into the darkness of Melbourne.

Rhiannon veered left, bashed open the door, the little bell jangling violently from the top of the frame, then barrelled though the middle of the line of washing machines and dryers, her sneakers squeaking on the lino as she dodged the swinging machine doors and baskets, while ignoring the owner's yell, and crashed through a back door that was covered in signage advertising slippery surfaces and chemicals.

Only to land, knees first, on lush grass worthy of a golf course. Even though her brain registered the strangeness of a small business back entrance being covered in well-maintained turf, she knew the most pressing problem was the pair of very angry men chasing her. She spun on her knees to catch the door in its final stages of closing, the stunned expressions on the men's faces gradually narrowing until the door snapped shut and disappeared. The vision was replaced by trees and even more lush grass.

Her sigh of relief didn't make it out of her throat because a second worry bubbled to the surface.

A soft cough, loud in the stillness, shimmered in the air. Rhiannon turned slowly, standing with the movement, and found herself face to face with a group of men and women, clad in leather—which would have been sexy but clearly not right now—astride horses. Rhiannon assumed the warrior—the sword gave it away—at the centre of the group was the one with early onset laryngitis, and she blinked as she took in the very detailed cos play. Except they weren't costumes. Somehow she knew that.

"Well, crap."

"You are a Trespasser," the sword-wearing, horse-riding, obviously-not-from-Melbourne warrior woman declared.

"A what?"

"You have illegally entered the realm of Breula."

Rhiannon stared in incomprehension.

Then the arrow struck and everything went black.

CHAPTER TWO

Orilaevar gazed moodily at her water glass. The afternoon's Council meeting was dragging on as each Councillor made a case for their policy to be adopted and made into law by her father.

"I speak for the entire Council when I say that the uniforms of the Guard require updating, particularly the armbands. The design is outdated."

Orilaevar lifted her head and stared in disbelief at the tall, angular man standing in front of his seat across from her in the large room. The uniform design? Again? This was Councillor Buwrec Robrong Breula's urgent matter? He'd brought it up last meeting. It was puerile and wasted Council time; time that could be spent on more important matters such as the recent increase in trespassers, maintaining the balance in the realm, or the stone repairs on the Facility, or the ongoing creation of the Elemental orbs, or the amount of salt at breakfast.

She returned to glaring at the water glass and shook her head. Orilaevar hadn't really taken to Councillor Buwrec Robrong Breula when first introduced at the welcoming ceremony for the new candidates. He gave the impression of a person with hidden agendas. As if he'd present an idea, then tack on an addendum, then another, then a rewording until you became so overwhelmed that you'd agree to the original idea out of sheer discombobulation. It was an excellent strategy for getting his way and unfortunately perfectly within the rules of the Council meetings.

He'd done it last month when he'd prattled on about invading Guards and hundreds of portals randomly manifesting at each corner of the realm. There had been many confused expressions on the faces of the other Council members. Then, moving on from the portals and marauding Guards, he'd suggested that the Guard uniform was last year's fashion, and the Councillors had promptly forgotten the first item he'd mentioned.

If only her father, King Rodlamar Reytoris Breula, could see past the facade of sycophants. She'd mentioned it many times and while he agreed somewhat with her opinion, he generally fobbed off her worry with misplaced trust in the process. The Councillors were her father's advisors and he valued their thoughts and opinions. He trusted tradition.

Orilaevar grumbled softly and played with the yellow orb sitting in the hollow at the base of her throat. She had an interest in the unlikely possibility of an invasion, seeing as it affected the whole of the realm, but she had absolutely no interest in the Council mucking about with the uniform of the Guard, *her* Guard. It was fine as it was and she'd only been saying so to her mother that morning.

***

"The leather we have chosen this year is more sturdy." She dipped her shoulder so that her mother could rub her fingertips across the fabric.

"Yes, it is wearing well." Then her mother stepped back, took in the leather riding pants and leather jerkin with the white short-sleeved shirt—tight over her biceps—peeking out from underneath. She tilted her head quizzically. "Why are you in uniform, Orilaevar? I thought you were on leave today."

"I have a Council meeting this afternoon, and I cannot get away with a more casual look anymore. Father suggested that my Guard riding pants are more appropriate for the occasion."

Her mother gave a small laugh. "He does get these fanciful ideas in his head," she stated affectionately, and sat on the small velvet two-seater couch in the lounge area of her quarters. Her simple loose pants and shirt settled elegantly on her body.

The love inside her mother's gentle admonishment of her father was strong despite her parents living in seperate quarters. They were each other's best friends, frequently attending events together, holding hands, embracing, but had long ago realised that a more intimate relationship was not something that interested either of them. Orilaevar didn't question further. No child really wanted *all* the details of their parent's sex life.

Queen Sermeh Reytoris Breula did not attend the Council meetings. Not because she wasn't allowed to. She simply chose not to as politics was of little interest to her. Orilaevar's mother had decided last year that the meetings were full of obsequious buffoons, and so she was perfectly happy for them to cast their arguments about the room, and let the words echo off the walls without her. Instead, she created blankets and quilts for the Arcanix in the villages, infusing her Heat element into each creation so that the recipient would be warm for the entirety of the winter. Social programs for the freed trespassers—the Arcanix—were the Queen's first love.

Orilaevar went to sit and heard the quiet 'tut'.

"Sword," her mother said evenly.

Orilaevar sighed, but nodded. Her mother wasn't overly fond of sword indentations in the furniture. She drew the weapon and laid it across her lap as she sat on the red velvet chair.

"It is getting cooler in the day, Mother. I imagine you have a lot of stock to deliver. Should I assign more of the Guard to assist?"

Her mother thought for a moment. "Yes, I think you should, darling. There has been an increase in Arcanix this year, so we have made quite a lot." She frowned, then smiled broadly. "And my assistants and I created small hats for the children." Orilaevar returned the smile, tracing the yellow gem in the hilt of her sword. Her mother had a veritable army of staff who could create the gifts, leaving her to infuse her Elemental energy as the only task, but she had always been a woman who believed in participating in her own initiatives and not simply delegating to others.

"All right. Well, let me know the amount before your delivery day."

"Yes, good." Her mother folded her hands into her lap. "Now, tell me about your own gossip."

Orilaevar sighed. "You saw me two days ago. I had no gossip then and it has not accumulated in the last forty-eight hours."

"So, a beautiful woman has not become smitten with your charms," her mother said innocently.

"Mother."

"I am teasing. I simply want you to be happy, darling. I was married and about to give birth at your age, which I know is irrelevant, but I was hoping you would have found someone special by now."

"I am not looking for anyone. I am thirty, Mother, which is still young, so there is no need to find a woman to wife up."

"Wife up?" Her mother's blue eyes sparkled with barely suppressed laughter.

Orilaevar waved her hand dismissively, knowing that her own blue eyes wouldn't be as sparkly but, even still, she held a small smile on her lips. "Besides, I am much too busy with the Guard to —"

"Oh, you are not. Darling, you are far too serious and you refuse to give yourself time to enjoy leisure. To enjoy frivolities. A striking young woman like yourself should play. Relax."

Orilaevar frowned. "I relax."

Her mother sat back, raising an eyebrow in a quick gesture of disbelief. Her hand drifted to the red orb at her throat; an unconscious movement that most Elementals made in response to anything from a small worry to cataclysmic disaster. Not that Breula had any experience with the latter thank goodness.

But her mother was clearly worried for her, even though Orilaevar had tried to explain that there hadn't been anyone who might stimulate her intellect, fire up her libido, make her laugh, make her want to protect, give and take with honesty and passion, challenge her, make her feel like she could be the best version of herself, and was her equal.

It came as no surprise that because she hadn't been looking, she was hardly going to find someone who met that criteria. They'd have to fall out of the sky and land in her lap, which was about as likely as her father granting free passage to every trespasser who arrived in Breula.

***

While she waited for her imaginary wife to arrive, she occupied her days organising the Guard to protect the realm, checking on the status of portals, maintaining borders, escorting trespassers to the Facility. And attending pointless Council meetings. She thought about rolling her eyes but she'd run out of rolls. There were only so many inside a person's head.

Her father must have heard the grumble because he leaned sideways to balance his elbow on the armrest of Orilaevar's chair.

"Orilaevar, please attend to the proceedings. Each item is of equal importance."

She turned her head to catch the look of disappointment drift across his light blue eyes and over the small wrinkles on his face. Even his black and silver beard exuded displeasure.

"The Guard uniform is hardly of equal importance to the recent influx of trespassers," she murmured. "Surely the Council could be debating my suggestion about increasing patrols."

He held her gaze. "Your suggestion is next on the agenda and also of equal importance."

Orilaevar repressed another head shake. She'd sprain her neck if she kept that up.

"Yes, Father."

True to his word, as soon as Councillor Buwrec Robrong Breula finished his speech and had reclaimed his seat on the other side of the room, her father rose.

"Orilaevar Reysandoral Breula will bring forth her agenda item."

Orilaevar breathed deeply, stood, adjusted her belt and scabbard, then marched down two steps, and across the marble floor to the centre of the large room. Despite their hardened soles, her boots made no noise, and she turned slowly, executing a full circle so that all fifty of the Councillors were aware of her presence. Her nearly six-foot-tall royal presence, with her long blonde hair cascading down her back, gold band about her forehead, and her arms crossed which she knew made her chest seem even broader.

Orilaevar wasn't averse to making a point.

"The number of trespassers has increased in the last month, and the patrols are not able to keep up. I would like the Council to agree to my proposal to deploy some of the Guard from the palace to form groups at the boundary to monitor these anomalies." It irritated her no end that she needed to appeal to the Council for something that she should be able to enact herself. Just another issue she had raised many times with her father, and another time when his reply was to trust in tradition.

"That seems excessive, Orilaevar Reysandoral Breula. Perhaps the Guard are simply not fast enough." The high-pitched voice, unctuous and condescending, came from behind her, and she turned.

Councillor Dasoskach Vaern Breula smiled, the gesture stopping at her lips, which she covered with two fingers as if caught sharing a secret. Again, Orilaevar growled very softly. The woman was a menace. Another Breulan who harboured ideas that weren't in the realm's best interests and Orilaevar was yet to discover her motivation. Another Breulan who had the luxury of becoming a Councillor through birth rather than by some sort of assessment process.

"They are fast enough, Councillor Dasoskach Vaern Breula. Thank you for your concern." She narrowed her eyes. "But we have more and more trespassers gaining entry into Breula in the hope of freedom and accessing permanent elemental strengths. It will place a strain on our resources." She thought of her mother, lovingly creating items for the trespassers who became Arcanix, and wondered how she would keep up with the population growth.

"Oh, there are only one or two extra. Hardly an explosion from the regular ten per month. I am sure we can make that judgement after we have toured the realm to inspect the gateways."

"That will take much too long!" She threw her arms out in frustration, then quickly regained her composure. It wouldn't do to lose control of herself, and create an unfortunate halo of Light around her body. Having control of an element was of utmost importance.

"Orilaevar." Her father's deep voice filled the space. "We will vote on this after we have conducted the tour. The decision will be made at next month's meeting."

"But—" The single word conveyed so much.

"I would like to move on."

She stared at her father seated in the high-backed wooden chair, his own glass of water centred on the armrest table to his right, and clenched her jaw. She loved him dearly but constantly wondered why he entertained a Council with so many members; members who were about to count portals and vacillate about the decision with too much rhetoric. Halving the number of Councillors would be a start—it was true that the more people involved in anything, the fewer decisions were made.

It was a point that she actually agreed upon with Councillors Dasoskach Vaern Breula and Buwrec Robrong Breula. Annoyingly. They'd put forward the idea of reducing the Council by half, suggesting that there should be a hierarchy, a ranking, so that any idea could easily and smoothly become law with only a few to vote upon it. They'd put themselves forward as candidates should the law be enacted.

Orilaevar didn't agree with all of the details because those two particular Councillors shouldn't have that much control over decisions that affected the people. But the idea had merit.

However, even expressing her thoughts about why her father couldn't simply pass laws himself was met with the same answer each time; upholding tradition was the most significant Breulan custom. Orilaevar was beginning to find that answer repetitive. And wearing thin.

***

After another drawn-out, unsatisfying two hours, Orilaevar marched through the double doors into the enormous Great Hall. A Guard member fell into step beside her, matching her long strides.

"Thought-provoking?"

Orilaevar stopped abruptly, and turned to Privana Trissandoral Breula. Her friend was clothed in an identical uniform apart from the single intricate armband representing his role as Deputy of the Guard.

"Privana. If I was not required to attend those things and if I was not so invested in the protection of the people, then I would build a hut in the Bytrec Valley and grow corn."

"Interesting choice."

Orilaevar allowed a wry smile to settle on her lips, which Privana mirrored, his white teeth flashing against his tanned skin. They'd been friends since childhood and so Privana's teasing was comfortable and familiar. Her friend folded his arms, relaxing his lean body into a stance that indicated that a long chat was imminent.

"I have some news about the latest group of trespassers."

"It needs to be good news."

"It is interesting news."

"Oh?" Orilaevar lifted her eyebrows.

"Mm. There are three trespassers from Baregi, all claiming banishment from their realm."

"Okay?" This was not news at all. There were always one or two trespassers a month from Baregi, all claiming banishment.

"We have two trespassers from the east." Orilaevar pursed her lips in response to this, and Privana nodded. "And one very unusual trespasser from the northern portal."

She blinked. "The northern portal?"

"Yes."

"That has not opened in decades."

"It is interesting." Privana said.

"Very."

"She claims to be lost and that crossing the gateway was an accident."

"That is a new one," Orilaevar said.

"Quite." Privana hummed. "The Guard members say that she is quite the individual. If you have nothing further to do today, perhaps we can go to the Facility and observe her."

Orilaevar glared. "Privana, trespassers are people. They are not oddities to stare at. It is disrespectful."

Her friend looked suitably contrite. "Yes. Sorry. Then how about we say hello? Have a conversation. Find out what they mean when they say she is an *interesting individual*."

"Fine. A conversation it is. Although," she gave her friend a long look and pointed, "you know I do not like to get attached to anyone in case they are unsuccessful in their application."

"Then do not get attached."

Chapter Three

"None of this is real."

It was probably the thirtieth time that she'd said it but repeating the sentence felt necessary. Because this whole situation was—

"Beyond normal. That's it. It's not normal." Rhiannon paced about her room. A room she'd woken up in this morning after however many hours of unconsciousness but at least not dead in a foreign land or realm or whatever the woman with the sword had said and it had been a really nice sword from what she'd seen of it and—

"Jesus! Okay. Okay. Stop." She paused, breathed deeply, interlaced her fingers, and stretched her arms, then dropped them to shake out her hands. Another scan of the room. Bed. Walls. A sort of lumpy fibrous carpet. Ensuite with an odd burnished metal receptacle that looked too fancy to take a crap in but was clearly a toilet. There was no flush button but her waste had been magicked away by the time she looked back. Then there was a bidet-type cylinder next to the toilet.

"How very French."

A sort of shower with what looked like a lamp fitted into the ceiling that delivered beautifully hot water after she'd mucked about with the metal lever on the wall. Despite the fact that she'd have to put her day-old sweaty clothes back on, she'd luxuriated in the water, squeezing her toes onto the small river stones layered on the base. The towel was made of a similar rough material as the carpet and was annoyingly invigorating. *Nothing about this place should be invigorating, beautiful, or luxurious.*

The entire space and its fixtures reminded Rhiannon of a nice room in a nice hotel that catered to business consultants.

Except this place didn't have a television or a folder listing nearby tourist attractions.

"Just a big-arse window." Which was where her pacing had led. The view of the open fields with a distant mountain was exquisite.

The marbled pink and white sky, which was again beyond normal, created a riveting panorama. For a second she lost herself in its beauty before more events came crashing back into her mind. Like this morning when the man had shaken her shoulder.

"Wake up, please," he'd said.

Rhiannon's eyes flew open and she bent her legs to scramble up the bed, before losing her balance and falling to the floor on the other side. She sprang up instantly.

"What the hell?"

The man, garbed in thick cotton pants and a red shirt with intricate stitching across the front, held up a hand. "Please be calm, trespasser. I will not hurt you. While you are here in the Facility, you are safe."

Rhiannon stared. The power of speech suddenly vanished, because this man, his dark eyes crinkling with compassion, was standing with his arms crossed over that beautiful stitching, and seemed to be waiting for a response.

"Right. Good. You're a guard-type person. Excellent." Rhiannon flapped her hands in agitation. "Okay. There's been a massive mistake. I was running through a laundromat and then I fell out the back door into," she flung her arms sideways to gesture dramatically at the window, "here, and then some guard-warrior-people," she flapped her hands again, "captured me. No, kind of like stopped me and then one said I was trespassing and I had no idea what on earth she was talking about and then one of them shot me with an arrow!" Rhiannon glared and clutched at her arm, squeezing the skin in search of an arrow wound. But there wasn't a mark. Clearly whatever freaky drug that had coated the end of the arrow had skimmed her T-shirt, knocking her out for a day, but not killing her or leaving her to die.

"Shot me with a freaking arrow!" she repeated, and rolled her fingers into her palms.

The guard held up his hand. "It is not a mistake."

Rhiannon clenched her teeth, then inhaled, and exhaled very carefully through the gaps. "Yes. It. Is."

"No, it is not. You entered Breula illegally through a portal from your realm and were captured by members of the Guard. It is of little consequence which realm you originated from."

Only one word stood out. "A laundromat is not a freaking realm, for Christ's sake!" Her voice sounded too loud and colourful for such a small room "And Melbourne is not a realm. It's a city and my friend is back there and—"

He tilted his head in confusion as she shouted "realm" for the second time.

"I feel an explanation is necessary."

Rhiannon glared again, swept her hand through the air in a 'please go ahead' gesture, then she crossed her arms.

The guard matched her stance. "Breula is a realm with portals to other realms. We use the portals for observational purposes, and, on rare occasions, for legitimate travel. You accessed a portal without authorisation and therefore you are a trespasser. This building is called the Facility. It houses you for a small duration of time until you participate in the application process for free passage into this realm."

"I have absolutely zero interest in passage into Bre-whatever. Seriously, I'd love to be tossed back through my portal into a rinse cycle."

The guard looked apologetic.

"I am sorry. That is not my decision." He cleared his throat and straightened. "I must speak with you about your weapons."

"What the ever-loving...? I don't have weapons! They did! Arrows and swords!" The agitated hand gestures restarted.

"You had weaponry."

Suddenly, it hit her, and she flicked a glance about the room.

"My tools." She turned back. "My tools. They're for my art. I make metal art. You took my tools?" Her voice broke. Not only Alex but her cold chisel and her files and the comforting weight of the bag against her body. "Do you still have them?" she asked quietly.

"Yes. We also confiscated this weapon." Reaching into his pocket, he pulled out a rectangular item and held it up. "You were armed with this."

Rhiannon nearly laughed but the situation was not at all humorous. "What? That's my phone. It's not a weapon. It's for communicating with people."

The guard wiggled the phone in front of his chest, staring into the screen. "This device communicates with people?"

"Absolutely. You call someone to tell them—"

"Well, you are here now. In Breula." It was all so very logical. "Who are you going to call?"

The response was almost Pavlovian. "Ghostbusters," she mumbled.

The guard had given her another strange look, then left through the wooden door.

***

Later in the afternoon, after donning heavy cotton pants, a loose overshirt, and a pair of leather moccasin-style shoes which had been delivered to her room, Rhiannon was escorted to the large communal space with wood and metal tables and stools dotted, like lilypads, across the intricate floor tiles. The tiles reminded her of Turkey or Crete and when she dropped her head back onto her neck, the pale-wood beams curved over the space so it felt somewhat like being in the lungs of a whale.

She garnered a few odd looks from other trespassers despite being dressed in the same clothing, but most of the stares were of curiosity, which she understood completely. Questions filled her mind.

The nearest table was occupied by a group of young people, possibly mid-twenties but it was hard to tell. They could have been three-thousand-years-old for all Rhiannon knew.

"Hi. Ah, can I sit here?" She gestured at the stool closest, and smiled hopefully. The group of four—three women and a man—paused in their conversation and studied her, then the man's face relaxed into one of friendliness.

"Yes. You may join us." He flicked long black hair off his face and a stab of sadness plunged into Rhiannon's heart. The gesture, the hair, the friendly smile reminded her so much of Alex that she thought she'd burst into tears. God, Alex! He'd be distraught. What a horrible situation, particularly because he was basically the only family she had. The idea of having to run away, albeit from thugs, was so reminiscent of her teenage years that it took her breath for a moment.

Alex knew the reason for her distrust of people. Rhiannon's parents had not responded well to the news that she was a lesbian, throwing her out of home at seventeen so she'd ended up on the streets, moving from shelter to shelter as she outstayed her time. Living by her wits, her cunning and not without a small amount of illegal activity, she managed to finish high school, forging permission or absence notes as required. It had been an incredibly stressful and heartbreaking ordeal, and it was only alleviated when, just after her eighteenth birthday, twenty-four-year-old Alex responded to her advertisement at the local queer youth centre to rent a room in his flat.

Something about Rhiannon must have resonated with him—he said that he felt drawn to her—because he suggested a rental payment that would increase in yearly increments in line with her income. Alex wouldn't tell her how they managed to pay for a whole flat on the wages of a call centre employee and a metal worker selling her wares at the local market three days a week. But whatever it was, it worked. They'd been flat mates for twelve years. Alex was special. He brought warmth to their home. During winter, whenever he was in the flat, his presence seemed to increase the temperature by at least two degrees. Alex brought a glow that made her heart settle. Alex was her family. And Alex was going to be beside himself.

It made her even more determined to get out of this mess. Get out of Breula with its pink and white sky.

"Thanks. I'm." She sat and shuffled the stool closer so her elbows rested on the wooden table top. "New here."

The two women at the other end of the table, identical with spiky red hair and the most incredible violet eyes, leaned forward, shared a glance, then the one on the left pinned Rhiannon with a long look. "Which realm are you from?"

Rhiannon chewed her lip. "I'm...not?"

The long look narrowed. "You are Breulan?"

"No!" Rhiannon must have looked appalled because her table companions grinned. "I'm Australian."

"I do not know that realm." The other red-haired, violet-eyed woman frowned.

"Well, it's not exactly a rea—"

"What is your name?" The question, fired as if from a bow, came from her left. The third woman, a veritable pixie, levelled a pair of suspicious eyebrows and stare combination, her slight body seeming to vibrate energy.

"Rhiannon." Then Rhiannon took hold of her courage. "What's your's?"

Pixie-woman relaxed her eyebrows. "My Breulan name is Jilh." Then she pointed to each person. "Hygt." The man. "Kolst." Violet-eyed red-haired number one. "Setyl." Violet-eyed red-haired number two. *Breulan name?* Rhiannon let that slide.

If the situation hadn't been so weird, and sad, and awful, having a long chat with Jilh, Hygt, Kolst, and Setyl would have been an awesome way to spend an afternoon. But there were questions to ask. Like why no-one had been introduced to a contraction. Perhaps later.

"What year is it?"

Jilh looked at her like she'd lost her mind. "It is year two thousand, five hundred and sixty-two of the Breaulan calendar." The 'duh' was silent but incredibly loud.

Rhiannon blinked. "So I'm in the future?" *You have got to be kidding.*

Hygt laughed. "You are neither in the past nor the future. You simply are. The realms exist on parallel consentient planes. Time exists as a social construct. How is time constructed in your realm?"

Rhiannon was still trying to process realms existing in places at the same time as Earth so she fell back on primary school science.

"Uh, there are years and each year is based on earth's orbit of the sun and in each year there are twelve months although there used to be ten but Julius Caesar's astronomers worked out that there were twelve lunar cycles, although our months are pretty much useless now that there's global warming. Each day is twenty-four hours because that's…" She trailed off as the silence registered. All four table companions wore various versions of slightly stunned and Rhiannon grimaced. "Yeah. Well, there you go."

Hygt broke the moment. "Your time seems complicated."

Rhiannon shrugged. "We learn our twelve times table quickly. So, why are you here?" She flicked her hand out to indicate the here and the everything out there.

All four faces fell. "We," Hygt pointed to himself and then at Kolst and Setyl, "are Arcanix from Miotral so it was necessary to escape. Our kind is not welcome in our realm," he said sadly.

"I am an Arcanix from a realm at the farthest border of Breula. Klytra," added Jilh.

"Arcanix?" Rhiannon blinked in confusion at Jilh.

"Yes." Hygt brought her attention back. "I assume you are as well. Arcanix are free people in their own realm. Free to hold energy. Here we are trespassers until we are granted freedom. Then we are Arcanix again. Our wish is to be Elementals." She pointed to her chest, then flicked her finger at her companions. "We have temporary elemental energy and since Breula is the only realm which encourages elemental energy, we need to seek refuge here in the hope of gaining our freedom in the application process. We know that we will never be able to realise our full Elemental status, but at least we will be recognised and safe."

"We might be able to reach that status, Hygt," Setyl said fiercely, tapping the table in front of him to reinforce her point. "You never know. Trespassers who become Arcanix could receive an orb if their energy is strong enough or if the society changed." Her eyes flashed with fervour.

"Ha." Kolst grumbled into the wooden tabletop. "My sister and her dreams."

Rhiannon's mind was reeling as if it was running through the final cycle of one of the dryers she'd bashed her head on when she'd escaped through the portal. But thoughts of how to decipher their word salad were halted when all four straightened and stared in wonder at the steps leading from a corridor down to the beautifully tiled floor.

Rhiannon whipped around and took in the sight of a tall woman, ramrod straight, with long blonde hair loose about her shoulders, a gold circlet around her forehead. Matching gold arm bands, the etched design visible from metres away, circled her biceps. She was dressed in leather pants, a short sleeve white shirt which would have been rakish except it was tucked inside a leather jerkin that hugged her incredibly buff frame. Her entire bearing vibrated with authority.

Rhiannon was now positive this whole situation was due to concussion. The woman was literally the embodiment of Tahlia from the market and like her fantasies about Tahlia, Rhiannon imagined this woman flinging off her armour, tossing Rhiannon onto a bed and, in five minutes, making her boneless from multiple orgasms. She dashed the thought away. Hardly the time.

"Thank Christ! Finally a person who can get me out of this mess," she muttered.

Ignoring the collective gasps of her companions and apparently the entire room, Rhiannon pushed back her stool and strode over to the woman who had descended the small set of steps.

Rhiannon registered the serious expression, the tall, muscular body, the intense blue eyes filled with curiosity, and the necklace with a beautiful yellow gem at her throat. Definitely a person of authority. A man, similarly dressed, with closely cropped black hair and wearing a white gem instead of yellow stood slightly to the left. He also had a serious face but his eyes held a touch of wariness.

"Trespa—"

"I'm sorry," Rhiannon began. "Normally I wouldn't be so rude but I think this situation calls for a person hitting the ejector seat on manners. This is all a big mistake. I'm from Melbourne and I fell through a portal into Breula. This place. And the only reason I landed here is because I was being chased by two guys who wanted to kidnap me because apparently I owed money which I didn't but someone stole my identity so I've lost my name, which is so shitty. But then I landed here after escaping through a laundromat and someone shot me with some type of poisonous arrow and apparently

I'm now a trespasser and you look like someone who could fix this situation." Rhiannon ran out of puff.

The woman's eyes were wide which Rhiannon hoped was concern but she didn't think so. Probably confusion. Then the woman squinted. Okay. Definitely confusion. Rhiannon slid her gaze to the guard person who was staring at her in fascination in that manner people have when they've come across a train wreck. Rhiannon's skin prickled, then her gaze found the tall woman's again.

"I look like someone who could help you?" the woman asked.

She sure did. Her whole demeanour was businesslike and her voice was smooth and low and created goosebumps and Rhiannon slapped at her common sense to wake it up.

"Absolutely." Rhiannon waved her hand up and down in front of the woman. "You look like someone in charge." Then patting her own chest, Rhiannon smiled winningly. "I'm Rhiannon Clarke, by the way."

"But you said you have no name." The woman studied her.

"I do. Sort of. Someone stole it," Rhiannon replied, sighing through her teeth.

"So you have no name."

Rhiannon spluttered. "Yes, I do! It's—"

"I do not understand." The woman frowned and her guard flicked his eyes between them.

"Oh, for the love of all that is holy."

"Tell me again, what is your name?"

"Rhiannon Clarke."

"Your name is not easy to pronounce." The woman frowned again. She'd dislocate her eyebrows at this rate.

"Rhiannon?"

"Yes."

Rhiannon nearly laughed. "Really? What's your name?"

The guard inhaled sharply and Rhiannon figured she'd stepped over some sort of line. *Too bad.* The woman straightened her shoulders which wasn't really necessary considering the almost military bearing she held. Her nearly six feet of height was impressive, and she fixed her blue-eyed gaze on Rhiannon.

"I am Orilaevar Reysandoral, daughter of Rodlamar Reytoris Breula, King of our realm."

Rhiannon blinked, then blinked again. King. *Well, shit.* "Ori… laevar Rey…sandoral."

"Yes. Also, Breula. On the end." Orilaevar's finger flicked to the side to indicate the word's location.

"So…Orilaevar…Reysandoral…Breula." Rhiannon tipped her head, making sure she'd pronounced it correctly.

The woman nodded seriously.

"Uh huh. And yet Rhiannon is superdocper difficult." Rhiannon rolled her eyes which, she realised a second later, probably wasn't a gesture to aim at royalty, and she wondered why the King's daughter was continuing to entertain her blathering.

There was a pause while they held each other's gaze.

After a moment, Orilaevar nodded, looked at Rhiannon quizzically, then folded her arms. "Your new name is—"

Rhiannon thrust out two hands, palms up, which made the guard twitch. "Woah! You can't just change my name!"

"You said that your name no longer belongs to you." The statement, dry and logical, hit Rhiannon in the chest.

"Well, yeah. But—"

"Therefore, your new name is Sevich."

Rhiannon stared for a full five seconds as her mouth fell open. No sound would come out so she slid her gaze from the ridiculously attractive warrior woman with the excessive amount of muscles to process this new information.

If there was anyone who could help get her back to Melbourne, back to her life, back to her flat with Alex and his warmth, it was the daughter of the King and if a name change was going to assist in that process, then so be it. She rolled her new name around inside her head. It wasn't awful. Pretty good, actually, if a name was to be foisted upon her. *Okay. So long, Rhiannon. Hello, Sevich.*

"Fair enough." She brought her gaze back and stuck out her hand. "How're you doing, Ori? My name's Sev." Another collective gasp from the now enthralled audience echoed about the room.

Ori blinked a couple of times, looked from Sev's face to her hand then back to her face and Sev wiggled her hand from side to side. "You're supposed to shake it," she said, and nodded emphatically to demonstrate the importance of the gesture.

Tentatively, as though it was about to explode, Ori clasped Sev's hand and held it still, then Sev shrugged. Close enough for a princess clearly not used to these types of interactions and let go. Sev had never regarded royalty as any more important than regular people. Just because a person was born in the right place, to the right family, in the right time, didn't make them extra special. Generally it made them pretty ordinary in the truest sense of the word.

"Why have you shortened my name?" Ori recrossed her arms, seemingly increasing the size of her muscles, which Sev thought incredibly unfair. She'd never felt so physically small, and she wasn't a small person. Well, tall, but not nearly as wide. And she had muscles, too, thanks very much.

She looked at Ori in disbelief. "Because I can't very well shout 'hey, watch out for the bus, Orilaevar Reysandoral Breula.' By the time I finished, you'd be road kill." She huffed as if the answer was obvious. "Therefore…Ori."

Ori stared in silence, then her lips—it hadn't escaped Sev's notice at how sensuous they were. *Really?*—quirked. "I have not experienced anyone like you," she said, her voice laden with fascination.

"And you haven't experienced me either, thanks," Sev parried with a long look. "So, cheers for the new name. Are we able to work out something so that I can return to my…realm?" She flipped her hands in query.

After a moment of contemplation, Ori ground out a "We will see," as if she hadn't really meant to respond but somehow felt compelled to say something. Then with a shake of her head, a final stare—more a narrowing of her eyes—and a wrinkling of her eyebrows, probably in bafflement, Ori turned on her heel, her guard falling into place beside her and strode away.

A thought flashed through Sev's mind. "Hey! Does Sevich mean anything?" The room stilled as people froze, their very breath caught in their throats.

Ori paused at the top step, and turned, one eyebrow raised. "Yes. It means mouse." Then, with a small smile, she walked away without looking back.

"Mouse?" Sev flicked her hands outwards. "Seriously?" Her incredulous shout would have carried up the corridor hopefully to ring in the princess's ears. Then she dropped her head. "Unbelievable."

CHAPTER FOUR

"So, that is our interesting trespasser," Privana commented, keeping up with Ori as they made their way through the Great Hall.

Ori caught Privana's grin and stopped abruptly. "She is not afraid to speak her mind," she said, and recalled the short tousled brown hair, the tall, wiry body dressed in standard trespasser garb, and the angriest pair of brown eyes she'd ever seen.

"She is abrasive," Privana said with a smirk. "And insolent. Calling you Ori. That is disrespectful."

Ori tapped her thigh in contemplation. Shortening her name hadn't grated at all. In fact, the familiarity inside the fury was almost a breath of fresh air.

"Well, yes. But understandable. Besides, if her story is true, then accidentally crossing into Breula would definitely cause distress."

"Orilaevar, trespassers rarely state the truth. Why should this one be any different?"

Exactly. Why should this one be any different? But Ori's gut instinct said that this trespasser *was* different and *was* telling the truth. Why?

***

Later that night, Ori lay on her back, head resting on her interlaced fingers. The white sheets draped loosely across her body; a whisper of fabric caressing her skin. She thought about Sevich's—Sev's—spirit, her unwillingness to back away, her reluctance to demonstrate deference to Ori's royal status, her unrelenting gaze, her outrage at the meaning of her name evident in the final shouted word that had made Ori smile as she walked back up the corridor.

Ori replayed their conversation. Most of it she'd understood, but some of Sev's phrases were incomprehensible, although given the tone, she assumed that Sev was either being sarcastic, channeling even more fury, or sending forth a combination of both, which would be a feat. Based entirely on one interaction, Ori knew that Sev could pull off fury and sarcasm with great aplomb.

She smiled. Revealing that Sevich meant mouse, albeit a frustrated, impolite, tall-enough-to-eyeball-Ori's-chin mouse, had been entertaining. But Privana bristling with displeasure beside her, coupled with Sev clasping Ori's hand in some sort of greeting, had been confusing.

Suddenly, and against her better judgement, Ori wanted Sev to win her application for freedom because there was much to learn about her realm, her people, her society. And much to learn about Sev. She chewed the inside of her cheek. The fire in Sev's eyes, the electricity sparking from her body, flickered against Ori's skin.

Apparently, this was *not* getting attached. Privana would thump her in the shoulder if he knew. But what if she did become attached? What if Sev was telling the truth and had come through a portal by accident? How was that even possible? The other trespassers snuck through when the portals were opened by Elementals who had visited to observe the realm on the other side. Ori had never heard of portals opening spontaneously. It just seemed so far-fetched, and made her skin prickle with unease at the idea. But if Sev was telling the truth, was it possible that the excuses and reasons from other trespassers were authentic as well? That thought had her head rolling softly about in her palms. No. She'd been told since she was old enough to comprehend that the trespassers came to Breula to gain freedom and to steal orbs as an end goal and that was that. If Sev won her application, then Ori would ask her to reveal her elemental energy and why she was seeking an orb as well.

Ending more fruitless thinking, Ori smoothed her palm over the glass globe hovering above her beautifully carved bedside table.

"Thank you for the Light," she whispered, then in the sudden darkness, sleep claimed her.

***

After a week stewing over the idea of spontaneous portal openings and an angry trespasser, Ori decided to slide the topic into a conversation with her mother when they were at the stables preparing for a ride. Her mother was more flexible in her thinking than her father and tossing about ideas was always welcome.

Ori waited until her mother looked up from the stirrup she was adjusting. "Have you ever heard of a portal opening purely by chance?"

Her mother clasped the reins of her horse and inhaled deeply, as if in thought. "I cannot say I have. That is not to say it cannot. The portals are ancient and I am convinced we do not know as much as we think we do. Why do you ask?"

Ori fiddled with the reins of her own horse, Ukih; a beautiful chestnut beast, eyes filled with mischief and high spirits, as if he rather enjoyed creating chaos at full gallop. He did, often insisting Ori let loose across the plains in celebration of life around them.

"You must have heard of the latest group of trespassers at the Facility."

"Of course. I do keep up to date with such things." Her mother indicated, with a nod of her head, for Ori to follow as she led her horse from the stables. "A few from the west and east portals and one from—" She stopped abruptly, pulling slightly on the reins and gave Ori a sharp look. "And one from the north."

"Yes, that trespasser claims to have arrived by accident. I have not ever inspected that particular portal because we thought it was dormant. The Guard members simply glanced at it as they rode past but this time it opened spontaneously." Ori smoothed the nose of her horse, keeping one eye on her mother. Ignoring Queen Sermeh Reytoris Breula's sharp looks was not a good decision.

"Yes, I had heard." Queen Sermeh delivered another sharp look, then raised her eyebrows. "Apparently, the trespasser is quite the character."

"Mother, I am speaking about the portal, not the person who came through it," Ori huffed, and her mother grinned.

"I am teasing, Orilaevar darling."

"Okay, then."

"Is she pretty?"

"Mother!"

Queen Sermeh's laughter echoed between the stalls. "I am teasing again." Her laughter subsided. "But in all seriousness, no, I have not heard of portals opening spontaneously. There are tales—legends and infant's stories—of an Elemental, able to harness the powers of all ten elements, who will suddenly arrive in Breula at a time of peril." Ori nodded to herself. She'd listened to those tales growing up. "But I am sure it is not Sevich from the laundromat."

Ori's head jerked up. "You spoke to her?"

"I spoke to the head of the Facility who informed me of your conversation with…Sev." This time she held the smile with pressed lips. "I rather like the name of Ori. It is casual and makes you sound relaxed."

Ori huffed again, then shook her head. "She is confusing and impolite and does not contain her emotions and…" She trailed off as her mother's smile grew, and Ori closed her eyes. "Well, besides all that, the Councillors who inspect the portals now have another one to add to their roster. It is becoming a problem. The members of the Guard are stretched thin, as are the Councillors—with some even inspecting by themselves. We have always looked through in pairs. Now, a single person might step through too far, and not be able to return." She could hear the agitation in her voice.

"Orilaevar, let us go for our ride, and have the wind blow disjointed thoughts away. We can fill our mind with logic, because I am sure there is logic in all this confusion. There always is."

***

Logic decided to not make itself known for the next few days. It was maddening how much space Sev took up in Ori's thoughts, leaving very little for her responsibilities. Forgetting to enhance the light from the lit torches at the night archery assessment for one.

"Orilaevar Reysandoral Breula. I am sorry to interrupt your contemplation, but the archers request a little more light to begin proceedings." Ori jerked and brought her attention to the assessor, an orange orb glinting at his throat, who was standing to attention at the first lit torch; the flame casting its light as a small flickering circle.

She looked up at the line of archers, all Metal Elementals, their bows hanging loosely, with three arrows threaded through the fingers of the other hand, and gazing expectantly at their Captain.

"Yes. Of course," Ori muttered, as if the Guard member had actually interrupted an important and serious and leader-ish collection of thoughts, rather than the musings of a woman enjoying mental images of another woman. She held her hands about the edges of the flame. "Thank you for the Light. The balance will be restored."

The flame held its shape, yet the light it cast doubled, spreading out and above so that the features of the recruits were no longer hidden in shadows. No wonder they'd been waiting. None of them could manipulate Light. Ori glared at herself. She must have looked like a gormless fool, staring off into the distance like that.

With an instruction from the Guard assessor, the archers quickly readied then loosed their arrows, sending all three skimming through the air to skewer a tall sapling; a small staccato the only noise indicating that the arrow tips had met the wood. This group of would-be members would bolster an already stretched portal Guard. Excellent.

***

The following Sunday was the Day of Application, which Ori normally found exciting, but at breakfast, she pushed her final piece of fruit about her plate as if she were designing a new dressage routine for Ukih at the next festival.

"Orilaevar, what troubles you this morning?" Her father's voice carried curiosity and compassion. His inflexibility was only apparent in the governing and maintaining of the structure of Breula. But inflexibility did not equal lack of compassion or care.

"Father, what is the reason for the application?" Ori looked up from her plate littered with fruit tracks.

"That is quite the question, but you know the answer." He frowned.

"I do. But…" She shrugged, which her father seemed to interpret as 'I've forgotten even though I'm thirty-years-old and have lived with this law all my life but please remind me'.

He laid his cutlery down. "Well, it sorts the trespassers into two groups; those who have enough elemental energy to stay and work here as Arcanix and those who don't. We accept those who are able to generate enough elemental energy to fulfil their roles each day. The balance is maintained when this happens."

"And those whose applications are not endorsed are returned to their own realms," Ori said, although it was more a question because she heard the lift in her final word.

Her father frowned. "Yes, of course they are. It is the most logical and compassionate consequence." He fiddled with the orange orb at his throat.

"It still seems harsh to send them back to their own realms when they claim to have run from persecution."

"Orilaevar, the trespassers will give this reason every time, and it is always said with such conviction, but we have never seen any evidence of this when we inspect the portals and look into the relevant realm. We would have to enter the realm to investigate further, and of course that will not happen. What a dire situation for any Breulan to be stranded forever in another realm that is not ours." He waved to the server to clear the plates, thanking her with genuine gratitude. Arcanix worked in the more everyday professions but their role was important, and common courtesy was encouraged. And frankly, expected. As her father said; the Arcanix helped to maintain the balance. "It is tradition and tradition must be upheld," he said, and pushed away from the table. "The applications begin in a few hours so I must get ready. I will meet you in the Great Hall."

***

Outfitted in full uniform—even more formal than that worn in the Council meetings—Ori made her way down the main road into the township, beside her father and mother as befitting her position. Her parents wore full regalia including cloaks, jodhpurs, riding boots;

everything Ori was wearing except a sword. Crowns to indicate the heads of state had been eschewed long ago, and so their place as rulers of the realm was indicated with gold clasps that closed their cloaks and the gold circlets about their foreheads.

Ori adjusted her belt, fiddled with the circlet, reached around and smoothed her left bicep band, then clenched her jaw. Pomp and circumstance didn't fit comfortably, even though the once-a-month ceremony leant itself to formality.

"You are twitching, darling," her mother said without taking her eyes off the line of Guard members ahead of her.

Ori instantly slipped back into a more military bearing and grumbled. "I dislike this, yet I like this, which irritates me."

"What is the 'this'?" The conversation continued without a sideways glance from either of them.

"This." Ori's hand jerked. She wanted to sweep her arm about to encompass the cavalcade of Guard members, the fifty Councillors, some accompanied by their partners or guests, then the approximately thirty Elementals who had requested to attend this month's application, and then the royal party of three. Her mother seemed to understand the undelivered gesture.

"Orilaevar, the trespassers expect their application to be valued, to be given significance. It is only fair. We are a peaceful realm, darling, and if the trespassers return to their own realms, they know that they were given every opportunity to prove themselves."

"Elemental strength," Ori muttered. What was wrong with her? Only recently had she become twitchy, as her mother put it, about the application process. Not doubts as such. Doubts required unpicking the fabric of tradition. It was more an analysis of the process. There had been whispers of trespassers being returned through the incorrect portal, finding themselves in another realm, just as foreign as Breula. It was gossip and she chose to ignore it. Hardly the practice of a realm that prided itself on benevolent tradition, even if that tradition gave her twitches.

The townspeople, and the Arcanix, waited at the side of the main road, with expressions of cheerfulness aimed at the royal family, and pressing their hands to their chests in deference to the King and

Queen; Ori received wide grins. Some chose not to make eye contact with many of the Councillors in the following line of Elementals. There was a feeling of distrust towards those Elementals, and sometimes Ori felt it justified.

There were a few Councillors who considered the wearing of an orb meant that sitting in a chair in the Council chamber their only responsibility. It annoyed Ori. Wearing an orb was more than prattling on and filling the silence once a month in that beautiful room. It was about realising that the townspeople relied on their decisions to impact favourably on their lives. Hence the lack of eye contact.

The lack of eye contact brought a memory from a couple of weeks ago of a trespasser whose eye contact had not wavered at all. It had challenged, in fact. It had caused Ori's lungs to hold a quick breath.

She then recalled a conversation with the head of the Facility only a few days ago when she'd asked after Sev. For no reason at all. Just because. In her role as Captain of the Guard, perhaps. Yes.

"Your intake this month is more than usual, Jarrion Enfiel Breula. Have you been able to house everyone?" Ori stood at ease in the entrance to the building, alongside Privana.

"Yes, Orilaevar Reysandoral Breula. Earth Elementals and quite a number of the Earth Arcanix were able to quickly create another wing." He smiled at that fact, then frowned. "This month, we will have twenty applying for freedom."

Ori raised her eyebrows. "Twenty? That is …that is quite a few."

The Guard member crossed his arms, mirroring Ori's pose. "I am sure we will be able to create matched applications, though," he chuckled. "I have no idea how the trespasser from the northern portal will fare. She seems to have a fire that does not bode well for when it is her turn."

Ori felt rather than heard Privana's hum of interest. "Oh? Can you elaborate?" Ori guessed, probably knew if she thought about it, that Sev's fire would sit at simmering and rise quickly to incandescent.

Jarrion Enfiel Breula chuckled again. "She has been talking to a group of trespassers throughout the weeks as she waits for the upcoming application, asking quite sensible questions as one would if you were a person who had fallen, in a tangle of limbs and metalworking tools, through a portal from a realm that we have not inspected for years."

Ori blinked and latched onto the one piece of information that she hadn't known previously. "Metalworking tools?"

"Yes. She claims to be an artist."

"This is why she is here; to obtain a Metal orb." Privana grumbled under his breath.

With a quick sideways flick of her hand indicating that her Deputy should keep that opinion to himself; a gesture that Privana didn't seem to appreciate if the follow-up huff was any indication, Ori hunted for another question simply to maintain their chat.

"Well, thank you for the information. I will let you get on with your duties." She turned, ready to leave the unsatisfactory conversation, but turned back. "Ah. Can you make sure that the tools are returned to her whether her application is successful or not, please?" Ori figured that if Sev was carrying her tools and not storing them at whatever facility would house such items in her realm, then they must be very valuable.

The Guard member blinked in response. "Of...of course, Orilaevar Reysandoral Breula. We can arrange that. Highly unusual, th—" He flicked his gaze away from Ori's glare, "Yes, of course."

"Right. Well, I will let you get on. I hope you have an excellent day." She turned again and this time continued walking. Quickly. Away from one of the most contrived, awkward conversations she'd ever had. She caught Privana's look. "Do not even."

Hopefully, Ori thought as she gazed down the road lined with people, thoughts of that conversation would disappear, even if Privana had looked at her like she'd lost her mind. The large number of people in the group meant that the walk from the royal mansion took an hour so the sun was at its peak when they arrived at the application building.

Ori smiled indulgently at the white marble, the columns placed mathematically around the perimeter functioning as decoration more than substance. She entered, made her way to the royal seats, again admiring the slightly curved roof that rose above her. The building was not large; slightly smaller than the Great Hall. It held one hundred spectators comfortably but wouldn't allow for more. The soft rubbery surface of the arena floor was close enough to touch but only if she took two steps down and reached through the single wall of Guard members. Their protection felt unnecessary but her father had insisted, justifying the decision by saying that today the trespassers were also armed.

Chapter Five

"Oh, what fresh hell is this?"

Sev stared up at the arena, blinking at the condensed version of a basketball stadium. It was a squat, curricular shape with columns dotted about the exterior. What it did resemble, Sev realised, was a miniature colosseum and a feeling of dread settled in her stomach.

When a set of double doors opened, Sev and the other trespassers were escorted into a large room where a number of two-seater benches were spaced along the walls

An Elemental, clearly identified by the orange orb at his throat—Sev knew this now because the other trespassers had explained the importance of that particular piece of jewellery—gestured for the group of twenty to congregate in the middle of what was ostensibly a locker room.

"Before we begin, it is necessary to point out that the bathroom is over there." The Elemental, taller than the regular six feet and probably just as wide, indicated to a door off to the right. Sev noticed a number of alcoves set into the walls, which she thought bitterly were probably shallow prayer spaces. The building's vibe felt like a prayer space was necessary.

The Elemental crossed his arms. What was with this realm? All crossed arms, and glowering eyebrows, and confusion at accidental trespassers. A certain King's daughter with long blonde hair flitted through her shattered thoughts.

"Welcome to your application," the Elemental said, the proud smile belying his stance. "Today you will apply for entry into Breula and if successful, your life in this realm will begin." His smile flattened at the group's low hum and Sev figured the ripples were those of anxiety if the other trespassers were thinking the same thoughts she was.

"If your application is not successful, we will return you to your realm." At another low murmuring, he added a pair of annoyed eyebrows to his flat smile, which really couldn't be classed as a smile any more. "We are a just and peaceful realm and so returning you after your unsuccessful application is an act of peace."

Bullshit. Something was off about this process beyond the whole arena thing, despite the fact that she now had doubts about her bullshit-o-meter lately considering the stolen identity palaver. She felt compelled to speak up. Nothing unusual there.

"Unless we're going into a giant human resources interview, I don't get this," she circled her finger at the locker room, "situation."

The Elemental gave up on any semblance of his benevolent tour guide act. He returned to his crossed arms irritated-by-trespasser position.

"Today you will be applying for your entry into Breula and if successful, your life in this realm will begin," he repeated, enunciating each word as if Sev was an idiot. "Your application consists of a contest to demonstrate your awareness of your elemental strength. The application element is chosen at random each month. This month it is the Metal element." He pointed to the orange orb at his throat.

There were gasps of disbelief from the group, then the shouts started.

"Mine is not Metal."

"How can Flora win this contest?"

"Will my element of Heat be sufficient?"

Sev swivelled her head, taking in every appalled expression.

The Elemental held up his dinner plate-sized hand.

"Stop. The element is Metal. Therefore, for this contest, you will need these." He took one step to the wall, pushed on a hidden panel, and a tall door opened, swinging back to click into place. Every head peered into the void.

"Swords. They are very blunt so they will not injure you or your opponent. We are judging your utilisation of the element, not your ability to wound. Swords are metal," he added pointlessly. "You will wield the sword as a demonstration that you understand how to manipulate your strength.

"Swords?" Sev's mind was chaotic white noise. "Swords." She blinked at the Elemental who seemed to have reached his tolerance for the trespasser from the laundromat because he growled, leaned into the storage locker, yanked out a sword and a leather and metal helmet, then strode over to Sev.

"Here." He grabbed her wrist, shoved the hilt of the sword into her palm, then held the cheek plates of the helmet in each hand. Sev reflexively gripped the weapon, and stepped back.

"Christ. This is…I *make* swords. I don't wave them about." Her voice rose to an anxious squeak as her hand twitched, wanting to wave the sword about and therefore negate that last statement. "I certainly don't aim them at people."

"You will do so today." He glowered. "Without injury."

"But…no!" Sev couldn't tear her gaze from the Elemental's almost black eyes.

"There is no chat now."

"Yes. Now. We'll chat now."

He glared. "No. Put this on. It is in case of haphazard application of energy." The helmet was thrust against her chest.

"I don't—" A helmet would make it all too real despite the fact that she was clutching a reasonably large and very real sword.

The Elemental huffed. "Your skull is susceptible to breakage." He grabbed the helmet, shoved it over her head, then smacked the top. "Wear it."

Sev's ears rang.

Then he turned abruptly to the other trespassers and directed them into a line, handing out swords and helmets to the stunned group. He was clearly unperturbed that, if the group organised itself, there was the potential for twenty swords aimed at his chest. Sev imagined he could activate some type of personal forcefield.

Her feet felt glued to the ground. With the sword hanging loosely from her hand, Sev rummaged through her brain for all the information she'd gathered in the last two weeks simply to make sense of this situation. Information was power or something. At this moment, information was a way to cope.

That information had been collected over the weeks through daily conversations with Jilh, Hygt, and the sisters, Kolst and Setyl.

***

"So, this application. What's the story?" Sev picked at the food on her beautifully burnished wooden plate. The whorls of black and light brown swung about each other, rising to the shiny surface. At Kolst's hum, Sev lifted her head, then leaned on her palm, elbow resting on the table.

"I do not know. It seems to be something about explaining your element and how strong it manifests within you. That is all I know. You?" Kolst lifted her chin at Hygt.

"Same." He shrugged, and continued picking at the rim of his cup. Then he looked up. "What is your element? I have forgotten to ask." His quick head shake seemed to indicate his annoyance at his lapse.

Sev shrugged. "I have no idea."

Absolute silence greeted her response.

"You…you do not know your element?" Kolst and Setyl asked at the same time.

"Um…" Sev grimaced apologetically. "I'm sorry. I told you. I'm an accidental portal person. I don't know anything about elements, or orbs, or Breula, or realms, or portals. Well, I know about some of those now, but seriously, having an element? I don't have one."

"That is impossible," Setyl whispered, staring at Sev in wonder, which was disconcerting so Sev deflected.

"What are your elements?"

"Metal."

"Metal."

"Metal."

"Flora."

Kolst, Setyl, and Hygt grinned at each other. Apparently team Metal was in the house.

Sev cocked her head at Jilh. "Flora?"

"Mm. I request the service of nature in order to create a positive force which I then return to the element to re-establish the balance."

Sev blinked, mouth slightly ajar. "Right." Then she pointed at the others, circling her finger. "And the same goes?"

"Yes. We request the service of metal, and so on." Setyl smiled.

"That's…that's wow."

"And you really have no element?" Setyl's gaze displayed disbelief.

"Nope." Then it occurred to Sev. "The orbs are related to the elements. That's why some of the Breulans are called Elementals." She rolled her eyes at her own obtuseness.

"Exactly. The orbs help maintain the power of the element for as long as the person wears it. Arcanix can only use their strength for a day," Setyl hummed.

"That's not much."

"True, and rest does restore our strength, but to have unlimited strength to request the element's service would be incredible. The orbs are an energy source."

A spotlight of understanding lit up Sev's mind.

"Gotcha. So you run from a shit situation in your own realm to the only realm that values what you can do, but you're not that strong here and you have to tell the assessment people how strong your element is so they'll give you freedom or whatever but you'll never have a lot of strength like they do because they keep it for themselves." Sev nodded at the group.

"Essentially, yes. You have explained it well," Jilh said, studying Sev. "The desire to obtain an orb is high."

Sev returned Jilh's gaze; a gaze that revealed, for a second, how intense Jilh's desire for an orb actually was. Interesting. The others simply wanted to be accepted into Breulan society. Sev tucked that piece of not-at-all-a-fact away for later contemplation.

"Would you like to know more about the elements such as the colours?" Setyl's voice sounded eager.

Sev had discovered that Setyl was one of those people who would joyfully impart information to anyone who stood still long enough to listen. It was endearing.

"Absolutely. Shoot."

Setyl blinked and Sev grimaced. "Not, like…*shoot* shoot. I meant," she pointed a finger, "tell me more."

"Well." Setyl wiggled on the bench. "There are ten Elements." She tapped on a finger as she listed each one. "Earth, Water, Air, Fire or Heat, actually, then there is Metal." She flicked a finger at herself, her sister and Hygt. "And Ice, Fauna, Flora, Dark, and Light."

It was all a bit *Lord of the Rings*. Next she'd see elves wandering about the corridors and Cate Blanchett calling forth the service of her people. That last bit would be perfectly fine. She shook her head.

"And they've got colours?"

"Oh, yes!" Setyl grinned. "Earth is green, Water is a beautiful violet purple—"

"I love that element." Kolst interrupted with a lustful sigh.

Setyl ignored her. "Air is silver, Heat is red." She delivered a one shoulder shrug and Sev nodded.

"Makes sense."

"Then Metal is orange, Ice is white, Fauna is amber, Flora is a lavender pink—"

"Such a weak colour," Jilh grumbled.

"You know there is no control over the colours. They were determined long ago. Even the Elementals have no say in the colours, let alone what element they are gifted with. The same as the Arcanix," Setyl said, her hands flicked over, palms up, to represent the inevitability of everything.

"I know. But pink…"

"It does not matter, Jilh. You are not going to wear one, so do not get upset about something that is impossible."

Sev ping-ponged her gaze between Setyl and Jilh. If she didn't know any better, she'd swear that an undercurrent of tension, perhaps dislike, had developed between the two over the past few days. It could be the stress of the impending assessment. Not her concern.

"Oh! I have not finished." Setyl's good humour returned. "Dark is black, which makes perfect sense, and Light is yellow."

"Can an Elemental have more than one element?"

"No. That is impossible. Just as we Arcanix—we are trespassers at the moment—are imbued with only one as well," Kolst answered, interrupting Setyl's flow.

Sev blinked. "Is there anything else?" Her gaze took in both women.

"The elements should not be forced against each other." Setyl wrestled back the conversation with a glare at her sister. This was clearly her TED talk and she was not going to be interrupted. "It upsets the balance."

Sev nodded slowly. *Oh my God, this is a lot.*

***

It was still a lot, Sev thought, as the group huddled together in the centre of the room, clutching their pathetic collection of mismatched swords and helmets. The heavy cotton over-shirts and pants, coupled with leather sneaker-type shoes were hardly going to protect anybody from anything, even a blunt sword. Even if the Elemental had told them that nobody would get hurt, Sev knew that injuries of some description were imminent. Particularly psychological ones.

The ping on Sev's bullshit-o-meter was now a klaxon. Breula's Elementals chose the application element *at random*? Like a lottery? That sounded just too sketchy. They must know that the trespassers who didn't possess that particular element wouldn't succeed. It was almost as if they wanted to sift through the various trespassers to ensure certain groups achieved freedom each month. Yes, just like a lottery. Bloody hell. So much for the idea that the elements couldn't be forced against each other. They were deliberately mucking around with the balance that Setyl had spoken about.

"Sevich!"

Sev leapt a mile. "What? Shit!" She stared at the Elemental, her lips numb with anxiety.

"Your partner in the application is Jilh."

"What? But she's…" Sev whipped her head around and stared at the small woman whose shoulders had sagged and she leaned on the weapon in her hands.

The sound of names and the gasps of despair hung heavily as Sev crept over to Jilh.

"I'm so sorry. This is really messed up. I don't know what's going to happen but you'll be fine."

Jihl lifted her head and contemplated Sev. "No. I possess the Flora element. I will not succeed in this application because I cannot compete against Metal. The elements do not fight each other, remember?"

"Well, that's debatable." Sev widened her eyes in realisation. "I don't have an element so you're not fighting against one! You'll be fine. You'll stay here and I'll go back to Melbourne and it's all good." She sighed in relief as the pieces fit together. This made sense.

Jihl gave a short, quiet laugh. "You really do not know, do you?"

"What?"

Jihl paused. "It was good to make your acquaintance, Sevich. You will do well in Breula." She dropped her head and turned away.

Acid bile rose in Sev's throat. Jihl had given up already but why? Suddenly she needed to vomit. Skirting the edge of the group, she made her way into a two-stall bathroom, and crashed into the closest one, slamming the door with her foot as she leaned over the bowl. The sour warmth in her throat trickled into the water.

"This is…!" Her hiss sizzled across the tiles. "So freaking, freaking shitty, crap shit!" The ridges in the hilt of her sword dug into her palm, and her thumb ring pressed on the exposed metal. She squeezed even tighter, welcoming the pain. Running the back of her hand across her mouth, Sev straightened, her breath shallow, and whistling wetly through her teeth.

"I hate this!"

She lifted the sword and jabbed it at the wall simply to release a skerrick of the anxiety that was churning in her heart. Then, as if in slow motion, the blade bent awkwardly at the tip, ripples undulating back up to her hand, and without a doubt, Sev knew the weapon was in pain simply because she was in pain. Psychological pain. She dropped the twisted wreckage on the floor.

"What the living hell?" Her gaze darted from her hand to the broken sword then back to her hand. The silence was deafening.

"Oh, God. I'm…I'm a Metal thingy. Metal element. Metal trespasser. Whatever." Her throat closed. "You can't be serious." She clapped both hands over her mouth to stifle the sob that was threatening to burst from her lungs. She stared wide-eyed at the mess of steel on the ground.

After breathing through shaking fingers for a minute, Sev's brain sorted through a number of pertinent facts. Mainly that she possessed an element. Metal. That thought shouted from its place on the podium in her brain. But other thoughts clamoured for attention; Jihl had clearly realised what Sev was and knew that she would lose the application with her Flora element.

"Oh, Christ."

Other realisations crashed in. She needed to hide the damaged sword because there'd be questions if she marched out to the main room with a steel infinity symbol. Sev toed the weapon to the corner of the stall then pushed it behind the toilet bidet combination.

"Sorry," she whispered. It felt right to apologise. After all, the metal was sort of alive. What an irrational thought.

It really wasn't irrational, she thought, as she attempted to nonchalantly walk from the bathroom. Hadn't she always felt the warm metal under her fingers as if it was happy to be handled? To be crafted into beauty? To be loved?

"Yep," she breathed. "Holy crap." Calmly, as if curious, she looked inside the cupboard and surreptitiously released a sword from its runners. Then holding it behind her leg, she slid her body along the wall, to eventually collapse onto a bench. Her body shook.

***

The application was everything Sev had visualised. The floor covered in what looked like Astro turf. The seating wrapped around the perimeter and Sev breathed through an instant feeling of claustrophobia.

Standing in the middle, Jihl by her side, their swords dangling from loose fingers, Sev took in the section of seating in front of her.

People in coloured shirts, matching the orbs at their throats, the same heavy cotton pants but in more interesting shades than dark cream. Curious and eager expressions, bodies leaning forward in anticipation. Sev bared her teeth. Then her gaze fell on the King's daughter, Ori, who sat next to a man who could only be her father and a woman of similar age who was probably the Queen but who knew with these people.

Sev held Ori's gaze for a long time, until finally Ori looked away. After a tiny celebration at outstaring royalty, Sev lifted her chin and glared at the King and Queen, who were responsible for her predicament. The spectators fell silent as if responding to the tension.

Finally, Ori looked up and Sev was close enough to see her swallow. Her mouth opened slightly like she was about to say something, but she closed it again.

"The applications will begin," the King stated, and languidly waved his hand.

With a final stare at Ori, Sev turned to Jihl, and realised just how short and small the woman was compared to Sev's lithe, tall frame. The situation couldn't have been worse.

"Begin." The instruction was repeated by the Elemental at the tunnel entrance. The words hit Sev's chest and she jerked her head as Jihl lifted her sword and swung.

"Christ! Damn!" Sev automatically knocked Jihl's blade away. "Jihl, I want you to win. You need to so I can go home."

"It is no use," she replied, using the same low voice as Sev. "I will not win, and I think you know that. But I will try." She swung again and Sev's blade crashed against it, almost as if it had made the decision by itself.

In a small part of her brain, she had the impression that the air had parted allowing the sword to whisk through the gap faster that normal, which was surely an impression produced by stress because to believe that air was sentient was ridiculous.

The back swing from the deflection caught Jihl at her knee and she fell, landing awkwardly. Sev gasped.

"Shit! I'm sorry. I didn't mean that. My sword and the air…" she trailed off when she realised how idiotic the end of that sentence was going to sound.

"I know." Jihl's eyes filled with tears. "I cannot go back. Please."

Sev stood over the woman. "What do I do?"

"If I am wounded enough, they will allow me to stay longer in the Facility." A flash of something—triumph?—whisked through her gaze.

Sev's hands shook. "But you're not injured. They said no-one got —" The realisation hit her. "Oh, God. I can't." Her mouth dried as a bitter taste filled her throat.

"You need to," Jihl pleaded.

Sev became aware of a murmuring in the crowd. Obviously she and Jihl were wasting good entertainment time.

"This is so messed up," Sev whispered. "Okay. Hold out your palm." Then, as Jihl turned her hand over, and Sev concentrated on the end of the sword. Somehow knowing the words to say, she whispered to the metal, "I'm sorry to make you do this but I'm trying to do a good thing. I promise to return you to your form." As she spoke, the tip of the sword slowly narrowed to such a point that it was needle thin, and Sev quickly drew the point across Jihl's skin. The blood bubbled to the surface and the kneeling woman dropped her sword and clutched at her palm, bowing her head.

An explosion of anger lit up Sev's brain and she whirled around, her reformed sword cutting through the air like erratic lightning.

"This is so freaking awful! You call yourself a peaceful society but look at this!" The sword, an extension of her arm, swept around to encompass the spectators. "This is the most insane thing I have ever seen. These are people and you're making them—us—fight to win our freedom! Like caged animals. This is not an application." Her eyes found Ori and she made sure to aim the next sentence directly at the princess. "This is an abomination."

They stared at each other.

Perhaps her words echoing about the space were the only sounds. She didn't know because her furious breathing, rasping through her teeth, filled her ears.

But in that silence, Sev took the chance to turn back to Jihl, who was now standing, having left her sword on the ground.

"Thank you, Sevich." She lifted her joined hands, blood trickling down her arm, and a sly smile slid onto her lips. "I am able to stay in Breula now, even if only at the Facility, and make another application next month." Her eyes narrowed. "One step closer to my goal." Jihl winked, then turned towards the Elemental who had come to lead her away.

Sev gasped. She'd been played. She'd been played and now she was free and both of those events were awful.

The sword fell from her grasp.

It was too much and, mortifyingly, for the first time in her life and, without the aid of poisoned arrows, her eyes rolled back in her head and she fainted.

CHAPTER SIX

Her father's line of Guard members in front of their seats hadn't stopped the potential, albeit highly unlikely, onslaught of twenty haphazardly-armed trespassers. However, it had stopped Ori vaulting over the seats in front of her so she could race to Sev who had crumpled to the green flooring. She, along with her parents and nearly half the spectators, had gasped and leapt to her feet, then watched as the Elemental had lifted Sev's limp body and carried her away through the tunnel.

Later that night, Ori leaned on the intricate metal railing of the balcony attached to her quarters. The twin moons, and stars, bright in the dark purple night sky, were a pretty representation of her scattered thoughts. Sev's apprenticeship placement. Sev's health. Sev's mysteriousness. Sev with her sword slicing through the air. Sev being utterly…

"Magnificent," Ori murmured. With her inflamed words, Sev had taken hold of Ori's breath, her gaze, her consciousness. The fury sparking from every pore had awoken something in Ori's heart, and while the message she'd conveyed was serious and worthy of contemplation, it was Sev's fire that sent swoops and swirls low in her stomach.

Ori straightened, slid her hands into her hair, and pulled it back, holding it in a loose ponytail. She flexed her shoulders, pushing her elbows back, and closed her eyes at the soft pop from the vertebrae in her spine. Then made a decision. She'd be responsible for Sev's placement with a metalworker.

"Askal Kirmiz," she said, and nodded decisively. He was perfect. Favoured by the Queen, a true craftsman, and a steady, even-tempered townsperson who lived with his elderly mother. Perhaps Sev might find solace in the calm of his home. She doubted it but it was worth a shot.

Because Sev would need to be calm if she was to agree to the idea distilling in Ori's mind.

**

"Riding across the plains?" Privana's incredulous tone echoed inside the empty training arena a week later. "That is your idea?"

"I think it is important to understand Sev's world and gather knowledge about how that realm functions."

Privana looked askance, and Ori squeezed one eye shut as she reviewed that sentence in her mind. Transparent as a window. She waved her hand in dismissal.

"It will be her decision, of course, but I thought that she would enjoy some time away from her work. Perhaps it will take her mind off being absent from her home."

Luckily, the Guard members for that day's skills session arrived, saving Ori from the uncomfortable conversation. They appeared from the tunnel entrance in groups of three or four, settling into lines in the centre of the arena. Ori delivered a courteous nod at the team of men and women who made up the defences in the west of the town.

She knew town defences seemed extraneous, particularly when insurgent forces were unlikely, but it assisted in the rotation of the Guard from patrolling the borders through to Facility escorts or overseeing the town defences. Of course the members of the Guard at the Juith River Orb Lagoon were never rotated. They were sworn to secrecy and having an elite permanent group of the Guard was essential. And logical. Despite any unlikely danger.

But each location required a skill set that was unique and so the rotation worked to create a well-rounded Guard. Ori was proud of that and it earned her respect from the members. They appreciated the variety, too.

Ori knew she was held in high esteem. It was evident in the deference they paid to her as their Leader, and not as the daughter of the King. The difference between the two meant so much and filled her heart with pride.

"So, how are you going to go about making these rides happen? Will you deliver an order?"

Ori imagined Sev's response to a royal order and almost laughed out loud. The woman would most likely wrench Ori's sword from its scabbard and plunge it through Ori's foot or somewhere as equally uncomfortable. She doubted that Sev would cause a fatal injury. She seemed like the sort to wound the person so that they'd stay still long enough for her to shred them to pieces with a tirade of furious sentences.

"I do not think so. I have not worked that part out yet. Perhaps I will think further on a strategy because I really believe that if I gather information, then I can help her return to this Melbourne and to her friend."

"You are still going ahead with that?" Privana blinked in confusion, then continued. "I do not know how. No Arcanix returns to their realm once they're free in Breula."

"Which rather cancels out the concept of freedom." Ori studied Privana. Her friend frowned, then frowned again, pushing his eyebrows lower, as if he had experienced an epiphany.

"Well, true. But it has never happened before," he repeated. Privana believed strongly in rules and tradition, which was a point of contention between them. Whenever Ori criticised tradition, Privana always pushed back. Their friendship was too robust for cracks to appear simply due to differences of opinion, but Ori wished Privana would at least be open to alternative mindsets.

Privana continued. "Perhaps it will happen. I suppose sometimes tradition experiences an anomaly and redirects its path." Ori blinked. Clearly, Privana could open his mind.

"Okay?"

"Yes." Privana turned square on to Ori and stared at her fervently. "An Arcanix could return if the Councillors agreed to your suggestion. Then you will have fulfilled your obligation and Breula can regain balance. Then you will be, once again, able to focus on m —your Guard. You could make the suggestion at the next meeting."

Ori tilted her head at her friend. It wasn't the first time he'd redirected her attention towards her leadership and away from pleasant interludes with women. Not that Sev was a 'pleasant interlude'. That conjured all sorts of scenarios. Besides holding fast to tradition, Privana was very loyal to the Guard and his role as the Deputy. And therefore Ori's wellbeing.

"Well, finding out about other realms and other people is always wise."

"Perhaps she will not be receptive."

Ori sighed.

"I can only try."

***

"Riding across the plains?" Her mother paused in the middle of the street as Guard members, carrying as many blankets in their arms as the Queen, marched past. Ori grimaced as Privana's question from a few days ago was repeated.

"Yes. I thought it would…" She trailed off. It wasn't as easy to stifle her mother's curiosity as she could with her Deputy. She shifted the blankets in her arms, and looked at her mother, who smiled.

"How is Sevich? Is she settling in?"

"I wouldn't know. I can't very well just knock on Askal Kirmiz's door and ask after his apprentice."

Which is exactly what she had planned to do but an irrational bout of nerves had hit and so she'd berated herself because she was the Captain of the Guard and to feel anxious about initiating a conversation with Sev would—

"Why not?"

"What?"

"What is stopping you from asking her?" Her mother was a mind-reader. It was completely unfair.

"I…"

Her mother pointed to the Guard members, to the street in general. "Darling, we are knocking on doors and asking if the occupants would appreciate some blankets and assorted knitted goods for winter. You simply need to apply the same process, just without the knitted goods."

Ori couldn't help herself. She laughed, then grinned at her mother whose eyes were twinkling with amusement and love.

"You're a meddling matchmaker," Ori said, holding her grin.

Her mother gave a single nod. "Of course I am. It is in the job description."

"Fine. I'll go to Askal Kirmiz's residence and ask after Sev's welfare."

"Perhaps you should ask about her willingness to traverse the vastness of Breula astride a horse; a mode of transport which could potentially carry her to the Northern portal where she might run away and therefore defeat your purpose of finding out about her realm." She raised her eyebrows and Ori hummed, then her mother leaned in to bump her shoulder against her daughter's. "Just be relaxed, darling. I feel you will need to be, as somehow I doubt that Sevich will be a willing participant in your idea." Ori agreed with that assessment. "Does she know how to ride a horse?"

Ori blinked. The thought hadn't occurred to her. Everyone knew how to ride a horse.

"I…"

"You might want to ask that question first, darling," her mother said, as they turned to walk towards the next house. "By the way, I have noticed that you are speaking rather casually lately. Very much like a certain Arcanix," she said, focused on the front door.

Ori ran the last few sentences she'd said through her mind and blinked. Yes. Contractions were peppering her speech.

"I hadn't realised I was." *Liar.*

"Perhaps you are preparing for your conversation with Sevich."

Her mother paused before lifting the metal knocker on the door, then winked. Ori shook her head. Her mother was incorrigible.

***

Striding into the Great Hall only to turn around, disappear up the staircase, then glare at herself in the floor to ceiling mirror in her bedroom felt as if she was channelling her pubescent teenage self.

"Oh, for…this is ridiculous," Ori muttered, pacing across the flooring from the balcony doors to the curtains at the entrance to her inner sanctuary. She rubbed her forehead with her fingertips.

Sev fuelled this behaviour but the tension also came from the idea of gathering more knowledge. She loved Breula and was curious about the other realms. It frightened her when the Councillors reported to the meetings about their findings from the other realms. Yet her curiosity festered. It frightened her when she read the books in the library of the research gathered from each world over the years. And yet the curiosity always won.

New knowledge equalled change, and change equalled unbalance and therefore stepping through the portals brought fluctuations to the stability; a situation she was loath to contemplate. But she was curious to know because curiosity also rattled tradition, and didn't she want that? Just a little.

The logical section of her brain reminded her that Sev was from another realm. Here by accident. And therefore had brought unbalance until she'd achieved success in the application. She brushed the thought away. Sev was now an Arcanix in Breula and so her success allowed the realm to rebalance because she was now absorbed into society and a member of Breulan society.

"That is the biggest load of garbage I've ever heard," she growled later as she and Privana made their way down to Askal Kirmiz's residence and studio.

***

Ori lifted the knocker but paused before she released it. She stared at the wood. This was completely insane. What was her motivation? Yes, she wanted to get to know Sev better. Yes, she wanted to find out about her realm. But a small part of her wanted to discover why her mind had sorted thoughts more clearly when Sev had shouted in rage at the audience.

She knocked, and, as if she been waiting just inside the door, Jino Kirmiz, Askal Kirmiz's mother, pulled the door open.

"Orilaevar Reysandoral Breula, and Privana Trissandoral Breula."
She smiled, the topographical map of wrinkles curving with the
action. "We are honoured to have you visit our home. Please come
in."

Jino Kirmiz stepped to the side and ushered Ori and Privana into
the space. The ground floor was arranged as if a foyer had been
erased from the original plans because they stepped through the door
and were immediately standing in the kitchen, pressed snugly against
the backs of chairs that were tucked under a table laden with platters
of food. Jino Kirmiz waved her hand at the display.

"We were not sure how many Guard members would be in
attendance so our catering may be somewhat excessive."

Ori smiled. "It looks wonderfully delicious, Jino Kirmiz. Thank
you so much." She tipped her head towards her Deputy. "I have no
other Guard members except Privana Trissandoral Breula who will
be more than happy to enjoy your hospitality."

Privana's eager expression reinforced that statement, as he
visually devoured a platter of fruit, and the elderly woman gave a
pleased nod. She reached into the middle of the veritable cornucopia
of food and plucked up a plate, handing it to Privana who
immediately pulled out a chair and selected cuts of meat, cheese and
the admired fruit.

Ori, lifting an eyebrow at Privana's manners, sat when Jino
Kirmiz had taken her seat, and accepted a plate as well.

"How is Askal Kirmiz? Does he have sufficient business?" Ori
speared three apple slices like a kebab with her fork and slid them
onto the surface of the metal crockery. The intricate design was
beautiful and a testament to Askal Kirmiz's attention to detail and
the excellent balance of his element.

"Askal is very well, thank you. He is in the studio at the moment
with his new apprentice, Sevich. I expect they will be here soon as it
is lunch, but I can ask them to finish now."

Ori wavered. Asking Sev to ride with her out of the township and
into the open fields felt like a request to make in private. Privana
already thought the idea completely daft, and Askal Kirmiz and his
mother probably would as well.

However, the opportunity didn't eventuate because footsteps sounded on the tiles, drew closer and the metal worker entered the kitchen, stopping short when he took in the sight of the King's daughter at the dining table. His open face, usually filled with a smile and sparkling eyes, dropped into one of puzzlement. Clearly, he hadn't received notice of the royal visit and Ori cut a glance at the inscrutable expression on Jino Kirmiz's face.

Askal Kirmiz jolted forward as he was bumped from behind.

"Oh! Sorry, Askal. Wasn't watching where I was going." Sev appeared, side-stepping around him and walked straight to the faucet to sluice water at her face. Drying her skin with a towel, Sev spoke over her shoulder. "I bet lunch is spectacular as normal, Jino." Then she turned and laid eyes on Ori. "Oh, hell no."

Privana leapt to his feet. "You cannot speak to—"

Ori touched Privana's forearm lightly. "It's fine." She made eye contact with Sev. "I am paying a visit to Askal and Jino Kirmiz, and of course yourself, but also I would like to talk to you about gathering knowledge of your realm if you have the time." She took in the heavy leather pants, typical of metal workers, and the loose green shirt that flowed about her torso. It was an industrial, yet enticing, combination.

"Really? That's nice. Talking to me about my *realm*." Sev enunciated the last word. "You've had two weeks since I've been at Askal and Jino's house, but apparently it's taken that long to find the guts to do so." Ori understood the gist of Sev's response, despite not really knowing what guts were, and winced at just how accurate the reply was.

"I'm sorry about that."

"Okay. Well, the answer is no," Sev said through very thin lips, and turned to leave.

Ori quickly pushed back her chair and stood. "Sevich…Sev, wait, please!" She heard the whoosh of three sets of eyebrows disappearing into hairlines.

"What?" Sev whirled around, glared at Ori and thrust her hands onto her hips.

"I…" She caught Privana's stunned expression, his fork frozen halfway to his mouth. "You don't have to speak to me about your realm if you don't want to, but I was—"

"Damn right." Sev leaned over Jino Kirmiz's shoulder, snagged a filled bread roll, whispered a "thank you, Jino", and stomped out of the room.

Askal Kirmiz swung back and forth on his feet, hands in his pockets, while his mother studied Ori with the same inscrutable expression as before.

"That went well," Jino Kirmiz said, leaning her elbow on the table and resting her cheek in her palm.

Ori reclaimed her seat, as Privana looked aghast at even more casual behaviour. Ori wasn't worried about the familiarity. Once they reached a certain age, a few Breulan women, such as Jino, were entirely comfortable displaying a complete lack of deference towards royalty. It was still respectful, yet bordered on mischief, and the dry humour and wit was quite amusing. Except when she was the brunt of the teasing. She rolled her eyes.

"I really would like to talk to Sev—Sevich about her realm. She is the first for so long through the northern portal, and it would be interesting to find out how her world is structured."

"You should probably make another attempt, Orilaevar Reysandoral Breula," Askal Kirmiz said, ungluing his feet from where he stood, then nodding as he sat next to his mother, smiling at her affectionately. "Some of the decorative framing she was crafting," he tipped his head towards the studio, then looked at Ori, "did not balance this morning and perhaps she is still smarting from the disappointment."

Learning to truly balance the elements was a process that could take months, but from the evidence at the application, Ori knew Sev would accomplish that balance very quickly.

"I imagine so. She is also homesick and has been through a dramatic experience."

The lunch and conversation was free-flowing—between Ori and Jino Kirmiz at least—and slightly stilted—with Privana and Askal Kirmiz. Privana's discomfort was likely due to the irregularity of the situation, and Askal Kirmiz's from an attack of nerves and shyness, which meant that the meal was brief. So soon after, Ori and Privana took their leave.

The Kirmiz household probably thought she was completely bonkers, although Jino Kirmiz, if Ori interpreted the long look that the older woman gave when she was saying goodbye, seemed to have read more into the visit than Ori would have wished. It didn't matter. Ori was determined to try again. With a more well-constructed plan.

***

It took Ori a week to revise that plan, which was essentially the same except that she'd decided to leave Privana behind. Privana seemed to irritate Sev, and Ori didn't want Sev irritated. She'd been on the end of Sev's irritation before and had not enjoyed the experience.

Ori hadn't given notice of her visit, hoping to catch Sev…what? Unaware? That thought didn't need analysing. Again, her knock was immediately answered by Jino Kirmiz.

"This is a surprise, Orilaevar Reysandoral Breula," Jino Kirmiz said, not looking surprised at all. "Are you here to ask after Sevich's wellbeing?"

The knowing look that Ori received reminded her much too strongly of those from her mother and she wondered if both women had been having morning teas together.

"Yes, among other matters, such as…" she darted her eyes about, "new door knockers for the Guard member's quarters," she replied eventually, drawing herself up to her full height in an attempt to regain the upper hand, which she immediately lost when Jino Kirmiz smiled broadly.

"It is a shame that they have worn away so quickly. I must remind Askal to work with the element more thoroughly if he is going to create products that cannot last longer than three months." Another smile bearing kindness and understanding appeared on her face, and

Ori couldn't help returning it albeit with a good dose of sheepishness because she'd been caught.

"Mm."

"Let me take you to the courtyard. The workshop is much too noisy to carry on any conversation." She turned to allow Ori into the kitchen, then closed the door. "Would you like a mug of…?"

Ori paused as well. "Water, please."

Her awkwardness felt ridiculous. She'd never experienced anxiety when asking after a woman. Pursuing and winning the affections of Hruti, her last girlfriend—*not* that Sev was applying for that position *at all*—had been a simple case of a raised eyebrow, a smirk, her royal position, and a stolen kiss in the forest away from her Guard. Simple.

Nothing about this was simple.

Mug in hand, Ori trailed after Jino Kirmiz—Queen Sermeh Reytoris Breula Mark Two, apparently—along the corridor, down two steps and into a lovely courtyard with red-leafed vines crawling up one wall, and vibrant blue, green and yellow tiles covering the ground.

"Oh, this is beautiful!" Ori stepped tentatively onto the tiles. They really were much too lovely to walk on.

"Askal finished laying the tiles last week. He was able to trade time and effort with Ralwi Jerth."

Ori nodded as she recognised the name of the Earth element craftsman.

"They're beautiful," Ori repeated.

"I am sorry we do not have chairs here yet. Askal and Sevich are currently crafting them, although with Sevich's assistance, Askal said he will be finished sooner than expected. He says that she is very gifted." She nodded at the steps. "I can sit with you while you wait."

The stone steps looked much too cold and harsh for an elderly woman to be sitting upon.

"I can't ask you to sit there. It wouldn't be comfortable at all."

The woman tutted. "Yes, I know I am old." Ori opened her mouth to protest. "You did not need to say, Orilaevar Reysandoral Breula."

She raised an eyebrow. "I will simply need to move slowly. I have discovered that if I move quickly nowadays, my breasts clap together."

Ori choked on her mouthful of water.

Jino Kirmiz grinned mischievously as she leaned in. Her eyes twinkled.

"And walking outside is a challenge. Hopping over uneven surfaces means I become a veritable percussion set."

Ori sprayed the remaining water onto the tiles, and the woman's cheeky grin showed just how much fun she was having teasing the King's daughter.

There was a snort of laughter at the doorway, and Ori turned to see Sev leaning against the wooden frame, smiling broadly. They gazed at each other and Sev's smile dimmed.

"Well, the dinner will not cook itself," Jino Kirmiz stated, then walked up the steps rather spritely for someone who claimed to suffer from breast applause. She squeezed past Sev and Ori caught the whispered instruction, "Just listen to what she has to say."

Sev frowned and flicked her hand at the steps, dropping onto the top one and squashing her body into the door frame.

Ori placed the mug on the ground beside her, unsheathed her sword, and laid it across her knees, the sharp tip pointing away from Sev. She lowered her body onto the other side of the step. She faced the courtyard. It felt easier to speak to the gorgeous tiles than the gorgeous woman. Again, ridiculous.

"So, you're back." Sev's tone was not welcoming, yet not really unwelcoming. Ori took that as a positive.

"Yes.

There was a long silence, and then Ori caught Sev's glance, then the second one. Ori had gathered her hair in a low ponytail, captured by a leather tie, and she'd forgone her head circlet to scale down the royal presence. Sev didn't seem to appreciate stately trappings. Ori hoped, however, that Sev's second look meant that she did appreciate today's overall presentation. Somehow it felt important.

She swivelled to study Sev who ignored her and continued to stare at the far wall, her arms crossed over her knees, her shoulder pushed firmly into the doorframe. She was wearing the heavy leather pants like last time—very similar to the pair Ori was currently wearing—along with the flowing shirt; this time in a soft orange.

She wore a bandana; the cloth twisted so that it fit snugly against her forehead to contain her wild hair. The choppy brown strands looked as if they'd experienced hours of Sev's tired, frustrated, yet pleased, and satisfied fingers running through them. It had resulted in chaotic spikes. There was a smudge on her cheek that Ori ached to wipe away. A smudge of dirt. A smudge that needed to be—oh, for the love of…Ori glared at herself.

"You're staring. How do I make it stop?" Sev said, frowning at the wall, then turned and leant her back against the wood. They regarded each other for a moment. "You're not very princess-y, you know."

Ori chuckled. "I haven't been told that before. Is royalty different in your realm?"

Sev flicked a hand dismissively. "Some countries still have royalty. They're mainly all pomp and circumstance and get a free ride for doing not much at all." She waved a finger at Ori. "Some of them volunteer for their country's military, and do a proper job, but a lot don't make any effort."

"I do a proper job," Ori said quietly.

"Yeah, I imagine that you do." Sev's shoulders suddenly relaxed. "So, you're on a fact-finding mission." She quirked a smile.

"Yes, it's taken much reconnaissance and strategising to come to this point." Ori gave a mock frown, her eyes sparkling.

Sev laughed. It was light, and delightful.

"What's your battle plan?" Sev rolled her lips, playing along.

"Well, I intend to ask the fact-holder," Ori said, and Sev laughed again, "to join me on some afternoon rides into the plains and wilderness of Breula so that she may also discover the wonders of our realm."

Sev's smile disappeared.

"Riding across the plains?"

The question was becoming tedious.

"I thought it would be a pleasant break from your work." Ori patted the flat of the blade across her thighs as if to demonstrate the work Sev would be having a break from.

Sev shook her head quickly. "That part's fine. It's the riding bit. As in being on a horse. The riding of such." Then her eyes widened. "It's a horse, right? There's no dragons or anything in Breula?"

Ori smothered a smile, and looked up at the pink and white sky through the square created by the edges of the metal roof. "Um..."

"There are?" Sev squeaked.

Ori dropped her gaze, and blinked seriously. "Well..." The she grinned. "No. No dragons."

Sev slapped her on the shoulder.

"You suck. It's not funny, Ori." She leapt up and marched about the small courtyard. "That was mean. I don't know anything about anything." She waved her arms randomly. "I know about the elements, and society, and..." Sev rounded on Ori. "But I really don't know anything at all. And I hate it. I'm so conflicted because I miss my home so much but I'm really enjoying working with Askal and trying out my capabilities with my element." She shoved her fingers into her hair in the gesture that Ori had imagined.

"I'm sorry."

Ori truly was. This wasn't Sev's fault. It wasn't as if she'd come through voluntarily, or so she claimed. Ori believed her. That truth sat well in her stomach. What also sat well in her stomach, actually a bit lower, was the slap to her shoulder. How an aggressive act could be so arousing was incomprehensible.

But it was. Arousing.

Sev paused her pacing. "I know you are. You're probably only a pawn in the giant chess board here, but you're the princess so you should have some clout." She pointed at Ori from where she stood in the middle of the tiled courtyard. "I know you're not solely responsible for the Facility and the injustice of that arena and application experience. But you're here and therefore handy to be pissed off at."

"Being pissed off is the same as severely annoyed?" Ori asked, which seemed to dissolve Sev's anger, because she huffed a laugh, shook her head, and walked over to reclaim her spot on the step.

"I don't particularly want to go on these rides with you. Why can't you come and chat to me here?"

Ori gazed at the ivy escaping over the wall. *Yes, why?*

"Because I would like to talk with you by myself without the Guard, metal workers and their mothers, Queens or townspeople. I'd like," she held Sev's gaze, "to talk with Sev from the Northern portal as Ori, a Breulan."

Sev pursed her lips in thought.

"No."

Ori let her head drop back.

"Not yet." Ori jerked her head up and stared in hope. "First, I want to find out some 'facts.'" Sev twitched her fingers in the air, emphasising the word. "Of my own. Before I go wandering the countryside to admire the sights of Breula like some bug-eyed tourist with a handful of brochures and a please-kidnap-me backpack because I'll be too worried about falling off the horse to take in anything informative."

Ori snorted. "Okay. I will be satisfied with a 'not yet.'"

Sev hummed irritably. "I don't like you," she said, and frowned. "I think? Maybe not." She shook her head again, and Ori had the distinct feeling that Sev did like her but didn't like the fact that she did.

"Okay."

The silence grew.

"But I trust you," Sev murmured. "Why?"

Ori studied Sev's perplexed expression. "I'm not sure, but I'm glad you do, Sev. I only ever tell the truth. It's a habit." She smiled, and Sev chuckled.

Then Sev's smile faded and she contemplated her hands. "I have elemental energy, Ori."

"Of course."

"No. You don't get it. This is such a big deal." Sev looked sideways. "Energy, which is not real."

"Here it is."

"Yes, but I'm not meant to be here."

"Your energy is."

Sev tossed her hands. "That's the thing. I hate that I feel, every now and then, a sense of being at home here. More than Melbourne. I feel so guilty."

"I'm sorry," Ori said again. There was another long silence. "You have elemental energy, Sev, because the portal opened for you, you succeeded in your application, you unbalanced the blade in the arena to help your opponent even if we found her to have trespassed for nefarious reasons. You are Arcanix."

Sev chewed on her top lip, then met Ori's gaze. "How did I know where to find the portal?"

"The portal called to you."

Sev rolled her eyes. *Lord of The Rings,* she whispered which meant nothing to Ori. "I didn't hear anything calling to me."

"Well, it doesn't really make an actual sound but the call can come from anywhere."

"So the back door of a laundromat is fine." Sev tilted her head and widened her eyes.

Sass. It was delicious, and Ori's eyes twinkled at the petulance. "The call came because your energy was listening and when it heard the call you knew where to find the portal because it always opens for one of us." It was very simple, although by the expression on Sev's face it wasn't very simple at all. Ori opened her mouth to try again, but Sev pinned her with a hard stare.

"I'm not one of you. I'm a trespasser."

"You were. Now you're not. And as you said, you have energy, Sev. Elemental energy."

"So does every trespasser."

Ori took her hands off the sword and lifted them, palms up, in compromise. "Not always."

They fell silent to stare at the beautiful tiles on the ground. Then Sev looked sideways at Ori. "How do you keep the portals, you know, portal-ly?" She circled her finger.

Ori lips twitched, then she chuckled. "Portal-ly. I like it. I'm taking that to the next Council meeting."

Sev laughed quietly. "So?"

Ori leaned solidly into the doorframe, ready to settle into an explanation that was going to sound incomprehensible. But somehow she knew Sev would get it because she was smart. Yes, she was abrasive, and sarcastic. Yes, the frustration and sadness simmered underneath which was understandable and Ori felt so much empathy for her. Yes, all of it combined was very attractive. But somehow she knew that Sev would understand the portal routine and structure quite quickly.

"Once a month, two Councillors attend to their designated portal and…" Ori tapped the blade looking for the word, "Peer? Yes, peer through."

"Peer through? Like through a window?"

"Essentially."

"Why?" Sev had turned her body completely so she faced Ori square on. She was clearly intrigued. Curiosity gleamed in her fabulous brown and gold eyes.

"To report on developments, disturbances that may impact on Breula and therefore disrupt the balance. Then they report to the Council and records are kept." Ori leaned her elbows on her knees, cradling the sword on her thighs. "We assume that the trespassers come through when the portals open. Except perhaps for you."

Sev mulled that over for a while, then her eyes widened. "How old do Breulans—how old are you?" She held her hand up. "I'm not being rude, but if Councillors are lurking at portals which have been around for donkeys years, then it wouldn't be the same pair, surely."

Ori quirked a smile, and held up three fingers. "Thirty." She watched as Sev blew out a breath. "And yes, there have been different pairs over the centuries." She frowned. "Although at the moment, there aren't enough Councillors to attend to the new portals in pairs. Some are observing by themselves. It's so dangerous." Ori hissed in consternation.

Sev studied Ori for a moment, then seemed to come to a decision. She leaned over and touched Ori's forearm. "Breula is your heart, isn't it? You care so much for these people. Do you see yourself as the protector of the population? A guardian?"

Ori felt the heat of Sev's hand through her shirt and shivered. A pleasant shiver. Only fifteen minutes ago, Sev had slapped Ori in the shoulder and told her she sucked. Now she was touching her forearm. Ori's body was rioting.

"I do. It's a self-imposed responsibility. I chose to become Captain of the Guard because it is a position where I can make a difference. I can guide and bring out the best in people. It's taken ten years, but I believe the Guard as it is right now is the finest group we've ever had."

"Why do you even need a Guard? There's nothing attacking you."

Ori knew the question was innocent, but it still made her teeth grind together. "There's potential for attack however unlikely and so preparing for potential is of utmost importance."

Sev pulled her hand back, and tucked her head into her neck. Her eyebrows rose.

"Okay." She lifted her hand as if to pacify. "I get it. Most armies have that philosophy." She spread her fingers. "So the Guard patrols the portals and capture trespassers accidental or otherwise." She tapped her forefinger to indicate number one, and quirked a smile. "They defend the castle—"

"Mansion."

"Same thing." Sev tapped the next finger. "They ride around the realm doing realm things." Tap number three. "Did I miss one?"

The answer sat at the tip of Ori's tongue. The role that Sev was missing was a secret and only the Council members and the permanent Guard knew of the location where the orbs grew in the lagoon created by the Juith River. She deflected.

"I'm assuming most armies have similar roles for their members."

It was a weak response and Sev's expression, the way she slowly curled her fingers back into her palm, the way she crossed her arms, indicated that she recognised the non-answer but accepted it nonetheless.

"How's it going with getting me back home to Alex?" Sev narrowed her gaze, pinning Ori to the door frame. Ori straightened and clutched her sword, sliding it up her thighs to her knees.

She couldn't really blurt out that she'd done nothing at all yet. But hesitation must have been written all over her face, because Sev growled and tossed her arms out as she shot up, taking the two steps in a single stride.

"God!" She marched into the middle of the courtyard. "I didn't think so." She whirled around, her hands chopping erratically in the air. "You haven't even thought about helping, let alone started asking people. Obviously people who have more decision-making power than you." More hand waving and tossing and pointing with upwards-facing palms. "You're the daughter of a King of a realm and you can't do anything with that title."

Sev marched forward, standing over Ori who gazed at her in wonder. Her anger lit up the small space and if Ori didn't know any better, she'd swear Sev was glowing as if she were a Light Elemental. It was obviously the sun bouncing off the newly-laid tiles, but it was no less spectacular.

"I'm going to try," Ori said softly.

"Sure you will. When?" Sev's hands curled into fists.

"There are procedures and protocols, Sev."

"No, there's posturing." She jerked her hand at the sword laying across Ori's knees. "Like that. All show and no substance."

"It's my everyday weapon, not my ceremonial—oh."

"See? You don't get it. This is my life you're not bothering with."

"I am botheri—"

"No, you're not!" Sev yelled, and slapped the blade, which shuddered from the force. Her thumb ring connected with the metal; the sound rang in the air. "You need to—" Sev's words stopped in her throat and her face paled. Ori watched in fascination as the flat surface of the sword wobbled like jelly then began to liquify, dipping into a silver 'U' between her knees.

"Well…"

"Oh, God! Oh, God. I'm so sorry." Ori lifted her head to take in Sev's horrified expression. "Ori, I'm so sorry. I didn't mean to." She patted the air as if the action would restore the blade. Ori stood, holding what was essentially a giant silver mug handle and twisted it about.

"Hmm. That's not going to work any more."

Sev wrung her hands. "I'm so sorry. That's beyond repair now. Seriously. I'll make you a new one."

Ori turned to her and grinned as an idea crystallised.

"Yes. You can make me a new sword."

Sev sagged in relief. "I feel awful. I'm so sorry. It's my fault because I let my emotions get the better of me. Of…of my element." Her lips turned down.

"You know? It's okay. But I think this means that you'll have to ride out to the plains to make up for it."

Sev jerked. "That's…I'm already replacing the sword!"

"But the guilt…"

Sev stepped closer. "I really don't like you." She mashed her lips together. "Fine. I'll ride a horse. Give me a placid, friendly one so I don't fall off *and* I'll make you a new sword." She glared, but Ori was positive she caught a glimmer of something—determination?—to somehow prove to Ori that she could ride a horse? To prove to herself that she'd like it?

"Excellent." Ori was enjoying Sev's proximity. "A brand new sword, a riding companion, and a horse with no more spark than a burnt matchstick." She grinned and Sev's faint smile, despite her narrowed eyes, was worth every melted sword.

"Just tell me we're not going to the forests. People tend to get shot there," Sev grumbled.

Ori laughed.

Chapter Seven

Sev gave herself a week to recreate Ori's sword. Seven days seemed a sensible allocation of time to have a chat with a lump of iron explaining her error and discussing the need for balance and the concept of guilt and a person's emotional reactions to the whole of everything.

At that point she'd actually swept her arm about to encompass the tools, the fire, the forge, the entire studio, and realised, after staring at the block in front of her, that she might be slowly and steadily losing her mind.

Askal peered at her work when he strolled over the day after the sword-melting saga. His black bushy eyebrows pushed together in confusion. The expression, including the confused luxuriant eyebrows, was almost a mirror image of Alex's bewilderment at some of her more dodgy decisions. She felt a stab of home sickness. She missed Alex, and Askal's resemblance was sometimes a comfort and a curse.

"I did not realise we had obtained a sword commission."

Sev paused mid-strike, her hammer hanging loosely in her hand. "We didn't."

"Then…" Askal squinted at her, then glanced at the blade that had begun to take shape.

"It's for Ori. I melted her sword."

Askal blinked. Then again. "Mm. I actually do not want to know how that happened, but I am glad you are replacing it. She would expect nothing less." He opened his mouth to speak again, then caught himself.

"What?"

"It surprises me that she allows such a casual abbreviation of her name."

"Ori?"

"Yes. Orilaevar Reysandoral Breula, daughter of the King." He slowly brought his thumb to his forefinger to indicate how short the name had become. "You call her Ori." Then he shook his head, a small smile on his lips. "And she lets you." He laughed then went back to his commission of door knockers for the Facility.

Sev watched him. A sudden warmth, a dart of goodwill and affection for the two people in the house, the town, the townsfolk, pricked her heart. Breula contained good people. She looked about the workshop. Good people who lived in a society that seemed medieval at first glance, but was anything but. It wasn't just the people and how they lived. It was the environment they lived in. It was the respect they paid to their element; a love where they gave and received energy to create conditions that enhanced their lives.

Such as the flooring.

The stone tiles adjoined each other without any grout. They'd simply been handled with care and elemental coaxing to sit quietly. The crushed rock on the roads had been asked to create the routes through the town, handled with such care that the surface was like a brand new autobahn in Germany. The trees supplying the wood for the furniture gave permission for their service.

No, Breula wasn't rough or medieval. It was advanced, clean and balanced. It was Scandinavian modern.

Sev worked on the sword in between her tasks for Askal, which meant that sometimes she was crafting right up until the metalsmith announced it was time to finish for the day. Sev had come to understand that the end of day call wasn't Arcanix union rules if such things existed. It was simply when everyone's energy waned, rendering them unable to focus and manipulate the element. The night was for regeneration and so at the first sign of evening, the township grew quiet.

The problem, Sev discovered early on, was that she didn't experience any waning in her energy at all. Nothing. She felt like a permanent battery, topped up and happy to work through the night.

Somehow she knew this was not information to share. It felt unsafe to inform everyone that she was the Arcanix equivalent of the Energizer Bunny. So she stopped work when Askal said to and followed him into the kitchen to share in another of Jino's amazing meals.

However, on day four of the 'I'm-so-sorry-for-turning-your-sword-into-goo' reparations, her attempt to blend in came undone.

"Yeakhorth Suurd expects these shoe lasts this afternoon," Askal said that day, late into the afternoon, indicating the crate of iron 'feet' that had been created for the tailor on the other side of the township. "I will be a little while so could you pack up at sunset before your energy dissipates?"

Sev gave a thumbs up—a gesture that still baffled the metalsmith —then she completely forgot the instruction, and continued to work on the sword. Quietly and carefully, she stamped and scored a series of intricate whorls into the steel, whispering to the blade, and complimenting its beauty. And soon the sky was dark.

The forge was low, heat drifting into the workshop in soft, tiny waves, and the globe beside Sev's head was the only light in the space.

"Sevich!" Askal's horrified hiss sounded next to her ear and Sev dropped the small scorer onto the bench.

"Shit!"

She straightened, and blinked in the muted glow of the studio.

Askal's eyes were huge. "You must stop." His gaze flitted between her hands, the sword, the fine lines in the blade, back to her eyes. He pointed a trembling finger. "How?"

Damn. She'd been so careful. "Oh. The energy after dark thing?" A grimace twisted her mouth and her shoulders dropped in resignation.

Askal seemed lost for words. "How?" he repeated.

"I actually don't know. It's like—" she stared at the large patterned stone tiles on the floor, then at the stunned expression on her mentor's face.

Suddenly, Askal threw a thick blanket over the sword, gathered the tools into his hands, placed them into their individual sections of a large wooden tray, and pointed to the light. "Please rebalance it, then come up into the kitchen." He turned on his heel and hurried out of the room.

Sev sighed. "Well, crap."

Cupping her hands about the lantern, she blew the flame out—rebalanced—and followed her mentor up the stairs.

Clutching a mug of hot cocoa—coffee didn't exist in Breula which was another reason to return to Melbourne—she looked across the table at Askal whose horrified expression had been replaced by an interesting combination of curiosity and concern.

"You are an Elemental," he stated, and let out a short cough of disbelief.

"Mm. I'm probably not."

"You are. You are more than Arcanix and the only other possibility is an Elemental. But…" He circled his finger at her throat.

Sev touched the base of her neck. "Oh! An orb." That was difficult to explain. "I've never felt like I needed one."

Yes. Very difficult to explain.

"The Elementals must wear an orb to retain permanent energy."

"I know." She sipped at her rapidly cooling drink and wished that hot chocolate would stay hot.

"And yet, you maintain your energy without an orb." Askal continued to stare and Sev figured he was stating facts before he put forward any potential theories.

"Yes, I do." She sipped again. "Look, Askal. I'm just as confused as you are."

Askal pushed his mug away and folded his hands together on the table. "Tell me what you feel when you work with the Metal element. Even in your realm."

Sev hummed. "I've always felt an affinity with my element in Melbourne. But," she tapped the table, "here in Breula I feel like I'm more in touch with it. Much more than back home."

Askal angled his head. "You were not as…" His eyes roved across her face. "Powerful?" He nodded as if satisfied with his word choice.

"Powerful." Sev huffed a single laugh, then sobered. "Yeah, okay. That's probably the right word." Another sip of her drink. "Metal feels alive to me. It always has. I completed a metalwork course when I was nineteen, and when I walked into the workshop at the college," she smiled at the memory, "it felt like coming home."

Askal nodded slowly.

Sev continued. "I can remember the first time the Metal spoke to me." Askal's eyebrows lifted and Sev bobbed her head from side to side. "You know what I mean. It didn't speak to me as such, but we definitely communed. Anyway, I'd cast and polished a small silver cat and it kind of vibrated in my hand. I nearly dropped the thing. The teacher was walking by and laughed. Said something like if I dropped it, I wouldn't pass the certificate." She held Askal's gaze. "I didn't drop it. I held that little cat for hours afterwards, and that piece of art was warm and glowed and it felt right."

They stared at each other for a while until Askal exhaled very slowly. "We cannot tell anyone about your energy."

"Yeah, I figured." Sev scratched the side of her neck, then rubbed her lips with her palm. Thinking gestures. "It would make a few people uncomfortable."

"And jealous."

"Really?"

"Yes. Many Arcanix will assume that you have stolen, or been given, an orb and I would hate to see you in danger."

Sev pressed her lips together and delivered a short hum. "Or you and Jino."

"Yes," Askal admitted. "Yes. I would be accused of assisting you or harbouring you." He flipped his hands slightly on the table and gave a soft shrug. "The latter of which I am going to do, anyway." He smiled. "The harbouring part. The assisting?" Another hand flip. "I have no idea what your energy really is but I feel experimenting with it for curiosity's sake is careless. The Council would not be so lenient."

"What...what would they do?" Tingles of apprehension shivered in her spine. She didn't want this gift, this energy. The fact that it had been growing in the eight weeks that she'd been living in Breula was worrying.

"There is no telling, really. You would certainly be made to demonstrate your capabilities so that they can decide on their plan of action."

"I'm not a science experiment!" Sev ground out.

"I rather think you would be."

They abruptly turned at the calm words issuing from the doorway.

"Mother, I thought you were asleep."

Jino strolled over to the kettle, felt the side, and must have decided it was still warm enough because she poured a mug of the milky drink, then joined them at the table.

"Whispering about the important can be as loud as shouting about the irrelevant." She sipped, placed her mug gently on the wood, then interlaced her fingers, and looked pointedly at Sev. "I missed the first part but I gather you are an Elemental without an orb which means the Council must not be told because you will be taken and studied and your presence will concern many. An important reason for secrecy. The inconvenience to Askal at the loss of the best apprentice he has ever known, and the fact that I am fond of you is also important." She smiled and reached across to cover Sev's hand.

Sev swallowed. The sense of family she felt with these people was overwhelming. "Besides the studying part," Sev turned her hand so she could hold the older woman's, "what else would happen?"

"I do not know," Askal answered. "There has never been one such as you."

"Terrific." Sev rolled her eyes. Her life in Melbourne was so ordinary compared to this.

"Most likely you would be sent back to your own realm because here you are upsetting the balance," Jino supplied, releasing Sev's hand to wrap her fingers around her mug.

Sev sat straighter in her chair. "But that's a good thing. I get to go back to Melbourne and everything's all fine again." Her heart twisted at the thought of leaving Askal and Jino and some of the townsfolk that she'd come to know. And even Ori which was silly because she didn't really like Ori. Probably. Maybe. Fine, she did.

Jino shook her head. "No, you might not go home. You might be sent to another realm."

Sev was horrified. "Why?"

"There are some in the Council who have hidden agendas. They feign deference and allegiance to Breula yet it is somewhat of a ruse. There are whispers that some trespassers are escorted to other realms to ensure that they cannot return."

"That's crazy. I'm not a threat!" Sev shoved back her chair and stalked about the kitchen, then tucked her hands into her armpits. "And why can't the King or the citizens get rid of the dodgy Councillors, particularly if you know about them? Isn't there a type of voting?" Then she halted, inhaled quickly, and studied Jino. "Ori's a Councillor. What if she's corrupt?"

"She is not. I would absolutely state that under any oath." Askal's lips were set in a stern line. "A voting system does not exist in Breula. Elementals become Councillors through birth, through recommendations from other Councillors and generally only when a Councillor retires or relinquishes their position. We are not..." He seemed to search for a word. "A fair system."

"You're not a democracy or even a constitutional monarchy." Sev reclaimed her seat, leaning heavily on her elbows.

"No. The Councillors act as advisors, and with a Council of fifty, much of the King's time is taken up with listening."

"God, this society is so messed up. The Trespassers being held in the Facility, then the winners becoming Arcanix who then become townsfolk who can only *exist*." Her fingers air-quoted the word. "In the daytime like reverse vampires." Sev grimaced at Jino and Askal. "Sorry. And then there's the Elementals who are born in Breula and just waltz along in life wearing an orb like it's a jewel at the Met Gala. What about the townsfolk who are born here? They're Breulans just as much as Elementals." She ran out of puff.

They contemplated each other, then Askal folded his arms and laid them on the table. "Yes. We are Breulans, but we are not Elementals. Our energy is not strong enough or rather our energy is not sustained."

"But wouldn't an orb increase the power?"

"No. It simply makes it last longer. An Elemental's power remains the same."

"So the Elementals are the only people who can maintain the balance of the entire realm's elements even though all the Arcanix and regular citizens balance elements every day."

"Yes."

A thought occurred to her. "That's why townspeople don't get a last name, isn't it? The Elementals and Guard members do."

"Yes," Askal repeated.

Sev rolled her eyes. "Elementals are simply Arcanix with privilege."

Mother and son laughed. "You are adept at finding the sharp edge of the chisel," Askal said and Sev grinned at the nail on the head idiom. It seemed turns of phrase could be translated across realms.

"What happens if an Arcanix or citizen gets together with an Elemental and they decide to have a child?" Sev's questions continued to multiply in her head.

Jino raised a finger. "It is uncommon, but does happen." She delivered a smile. "You cannot help who you fall in love with, can you?"

Sev dwelt on that very true statement.

Jino continued. "The child is an Elemental but does not receive an orb."

"Far out. That's harsh. Mum or Dad or whoever are parading about with a necklace and the other parent and the kid are second-class citizens." Then a thought occurred to her. "How do people know that the Elemental is strong enough to hold that energy? Strong enough to wear the orb? Do they have a practical test as well?"

Askal scoffed. "No. It is assumed."

"That's…"

"Unfair?" said Jino.

"Yeah."

"Mm. It is, but this is how our society is structured." Jino cocked her head. "You, my dear, are an anomaly. You do not need an orb because you seem to have unlimited energy. You can manipulate the Metal element in a manner that most Metal Elementals could only dream of."

"Metal superhero." Sev smirked, then realised that a smirk really wasn't appropriate for the moment and let it fall. "Well, you're right. It isn't fair. God, the societal structure here can bite my arse."

Jino and Askal blinked. It seemed not every turn of phrase translated across realms.

Sev pointed at Askal. "Don't you want to…?" Overthrow seemed a little extreme. "Change the system?"

"No. It would be counter-productive. We are happy, healthy, with benevolent leadership despite a few exceptions, and we have balance in our land. All the elements are at peace and to destabilise that would be catastrophic." Askal's fingers flattened on the table. "But you, Sevich? You are unusual and therefore could disrupt the balance."

"I'm not doing it on purpose," Sev said, defensively.

"We know, my dear." Jino reclaimed Sev's hand. "It is why we will continue like we have until we decide on a plan." She looked at Askal, then back to Sev. "Because there will need to be a plan as I feel there is much we do not know."

***

After the others had retired to their bedrooms, Sev checked the mechanism on the front door as she did most nights, admiring the clever simplicity of the lock; the bar on the inside of the handle which dropped into a groove while the other end cleverly slotted into the opposite groove on the upward swing, then the latch that slid across to prevent any movement.

The discovery of her unintentional power had clearly thrown Askal; his initial fear had been palpable. Jino seemed less horrified. In fact, when Sev thought back to the conversation, Jino had been calm, analytical, and all too knowing. Interesting. It was as if she'd been waiting for this revelation which was absurd. Jino seemed to be a deep vessel. Sev bit at her top lip. It occurred to her that in eight weeks Jino hadn't shared what element she possessed, but something had stopped Sev from asking. Not only had Jino not mentioned her element, she hadn't demonstrated her element either. Which was weird. What Jino had shown, though, was her ability to hug. To protect. To wrap Sev in soft words that soothed.

A pang of loss, of a desire for something she'd never experienced, stabbed at her soul. Jino was the mother figure she'd wanted throughout her life in Melbourne. A mother to confide in. To depend upon. To love.

Later, as Sev lay in bed, tears pricked at her eyes. It took her a long time to get to sleep, and the Breulan version of counting sheep —numbering the knots in the planks of wood lining the ceiling— finally did its job.

In the next few days, Jino was more successful at maintaining normality than Askal, although beheading the strawberries at breakfast as if she were in charge of a Revolutionary guillotine hinted at her agitation. The potential of Sev being exposed and the ensuing consequences probably spurred Jino's aggressive precision.

Askal was less circumspect, stiffening his spine when a customer arrived to place or collect an order, and darting his eyes at Sev, who rolled hers in response. She wasn't about to chuck anvils around. Hardly subtle.

Instead, she continued with the sword, adding the final touches, and polishing the metal so her reflection shimmered in the ridged line running down the centre of the blade. Then, at the end of the day, as Askal hovered, twitching from one foot to the other, she carefully hung her tools, and apron, and extinguished the light over her work station.

The sword was finished and ready to present to Ori the following day when they embarked on the ride through the wilderness. Sev chewed her lip. That section of the day would be interesting and she wondered what Ori's idea was of a placid and friendly horse. Probably last year's winner of the Melbourne Cup.

***

Ori had been staring at the sword, held across her palms, for at least two minutes, and Sev began to panic. Was the sword the wrong length? The wrong pattern? The wrong everything? She was sure that she'd copied it exactly. Her memory for Metal was perfect.

"Is it…?"

Ori's head lifted, and a slow smile crept onto her lips. Sev's skin tingled.

"It's beautiful. Thank you." The smile bloomed properly. "You are a revelation. I haven't ever possessed such a piece. Even my ceremonial sword is not so well crafted." She shifted to slide it into her scabbard, holding Sev's gaze at the same time, which was all a bit sexy when combined with the riding pants, the casual wool over-shirt, her hair tied back with the black leather band that Sev had admired at the beginning of the week. Sexy thoughts were unexpected, particularly when she wasn't sure if she actually liked… Sev sighed to herself. Sexy thoughts were really nice.

"Well, I'm glad you like it. I try not to go around melting swords as a rule. It tends to upset people."

Ori grinned, white teeth blazing, then gestured at Sev's satchel. "Snacks for the journey?"

Sev's eyebrows lifted, her lips twitching with amusement. "When did this little ride go from a bit of a jaunt to a journey requiring food?"

Ori laughed and Sev warmed to the sound. Ori had a great laugh.

"I just assumed. I don't know if your people require—".

"Ori."

"Teasing," Ori said, her voice laced with amusement.

Sev grumbled. "If you must know, it's." She reached into the satchel and plucked out one of five metal mice that she'd made that morning. "A handful of these." She placed the ornament into Ori's palm. Since that lesson during her diploma, she'd created hundreds of the pieces over the years, and noticed that since she'd been living in Breula, her skill had increased so much that the animals seemed almost alive. The pieces were quick and enjoyable to make and giving them to the children warmed her heart.

The metal held Ori's attention.

"There are six kiddos living here next to the stables," Sev indicated with her chin, "that missed out last week so I said I'd bring theirs today. I whipped up these guys yesterday." Sev took in the strange look on Ori's face and sighed. "You're not listening."

Ori blinked. "Yes, I am."

"What did I say?"

"Kids. Gifts." Ori glanced at the mouse, then shot Sev a mischievous look. "You've created yourself."

Sev glared. "Shut up. You're not funny."

A passing townsperson stared at Sev. He'd probably never heard someone talk to the princess like that, particularly with her arms crossed, feet shoulder-width apart, growly words, and eyebrows furrowed in pissed-off-ness.

"I'm sorry." Ori delivered the little animal to Sev's palm. "It wasn't a very good tease." She smiled and pointed to the mouse. "Your work is incredibly intricate. They are almost sentient." Another smile. The same smile. Her eyes holding Sev's gaze. Sexy thoughts.

"You're very gifted," Ori whispered, which forced an army of tingles to march up and down Sev's skin. Oh boy.

The silver mice were duly delivered to six very excited children who hugged Sev about her hips, then joined their parents at their respective front doors to gaze, eyes wide with awe and adoration, at the daughter of the King leaning against their garden gates.

"They love you," Sev said, as the pair strode down the back lane towards the stables.

Ori gave a kind of contemplative hum. "Not love as such, really. Probably it's more that I'm easier to relate to than some of the other Elementals or Councillors. I dislike the idea of an aloof, condescending, royal snob because it disrespects people no matter where they exist in Breulan society."

Sev silently sucked in a breath. How conflicting. The first half of the statement was lovely and made her warm towards Ori even further, but the second half made her growl. Thinking about where people existed in the society brought back the conversation with Jino and Askal and permanent energy and keeping secrets.

***

Kotrol sneezed, spraying wet unimaginable into Sev's ear.

"Oh, ew." Her hands were busy adjusting leather straps, metal clips and other paraphernalia, which meant that she had to lift her shoulder in an attempt to wipe the mess away, then try, for the second time, to haul her body up and over the horse's back.

"Do you need help?" Ori's voice held barely contained laughter and that alone made Sev more determined to achieve the feat by herself.

"Nope."

Sev stuck her foot into the stirrup and flung her body up and over. That was the plan, anyway. She hopped about on her free foot having ricocheted off Kotrol's side.

"For God's sake."

There were many skills in Sev's personal toolbox of expertise but mounting a horse was not one of them.

"Seriously, Sev. Stop being so stubborn," Ori said, her voice close.

Sev yanked her stuck foot from the stirrup and spun around.

"I said I can…" She faded off, taking in Ori's presence; so near—Sev could have lifted her hand to run it down Ori's chest—and so blonde and blue-eyed and tall and strong and leather-clad and—"Um." She dragged her gaze from the beautiful yellow sphere at the base of Ori's throat up to her gorgeous blue eyes, then cleared her throat. "Wow, there's a lot of you, isn't there?"

A slow smile lifted Ori's lips.

"So, can I help?"

CHAPTER EIGHT

"These really are the best pants I've ever worn, and, trust me, I've worn all the pants."

Sev waved vaguely at her thighs and the region above it, as her body rocked in the saddle. Ori cast an appreciative glance at the indicated area and then took in Sev's body in general. She'd been sneaking glances since they'd started the ride and being granted permission to look more openly was quite the gift. She grinned.

"Yes, they have an assortment of redeeming features. There is the inclusion of ties, and pockets."

"Exactly! Pockets!" Sev gestured elaborately, accidentally tugging on her reins. "The dilemma for women since forever."

Ori shrugged with incomprehension. Pockets were a sensible inclusion in all outer garments. Perhaps Sev's realm was riddled with many clothing controversies.

Spotting the rocky outcrop where she'd planned to stop, Ori twitched her hand, guiding Ukih towards it. Sev followed suit, then slid off Kotrol, the grey and white horse Ori had chosen for her. She'd hoped his soft, quiet nature would suit Sev's inexperience. Surprisingly, once Ori had helped Sev onto Kotrol's back, it was as if Sev had been riding for years, such was her almost instant understanding of his gait. Kotrol seemed to listen to every word she whispered into his ear when she leant forward, and responded favourably when she rubbed his neck. Ori smiled softly. Sev was a quick learner.

Ori jumped down, slid her sword into a scabbard attached to the saddle, then arranged the reins into a loose knot. "Stay close, Ukih. I don't need to chase you all over the plains like last time."

The horse huffed, his lips wobbling as if he was laughing, and Sev chuckled.

"Sounds like he's got your number."

Ori squinted, unsure of the phrase, but assumed it meant that Ukih simply made up his own mind.

"Yes, he's wilful." She delivered a look of admonishment at her horse.

Sev laughed again, then turned to Kotrol. "Would you mind staying near, please?" she asked as she smoothed her hand down his neck. She paused for a moment, her hand resting on his coat, then nodded, and Ori could have sworn Sev and Kotrol had just had a quick conversation.

Ori shook away the impossible idea, and cast her arm about to take in the landscape.

"The view from here is beautiful. It's the highlight of the tour," she said playfully, indicating to Sev to join her at the largest rock, its flat face directed towards the horizon where the sun would soon be falling over its edge.

They rested their backs against its rough surface, and Sev bumped Ori's shoulder to acknowledge the sass. Ori's stomach swooped. This Arcanix was getting under her skin in a rather pleasant way and Privana's advice came tumbling back into her mind. Don't get attached. But she was getting attached. The loudest thought in her mind was that she had no plans to detach.

"We're on a tour?" Sev replied just as playfully, her eyes sparkling.

The banter nearly dipped its toes into the pond of flirting. Ori held Sev's gaze. "Absolutely."

Sev lifted the corners of her lips. "Do I get a t-shirt?" Ori blinked and Sev laughed. "I'm sorry. That's a terrible line. I know you don't know what a t-shirt is." She bumped Ori's shoulder again.

"Hmm. I know what a t-shirt is," Ori said, tilting her head and frowning. "I'm simply wondering why you chose such a cliched souvenir."

Sev laughed. "Oh, touchè." Then she winked, and a soft blush dusted her cheeks as if she thought she'd gone too far with the gesture. Ori was perfectly happy with the distance of that gesture if her tingling goosebumps were any indication.

A comfortable silence fell between them as they stared into the vast fields, and Sev looked to be admiring the far away hills rolling up into the gorgeous pink and white sky.

"The wind wolves are restless," Ori whispered after a while, then assumed that Sev's silence meant the phrase was not common in her land.

"Do you hear the cry as the pack goes by, The wind-wolves hunting across the sky?" Sev murmured, leaning into Ori's shoulder.

"You know the phrase?"

"Not well. It's the first line from a poem by William Sargent. I had to learn it at school. The whole poem is a giant metaphor for kids seeing animals in the clouds." She pulled away and regarded Ori. "What does it mean here?"

Sev's eyes, almost amber as they reflected the ball of sunlight at the horizon, paralysed Ori and the temptation to simply lean over and kiss Sev's lips was all encompassing. It was completely irrational. Yes, she was attracted to the woman but this was ridiculous. It was almost as if she had no say in any of her feelings at all. She wrenched her gaze away and continued to take in the landscape below them.

"Here it means the heads of the tall grass. It rustles and howls like a pack of wolves."

"Do you have wolves here?"

"Yes, but much further away in the Rifth Valley."

Sev's lips formed an 'O', then she hummed, obviously satisfied at the distance between her and packs of wolves.

They resumed their contemplation.

"How many people live in Breula?"

"In the town? Probably five thousand people? But in the realm? Most likely another thousand or so." Ori met Sev's quizzical gaze.

"Probably?"

"Yes. The last census conducted was over one hundred years ago. You'd think a census would be an excellent tool for maintaining balance or tracking mastery of the elements but the results of that census were used dangerously."

"How?" Sev's face expressed concern.

"A group of Elementals," Ori's face darkened in anger, "members of the Guard, in fact, had taken it upon themselves to rank," she hissed the word, "the elements in order of importance, of their value to Breulan society. They were going to use the census to cast out the element they regarded as least important so that more trespassers could enter the realm to become Arcanix with the favourable elements."

Sev's hand crept onto Ori's forearm.

"God, that's awful. The elements can't be ranked. That's terrible!"

It was touch-and-go; Ori wanted to haul Sev upright, wrap her in the strongest, warmest hug and never let her go. She only just restrained herself, because in that moment, Sev was perfect. Of course, the elements couldn't be ranked. Yes, the misuse of census data was appalling. Sev was right. But beyond that, Sev hadn't asked which element had placed at the end of that list as if she knew the betrayal by the Guard, Ori's Guard, albeit one hundred years ago, was the most distressful. And that said so much about this wonderfully astute woman.

"It was an unpleasant moment in our history. Therefore," Ori shrugged, "we were, and still are, a realm attuned to balance rather than restrained by numbers. It seems the former tends to look after the latter, anyway."

Sev studied her for a bit, then nodded slowly. After quickly squeezing Ori's forearm, she moved back and smiled.

"What were you like as a teenager?"

Ori blinked. "If a teenager is before adulthood, then I was already training to be a Guard member."

"Really?" Sev's eyes sparkled.

"Yes. I attended schooling, of course, but our schooling includes elemental energy and manipulation and for Elementals who wish to join the Guard, there is a need to learn preliminary skills before the trials."

"Were you a bit obnoxious and full of yourself about being the princess and on track to become the next Guard Leader?"

Sev grinned, and Ori returned it. The tension was lovely.

"No. I took myself very seriously."

Sev gasped. "You? No!"

Ori lifted an eyebrow at her. Another moment of wanting to grab her and hold her close, and Ori congratulated herself on her restraint.

"Ha ha! What about you? Were you obnoxious?"

"I didn't get a chance to be obnoxious. I had to fend for myself." She waved her hand in dismissal and pointed to Ori's throat. "I like your orb. The colours, I mean. The yellows remind me of a gem called citrine or even a yellow Cape diamond. It's beautiful." She turned away before Ori could respond, as if she'd said enough and wanted to study the landscape further.

They sat in silence.

"Why did you name me Sevich?" Sev asked, the question aimed at the ground.

"Because you are brave." Ori dared to touch Sev's forearm, thrilled that Sev didn't flinch. "Mice are fearless and inventive and adaptable. I saw that the first time we met." She removed her hand and smiled as Sev turned towards her. "I'm a good judge of character," she finished.

Sev's gaze roamed across Ori's face. "I don't feel brave, Ori. I hate that I've come to like this place so much and sometimes I catch myself not thinking about Alex." Her eyes filled with tears. "How awful is that? He's my family. But I feel the energy here, and the balance, in my bones. I feel like Askal and Jino are my family but I've only been here just over eight weeks. I've known Alex twelve years. I'm a horrible person."

Tears, held back stoically, now fell slowly down her cheeks. Sev swiped at them aggressively and dropped her head as if embarrassed to reveal her despair.

"You're not a horrible person, Sev. I happen to think you're rather amazing and fearless and adaptable and…"

Sev slowly lifted her head and studied Ori. "And?"

Ori went for it. "And just so wonderful," she whispered, and the sensation of slowly being pulled towards the woman beside her was overpowering. "Can I give you a hug?"

Sev blinked, the final tears disappearing with the action. "Why?"

Ori eased back. That hadn't gone well. "Um, because you are—"

"Yes, please." Sev leaned in, wriggling a little so Ori could adjust her arm and curl it about Sev's shoulders.

"I promise I'm working on getting you home," Ori murmured into her hair and swallowed the sadness at the idea of Sev leaving.

One of the 'working on' situations had occurred only three days after Sev had melted Ori's sword. Ori's irritation at the Councillors still prickled her mind even four days later. She rolled the memory of the meeting around in her brain while Sev leaned into her side.

***

"She has requested to return to her realm," Ori stated calmly from where she stood in the centre of the Council chamber. "I see no harm in it. We return trespassers to their own realms when they are not successful in their application. Why not an Arcanix living in Breula?"

The mumbling of fifty Councillors who had never heard of such a concept reverberated about the Chamber.

"I think that it is reckless, Orilaevar Reysandoral Breula." Councillor Dasoskach Vaern Breula met Ori's narrowed eyes, the squat woman's shoulder lifted as if to suggest coyness or innocence, and a tiny smile slipped onto her painted lips.

Ori ground her teeth.

"It isn't." She jerked her hands forward in frustration. "If we say the trespassers have won their freedom into Breula, but we don't let them return then they're hardly free, are they?"

More mumbling.

"Orilaevar, perhaps we should—" The King began.

"No, Father, we need to solve this because Sev—Sevich is becoming more distressed each day. She has family—found family —in Melbourne, and because she is an accidental trespasser, they will be very concerned for her safety." She took in her father's thoroughly unimpressed expression at her impoliteness. "Sorry. That's…sorry."

"But she is adapting well?" asked a Councillor to her right.

"I have heard she is a Metal Arcanix and is quite popular with the townspeople," said another.

Ori growled. "That's not the—"

"Perhaps you have not thought this scenario through," Councillor Buwrec Robrong Breula suggested, his deep voice resonating across the floor. Ori thought she heard a subtle warning in the sentence but dismissed it. Hearing hidden threats from that particular Councillor was simply due to her dislike of the man.

"What possible scenario is that?" She twisted her lips to the side so she could chew the inside of cheek rather than march across the chamber and knock the man off his chair.

He smiled patronisingly. "This Sevich has resided in Breula eight weeks, including her time in the Facility. She now has knowledge about our realm; knowledge that trespassers who are unsuccessful do not have. When they return to their realm, they take nothing of value with them. Nothing that could be used against us. Therefore the balance is maintained. However," his smile lifted at one side, "Sevich could return to Breula with others. She could share intimate knowledge of our society and therefore balance will be lost. Think of the people."

Ori gave him a long look. She doubted that Councillor Buwrec Robrong Breula had thought of the people during his entire tenure as a Councillor.

"That would never happen. Sev wasn't fleeing persecution. She wasn't on some sort of reconnaissance mission. She has no desire to steal orbs or bring a gang of people back to disrupt anything. Her existence in this realm is an accident."

"I am curious why this particular Arcanix has caught your attention, Orilaevar Reysandoral Breula," Councillor Dasoskach Vaern Breula said, then giggled as if sharing a secret with those around her.

Ori flushed. "Councillor Dasoskach Vaern, Sev has caught my attention, in the mundane definition of the phrase, because she is an anomaly, and anomalies do not assist in maintaining the balance in Breulan society. Therefore, Sev should be returned to her realm for her own benefit, but more importantly, she should be returned for the benefit of Breula because she has no place here."

Horrible words that hurt and stabbed. *I'm sorry, Sev.* But harsh words were the only tools to use when chipping away at tradition.

"Not that it is any of my—the Council's—business, of course, but if the daughter of the King is showing an inter—"

"The discussion has finished." King Rodlamar Reytoris Breula projected his deep voice above Councillor Dasoskach Vaern's simpering commentary. "I think we have enough information." His gaze took in each Elemental, the slow survey reducing the grumbling to silence. "I am of the opinion that our accidental Arcanix poses no threat. If it is within the bounds of our current laws, we should look for a positive outcome for her as soon as possible. Let us table it for our next meeting."

Ori breathed out, shook off the film of frustration that always settled over her after Council meetings, then returned to her seat. The next meeting would have to do.

"Thank you, father," she murmured. He cast a stern look at her, then leaned into her space.

"You are antagonising the Council, Orilaevar. Some of your suggestions are beyond what our laws allow. Yes, I may agree with you, but I must listen to the Council's advice. Please trust the process."

Trusting the process was doing not much at all, which meant that the next morning, while creating more fruit routines on the patterned crockery in front of her, she'd led the family small talk.

"What would happen if a horde of people from another realm decided to invade so they could steal the orbs?" Ori wasn't stupid. She hadn't become Captain of the Guard for no reason, and she knew exactly what would happen if a collection of armed people arrived en masse intent on the grand heist of their vital energy source.

But she needed her father, and mother, who had resettled her teacup on its saucer, to understand the not-marauding nature of Sev's desire to return home. No matter how much it hurt to think of Sev returning home.

"All the orbs?" her father asked, pushing his plate away.

"Yes."

"I cannot even begin to imagine." He lightly tip-tapped the table top, little finger to thumb, and frowned in contemplation. "They would gain a mighty power source, which would supply energy to their realm for millennia, and in the process devastate Breula." Her father eyes made contact with hers and their gaze spoke of the magnitude of such a cataclysmic event.

"We would be incredibly vulnerable as an incursion would be beyond the capacity of our Arcanix. Only the Elementals would be able to protect the realm on a constant basis," her mother added.

"The Guard are all Elementals as are the Councillors, and us," Ori said.

"Exactly. We are the protectors of the realm but a horde of people intent on taking our energy source would eventually overwhelm us. I imagine that if I was an invading realm, I would seize the orbs, then direct my forces to eradicate the largest threat first.

"Elementals." Ori said, circling her finger at the three of them, then dwelt on the scenario and shuddered. "We wouldn't survive," she said, echoing her father's words. "There would have to be a miracle."

"All of this is hypothetical. We have never experienced an invasion, and none of the Councillors or members of the Guard have heard anything about one in the near future," her father said, sighing as if the conversation was starting to become slightly pointless. "Orilaevar, I know you are only wanting the best for Sevich, and I know the likelihood of her leading an invasion through the northern laundromat portal is minimal." He delivered an indulgent smile and Ori shifted uncomfortably. "I also know where this line of questioning is stemming from. I am on your side here, but quite a few of the Councillors need to be convinced."

Ori sighed. "I know. I just wish there was a way to streamline these things. It's so drawn out."

"It is as it has always been."

"That's what I said. Drawn out."

Queen Sermeh Reytoris Breula chuckled quietly. "Darling, you are impatient." She held up a finger halting Ori's protest. "And, of course, I agree with you." She turned to her husband. "Rodlamar Reytoris, darling, you have said yourself how frustrated you are at the lengthy process and how you sometimes wish for change."

The King widened his eyes at his wife as if she'd blurted out a tightly held secret.

Ori's eyebrows lifted. "You have?" she asked in amazement.

Inhaling deeply, he flicked a glance from his wife to his daughter. "Yes. I have wished that our governing system could be more efficient yet continue to maintain the integrity of our laws and traditions. Efficiency and tradition seem disharmonious at the moment."

Ori willed her hands to remain still, because she desperately wanted to clutch her cutlery, thrust her fists into the air and shout, "Finally!"

Instead, she smiled broadly. "Okay, then. Now to convince those stubborn Councillors that Sev isn't a concern, and she can head back to her realm, and not," her smile faltered, "return, leading a collection of tall Sev clones with chaotic emotional hair, brown eyes that see everything, bearing metal-working tools and sarcastic wit." She dropped her eyes to her plate, but didn't miss her mother's long look.

***

Meanwhile, she was holding a woman who created all sorts of enjoyable responses in her body. The wind wolves dancing across the tops of the grass on the plains matched the volume of Sev's whispered words.

"Are we friends?"

Ori breathed deeply, leaned back into the rock, lifting Sev's head from her shoulder in the process. They stared at each other. "I think so," Ori replied, then amended her answer. "Yes."

Sev slid her gaze over Ori's shoulder. "Okay, then." She brought her eyes back and nodded. "Okay," she repeated, then tucked her legs into her chest, one leg under the other and stood. Ori wished friendship was just the beginning but clearly Sev wasn't interested in making wishes.

They walked slowly, their horses tagging along, down the slope towards a large stand of trees which, when they skirted the perimeter, would lead them to the road back to the town.

"So, after chatting to the Councillors, there's a bunch who reckon I'm a massive threat." Sev waved her hand in front of her torso.

Ori tilted her head in resignation, then nodded, having relayed the entire Council meeting proceedings and then the conversation with her parents.

"Ori, you know I wouldn't. First of all, I don't know that many people in Melbourne to create a marauding mob even if I wanted to, and secondly, it would never happen because you and I are friends now and friends don't raid each other's realms, unless that friend's got more followers on TikTok." She grinned, but the smile dissolved quickly, and she stopped, pressing a hand to Ori's shoulder. They stood, contemplating each other's faces, and Ori marvelled again at the gold in Sev's brown eyes. She congratulated herself on the restraint she was showing by not leaning in and softly kissing Sev's lips. The location seemed a perfect kissing spot. It was a perfect kissing moment. A completely inappropriate kissing moment.

"I know. In all seriousness, I know." She was conscious of Sev's hand on her shoulder. "I'm sorry you're in this predicament. It's creating such agitation for you. Such imbalance." An idea struck her. "Would you like to talk to the trees?"

Sev blinked and withdrew her hand. "That's got to be the weirdest invitation I've ever received."

"Oh." Ori rolled her lips in. "If a Breulan is feeling unbalanced, it is recommended that they sit inside a grove of trees and breathe." She rolled her eyes. "Obviously they breathe. But it's more a—"

"Meditation?"

"Yes. That."

"Tree meditation."

"Yes."

Sev's mouth opened slightly. "Ori. Come on, really?"

"I'm being sincere." She frowned. "Do you not have contemplative places in your realm? I don't understand—"

"Ori, I'm in a foreign land in which I had to fight for my right to remain even though I didn't want to. A bunch of Elemental folk refuse to let me leave but some reckon it's okay that I do. I find out I can manipulate Metal by talking nicely to it and now I'm being escorted about the countryside by the daughter of the King who's telling me I'm unbalanced and all I need to do is have a coffee and a chat with a bunch of trees." A small smile tugged at her lips. "You can see my dilemma."

Ori nodded slowly, struggling to contain her smile. "Yes, when you put it like that it does make my suggestion sound very strange."

Sev's smile grew into a grin. "Yes. But!" She poked Ori's bicep then flicked the same finger towards a stand of trees not far away. "I'll try some tree meditation. Maybe it will help settle my thoughts." This time she briefly wrapped her fingers around Ori's forearm, then marched down the slope, paused at the first tree, rubbed its bark then sat against its trunk, legs crossed.

Ori stared. Sev was a tall person, but looked small huddled at the entrance to the grove. She wanted to stride down to Sev—her friend —pull her to her feet and hold her. And hope for more forearm holding and bicep touching and contemplative looks and shoulder pressing. Instead Ori watched as minutes passed, then Sev straightened her back as if struck by an idea or when something unexpected occurs. Sev bounded to her feet and walked quickly back to Ori and the two horses.

"Right. Communing done." She frowned. "So the trees said that there is an imbalance in the realm but it's not me, apparently. So those Councillors can—"

Ori's quiet laughter cut her off.

"What?"

"The trees don't actually talk, Sev. It's a form of mindfulness. Only Flora Elementals communicate with nature and even then it's an understanding, rather than actual words."

Sev looked like she wanted to say something but stopped herself. Instead she gave a single hum.

Ori filled the silence. "I'm glad you found harmony at least for a moment." Sev gave another hum. "You know I'm making every effort. I promise." Ori murmured the last two words, then noticed a leaf in the nest that was Sev's spiky hair. She gently plucked it out and held it between them, surely imagining Sev's soft, tiny gasp.

"You were wearing a leaf." The moment was one of those kissing moments. Holding a leaf. Kissing while holding a leaf.

"It's the latest fashion." Sev's voice was just as quiet.

"Then I'm sorry for removing it," Ori said.

The leaf fluttered from Ori's fingers, and they gazed at each other for a second. Ori hadn't made an actual decision to become so attracted to Sev but there it was. A hot wave of lust rolled through her abdomen as her libido booted common sense into a box. All of which meant her next sentence was entirely inappropriate.

"Is there any more latest fashion that I can—?" Oh dear. Ori cringed inside her head as common sense looked on in horror.

Sev blushed, then cleared her throat. "I thought you wanted to know things about my realm. We seem to have spent the entire ride chatting about Breula."

"True. Perhaps on our next ride. It's a bit late now," Ori said, taking in the darkening sky.

"There's going to be a next ride?"

"I'd like that."

Sev gathered Kotrol's reins. "I'd like that, too."

***

As they arrived at the entrance to the stables, Sev tipped her chin at the sky.

"I can't get used to that."

"What?" Ori slid off Ukih.

Sev dismounted as well, and patted Kotrol's nose. "The moons. Two of them, Ori."

"Oh, that's right. Your world only has one, doesn't it?"

Ori grinned as Sev gave her a sideways look. Her eyes narrowed. "I'll have you know I will defend my realm's single solitary moon." Sev growled as she came around to stand in front of Ori, her lips slowly curling into a mischievous smile. Ori's skin tingled. "You like teasing me."

Ori breathed carefully and leaned a little further into Sev's space.

"Yes. I do." This time she didn't imagine Sev's shudder, but after a beat, she decided to pull away and resume the conversation because…because she wasn't going to push and perhaps Sev wasn't ready for that yet either.

"So what else is difficult to get used to?" Ori asked, ignoring the way Sev's gaze dropped from her eyes to her lips.

Sev breathed in and turned to look up at the night sky. "The colour. It's such a deep purple."

"What colour is it in your world?"

"Black. Particularly if you go out into the middle of nowhere. It's the blackest black with a million stars like sprinkles of silver."

Ori stood close next to Sev's shoulder staring out at the dark plum. "It sounds beautiful."

"It is." Sev turned square on again. "Can a Dark Elemental make the sky darker if they want to?"

Ori blinked at the sudden change in direction, then shook her head.

"No. However, they wouldn't even if they could. It would upset the balance, but a Dark Elemental can enhance shadows if the need arises."

"Handy, and a bit niche." Sev's lips quirked.

"Oh?"

"Yeah. The townspeople who have the Dark element can only use it in the daytime. Bit pointless, don't you think, considering they can't use it at night?"

Ori's laughter echoed into the stables. "It sounds like it would be, but it's not pointless. All elements have their place and sometimes shadows are very important."

Sev absently smoothed the fabric on her thighs. "Can the elements be used together? All at once?"

"By one person? No, that would be impossible. No one could hold that much energy."

Sev nodded slowly as if mulling that thought over. Then she held Ori's gaze.

"Thanks for today. I actually really enjoyed it." She gave a wry smile as if coming around to the idea of riding across the plains.

Ori reached for Sev's hand and squeezed it. "You're welcome. We'll go a different direction next time." She grinned. "For variety." Then she released Sev's hand.

After a small pause where Sev made a little movement forward, then stopped, then seemed to come a decision, Ori was enveloped in a hug that was more than friends if the non-existent distance between their bodies was anything to go by. She slowly curled her arms around Sev's torso, breathing in the scent of her hair. They held each other quietly at the entrance of the stables under the dark purple sky with the two moons eavesdropping on the sensuality of such a simple hug.

Then Sev pulled away. "I…thanks, you know, for today."

"You've said that already," Ori replied, a small smile lifting the side of her mouth.

"It's okay to repeat gratitude." Sev shrugged. "I…" She shook her head as if to dislodge some words, then waved her hand as she sighed. "I like you."

Ori let her smile grow, and reached for Sev's hand again. "I like you, too."

"Well, good. Good. That's good."

Ori smiled internally at Sev's babbling. It was cute; not an adjective she'd thought she'd ever apply to the feisty, determined, talented Arcanix, but in that moment, Sev was cute. Particularly with the blush on her cheeks, visible even in the evening light.

They held each other's hand. Just the one. They held each other's gaze. Just for a moment. A weighted moment. Ori drowned in Sev's brown eyes. For more than a moment. Then she let go and reached for Ukih's reins.

"Come on. Let's get you back to Askal Kirmiz's. Your element needs replenishing and I doubt that your mentor would be thrilled if his apprentice was unable to complete her work tomorrow."

There was another pause and Ori was convinced Sev wanted to say something more. She thought about asking but it was late and perhaps Sev had decided further conversation should be kept for their next ride.

CHAPTER NINE

The week after chatting to Ori out on the plains was busy, which was just as well because her brain really *really* wanted to run a continuous slideshow of Ori's face lighting up as she spoke about her realm, of them sitting together with Sev tucked under Ori's arm, of that hug at the stables—*that hug!*

Flattening metal into strips thin enough for her and Askal to create hinges for the massive front doors of the mansion had been an excellent distraction for what was foremost in Sev's mind; Ori had been wrong. Trees, in fact, did talk and she'd had a fairly insightful chat with the one she'd been slumped against.

Sev decided to keep that particular piece of information to herself. Another secret. She was beginning to feel like an elemental spy. But it was absolutely necessary. If Jino and Askal were concerned about her permanent Metal energy, she was loathe to think how they'd react when told that she could discuss her emotional state with plants.

And animals if she was being incredibly honest. Sev had told Kotrol that she didn't know one end of a horse from the other, then somehow an exchange of energy, little waves of thought, had occurred and suddenly Sev and Kotrol had developed an instant understanding. Another secret to tuck into the mental dossier.

Ori had been right about one thing, though. Trees didn't actually use words as such and neither had Sev. Much like her interaction with Kotrol. It had been more a change in the air pressure with the trees as if something solid had cupped her cheek, cradled it like a hand. Then, without words at all, the trees had told her about their concerns for Breula, of a future imbalance. But she wasn't the imbalance, which was reassuring.

It had all been a bit vague when she thought about it, and it seemed like the trees were predicting future events, like a weather forecast. The pressure on her cheek had left almost as soon as it had arrived, and she'd breathed deeply, then stared at the grass for a solid minute while trying to process the experience.

Talking to trees. Something only Flora Arcanix and Elementals could do. Chatting to horses. Something only Fauna Arcanix and Elementals could do. Playing about with metal into the night. Something only Metal Elementals could do. Sev's suitcase of elements. It was getting pretty full.

She nodded slowly, the hammer swinging lightly from her hand. To say that she was a tad conflicted was hilarious because on one hand she desperately wanted to tell Jino and Askal. They were her closest friends—family, if she was being completely truthful—and probably needed to know. On the other hand, telling them would be unfair because it would create even more pressure for them to keep her energy under wraps. Sev ground her teeth.

"Elemental super powers? Just no," she muttered, laying the hammer in the box of tools. Pulling off her leather apron and hanging it on the hook near the benches and shelves dedicated to finished items, she turned to see Askal descending the three steps into the workshop. A lump formed in her throat, and without any thought, she walked over and flung her arms about his shoulders, leaning the side of her head into his.

Askal stiffened for a moment then completed the embrace, his arms tightening about her torso.

"Is everything alright, Sevich?"

Sev pulled away, and let out a breath. "Yeah. Just needed a hug. You're a good person, Askal, and good people give good hugs."

He chuckled. "I am glad I could assist you. I feel somewhat of a bond with you, Sevich, so you are welcome to have a hug at any time."

Sev hummed. "Yeah. A bond. That's exactly what it's like. I mean, at thirty-six you're not much older than I am. Maybe that's the bond. But I feel like you're more than my mentor. You're like a protector, I guess? Particularly with…" she waved vaguely at the workshop.

Askal pursed his lips in a gesture of thought. "Yes. That is exactly right. I have a strong sense of responsibility for you." He studied her, then delivered an honest, soft smile. "I like this responsibility."

Sev smiled in return. "You remind me of Alex. You even have a passing resemblance." Then she patted his shoulder and side-stepped around him to make her way to the kitchen.

***

Two days later, Sev leaned in the doorway of the kitchen and eavesdropped on a conversation between Ori and Jino. The older woman caught Sev's eye and winked.

"Sevich will enjoy your visit this morning," Jino said, a smile tugging at the corners of her lips.

Ori sipped her water. "I hope so. I would like to invite her for another ride."

"Oh? Sevich mentioned your Sunday activity was already organised." Jino frowned, then slowly her eyebrows lifted, and Sev watched with amusement as Ori straightened her back, adjusting her backside on the seat. She was actually squirming and Sev grinned. It was so much fun seeing the princess—the six foot tall, buff, blonde princess—pinned by one of Jino's pointed looks.

"Ah. I just wanted to make sure that…"

Sev took pity on her. "To make sure I didn't back out?" She walked into the room and sat at the table opposite Ori. They traded smiles that said 'hello' and 'I see you' and 'Gosh, you're delightful' and more 'hello'.

"This is nice," Sev added, continuing to smile into the friendly blue eyes. Unbidden goosebumps travelled up her arms.

So subtle.

Jino's soft, very brief, hum fell onto the table, so Sev and Ori turned to her, finding the woman clasping her hands in her lap, crossing her legs and settling into her chair. She stared benevolently at both of them.

"Sevich, it is such a coincidence that Askal does not need your assistance at this moment while he is working on today's pieces. You have time for a drink or something to eat," Jino said, beaming at Sev.

Sev frowned which had little effect on Jino whose eyes sparkled with merriment. Then Jino pointed to Ori's orb.

"Sevich exhibited some curiosity about the orbs this week. You should tell her about them." Jino nodded encouragingly at Ori, then met Sev's gaze whose eyes were wide like saucers. What was Jino doing? What happened to secrets and protection and under the cloak of darkness and subterfuge?

Ori missed the silent interaction or chose to ignore it, seemingly happy to just stay seated at the table, holding Sev's attention.

"What do you want to know?"

"Where do they come from?" Sev asked, angling her head, then circling her finger at the orb at Ori's throat. Opening with a substantial and solid question seemed a good first move. Jino must have thought so as well because Sev caught the subtle nod of approval. It looked like the woman had settled in for the duration. Sev wouldn't put it past her.

Ori twisted her lips. "I can't tell you."

Not such a solid start after all, but Sev chuckled. "What? If you tell me, you'd have to kill me?"

There was a pause, then, "Yes."

Sev's mouth fell open. "Really?" *Mission Impossible. Maybe James Bond.*

After another long pause and delicious eye contact—this time Sev's goosebumps travelled up her spine—Ori laughed.

"No. That's quite dramatic." She bit her bottom lip in apology. *Yum.* "But I really can't tell you because it's a secret location. The Guard protect the—" She flicked her hand about as if searching for a word, or perhaps searching for a word that hid the actual word. "Outside barrier and the Elementals access the source when they are due to receive their orb. All Elementals have this access but usually wait until they can participate in the orb presentation ceremony presided over by my father."

"When do you get it?" Sev's question must have been another good one because Jino was back to nodding in approval.

Ori didn't answer straight away and Sev couldn't help staring at that gorgeous face, the cheekbones, the—Jino and the kitchen faded into the background.

"Eighteen," Ori said finally.

The thick chemistry was astonishing. Sev took in the long blonde hair collected in a ponytail, the muscular forearms leaning on the table, the soft smile on those sensuous lips, the startling blue, kind, and sexy eyes. Could eyes be kind and sexy at the same ti—Sev blinked and straightened on her chair.

Jino cleared her throat; more a grunt of laughter, and Ori dropped her gaze to study the mug in her hand. A dusting of pink coated her cheeks

"Eighteen? That's the same as Melbourne."

Ori jerked her head up. "For an orb?"

"Yes, Ori. For an orb." Sev rolled her eyes, and Ori gave her a mock glare. Then they grinned at each other and again Jino and the kitchen, maybe the entire house, disappeared. "No, not an orb. For something just as important. A vote."

Ori's eyebrows lifted.

"Well, I think I will leave you two to chat. It has been wonderful to spectate this conversation, however there are many tasks I must suddenly create so I am able to depart somewhat authentically." Jino threw a look of innocence at both of them, pushed back her chair and sauntered out of the room. Ori and Sev watched her leave then turned to look at each other.

"She's matchmaking. I think," Sev said with a shrug.

"Is she? Do we need her to?"

"Ori."

"Sev."

"No, we don't." No, they didn't, because Ori's eyes had darkened and Sev's heart rate had kicked up. Who needed matchmaking? They were doing an excellent job of it all by themselves. An accomplishment that Sev wasn't sure she wanted to be proud of or despondent about. She shook off the uncomfortable feeling and pushed away the exquisite sexual tension.

"I didn't get to tell you much about my world on Sunday. I heard all about wind wolves and tree meditation and how rigid the rules are in Breula and then I cried on your shoulder. Super."

Ori chuckled.

"So," Sev laid her palms flat on the table, "what can I tell you since we've got all this time?" She flicked up an eyebrow in a flirty gesture and her common sense looked at her as if to say, "Really?"

Ori quirked her lips. "What's the main difference between Breula and your realm?" She leaned her elbows on the table and cupped her chin. It was totally adorable.

Sev stared at the ceiling. "Direction. I wish my realm had taken a different path than it did." That was all a bit serious, but it was true. She dropped her gaze. "I look at Breula and I see what my world could have been. My world grew into itself pretty quickly, Ori. All electric this and machines that. Then it outgrew itself and ran. People didn't care about balance. They didn't want it, not when so many technological advancements were galloping along making life easier and faster and…so much. Just so much." Sev drew a shaky breath. "This." She waved her hand to encompass the kitchen and Ori nodded, clearly understanding that the gesture meant all of Breula. "Is unusual. You have to work really hard to find something as balanced as this back home."

"There is no balance in your realm?"

Sev scoffed. "Nope. I don't think my realm's been balanced since…well, for a very, very long time. The world's a bit of a shit show at the moment."

She let out a long breath as Ori contemplated that statement.

"So no-one is an Elemental or has an affinity with an element in your Melbourne?" Ori said in puzzlement.

"Well, yes. Some have an affinity. I don't think anyone is a capital 'e' Elemental." Sev flipped both hands over themselves. "I have an affinity, as you know. Artists and creatives generally do. People who meditate or have an inner balance seem to have an affinity with Air or something as equally delicate. The CEO of a steel company, for example, would say they have a strong connection with the Metal element which is such utter bullshit because they don't touch metal, not in its wonderful raw state. They don't work with the metal, they…" Sev grunted in annoyance and lightly thumped the table, "they simply take the money from the sale of vast reserves of iron ore. Take and take because it's needed to supply the machine that we call technology. But it's not technology at all. This is technology." She waved her hand about again. "In my realm, your amazing technology is sneered at. People would think it old-fashioned. Too slow. But it's not. It's brilliant and beautiful and so very clever. In my realm, I think technology is ugly no matter what people say about how fast and sleek it is. Technology feeds industrial capitalism and in return industrial capitalism feeds technology. It's a sick cycle." She growled. "Great. Now I'm grumpy. Where are some trees when you need them?"

***

Sev's next visitors weren't nearly as enjoyable. The knock on the door interrupted Askal's retelling of the latest commission Sev had received and the pride he had for his apprentice. Abandoning his dinner, Askal pushed back his chair to open the door. Sev felt a strange prickle of foreboding because the only people who would be out and about at night were Elementals and for some reason she knew it wasn't Ori.

"Councillor Buwrec Robrong Breula. What a welcome visit. Please come in. Oh, and Privana Trissandoral Breula! How nice to see you again." Askal held the door open and a tall man, black orb balanced at his throat, strode in, the sallow skin on his face pulled tightly over his bones. Ori's bodyguard stopped just behind the Councillor and both took in the domestic scene playing out in the kitchen.

Jino stood slowly.

"Please join us. We have only just begun to eat and have plenty to share." She waved towards the empty chairs at the end of the table, then reclaimed her seat when the two men took her up on the offer.

Askal sat warily, and Sev ping-ponged her gaze between all four of them. This was not a welcome visit at all, no matter what Askal said.

The Councillor swallowed his mouthful, and smiled benignly at Sev.

"I understand from Orilaevar Reysandoral Breula that you are enjoying life in Breulan society."

His tone was slick like those of gallery owners ready to skim extra commission, or the market manager who insisted on raising stall rents for no reason at all. Her alarm bells clanged.

Sev mimicked the speech patterns of the Councillor because pausing to form careful sentences felt suddenly important.

"I am, thank you. I have friends," she indicated to Askal and Jino, "and fulfilling tasks utilising my element." She held his gaze, then cocked her head innocently. "Sorry, I did not catch your name. I know Privana here." She casually flicked her hand, greatly enjoying the narrowed eyes, the lips compressing abruptly to thin lines, and two sets of cutlery slowly lowered onto plates. Then she caught the look on Jino's face. Wide eyes and the tiniest shake of her head. Her breath caught. The plea in her eyes stabbed at Sev's heart.

"Sorry." She wasn't but it was essential to calm the situation. "That was rude. I am feeling slightly intimidated by a visit from a Councillor and Ori's— Orilaevar Reysandoral Breula's Deputy. This is an honour." Okay, that was a bit much, but seemed to work, because everybody relaxed, and the cagey expression returned to the Councillor's face. It seemed to be his default.

"Apology accepted, Sevich. Now, I am Councillor Buwrec Robrong Breula. During visits to townspeople, my presence as an Elemental can be startling but the visit quickly becomes amicable." Based on Askal's reaction, visits from Elemental Councillors were unheard of, and if they did occur, they were hardly amicable. Interesting.

"So—" Sev began.

"We understand that an anomaly is developing within Breula. The Flora Elementals have indicated as such." Sev held back her nod of agreement. That would reveal a lot. "And this concerns the Council." Ori hadn't mentioned anything about concerned Councillors and she trusted Ori. That was a thought for later. Meanwhile, she knew without any evidence that it wasn't the Council that was concerned about anomalies; it was this guy in front of her.

"I imagine it does," Askal said, joining the conversation now that his eyes had settled back to their original size.

Privana scowled at Askal which seemed excessive. All Askal had done was agree with Councillor Buwrec Robrong Breula. Perhaps Privana was a perpetually cranky person.

"I understand that you are interested in returning to your realm," the Councillor continued and Sev blinked. The sudden turn in the conversation threw her for a minute.

"I am." Askal, and Jino's shoulders dropped at her reply and she swallowed the lump in her throat. Every day the wish to clone herself or split herself in two grew stronger. It would solve all her problems. "Yeah, I'd like to go back to Melbourne. Ori—Orilaevar Reysandoral Breula is working on it."

"Yes, I know," Councillor Buwrec Robrong Breula said softly. "I am assisting her by speaking to the Council, making petitions, putting forward arguments for your return, accessing the portal, etcetera. Another Elemental, Councillor Dasoskach Vaern Breula, has also joined us in actioning your case. She has been most helpful."

She had? They were? He was? That was good. Maybe he wasn't such a creepy person after all. It still didn't explain Askal and Jino's reaction to the visit. They were frozen mice. Ironic.

Sev called on her namesake. "Well, that's awesome. With you on board, the Council will be in agreement in no time." More excessiveness but he looked like the sort to respond to ridiculous over-the-top baloney.

Councillor Buwrec Robrong Breula preened and Sev gave herself a pat on the back.

"As a side note," he smiled, all teeth, "we will be conducting a census of the Arcanix and the townspeople which may impact negatively on the speed of your plea. However, be reassured that we will push forward your—"

"A census!" Jino gasped as Sev whipped her head sideways to catch the woman's face losing all colour. She suddenly looked much older than her seventy-five years.

Councillor Buwrec Robrong Breula regarded Jino, his innocent expression making Sev shudder. It was like a snake calmly inspecting prey. So much for not being a creepy guy. Jino's normally mischievous, sassy disposition had completely disappeared.

"Oh, yes. We have not conducted a census in over one-hundred years. The results of that census were enlightening and after acting on those results Breula was rebalanced at a time when imbalance was strong in the land."

Curiosity, plus the need to take the focus off Jino, fed Sev's next question.

"How?"

"How what?" Privana frowned. Sev frowned in return, amping up the gesture to the point where her eyebrows almost fell into her eye sockets.

"How did the census rebalance Breula?" she elaborated.

Councillor Buwrec Robrong Breula wrestled the conversation back. "The Elementals found three Arcanix who had managed to remain in Breula despite possessing no elements at all. They also discovered one who possessed more than one element and so these two situations created a dreadful imbalance." He smiled as if thrilled with the achievements of his ancestors.

The information-dump filled Sev's mind. Oh, shit. Here she sat possessing more than one element. She was the imbalance. What did a bunch of trees know?

"Of course, they returned those townspeople to their own realms."

Sev tamped down her jolt of horror.

"But what if those people were born here?"

"The imbalance had to be addressed. I am telling you this since you are new to Breula. Much of our history is unknown to you and it is important for citizens to understand how we came to be such a wonderful society."

Sev stared incredulously.

The Councillor hadn't finished.

"Of course, at that time the Elementals were still discovering how the newer portals operated and simple errors occurred."

Jino gasped. "What errors?"

"Oh, mainly the one we are investigating now. People being returned through the wrong portal, so that there is no possibility of return. That sort of thing. Journeying through your realm's portal means the potential of return, though nearly all returned Arcanix or false townspeople do not attempt a re-entry to Breula."

"Is that what they are called? False townspeople?" Jino whispered. Sev watched her sink further into her chair.

"Not yet. I have not found a descriptive label in the annals. Councillor Dasoskach Vaern Breula and I are petitioning for that particular label to become the standard."

He beamed again. "But the placement of people through incorrect portals does happen. It is unfortunate." He was obviously enjoying the retelling of such an awful period in time and the fact that it was still happening was unconscionable. His cavalier attitude was sickening. It felt like a warning.

Then she slid her gaze to Privana who had shifted slightly, his jaw muscles clenched, perhaps in agitation, and Sev wondered distantly if the Deputy found the whole business just as appalling.

Sev grit her teeth. "So you actually can return people to their realm, but only if you conduct a census."

"Exactly, Sevich. For us to return you to your realm of Melbourne, you will need to participate in the census. You will be asked to demonstrate your element and questioned about additional elements you may possess which of course is highly unlikely but we must be thorough, you see. You were able to demonstrate your Metal element in the application but it is always prudent to retest since your return would create an imbalance in the realm. We would be missing a Metal Arcanix. You will need to be replaced and if you possess any other elements," he chuckled at the absurdity of the notion, "then we would need to rebalance those as well." Then he shook his head as if the required workload was enormously tiring.

Shit.

Her hands shook and she tucked them under her thighs. If they found out what she could do with the elements, including the permanent Elemental energy she wasn't supposed to possess, they'd return her, which was good, but maybe they'd stick her through another portal because Privana might have a word in the two Councillors' ears. He was looking at her like he might not enjoy his Leader of the Guard hanging out with a sarcastic Arcanix.

Although the Councillor probably didn't need any help making an accidental-on-purpose portal oops. She wouldn't put it past the piece of slime in front of her.

***

Privana and Councillor Buwrec Robrong Breula departed soon after the warning had been delivered. It was definitely a warning. If the purpose of their so-called spontaneous visit was to scare the bejesus out of her, then it succeeded. It clearly scared Askal and Jino because as soon as the front door was locked both moved as one, pushing chairs under the table, wishing Sev a goodnight, then retiring to their own bedrooms, and refusing to talk about it for the remainder of the week.

She'd tried cornering Askal in the workshop to demand that he tell her what was going on, but he'd simply looked right through her.

"It is not my place to impart that knowledge."

Then he headed off to hammer aggressively at things.

Sev had gaped after him. He'd completely shut her down.

Jino was less abrupt but no more forthcoming. "I need to sort many thoughts, Sevich. I will be able to elaborate soon."

The frustration continued to sizzle inside as, early the next morning, she stomped along the road towards the market gardens where the Flora townspeople cared for an extraordinary range of fruit, vegetables, herbs, and plants that looked like weeds but weren't.

Annoyed, she scraped the sole of her leather moccasin on the road in an attempt to dislodge stones and scoot them along the sleek surface, like she did on the Melbourne paths that snaked their way through the city gardens. But these roads were created by Earth townsfolk and the stones were set like the smoothest concrete. Kicking at the road had no effect. Sev scuffed her foot again simply for the sake of it. And froze. A hole stared back at her, and Sev's eyes widened as her lips formed an 'O'. A long breath escaped from her lungs.

"Mm. Yep. Okay." She looked around. Most people were going about their business, and not paying any attention to a Metal Arcanix standing stock-still in the middle of the road, like she'd been struck by lightning. One woman, short and squat, was standing on the corner, looking intently down the road, then turned away, probably realising what a non-event Sev was.

Slowly sinking to her heels, Sev stared at the fist-sized hole.

"Yep. That's a hole." She gently poked her finger into the bottom. Loose stones. Bit of gravel. "Uh huh. A hole. In a road that shouldn't have holes because Earth townsfolk made this road, and they make perfect roads. Indestructible roads. But there's a hole. Right there," she murmured.

Somehow she had to fill it in because if a townsperson stumbled across it, there'd be all sorts of questions raised. Why is there a hole? Yes, good question. Which Earth townsperson was mucking about making holes? Well, it wasn't an Earth townsperson, actually.

Sev didn't have Earth tools handy. Of course not. *Chisel, anyone?* Those with Earth energy worked with tools. Just like those with Metal. Just like Flora and Fauna—when those two elements weren't living anymore. *That's how it works.* But a little thought told her she didn't need a tool and lately Sev wasn't ignoring little thoughts. She laid her hand on the road, next to the newly created cavity, ready to brush the sand and stones back into place. It felt right to apologise to the accidentally unbalanced Earth.

"Sorry," she whispered.

The loose material shivered under her palm and ever so slowly the divot filled with the sand and pebbles as if the rest of the road was sharing some of its innards. The edges drew together, and to Sev's disbelief, the surface reformed. If anyone had wandered across to look at that bit of road, they'd never suspect that a minute ago there'd been a hole at all.

Sev jerked her hand away as if the surface was on fire and stood up so abruptly that she felt lightheaded.

"Okay." She clenched her hand. "Okay. Okay." Then clenched her other hand. A double hand clench. Other body parts clenched. "Oh, come on. I'm Earth element, too? Without tools? Really?"

She looked about, a little frantically, and noticed a few people tossing interested looks her way. But nobody was galloping over with horrified expressions and pitchforks.

When Sev arrived back at the house, she placed the cloth bags of produce on top of the kitchen table, mumbled a response to Jino's thanks, then hurried down to the workshop. She needed to work with some metal, needed to create something, maybe the little animals for the kids. Anything to still her reeling mind.

Stones. Trees. Horses. Metal. "Earth. Look, everyone! No tools!" Sev flicked out fingers to count the elements currently sitting in her Elemental toolbox. "Flora. Fauna. Earth. Metal. The permanent kind." She nodded. "Oh my God."

It was time to get on with burying her head in the sand. The art work in the studio. Processing could come later.

She checked on the cooling barrels. They were her responsibility; making sure the water was cool enough for when the hot cast iron was thrust inside. Usually she asked Tuarn, the Ice Arcanix next door, to call by in the mornings and drop the temperature dramatically, ready for the day's work. Tuarn didn't mind at all. She was always thrilled to spend time chatting to Askal. The crush that the Ice Arcanix had on Sev's mentor was all encompassing. Too bad it wasn't returned. Maybe Jino could work her matchmaking magic.

After a quick swirl about with her finger, Sev found the water much too warm and sighed. Time for a quick visit to their neighbour.

Something made her pause. "Why not? I'm collecting the rest of them like baseball cards. Wouldn't that just top off the day," she whispered, ironically acknowledging that it was still morning. She looked into the barrel. "I'm just testing something, okay? I'm sorry to unbalance you for no reason." *I'm talking to Water. Great.*

She spread her fingers and lowered her hand onto the surface. At first nothing happened, then slowly tiny lines like spider webs radiated from her fingers to create a fog of ice across the liquid. Sev sucked in a breath as she yanked her hand away, then flipped it over to stare at her palm. She tentatively poked at the hard skin in the barrel, which cracked, the shards sinking, leaving her fingertips dangling in the cold water.

Well, that saved time. No need to knock on Tuarn's door. She gave a short, slightly hysterical laugh.

"Holy hell," she breathed. "I'm Elsa."

It was at that moment that Askal arrived, walked over to Sev standing at the barrels, and smiled.

"Oh, excellent. Thank you, Sevich. We can get started straight away although I am sorry I missed seeing Tuarn." His smile reached his eyes which held regret at not being able to greet their neighbour.

Sev blinked at him and came to a decision. She took two steps towards her mentor, grabbed his shoulders, spun him around as his mouth opened in surprise, then steered him up the stairs, down the corridor to the kitchen, to eventually plonk him onto a chair. All without saying a word.

But now she had words.

"Right." She paced the room, shaking her hands in front of her chest as if to remove a sticky substance. "Right. Okay. So, I need answers." Jino appeared in the doorway and Sev pointed at her. "Jino, can you have a seat, please? I have so, so many questions about weird stuff, which is a really poor choice of words because it's not helpful but it's all I've got at—"

"Sevich," Jino interrupted, having pulled out a chair, and was now in the process of crossing her legs.

"Sevich," Askal repeated her name, and gestured to the chair opposite him so she'd be facing both mother and son.

After a moment of silence, which gave time for her words to finish echoing about the room, Sev sat heavily. "I've got something to tell you that's beyond normal and I need to talk right now."

"Yes, your manhandling of Askal would indicate that." Jino tipped her chin at her son.

"I've got more than Metal element," Sev blurted.

Askal's eyebrows lifted in surprise. More in astonishment.

Jino's eyebrows stayed in place. She looked not at all surprised or astonished.

"Yeah," Sev continued. "So I've got the permanent Metal business going on, but just then, not five minutes ago, I froze the water in the cooling barrel. It was the only time I've actively tried to manipulate an element. It was easy, which freaks me out. Ice, Jino!" She bounced her hands in and out from the space in front of her chest towards Askal and Jino.

Jino nodded and Askal's eyebrows returned to their original position.

"But you have manipulated other elements by accident?" It seemed Askal's curiosity overrode his shock.

"Yes, and again it was intuitive. I had a chat with Kotrol, the horse I rode last Sunday. I told him I wasn't that confident and he understood, then I asked him not to run away with Ukih when we stopped at the large collection of rocks and he said he wouldn't."

Askal's eyebrows disappeared again and Sev flapped her hand. "I didn't use words. It's like communication with emotion. Like with metal." She swallowed, and Jino rose to fetch a cup of water and Sev clutched at it like a lost traveller in the desert. "Then I spoke." Jino and Askal nodded at another hand-flap, obviously understanding that there'd been no speaking at all. "To the trees when Ori told me I was unbalanced and they told me there was an imbalance in Breula but it wasn't me despite the fact that I think I am." Sev's voice cracked a little at the final word.

Jino leant across, tugged one of Sev's hands from around the cup and held it tightly in her own. Tears gathered in Sev's eyes.

"I can imagine that this is very confusing for you. Frightening as well."

"You can say that." Then Sev dropped her head. "I shifted some of the road this morning." She looked up. "I made a hole." Askal and Jino gaped. Apparently no one made holes in the road which confirmed her suspicion. "And then I apologised to the dirt because it seemed like the right thing to do and the stones and stuff shifted by themselves." She held her palm up. "I put my hand next to the hole, and the hole sealed by itself."

"Not by itself. You rebalanced the Earth." Jino released Sev's other hand and leaned back into her chair.

"Sevich, what did you just say?" Askal's voice trembled.

"What? The hole sealed itself?"

"Yes, but how did you do it?"

"I touched the bit of road next to it and the Earth shifted." Sev frowned at Askal's expression.

"That is impossible."

"Um, no, it's no—." Sev gasped. "Oh!" A small detail she'd forgotten until then.

"Four elements must use tools. Metal, Flora, Fauna, Earth." Askal counted on his fingers at each word.

"And I don't need a tool for Earth." Sev breathed deeply. "This is getting fun, isn't it?"

"You have not shown the ability to manipulate Metal by hand?" He frowned as if Sev might have hidden that skill.

She frowned in return. "No."

"Flora or Fauna?"

"Nope."

Askal stood, walked across to the bench, hefted the pot which held an uncooked leg of lamb, ready for the night's dinner, and returned to his seat. He slid the pot towards Sev.

"I dislike the idea of asking you to demonstrate as if to provide evidence, but I feel this is important. Are you able to manipulate Fauna by hand when it is in this form?"

Sev knew he meant dead fauna, not a quick 'how's-your-day-going?' with Kotrol.

"Askal…"

Both mother and son stared at her and she sighed, pulled the pot closer, and peered at the pink meat. Small chunks? That'd be handy. Save Jino a bit of time. With a deep breath, she ran her index finger along the flesh closest to the bone and watched in fascination as it separated, falling away and laying flat in the bottom of the pot. Sev gazed at the precision, then wiped her finger on her thigh. Ick. That definitely wasn't her favourite hands-on manipulation. It was a bit knife-wielding serial killer-ish if she were honest.

"Well," she said. "There you go. I'll be handy at barbecues."

She caught Askal and Jino's shared glance.

"Interesting," Jino murmured.

"I can think of other words," Sev said, and pushed the pot away.

"I wonder why Earth was the first non-tool element to show itself," Jino mused.

"Okay," Sev growled. "That right there?" She clenched her hands. "What makes you think there's going to be more non-tool moments? Actually, you know…" She tightened her fingers into her palms, then flicked them out, relieving the tension. "I don't want to analyse this." She poked the table top for emphasis and all three watched as Sev slowly withdrew her finger from a freshly created divot in the wood.

"Oh, for—"

"That is…" Askal whispered.

"This is becoming absurd." Sev dragged her finger towards the small dent, repairing the grain as she whispered an apology and her gratitude, then slowly blinked.

Jino stared. "You are quite remarkable, Sevich." Then she breathed in sharply. "Did anyone see you move the particles in the road?"

Sev sighed. Good question. There'd been the woman on the corner but surely Sev's body would have shielded any of the stone moving. "No. I'm pretty sure no one did."

Jino nodded and hummed. "So, you are able to manipulate Flora, Fauna, and Earth by hand. If we look at just the elements, you have Metal obviously. Earth, Ice, Flora, Fauna. Any more?"

Sev regarded the woman. The lack of surprise coupled with the intensity of questioning was odd. There was more to this than simply being a magnet for elemental energy. She contemplated Jino's question. Had there been any more element moments? She took a minute. What was left? Air, Water, Heat, Dark, and Light. None of them stuck out in her memory.

"No. I've got the five you mentioned. The other five are missing." Then a thought struck her. "Perhaps it's temporary, like I'm new in Breula and susceptible to attracting elements and it'll all calm down soon."

The expression on Jino's face indicated what rubbish that sentence was.

"We all possess an element, Sevich. You simply possess more, and with additional energy levels." Her gaze never wavered, almost as if in challenge. Sev stared back and wondered. No, not everyone possessed an element.

"Jino?"

"Yes?"

"I've never seen you show your element. What is it?"

Jino exhaled. A long breath in which she looked to be gathering words for her reply.

"I do not have one," she said quietly.

The sadness, the touch of fear, hit Sev in her heart.

"Why?"

Deciding that getting up and fetching a mug of water for Askal and one for herself was necessary, Jino then returned, and studied her hands.

"There is a prophecy that tells of a Guardian who arrives in Breula to rescue the realm from great danger It is foretold that there is one who is tasked with protecting the Guardian until they are ready." Jino swallowed and flicked a gaze at Askal. "This Guardian is able to wield all ten elements with more power than the Elementals could ever imagine. The Elementals become worried about the powers so they conspire to capture the Guardian and cast them out of Breula. However, as in all good stories, the danger is avenged and Breula is rebalanced. Then, according to the prophecy, the Guardian's powers diminish and the Elementals allow the Guardian to stay. Of course, this Guardian has fallen in love," Jino raised an ironic eyebrow, "it is a prophecy for a reason. And chooses to stay in Breula because of the one they love."

Sev blinked. "Okay? So what does—" A terrifyingly cold realisation washed through her. "You think I'm the Guardian."

Jino's hand moved at lightning speed to clutch Sev's. "No! No, we do not."

Askal sighed. "No, we do not," he confirmed. "You cannot wield all ten elements. You have not fallen in love." Jino and Sev shared a long look at that statement. "And there is not a danger present."

"But there may be." Jino withdrew her hand and let her words sit on the table. The gravity of the sentence hung in the room.

"Does the prophecy say when the da—" Sev blinked. Her brain was on spin cycle. "I'm not the Guardian." She nodded and sighed in relief. "That's good." Another question rolled out. "Does the prophecy say what gender the Guardian is?" The next question followed much too quickly. "The Guardian is Breulan, right?" Then another. "What about the Guardian having permanent non-orb elemental energy?" Another. "What about the Guardian waving their hands about and manipulating all the elements?" And another. "How does this relate to you not having an element?"

Jino lifted her hand to halt the barrage. "No, the prophecy does not specify a gender. The Guardian may be Breulan or not. There is nothing in the prophecy that tells us about any permanency, nor non-tool manipulation. And yes, it does relate,"

Sev mentally matched the questions and answers, then she regarded the woman. "Bit light on the details, this prophecy of yours."

Jino laughed. "Oh, you are very delightful, Sevich, dear."

Sev grinned, then sobered. "So, no element, Jino. Why haven't you been found out?"

"The town protects me because I see the prophecy. I see details, despite your belief that details are missing."

"What?"

Askal gestured at Jino. "Many children's stories are cautionary tales that exist to explain societal rules. But this is a prophecy." Askal raised his bushy eyebrows in a 'it is what it is' gesture.

"You're a seer? But that's not an element."

"Oh, I know, which is why I have been kept secret by the townspeople since birth."

"The Elementals know you as Jino, a person."

"Yes. But all assume I have the Metal element since I am here with Askal."

That seemed sensible. People only saw what they wanted to see.

"So, what's something you saw?"

"I saw that Askal would become your mentor." Again, she cast another sharp look at her son.

Odd, but it wasn't Sev's place to get involved in family tension, if that's what it was.

"What's your energy?"

Jino tilted her head. "I am able to sense imbalances that may bring prophecies to light."

Sev closed her eyes. "I'm not the Guardian, but I'm an imbalance."

"Yes."

"Ori said the same thing."

"That you are an imbalance?"

"More like I'm unbalanced."

Jino quirked her lips.

"Yeah," Sev continued. "Probably because I yell at her every now and then and melt her swords." Then she dropped her head. "Okay, I'm very aware of the innuendo in that sentence."

Jino chuckled and Sev raised her head.

"Sevich, I like the two of you together. You fit well."

"We're not together." Sev frowned.

"You are not? At all? Not even a little bit?" Jino's slow smile grew and Askal gave a soft laugh.

Sev heaved a sigh at the woman's theatrics. "Fine. We might be heading that way."

Jino nodded. "You have already taken many steps in that direction. I hope both of you choose to stay on that road together and that neither of you shove the other into the forest."

With a glare at Jino, then at Askal who was grinning broadly, she flapped her hand at both of them. "Okay, well. Whatever. Let's get back to seers and prophecies."

***

Finding out that Jino could see into the future, albeit through a slightly foggy, fuzzy, not at all reliable lens which most fortune tellers seemed to possess, was astounding but not at all surprising when she thought about it. Jino seemed to know things.

But at least, she reassured herself later that night, she wasn't a Guardian or a knight in shining armour, because any danger that could befall Breula would surely be dire and Sev wasn't going to save the realm with a quick chat to some trees, some rocks, a leg of lamb, and hurling an anvil or two. She'd also be fairly useless with her hands-on skills. What good would that do? She still thought, maybe now only once a week, about leaving, but with every revelation, with every moment with Ori, with every connection with Jino and Askal, it was becoming more distant in her mind.

The reasons for running back to Melbourne were dissolving like candy floss while the reasons to stay were solid and steadfast. Like the metalwork which was wonderful and immersive. Like the fact that she'd never be able to find the portal, anyway. Like the fact that she'd miss Jino and Askal desperately. Like the fact that she'd disappoint Ori. And all of those reasons fuelled the tiny voice in her mind that maybe the Councillors didn't need to work so hard at reaching a resolution after all. But it still made her heart clench when she thought about poor Alex.

***

Sev stewed for the first hour of the ride with Ori on Sunday. Stewed was a terrific word because it described the casserole of thoughts in her mind. Prophecies and energy. Way too much energy. Yet, despite Sev being sucked into Breulan society, despite bouts of awful homesickness, despite all of it, riding about the countryside with Ori was a welcome distraction. Today, with Ori dressed in tight leather and a heavy over-shirt and boots, lusting after a Breulan princess was a lovely and welcome distraction.

Chapter Ten

Dressed in leather riding pants, a heavy beautifully embroidered over-shirt—a gift from the mother of one of the recipients of a small silver animal—and boots bequeathed to her by Askal Kirmiz, Sev was a welcome distraction from pressing thoughts such as a sudden and inexplicable census put forward by Councillor Dasoskach Vaern Breula and Councillor Buwrec Robrorg Breula, the Council continuing to debate Sev's departure, and the imbalance that many of the Flora Elementals were adamant currently existed in the realm.

Ori glanced at her riding partner. Sev was quiet. Contemplative. But Ori didn't mind. It was a clear day and such clarity often helped shine light on decisions hiding in the dark. Perhaps Sev needed to share her thoughts with the sky. It was also a cold day, and despite snow only ever falling on the mountains, the temperature was hovering at blowing-on-fingers level.

Ori broke into Sev's thoughts.

"Has your shirt been infused with warmth from a Heat Elemental?"

Sev started, and blinked, looking for all the world like a person who'd abruptly returned to their body after travelling from realm to realm on a zephyr.

"Oh! No. It's," Sev looked down at the patterns, "just a shirt. But I don't seem to feel the cold in Breula. It's like I've stuck a little hot water bottle over my heart. The effect is a bit sporadic, though. Same as in Melbourne." She laughed. "There I seem to only be warm when I'm standing in front of a forge or when Alex is in the flat. It's like he's a handy mobile furnace." She gave another short laugh. "Anyway, I'm nice and warm. Thanks for asking."

Ori caught and held the heavy gaze that Sev slid her way. The flirty looks were increasing and Ori was there for it. What she wasn't thrilled about was the fact that Sev used present tense to talk about Melbourne. And Ori's heart was exhausted from being wrenched from end to end of the emotional spectrum.

**

"And you're sure it was a threat?" They'd ridden further into the plains, passing through great tracts of grasses with the feathery tops brushing the hair on the horse's underbellies, and dismounted near the entrance to the forest of ancient trees south of the town. Ori stretched her legs and leaned back on her elbows, matching her companion's posture.

Sev turned her head.

"Hell, yes. I was subtly told to piss off back to my own realm but oops watch out I might get shoved through a different portal." Sev widened her eyes in a glare, and Ori shook her head. She dropped onto her side, bent her elbow, and rested her cheek on her palm.

"Which is a horrific thought," Ori said. "He mentioned that Councillor Dasoskach Vaern Breula was assisting him with the development of your case?"

Sev sighed, then to Ori's delight, Sev's body seemed to liquify causing her to flop onto her back, bringing her closer. Sev frowned at the sky, then rolled her head. Her brown eyes held confusion.

"Yes. Why are you asking? Councillor Buwrec said all three of you were working on getting the entire Council to agree with my appeal."

They were? This was news to Ori. Teaming up with both Councillors for any initiative was highly unlikely, let alone one that Ori was very passionate about. Passionate because she'd given her word to Sev. Passionate because it was Sev.

"I must confer with both Councillors later today to ascertain our progress for you," Ori said, and frowned. A chat would be very necessary, along with a great deal of diplomacy. She didn't trust either of them. There was more to this than a simple visit to an Arcanix. She gave Sev a long look. "And Privana was with him?"

"Mm. He didn't say much. Just scowled a lot. I got the feeling he was a bit uncomfortable about how odd the visit was."

"He would be. He likes rules. Gets a bit twitchy with anything odd."

"Hmm. Although I think he was on board with one thing mentioned. Councillor Buwrec seemed to dislike the idea that I was becoming mor—that I'm your friend." Sev darted her eyes about and Ori smiled to herself. She was positive Sev hadn't meant to make that small slip. Her skin warmed.

Sev hummed. "How long have you and Privana been friends?"

"Since we were children."

"Has he ever expressed a wish for more than friendship?"

"No. Well, I haven't noticed it."

"I think he came with Councillor Buwrec the other night to check out his competition."

Ori chuckled. "Really?"

"Yep. Just a feeling." Sev grinned.

"And you're his competition?"

Sev's smile faded and she paused, holding Ori's gaze. It was the sort of eye contact where the space about them shimmered, then drifted into the background, leaving their features, their faces, their lips, their eyes in stark contrast.

"Am I?" she murmured.

"I asked first," Ori said, leaning forward infinitesimally so that Sev was within kissing distance.

Another pause. "I could be. Maybe. I'm not..." Sev looked for all the world like she wanted to kiss Ori and stay, or kiss Ori and run, or simply just kiss. Her lips parted.

Ori took in the sensuality of Sev's mouth, her lips, the way her eyes had darkened. But she respected the indecision. What a conflict to carry, and one that occupied her mind just as fully. How was it possible to have so many feelings?

So she met Sev halfway. Sort of. Perhaps to give Sev's indecision a signpost and help calm some of the conflict that was occupying her mind.

Lifting Sev's hand, she turned it so the inside of her wrist was exposed, then closed her eyes and pressed her lips to Sev's soft skin, stayed, delayed, drowning in the intimacy of the moment, then held Sev's hand in her own while this woman, Privana's competition, this wonderful Arcanix, gaped at her.

"Sev," Ori breathed. Even her name had taken on shiver-inducing levels of delight. "That? That can mean absolutely nothing if that's your decision. I…I just wanted to and it pleased me and I hope it pleased you and that's all it needs to be if you want." Ori swallowed in panicked joy at what she'd just done and how ridiculous she sounded. Then, because she seemed to be incapable of forming sensible sentences and because Sev's stunned look was disconcerting, she released Sev's hand. "Do you want to return to the town?"

***

The next few Sundays felt like they linked seamlessly. Crossing plains. Lounging near forests or rocks. All the while their bodies slowly crept closer and closer, talking, sharing their wishes, their dreams, their history, and touching hands, which relieved Ori's nerves because the Wrist Kiss—capitalised in her head because her desire was now at incandescent levels so goodness knows where Sev's was—had altered their relationship significantly.

Now, Ori would kiss Sev's hand. Now, Sev would tighten her fingers in Ori's grip. Now, at the end of their rides, Sev would kiss Ori in the space between the corner of her mouth and plane of her cheek. Now, their hugs became commonplace. Now, their hands crept up higher on each other backs and Sev would tuck her forehead into Ori's neck. It all made for a wonderful nightly dreamscape that cycled through Ori's head as she was drifting off to sleep.

This whatever it was had migrated from the warm comfort of two friends spending time together to that tingle when you know your not-just-a-friend was looking at you even when they were looking at the clouds. Swooping electricity in all the best places.

With her back cushioned by the spongy grass, Ori knew she could lie here with Sev every day. All day. The thought gave her pause. Lying here with Sev all day, every day, meant seven days of all the weeks and oh, that felt good.

A featherlight touch skimmed her wrist and she turned to find Sev leaning on her elbow looking down at her. Sev held fast eye contact as she dragged her fingertip up Ori's arm, over the thousands of goosebumps that had broken out on Ori's skin, over the muscle in her forearms, over her biceps, to the arm band where she traced the pattern in the metal. Ori's breath hitched.

"What are you doing?" Ori whispered.

"I'm feeling the metal, the shape, the intricacy."

"And you needed to start at my wrist to do that?"

Sev paused, holding her finger still.

"Yes." Brown, gold-flecked eyes held her own.

Then—*then!*—Sev leaned down and gently kissed Ori, lightly touching her lips, lingering like a soft breeze, and Ori couldn't help the moan that fell out in response to the eroticism of the brief, delicate gesture.

"Oh," Sev breathed, drawing away, and the tip of her tongue ran across her bottom lip. "I really, really wanted to know how you tasted."

"How do I taste?" Ori licked her own bottom lip and Sev's eyes followed the movement.

"Like sunshine." A small smile drifted across Sev's mouth and Ori took the chance to prop herself up on her elbow so their faces aligned, then slide her free hand around the back of Sev's neck.

"I imagine you do as well," she murmured and pulled Sev towards her.

It felt incredibly natural to push into a kiss. Their lips fitted together perfectly, with none of that awkwardness when two mouths can't work out where to place the first pieces in a jigsaw puzzle.

She shuffled a little closer without breaking the kiss; noteworthy considering she was raging with desire which always affected coordination. Their heads were still cradled in their hands.

They paused to take a breath. To rest their foreheads together.

"I was right."

Their thrilled smiles were mirrors.

"I've wanted to do that for a while."

"Me too," Ori whispered.

Then lips slid against each other once again.

Sev's hand drifted up Ori's arm and wrapped around the metal band, and all Ori could think was how right Sev's lips felt, how right her skin felt, how right her hand felt, the thumb ring bumping against her skin, how right that felt on her Guard Leader's cuff. Their kiss became two, then three, then Ori felt the warmth on her bicep.

Sev jerked away.

"Oh! Oh, shit. Ori, I'm sorry." She leapt up, with Ori not far behind, and both watched as the band dripped from Ori's arm to the ground where it formed a small gold lump. Ori looked between Sev's appalled expression and the slowly hardening metal nestled in the grass.

"Oh my God!" Sev clutched at Ori's hand.

"Huh." Ori swung their joined hands back and forth. "I really liked that one, too. Oh, well."

"I'm sor—" Sev caught the grin, and shook off Ori's hand to punch her in the shoulder. "Fine. I'm still making you a new one even if you're being a smart arse about it."

Ori laughed and stepped closer. "This could become a habit, you know."

"What? Liquifying things?" Sev's eyes slowly darkened in realisation.

"Yes."

The rush of the wind wolves across the plains could not compete with the rush of desire that whisked through Ori's body.

***

The wind wolves were howling the next Sunday.

The sound of Sev's breathy whimper rolled up and down Ori's spine in successive waves as she pressed her to the tree trunk, pelvis to pelvis, heat radiating through the thick leather riding pants. Sev's fingers clutched at strands of her long hair, and the zap of electricity whisked through her sex.

Then Ori felt Sev smile and she broke the kiss.

"What?"

Sev smiled into Ori's eyes. "You know how to kiss a woman."

Ori grinned.

"I know how to kiss you."

"Smooth."

"Like ice."

Sev laughed, a delightful sound. "This poor tree might be scandalised if we carry on like this."

Ori delivered a quick kiss, then another, and another. And it felt as if a sun shower pressed their bodies together.

"The tree will be thrilled," Ori declared, smiling against Sev's lips.

"I should ask permission," Sev said, then her grin suddenly fell away and her eyes widened. After a brief nod as if receiving advice, she delivered a quick kiss in return. "Yep. The tree totally approves of this idea."

Ori narrowed her eyes. Either Sev was an accomplished actor or there had definitely been communicati—No, Sev was an accomplished actor. That's all it could be.

The idea of performing reminded Ori of the upcoming festival.

She pulled back, leaving her hands on Sev's hips.

"Would you accompany me to this year's festival next week?"

"That sounds like a date." Sev's eyes danced with mirth, and Ori tightened her fingers in a light squeeze, which forced a set of giggles from Sev who twisted away.

"Yes, like a date," Ori answered, grabbing Sev's hand and pulling her back against the tree. Sev slid her arms about Ori's neck again, and Ori immediately forgot what she was going to ask next. She wanted Sev. She wanted Sev to always look at her like that. As if she was an exquisite dessert to be admired then consumed.

"I've heard about the festival. It's a chance for the Elementals to show off."

Ori hummed in self-deprecation. "A little. Since the festival starts late in the afternoon and continues into the night, we are able to demonstrate all ten elements in their entirety because of our orb energy. It is quite spectacular. There are displays, but also horse skills, sword dancing, music, singing, and the Arcanix participate, initially with their energy, then when it is dark by operating stalls that do not require elemental manipulation. The next day is a holiday so that everyone is able to recover. All citizens participate and it is a night that celebrates everything that's Breula."

Sev smiled. "It sounds wonderful, and seeing the sword dancing would be incredible. Okay, I'll be your date." She kissed Ori's hand, held tightly in her grasp, then narrowed her eyes as if in challenge. "Just so you know, I'm an expert at shoving a ping-pong ball down the throat of a laughing clown."

Ori furrowed her brow. More incomprehensible information. Laughing clowns?

Sev hugged Ori, planting a kiss on her lips. "I am not even explaining that. Come on, we need to get back before I run out of energy, etcetera, etcetera."

***

The gorgeous apparition that exited Askal and Jino Kirmiz's house the afternoon of the following Sunday caused Ori's lungs to lock her breath away. Sev wore sleek boots, black fitted pants, and a beautiful multi-coloured shirt; a series of triangles running horizontally across her torso. It too was fitted and showed off her strong shoulders and her small breasts to perfection. She'd also wrangled her brown hair into a sort of controlled chaos and it did things to Ori. So many things.

Ori congratulated herself on not stepping forward and sweeping Sev into a searing kiss, but apparently her containment wasn't particularly successful.

"Did you just whistle at me?" Sev cocked her head and a small smile threatened to break into a grin.

Ori blinked, then met the teasing head on. "Of course not. Air simply exited my pursed lips."

Sev fell about laughing.

"That was a clever answer, Orilaevar Reysandoral Breula," Jino Kirmiz said, having closed the front door after herself and Askal Kirmiz, and joined Sev and Ori at the edge of the road. The older woman looked Ori up and down. "Except for the absence of the cloak and your head circlet, it is full uniform, is it?" she observed. "I imagine the Guard will be dressed similarly?"

Jino Kirmiz had seen the Guard in full uniform at many events hence the lack of reaction, but Sev hadn't, not really, and Ori hoped that the soft pants, tight on her thighs, that were tucked into the tall boots, and the long buckskin jerkin which hung past her hips, clasped together with small gold tassels at various stages down her chest; the supple material contained with a braided red and gold ribbon made of tough, coarse fabric hefty enough to support her scabbard and sword, combined with the Leader of the Guard arm cuffs, and her hair held back in a beautiful multi-coloured clasp that had been her grandmother's, would impress Sev sufficiently that she would experience a somewhat more enthusiastic reaction than the one from Jino Kirmiz. Or Askal Kirmiz, for that matter, based on his bemused expression.

Sev seemed to enjoy the vision in front of her if her lips parting slightly and her eyes raking up and down Ori's body were any indication. Ori's blood sizzled, rushing to all sorts of interesting places. She dragged her gaze back to Jino Kirmiz, realising that she hadn't answered the woman's question.

"Yes. It is expected, but I'm the only one with a hand-crafted sorry sword."

Sev narrowed her eyes. "Excuse me? A sorry sword?"

Ori gave her an innocent look. "Catchy, hey?"

Askal Kirmiz laughed. "I hear that a Leader of the Guard arm cuff is also due."

"Okay, we can go now," Sev huffed, glaring at her mentor who laughed again. She took a step forwards and, without preamble, slid her hand into Ori's. Stomach butterflies tumbled and twisted, fighting for space, and Ori couldn't fight the grin that appeared on her lips. Right then, the very idea of Sev, the very idea of Sev and Ori, the very idea of Sev and Ori and a complete lack of clothing was seductively running its fingers up and down the veins under her skin and it felt marvellous.

"Happy festival, Orilaevar Reysandoral Breula, Sevich," Jino Kirmiz pointed down the road. "We are walking this way."

Askal Kirmiz frowned. "We are?"

His mother gave him a long look.

Askal Kirmiz's eyes opened, then he nodded quickly. "We are."

Ori and Sev shared a grin and turned to walk in the opposite direction. The smiles from the various townsfolk, and the surprised looks from some Elementals at their joined hands were welcome from the former and sigh-worthy from the latter. The hierarchy, locked by tradition, irritated Ori. She adored her realm, and the people, and the details that made a society strong, but it seemed that falling in love with a person not in the—woah, there. Ori blinked.

I'm thinking in the abstract. That unfinished statement was not specific to anyone in particular. Just a general observation of certain expectations about relationships. That's all. She nodded to herself. Good.

But the internal monologuing and non-specific thinking stirred a need.

"Let's take a short cut." Ori indicated to an opening in the line of Flora workshops. She led Sev into the alley, and the sides of the buildings, smooth with Earth energy, created shadows across the walls and ground.

"A shortcut, hey?" Sev said mischievously.

Ori stopped, spun Sev around, then pressed her gently against the wall. She slid her hands onto Sev's hips. "A shortcut."

There was enough light to watch Sev's pupils enlarge with desire, to hear her breathing shallow, and Ori couldn't stop herself. She leaned in and carefully ran the tip of her tongue across Sev's bottom lip, once, twice. Sev shuddered in her arms.

"Oh my God," Sev whispered, and snaked her arms around Ori's waist, mindful of the hilt of the sword, then around to her back. She splayed her fingers.

"I want to kiss you more and longer and more, but there's far too much light at the moment and people will be very entertained," Ori murmured against Sev's mouth, which curled into a smile.

"We can't have that," Sev said just as quietly.

The sounds of the festival drifted down their small lane, bouncing softly off the sleek surfaces.

"Oh well. We probably should be going," Ori sighed halfheartedly. Neither of them moved. Their breathing was soft against each other's lips.

Then, she watched in fascination as the light around them greyed, like a soft cloak draping itself about their space, quietly and lazily as if it had all the time in the world. She pulled back and looked up at the sky, the fading pink dotted with small clouds, then dropped her gaze to catch Sev's look of wonder along with a low, incredulous "No way," and nodded. Sev, even after three months, was probably still acclimatising to the concept of a pink and white sky, and the slow arrival of the dual moons. Ori touched Sev's cheek, bringing her attention back.

"It seems the clouds have gifted us some personal shadows." It really was darker. Perhaps rain? She hoped not. The Air Elementals had insisted that the festival night would be clear.

Looking for all the world like she was conducting an internal conversation, or, more likely, a shouty argument, Sev then blinked, shook her head as if to dismiss her thoughts, and hooded her gaze.

"Well. Let's not waste the generosity of the clouds."

Ori's lips were captured in a kiss filled with such heat that she expected to combust then and there. Sev slid her hands into Ori's hair, and tugged softly. Ori moaned, then angled her head, deepened the kiss, and swam joyously in the delicious sound of Sev's responding moan. Oh, her lips were so soft. And when Sev slipped her tongue inside, Ori clutched at the hem of Sev's shirt, bunching the fabric into her palms as white light filled her mind.

Their hands moved, driven by need, over torsos, over breasts, pausing as muscles tensed, pausing as breathy whimpers filled the alley, pausing to rub against nipples that were hard with desire, obvious even through the winter clothing. and, in Ori's case, so incredibly sensitive with arousal that she wondered if the Flora townspeople had ever had a member of royalty almost orgasm outside their shops. Simply because a wonderful, sassy, gorgeous, incredible woman was kissing her boneless.

She moaned again into Sev's mouth.

Ori wanted the kisses to last longer, to grow deeper, but Sev broke away, breathing heavily, and she touched her swollen lips.

"Wow," she whispered. "We're so good at this."

They made eye contact and shared a slow smile.

Ori cupped Sev's cheek. "I have adored getting to know you before we did...this."

"This?" Sev quickly kissed Ori's lips.

Ori chuckled. "Yes. This." And returned the kiss.

"I liked finding out about you as well. The hanging out, and the chatting, and the silences, and the kissing, the getting handsy bit, then the getting really turned on bit." Sev quirked an eyebrow. "Multitasking."

Ori laughed and pressed her body into Sev's, delivering another kiss that she hoped conveyed just how invested she was in travelling down this road of whatever this was. Then she pulled away and winked.

"Come on. People are expecting me to appear for at least some of the festival. We can," she smirked, "multitask later."

***

Sev tugged on Ori's hand, pulling her towards Denjern Sohe, who was surrounded by numerous barrels filled to their brims with coloured chalk.

"Hi, Denjern. Happy festival. What happens here?"

Ori grinned at Sev's enthusiasm. It was childlike and wonderful.

"Happy festival, Sevich and Orilaevar Reysandoral Breula." Denjern looked between Sev and Ori then at their joined hands and grinned. Another townsperson pleased to see their outward display of affection.

Earlier, Sev had checked with Ori about whether hand-holding in public was too much PDA. After Sev explained what PDA meant, Ori had laughed.

"It's fine. Delightful, in fact. Breulans celebrate lo— relationships," she corrected quickly, hoping that Sev didn't catch the slip. She hadn't seemed to, and they'd arrived at the festival, fingers entwined.

Denjern Sohe indicated to Ori's orb as he answered Sev's question. "You decorate your face to celebrate your element, and when everyone mingles, it looks like a beautiful painting, a representation of balance." Then he dipped his index and middle fingers into the barrel containing blue chalk, and dragged the dusty substance from his left temple, over his closed eye, and down his cheek, skimming the corner of his mouth. The chalk traced the blue lines already present but now they were even more vivid and stark.

Sev turned to Ori, her eyes sparkling.

"Yes?"

Ori grinned.

"Yes." She shuffled Sev along to the orange barrel, dipped her fingers into the chalk, then, as Sev closed her eyes, slowly ran her fingers in parallel lines down Sev's face.

Sev's eyes opened, and her lips parted. The utter sensuality of the moment was not lost on either of them. Ori wanted to drag Sev behind the nearest tree and rip her clothes off.

"My turn," Sev murmured, and tapped the pads of her fingers in the yellow chalk.

Ori shuddered as the chalk was pressed lightly into her skin, as Sev's soft breath whisked across her face, and her hand involuntarily reached for Sev's waist to steady the dizziness that overcame her.

She took in Sev's expression as she opened her eyes. "You look good in orange," Ori said, and Sev smiled.

"Yellow's definitely you."

Ori revelled in Sev's reaction to each display. Attached to Sev's hand, she was led from Elemental exhibits to arrays of artisan creations to children playing with toys engineered as the Elementals worked together. It was the best festival she'd ever attended.

Sev commented on the casual deference that was paid to Ori.

"They leave you alone, but recognise you. They smile and when you talk to people, they love it. You're loved."

Ori was reminded of Sev's similar observation weeks ago. "I like people. These people. I recognise them also."

Sev nodded contemplatively. "Before smart phones, selfies, Insta and TikTok, it was the same in Australia. We were known for being the one country that celebrities could wander around places without being hassled by the general public. We were proud of that reputation."

Ori studied Sev. "You miss your realm."

It was a loaded statement, because she knew that Sev absolutely missed Alex. But Ori had come to realise that Sev wasn't sure about the rest. She hadn't spoken about her realm for a while but that was a thought to pack into a box for later contemplation. Sev pointed to the lanterns hanging above their heads, deflecting Ori's statement.

"No strings or wires?"

Ori shook her head. "No. Light, Heat, and Air Elementals demonstrate their expertise when they create those. They float, so Air Elemental." She spread her fingers and raised her hand to indicate a lifting off the ground. "The flame is maintained. Heat Elemental, and then the brightness is enhanced to provide illumination over a larger space." She pointed to her orb. "Light."

Sev stared up for a beat then lowered her gaze. "Show off."

Ori cracked up. "Oh, you're not easily impressed," she said, a grin on her face, which slowly faded as she took in Sev's expression. They held fast eye contact.

"Yes, I am," Sev whispered.

Ori breathed carefully. Standing so close in the middle of the festival meant that they were already receiving a few looks, but Ori wanted to run both hands around the back of Sev's head so that her thumbs could trace Sev's cheekbones and kiss her deeply until both of them trembled. It wasn't the best idea but it sounded fabulous.

Therefore, Ori's common sense was thrilled when Sev chose to tuck her hand into the crook of Ori's elbow, curl her fingers around Ori's bicep, then point at the very large circular space of grass that had been marked out with dozens and dozens of fabric triangles in the ten elemental colours.

"What happens there?"

They wandered across to the perimeter of the circle.

"A number of performances. The sword dances mainly." Ori smiled.

"Sword dancing," Sev said, nodding slowly and tilting her head down to Ori's sword. "I'm looking forward to that."

Based on that one comment, Ori, who had already prepared a dance for the night, immediately changed her mind because suddenly she wanted to dedicate her dance to Sev and she knew the perfect choice. She hoped her new dance would fit with the program, but that was Privana's decision, since it was his role to coordinate the list. Members of the Guard spent months practicing their dances hoping their audition would make Privana's decision simple. Ori was an automatic inclusion despite telling Privana that she should audition as well. He wouldn't even entertain the notion.

"Speaking of..." Ori muttered happily, as she spotted her friend entering the orange tent where the sword dancers waited to be announced. She looked at Sev. "I need to ask Privana something about the sword dancing program. Do you mind if I dash off for a moment?"

Sev squeezed Ori's upper arm and withdrew her hand. "Of course not. I'll be here."

Ori flashed a grin then strode away towards the tent.

Privana was exiting as she arrived, and smiled in acknowledgement. "Happy festival, Orilaevar."

Ori clapped him on the shoulder. "And to you, Privana. I have a change to your program if I'm allowed."

Privana frowned. "Of course. You are the Leader of the Guard. You can choose to be wherever you like in the performance order. I simply assumed you would be the finale as you have been in previous years."

"I'm perfectly fine with going last, and it's always a great compliment. No, I'd like to change my dance."

Privana's eyebrows lifted. "You do? But..."

Ori waved her hand. "Yes, I know. Tradition, choice of dance, etcetera. Leadership and all. But I'd like to dance the Valwith."

With his eyebrows still entrenched at his hairline, Privana pulled his head into his neck. "But...but it is the courtship dance."

Ori tamped down the blush that threatened. Thank goodness for yellow chalk stripes. "Yes, I know. But the dance is beautiful and I think it will end the program quite nicely." Why she couldn't tell her best friend the true reason for the change of mind was baffling. Perhaps it was a tiny memory of Sev suggesting that Privana saw himself as Sev's romantic competition. That seemed silly.

Privana's eyebrows descended rapidly into sharp arrows that pointed to the bridge of his nose.

"I suppo—of course," he said, then he stared past Ori's shoulder and squinted as if trying to make out something in the evening light. He brought his gaze back and clenched his jaw, the joints bouncing on either side of his face. He shook his head, frowned again, then spoke through his teeth.

"So you have bedded the Arcanix?"

Ori gaped, her breath falling out as if punched from her lungs. "Privana! That's…you did not just say that!" Her hand twitched towards the hilt of her sword.

She registered the shock on Privana's face before her friend quickly hung his head. "I am so sorry. That was completely uncalled for." He spoke into his chest, his hands rolling into fists at his side.

"It was appalling, Privana! What has got into you?" Ori grabbed his shoulder and gave it a shake so he was forced to raise his head. A hot wave of anger washed over her and she knew, standing so close to the floating lantern at the tent's entrance, that a small halo of light was shimmering about her body. Thoughts of ploughing her fist into her friend's shoulder skittered through her mind. How dare he speak about Sev like that?

"Tell me what that was about," she demanded, hissing the words near his face, digging her fingers into the cloth covering his upper arm.

Quite unexpectedly, Privana's eyes filled with tears. "I am your Deputy, Orilaevar, and in that role I will defend and protect you with my life. But beyond that I value our friendship. We have been each other's mirrors for just about every major event in our lives. We share our thoughts and our worries." He swallowed, his throat moving quickly, and he breathed loudly through his nose. "We have helped each other realise that even though a distant idea seems a possibility, it is often the idea right in front of us that is the true path." He stared at Ori in dismay, clearly remorseful. But there was a hint of desperation in his eyes. "I was simply hoping that you would not be hurt, yet I have done so with my crude statement."

Was Sev the distant idea? Had jealousy spurred the question? Ori took in Privana's repentant expression.

"I'm so glad that Sev didn't hear what you said," Ori whispered and let out a slow breath.

"I am sorry. It was humiliating to you and to Sevich," Privana said, lowering his gaze.

"Yes." She shook his shoulder again. "You've made crass statements before but this one was personal, Privana. Look at me."

Her friend raised his eyes.

"I accept your apology. You are my lifelong friend and lifelong friends can make idiotic comments to each other and seek forgiveness, but then they must accept a consequence."

Privana's lips parted and his eyes widened, darting towards Ori's sword.

She rolled her eyes.

"This consequence," she said, then tightened her fist and drove it into his upper arm with enough force that Privana grunted in pain. Apparently, scattered thoughts could become solid ideas.

CHAPTER ELEVEN

The Dark element. Terrific. As she watched Ori striding towards her around the perimeter of the performance space, Sev replayed the whole collecting-shadows-to-make-them-darker moment in the alley earlier that afternoon. Ori had been kissing her. Liquifying her insides.

"Then, apparently, there's too much light for all that kissing so guess what? I'll just grab a bit of shadow and enhance it with my super powers which shouldn't be existing right here in my body," she murmured in surrender as Ori arrived beside her.

Sev smiled. "So, what's next?" she asked brightly, because super powers could be dealt with later.

"Music," Ori announced, then gave that smile Sev had nick-named 'The One That Forecasts Potential Pleasure' and grabbed Sev's hand.

The stage, wooden and clearly the handiwork of a Flora Elemental—given the lack of joinery—looked like it was rising naturally from the ground.

"It's like it's been made from one piece of wood. There's an energy to it," Sev said, indicating to the stage where a group of musicians were arranging chairs in preparation for their performance.

Ori raised an eyebrow, visible even in the muted light.

"M'kay. So Flora Elementals are big show offs as well."

Ori laughed and squeezed Sev's hand.

"Come on. Let's move to the side. The open area at the front is for dancing." Then Ori stopped short. "Oh." She looked at Sev, her expression questioning. "Unless you'd like to dance?"

"I'm more a spectator when it comes to dancing. Much less embarrassing." Sev grinned, then followed Ori to the edge of the ever-growing crowd. The musicians began, the sound of their instruments carrying further than seemed possible. Had to be the Air Element at work. Sound waves and all that. Sev shook her head.

That was an element she didn't possess. Yet. It was definitely a 'yet'. Sooner rather than later that element would make itself known because the others had appeared in such quick succession. She should be running about fully expecting photon blasts shooting out her palms like Captain Marvel.

Ori stood behind her and wrapped her arms across Sev's stomach, crossing them over so that Sev was pulled into Ori's chest. Then Sev broke out in goosebumps as Ori whispered in her ear.

"This is an excellent place for multitasking."

Sev gave a quiet gasp when she felt Ori's fingers creep under her shirt. "Ori. There are people and…people, and you're you."

"No one's watching."

"I'm sure there's a thousand pairs of eyeballs watching you reduce me to a hot, wet mess."

Ori gave a low chuckle. "Really?"

"As if you don't know." Sev breathed shallowly as Ori leaned into her back.

"You have the same effect on me," Ori whispered.

Sev's skin burned as those fingers continued their journey.

"Besides," Ori continued, "the music is quite hypnotic and generally everyone is caught up in the rhythm."

Oh God. Sev used the last bit of her concentration before her brain misfired completely to test a theory that had been percolating in her mind ever since the first element had appeared.

Thank you for the Dark.

She concentrated on the thought and waited. But the darkness didn't alter a single bit. Okay. Theory proven. She could only use the other elements in the daytime like regular people. It was the Metal element that was permanent. Good. Maybe. Hard to know if that was actually good or not. Didn't matter. Her brain misfired.

Soft fingertips continued to trace circles on her stomach, and she sank into the sensations rioting through her body.

"Ori," she whispered.

"I'm multitasking."

Sev chuckled breathlessly. "No. You're singularly focused."

The music drifted through the large group of people and they began to sing to the melody; their voices combining to create a harmonious choral piece. It was beautiful. Meanwhile, Ori meandered her fingers from the top of Sev's pants to the underside of her breasts in time with the rhythm. Sev shuddered.

Suddenly—*suddenly!*—Ori was singing and Sev's eyes widened.

"A je a Breula
A je a Breula
Suz radrap suz relgall
A Hodathis a ka la il"

It was haunting and Ori's fingers had slowed as she continued, her mouth close to Sev's ear, her soft breath against Sev's cheek.

"A je a Breula
A je a Breula
Onsa ukih A ekaver
A ekaver a je Breula

Finjuk Finjuk Bekhoarth
Yugud yugud pajoarth
Pal Palgru Palgruking
Mm Mm Mm Breula"

The stimulus, in Sev's ears, on her skin, in her heart, overwhelmed her and she turned in Ori's arms, which meant that Ori's hands had to change position, stopping to rest on Sev's lower back. Sev rested her hands on Ori's hips.

"You sing."

"I've been known to carry a note or two."

Sev chuckled. "That wasn't just carrying a note, Ori. That was amazing. What does it mean?" She leaned back to see Ori's face fill with pride.

"It is very old. Our language has changed significantly over centuries but the ancient songs remain. They celebrate our heritage.

That song is about..." She paused. "It's easier if I sing it in our modern language."

Then to Sev's delight, Ori held her gaze and sang.

"The truth has abandoned me
Haunted by the distant past
Spoke to the skies overcast
Lightning
I battled demons
But I found my way home"

The beat of silence was thick and Sev lifted her hands to cup Ori's face. "Thank you." She smoothed the skin on Ori's cheeks with her thumbs. "It's about carrying Breula in your heart even when you're away or lost."

Ori beamed. "Yes."

"It's beautiful. You're—"

"What?"

"You're beautiful."

Ori blushed, and Sev leaned up and kissed her lips. "You're also adorable."

The princess, daughter of the King of the realm of Breula, frowned. "I've not been called that before."

Sev laughed. "Well, you are. Utterly adorable."

***

Sev was surprised when Ori asked to dance for her but quickly reasoned that if Ori sounded like one of Enya's back-up singers then dancing was probably not a problem either.

"Sure. I'd love that. Back at the stage or here at the performance space or...?"

Ori turned Sev by her shoulders to place her at the border of flags, directly opposite the orange tent that she'd disappeared into earlier.

"Here."

Then she grinned and took off at a jog, long hair swaying, towards the far side of the circle. People smiled as she went past, lifting their hands in greeting. Sev sighed with happiness. If she ignored the uninvited element acquisition, like a random collection of baseball cards, then yes, happiness was in the box seat of her heart. Ori was wonderful and sexy and gorgeous and funny and under any other circumstances Sev could see herself completely and utterly falling for the woman. The idea that she was in a…whatever this was with the daughter of the King of the realm of Breula was absurd and fabulous and made her tingle all over.

But.

"Yeah," she breathed sadly. The 'but' was that some of her heart was still rooted so heavily in Melbourne.

Then it hit her. She'd said 'Melbourne', not 'home'.

That was the 'but'.

Shaking her head, Sev focused on the performance space as Privana marched out of the tent. He made his way to the middle as the crowd quickly doubled in size.

"Sword dancing is an ancient art form where the elements are manipulated through performances bringing the dancer and the sword together as one."

Loud applause greeted this statement and a fizz of excitement filled Sev's stomach. Privana raised his hand. "The exhibition features all the elements." His formal speech and commanding presence silenced the crowd. "As you know, each member of the Guard has been selected for their excellent skills and talent." There was another round of applause. "The opening dance is Ice."

Privana drew his sword and took on a stance that was reminiscent of tai chi. Another Guard member, carrying a small bucket, strode from the tent and placed it next to Privana's feet, who held the tip of his sword over the top for a moment. Suddenly crystals formed on the sword's blade and Privana nodded at the Guard member who picked up the bucket and rushed away.

Privana paused, then launched into a series of sideways flips and turns where his body curved through the air, chased by a trail of crystals which sparkled in the light of the lanterns. It was beautiful in its fury, and the audience gasped and murmured in appreciation. The murmurs were the only sounds. There was no accompanying music, and as Privana slowed his movements, the crowd held its breath, appreciating the reverence that Ori's Deputy held for his element. Eventually he centred his sword in front of his chest, chin raised, and closed his eyes.

Wow. Sev blinked as Privana bowed his head, acknowledging the applause, and strode from the circle into the tent. She'd never seen anything like it; the fluidity, the aggressive artistry.

The people behind her talked excitedly about the order of the dances, and Sev discovered that Ori was the final performance, so she spent the next half an hour enjoying the other eight elements until Privana called for the last dance of the evening. Sev's eyes rounded as Ori walked into the centre of the space, looking every inch the warrior princess and Leader of the Guard in those tight pants, the dark brown boots, the gold and the red and the arm bands and the hair clasp and…oh God. Even from a distance, Ori found Sev's eyes and held her gaze as she drew her sword slowly, almost sensually. Sev shivered with desire.

The same member of the Guard hurried out with a lit candle; its flame not wavering in the breeze. Magic.

Ori hovered her sword over the candle and then lifted it away as a golden glow made its way up the blade to the hilt. Ori's face reflected the metallic flush, and Sev couldn't take her eyes off her. Ori was ablaze with intensity and Sev felt it in every fibre of her body.

Ori paused then shifted to place one hand in the small of her back. Then she laid the sword across her broad shoulders; the weapon perfectly balanced and without making the blade give a single wobble, undulated her shoulders, the waves becoming more pronounced until she was able to roll her body over as if in a washing machine. The sword slid down her arm as she touched her fingertips to the ground and she spun the hilt about her wrist; a circular blaze of light. Not once did the sword touch the ground, or pause, or alter its journey about Ori's body unless she asked it to. She cradled it, sensually, the blade seemingly caught in the desire, and the fluidity. Ori was aglow, her expression intense, full of concentration. Radiating a need that curled in waves towards Sev.

Sev was entranced, until a quiet voice murmured near her ear.

"Are you enjoying the dances?"

Sev recognised Askal's voice, so only delivered a quick glance and smile as she responded.

"I am," she replied. "Very much."

Ori's dance steps became more intricate as she undulated her body, the lit sword now twisting over her shoulders again, the glow looking very much like the delayed arcs of white light created by sparklers waved in the air on Christmas Eve.

"Has anyone explained the meaning of each dance?" Denjern Sohe, the Arcanix who had been attending to the chalk barrels, had joined the conversation, standing near Askal's shoulder if the direction of his question was any indication.

"No, but it's about the element, right?" Sev continued to stare at the Leader of the Guard, whose dance steps brought her closer.

"Not completely," Askal murmured. "It is about what the dance means to the Elemental. What energy they are choosing to portray to those watching."

Sev ignored the butterflies in her stomach as she held eye contact with Ori and even though she was still a reasonable distance away, she caught the small smile on Ori's face.

"Yes," Denjern Sohe added, quietly. "Orilaevar Reysandoral Breula's dance, the Valwith, is rather special because it is not performed for the people."

"It isn't?" Sev swallowed.

"No. It is a performance for an audience of one."

Sev felt like an idiot asking the next question because she knew the answer. But she asked it anyway because the words needed to be said out loud. To make them real. To hear the answer.

"Who's she dancing for?" she whispered into the reverent silence.

Askal and Denjern Soho didn't respond for a moment.

"You," Askal said.

Sev released a very shaky breath, as Ori, only a few metres away, made eye contact and paused, feet together, the sword rotating slowly over and around her wrists.

It was like they were the only people at the festival.

Then Ori broke their gaze and took large, deliberate strides to the centre of the performance space.

"Me?" Sev replied.

"Really?" Askal's incredulous tone filled her ears. "It is as if you have stuck your head in our furnace and burnt your eyeballs."

Sev rolled her lips inwards as laughter bubbled in her mouth, breaking the exquisite tension. The confirmation of her suspicion, the delight in the direction of her thoughts, the breath she finally let out as Ori finished her performance, slowly sliding one finger down the blade to extinguish the light. All of it.

All. Of. It.

***

Ori's expression, in fact her whole body, radiated shyness when she joined Sev moments later. Sev almost expected Ori to drag her toe in circles on the grass and dart her gaze about. Adorable.

Sev, aware of eyes watching their every movement, reached for Ori's hands, to bring her gaze back.

"That was beautiful, and yes, I know what the dance means." She squeezed Ori's fingers and released her hands. "Thank you." The tender smile hovered between them.

"You're welcome," Ori said quietly, then flicked her eyes over Sev's shoulder and delivered a low hum. "Hello, Mother."

Sev whipped around. The Queen, wife to the King of the realm of Breula, and probably more importantly, Ori's mum, stood not half a metre away, with a member of the Guard—all leather and straight eyebrows—outfitted with a bow, a quiver of arrows and a small sword in its scabbard, positioned at a respectful distance to the rear. The Queen was a slightly shorter, more regal version of Ori, but with the same long blonde hair and blue eyes. She was radiant.

Sev's eyes widened.

"Mother, this is Sevich." Ori inclined her head at Sev. "Sev, this is my Mother, Queen Sermeh Reytoris Breula."

The elegant woman studied Sev with inquisitive eyes that sparkled with wit and mischief, and Sev felt compelled to deliver an awkward bow-curtsy combination which probably made her look like she was having a stroke.

"Sevich, dear, we do not stand on such ceremony here. Please, call me Sermeh Reytoris," the Queen said in a beautifully melodious voice. "I rather like the informality. Orilaevar has been educating me on the speech patterns and conventions of your society."

Sev caught Ori's grimace and she bit her lip. Clearly, Queen Sermeh Reytoris wasn't averse to teasing her daughter.

"I'm really pleased to meet you…" Sev paused as she worked around the idea of shortening the name of a member of the royal family. "Queen Sermeh Reytoris." She couldn't bring herself to drop the title. It felt wrong, even if she was really not a fan of royalty at all.

The townspeople flowing past gave the Queen a much wider berth than they did for her daughter, but still with the veneurative attitude; respectful smiles and nods and hands pressed to chests. Clearly the Queen was adored just as much as Ori. Sev wondered if the King inspired such devotion. Probably.

Turning to Ori, the Queen's eyes sparkled again. "That was a beautiful dance tonight, darling. Ardent and passionate. Three months is such a brief period to rehearse those steps."

"I only decided to—thank you, Mother," Ori muttered, her eyes closing in resignation. The lantern above their heads highlighted the flush of pink on her cheeks, and Sev grinned. Oh yes, the Queen was full of mischief.

"It has not been included in the program since Tua Jur Breula almost five years ago," the Queen continued. "His element is Dark which was an odd element for the Valwith but Ualwu Onsa Breula certainly appreciated it, judging by their union ceremony two months later."

"At least with the Light element, I could see the movements," Sev added. "I can't imagine that dance with a dark sword. It'd be like having a besotted ninja appear out of nowhere to scare the living daylights out of a person."

The Queen blinked, then let loose a peal of laughter. "Oh, I do like you, Sevich." She pointed to Ori, and hummed—the high to low version—through a smile and a single nod. Then she turned back to Sev. "I was hoping to speak with you regarding a new sculpture for the Great Hall."

"Me?" Sev wrinkled her forehead. The Queen needed design advice? From what Ori had told Sev about her mother's enjoyment of the arts, she hardly seemed the person who'd need guidance in interior decorating.

"Yes. I understand that you are quite gifted in metal art." The Queen pinned Sev with a long look, which was uncomfortable because it felt like the Queen had been having morning tea with Jino who'd told her all about Metal permanency and extra elements hanging about. Completely irrational.

"Um, thanks. Should I come up to the mansion on…?"

"Lovely. It is settled then." The Queen clasped her hands together, the sleeves of her gown swaying at her wrists. "Perhaps tomorrow?"

Ori stiffened. "I had hoped that Sev would join me on another ride tomorrow."

This time Ori was the recipient of a long look. "Of course, Orilaevar dear. I understand that you have visited many attractive landmarks." She turned to Sev. "Have you been to the warm pools?"

"Like hot springs?"

"Yes, that is also an applicable label."

Sev quickly faced Ori. "That sounds great. Tomorrow is sorted, then." She turned back to the Queen. "Would you mind if I visited the next day?"

The smile Sev received was affectionate, and when combined with a rather regal head tilt, she took that as a 'yes'.

Ori narrowed her eyes at her mother. "You're meddling."

"Oh, psh."

Sev caught the coy shrug. An elegant, coy shrug that probably only a Queen could pull off.

"Mother, I think I should escort Sev home. She's most likely tired and needs to rest to replenish her energy."

Sev couldn't very well announce that she was fine. Topped up. All permanent and everything. So she nodded.

"That's probably a good idea." Sev gave the Queen a warm smile. She liked Ori's mum a lot, and despite the noble bearing, she could visualise the two of them having a casual chat over a cup of tea and a TimTam. Well, whatever constituted a TimTam in Breula.

***

"My mother is quite invested in my love—in my personal life," Ori said, as they stood together outside Askal and Jino's house.

Sev laughed. "It's clear that she wants you to be happy."

Ori swung their joined hands. "I am."

The response thrilled Sev because she felt the same happiness, but it frightened her, so she deflected.

"I like how she teases you. You bite well."

"She is an expert." Ori rolled her eyes.

"So we're on for another ride tomorrow."

Ori's eyes darkened. "Yes, please."

Sev held her gaze. "I enjoyed tonight. Your singing, your dance—"

"Your dance," Ori corrected.

Slowly, Sev closed the gap between them, their faces close. "My dance," she whispered, then pressed her lips to Ori's, enjoying the softness, then pulled away, mindful that they were in the middle of the town, and she felt like she was saying goodnight outside her parents' house. The thought made her giggle.

"What?"

"Nothing. Seriously, I'm just happy."

Ori smiled. "Good." Then after a quick kiss, Ori stepped back. "Rest well, Sev."

"You, too." And she watched Ori turn and walk quickly up the street, pause at the corner to wave, then disappear from view.

It crossed her mind that she should have asked Ori how Operation *Return Sev To Melbourne* was coming along, then it occurred to her that maybe she'd forgotten to ask on purpose. An interesting development. And complicated.

***

Sev spied Jino in what constituted a lounge room in a Breulan house and veered left to say goodnight. She stopped in front of the seated older woman, taking in the outstretched legs, the tired expression on her face. Clearly the night had worn her out.

"Did you enjoy the festival?" Jino asked, her raised eyebrows loading the question with innuendo. It was Sev's turn to blush.

"Yes. Very much." Then she flopped down next to Jino on the curved wooden couch. The wood had been manipulated into such a soft texture that it dipped under her body as if it were foam padding. In her first week in the house, her brain hadn't been able to process the dichotomy. Like those cakes that looked like other things that shouldn't be cakes. Now, with her hands-on manipulation of Flora—the dead version—she appreciated the skills used even further.

"So." She rolled her head, directing her gaze at Jino's quizzical expression. "You can add Dark to my shopping list of elements."

Jino gasped and sat up, swivelling until she was square on. "Oh my!"

"That was my reaction as well," Sev sighed, and pushed back into the curve of the furniture, tucking her legs under her.

"You do not seem upset." Jino's gaze hadn't left Sev's face.

"You know? I'm really not. It's like I've started to see myself as some sort of science experiment, which is not healthy, I guess. I bet a psychologist would have a field day. They'd probably diagnose dissociative behaviour or something."

Jino's eyes widened in confusion.

Sev wriggled her shoulders to relieve the tension. "Anyway, I was…" She paused as a sudden rush of heat reminded her exactly what she'd been doing when she'd discovered her Dark element energy. "Ah…earlier this afternoon, I was thinking about wanting the space around us—me, to not be so bright, and it was like I was able to create more shadows from existing shadows, layering them to get the amount of darkness I wanted."

"Oh, Sevich." Jino reached across and held Sev's hand. "How many is that now?"

Sev breathed deeply. "Metal, Flora, Fauna, Earth, Ice, Dark." Then she swallowed and gave voice to the half-baked idea that had been whispering at her for weeks. "But I feel that there's more? Like, I can feel an unconscious energy with the others?" Suddenly unable to sit still, Sev leapt up and paced about. "There's Water, and Light, and what else?"

"Air, and Heat."

"Right," Sev said, pointing at Jino, then tucked her hands into her armpits.

Jino cocked her head.

"Think back throughout your time here so far. Has each element presented itself as strongly as the six you possess?"

Sev rocked on her feet and cast her mind back to her time in the Facility. *Water, Light, Air, Heat. Water, Light, Air, Heat. Water, Light, Air—*

"Oh my God," she breathed.

Jino leaned forward, sore feet obviously forgotten.

Sev pretended to grasp a sword and imitated cutting a swathe through an imaginary barrier. "Air."

"Air?"

"Yes. When I accidentally injured Jihl in the assessment, it felt like the air parted slightly so the sword's journey was smoother, faster, and…" Sev stared. "I moved air, Jino."

"It would seem so." She lifted her hand and pointed to her forefinger. "That is seven."

Sev's feet resumed see-sawing.

"Oh! When I yelled at Ori in the courtyard." Sev flapped her hand. "The day I melted her sword. I was so mad and homesick and frustrated that she wasn't helping me get back to Melbourne." Sev tried to ignore the way Jino's face dropped at the mention of Sev leaving. She didn't think Jino realised she'd shown any emotion. "I was standing over her and it was like I was glowing. I thought it was because it was a sunny day, but it wasn't, was it?"

Jino shook her head. "Most likely not. It will have been Light."

"Jesus Christ." Sev tucked her now shaking hands back into her armpits. "And I'm positive about one more. Heat." She received a raised eyebrow in response. "Riding in winter is supposed to be a tad cold, right? Nope. Me and my warm, toasty self are just fine. I told Ori that I had a mini hot water bottle over my heart and she thought I was insane. But I'd manipulated Heat. I know I did." Sev stared at the ceiling. "But I can't for the life of me think of an episode with water." She dropped her gaze. "There isn't one. Maybe I'll stop at nine?"

Jino delivered the longest look that Sev had ever received and it caused her to return dejectedly back on the couch.

"I doubt that, young Sevich."

"Yeah, so do I."

Then it felt completely natural to shuffle sideways and lean into Jino's shoulder, swallowing thickly as the tears welled.

"I don't know what to do. I have eight more elements than I should. My main element is permanent. I can mould three tool-based elements by hand. I'm in lo—I'm in a thing with Ori. I don't think she wants me to leave at all. I'm not sure I do either. But I miss Alex so much. I met the Queen tonight and she's really lovely and I'm liking Breula, particularly you and Askal and the townspeople and Ori. Actually most of what makes Breula what it is, even though I'm positive that there are couple of people who aren't thrilled I'm even in this realm." Jino brought her arms around Sev's shoulders and that did it. The tears fell over the edge of her eyes.

"My dear, you have such a lot in your heart. It is just as well it is very large to carry so much love. I feel many would not do well bearing your worries."

"I don't love all my worries. I'd be perfectly happy if a few left," Sev mumbled into Jino's side. The hug, protective and comforting, felt as if Sev could drop some of those worries for a moment and simply absorb the tenderness that came from a mother's embrace.

She wouldn't know but it felt like the kind that Sev had always imagined.

"You have love, Sevich. You would not hold the energy of each element if you did not love it. To manipulate an element is to nurture it, to care for its balance, to respect its place. To hold permanent energy? To use your hands? Goodness, that shows such devotion to the elements. They understand you as you do them. Your love for your friend, Alex, is unbreakable. Your burgeoning love for Orilaevar Reysandoral Breula—" Jino squeezed Sev's shoulders to hold her in place. "It is. I see it. Your burgeoning love for our people, for this place, for us. I see that as well and when the element of Water awakens, you will see that the love is returned."

This time Sev managed to pull away. "Returned by...?"

"In the prophecy, it is said that the Guardian is protected by love from the time they arrive until the time they are needed."

Ignoring the idea that adding the Water element to her repertoire would activate Guardian Girl, Sev squinted. "But isn't that the Guardian's job? To protect? To love Breula?"

Jino smiled gently. "Love is not a job, my dear Sevich."

CHAPTER TWELVE

Ori glanced back at the wide doorway to the stables complex. Privana had insisted on accompanying her more frequently lately which was not really outside his role but felt a little overbearing if Ori was being completely truthful. She was one of the most accomplished swords-people and archers in the realm so his continuous presence seemed extraneous. Perhaps today's hovering was due to feeling remorseful for his outburst at the Festival. Who knew?

Ori returned to her task at hand. She'd arrived at the stables earlier than usual as Ukih and Kotrol needed grooming. It was an enjoyable activity. Peaceful. And the horses clearly enjoyed it if the soft sighs as she dragged the brush across their hair was any indication.

Voices from Privana's post drew her attention, and she paused, holding the brush mid-sweep along Ukih's flank.

Councillor Dasoskach Vaern Breula was speaking with Privana, the words indistinct, but the stiffening in Privana's shoulders, the head shake of disagreement and the agitated gestures from the Councillor indicated that it wasn't a jovial interaction. She cocked her head, then frowned as Privana's voice carried down the long walkway.

"Orilaevar Reysandoral Breula, I must attend to a member of the Guard who has slipped and hurt their shoulder." And before Ori could respond, he disappeared from view.

The injury to the Guard member must have been the reason for the Councillor's presence and because Privana took his job very seriously, shuffling the Guard about to replace injured Guard members would be high on his list of priorities. Hence his quick departure. Ori hummed. She'd check in later after the ride with Sev.

Consternation for the hurt Elemental was put aside when Councillor Dasoskach Vaern Breula strolled towards Ori, her boots tapping along the smooth stone surface between the stalls, and stopped quite a few steps away from Ukih. She obviously had a respect for, or fear of, the large beasts.

"Good morning, Orilaevar Reysandoral Breula," she simpered, her voice echoing in the large space.

Ori lowered the brush and dangled it from her hand.

"It is a good morning, Councillor Dasoskach Vaern Breula. I hope the Guard member's injury is not too serious."

The Councillor blinked, frowned, then smiled broadly. "Oh! Yes, they are not badly hurt, actually, however Privana Trissandoral Breula wanted to ensure that they were receiving good care." The broad smile held for another moment.

Ori puffed out her lips and tossed the brush into a bucket. The interaction felt strange.

"Good. Good, well…I was not aware you had an interest in the horses of the realm. It is unusual to see you here."

The woman tittered. "Oh! I admire people who have an affinity with the animals. Fauna Elementals are simply wonderful. Oh, and those Arcanix who possess a smidgen of the Fauna element? Why, they are adorable. I wanted to visit today to view the beasts."

Ori breathed in slowly. The patronising tone, and the subtle put-down of Arcanix raised her hackles. She straightened her shoulders.

"Besides admiration for horses and those who ride them, to what do I owe this visit?" She did not like the woman, so drawing her body up to its full height and reverting to a sudden ignorance of contractions fortified her wariness.

"Well, Orilaevar Reysandoral Breula, I thought I should inform you that I have been granted a place in the agenda for us to present the Arcanix's case to leave Breula and return to her home realm."

It took Ori a moment to realise that she was talking about Sev and the realisation hit her in the chest.

"Oh. Right."

Councillor Dasoskach Vaern Breula gave Ori a sly look. "That is what we agreed upon, is it not? You put forward that plea many weeks ago."

Ori pinched the bridge of her nose. "Yes, I did."

There was no way she was going to admit to this Councillor that she'd had a change of heart. That Sev had slowly but surely settled in that heart and it was breaking at the thought of Sev leaving.

Her face, having a mind of its own, must have expressed that sentiment.

Councillor Dasoskach Vaern Breula laughed; a high pitched tittering that caused Ukih to snort and toss his head. The woman took a step back and clutched her hands together at her large bosom, the skin at her neck trembling as she huffed in surprise. Then she seemed to gather herself and fixed Ori with a narrow look, adding a coy smile.

"She is an intriguing character."

Ori grumbled. "Sev's a person, not a character from a book."

Then done with the odd conversation, she reached for Ukih's reins, ready to lead him into his stable.

"Perhaps she is from a children's story."

Ori paused and stared at Councillor Dasoskach Vaern Breula, whose green orb flashed in the light. Earth Elemental, Ori's brain registered vacantly.

"What?"

The Councillor waved her hand as if to dismiss the comment. It was clearly meant to be placating.

"I simply meant that she must seem as if she is from a fairytale." A simpering laugh. "A legend, if you will, to have arrived out of nowhere and caught your attention so quickly."

Ori stared at her, unable to think of any possible response. Familiarity from the citizens of Breula was fine. Incomprehensible snark wasn't. She blinked.

The Councillor continued, her voice overpowering the soft snuffles from Ukih and the other horses.

"I hope the Council is able to learn from this Sevich before she leaves. The technology in her realm sounds quite advanced."

Ori released Ukih's reins. She recalled what Sev had said about technology; the people's consumption of that technology while it consumed them. If some of the Council members got their hands on such technology, it would be devastating for Breula.

She stuck her thumbs into her belt, registering the space where her sword would normally be kept. She'd taken to leaving it behind when on the rides with Sev, and Privana had been horrified, convinced that Sev was a threat. Ori had informed him that he was being ridiculous and overprotective.

"I do not think that is a good idea, Councillor Dasoskach Vaern Breula. I am sure that Sev does not have all the knowledge about her realm and there is much danger in possessing only a small amount of information when attempting to create a vast societal system."

The Councillor stepped forward, eyeing Ukih carefully. "Oh, I am sure if you mentioned it to your father—"

Again with the unwelcome, snarky familiarity. "King Rodlamar Reytoris Breula," Ori corrected.

Councillor Dasoskach Vaern Breula pressed her fingertips to her lips. "Oh, yes. Of course. I forgot myself for a moment. Perhaps I was distracted by these beautiful animals."

Ori took in the rotund body, the narrowed eyes and the smile that stretched the woman's lips but did nothing to invite the other facial features to join in. She needed to be careful. Her father relied heavily on the Council's opinions and here was one member of that Council attempting to persuade Ori about…something. It felt threatening, particularly towards Sev which raised all sorts of alarm bells and Ori's sense of protectiveness kicked into gear.

Just then, as if conjured by Ori's thoughts, Sev appeared at the stables' wide opening and strolled along the walkway, pausing to rub Kotrol's nose.

Ori's smile outshone the Councillor's scowl.

"Orilaevar Reysandoral Breula," the Councillor said, her voice urgent. "I would also remind you that you agreed to assist in the organisation of the census."

I had?

"We would be grateful for the assistance of the Guard. As you yourself noted, often the Guard cannot attend to every portal and who knows how many trespassers are hidden in the town without passing the application and therefore are undocumented?" She gasped, and again, fingertips snapped to her lips as her eyes widened at the idea of hordes of trespassers gallivanting about the countryside.

Ori knew that a few trespassers slipped through the Guards' monitoring but it would be very unlikely that any of them continued to live within the six thousand citizens. The Guard eventually escorted all trespassers to the Facility, and so the census felt unnecessary. But oddly important.

Ori bobbed her head from side to side. "No, I have not forgotten. We will convene later this week to discuss logistics. I will also speak with my father." Then, done with the woman's theatrics and undercurrent of artifice, Ori peered over the Councillor's head—an advantage of her height—and grinned at Sev.

"Hi."

The smile in return was like the sun had found gaps between the beams to cast brilliant rays across the floor. Ori could have been consumed by that smile for every second of every day. Then Sev turned to the Councillor.

"Good morning." She squinted and frowned. "I think we've met but I'm not sure. I'm Sevich." She stuck out her hand, then, receiving no response, swung her hand so that it brushed against the outside of her thigh as if she'd discovered an itch or sore muscle. Ori smothered a smile. Sev's greeting still perplexed many.

"Hello, Sevich. I am Councillor Dasoskach Vaern Breula and I am sure I have seen you from afar, but it is good to make your acquaintance. I would remember if we had already been introduced. You are quite the celebrity." The Councillor gave a high-pitched giggle, and Sev's eyebrows rose.

"I am?"

"Oh, yes," Councillor Dasoskach Vaern Breula gushed. "Now that you are such an intimate part of Orilaevar Reysandoral Breula's life."

Sev blinked, then frowned. "Um. Wow, that's pretty personal. Normally you and I would be Starbucks buddies for at least a month before we got to good stuff like that."

The Councillor tipped her head slightly, clearly confused by Sev's comment. Ori grinned, because even though she didn't understand much of Sev's reply, she understood tone and Sev's response was layered in sarcasm, which meant she was not at all enamoured with the Councillor. Recovering her equilibrium, the Councillor gestured towards the end of the walkway.

"Well, I must leave. Thank you for your assistance, Orilaevar Reysandoral Breula. I look forward to presenting our cause to the Council." She smiled thinly at Ori and Sev, then strode away, walking in the centre of alleyway to avoid the noses of the horses poking over the half-doors to their stalls.

Sev turned back to Ori and slowly blinked. "She's delightful."

Ori laughed. "She is one who must be treated carefully, but yes, not an overly pleasant person." Ori ran her hands up and down Sev's arms. She'd wanted to touch Sev since she'd arrived at Ukih's stall. "I get the feeling you've met her before."

Sev stepped into Ori's space, resting her hands lightly on Ori's hips. "I'm not sure. I feel like I've seen her somewhere but I can't place her. Maybe at the Festival." A shrug. "Never mind." She lifted up on her toes and kissed Ori's lips. "Where are Ukih and Kotrol taking us today?"

Ori smiled, returning the kiss. "Ukih and Kotrol have no say in the matter."

"Rubbish."

***

Strongly reminded of her own twitchiness when she was dressed in full regalia and attending the assessments, Sev's fidgeting—tiny grimaces, hands clenching unnecessarily about the leather reins, and minute head shaking as if having an internal argument—continued for at least the first few hours. She wasn't distracted as such, Ori decided. It was more like she was waiting for something to happen.

Whatever it was eventually dissipated and Sev flicked a flirty smile at Ori, then because the horses were close enough, leaned slightly and ran her finger up Ori's thigh.

"I'd like to kiss you again," she said. "And other things." Her eyes rested on Ori for a long moment.

Ori breathed slowly through a smile. "So we're mind-reading now?" Then she gestured to a small hill. "How about over that rise?"

Sev encouraged Kotrol into a trot. "I really, really want to get to the other things," she said over her shoulder, and crested the rise before Ukih had even contemplated joining his stable mate. Ori heard the gasp as it travelled on the breeze.

"Oh my God, Ori. This is gorgeous!"

Coming to a stop, Ori flashed a grin at the look of awe on Sev's face, then stared at the scene before them. The Juith river cascaded over the jumbled rock formations in a series of waterfalls, each tumbling into individual pools of various sizes and depths. The pool that Ori was interested in was off to the side, and even though all eleven pools were devoid of people, she wanted privacy and the Giord, with its rocks, trees, walls of grasses and mossy platforms— one behind the curtain of water—was secluded and her favourite.

"The water is warm if you'd like to swim," Ori said, casting a hooded gaze at Sev who parted her lips, snapped them shut, then gave a slow smile.

"I'd like that."

They flicked quick, seductive glances at each other as they made their way down the slope, then dismounted at a large boulder several metres away from the water's edge.

Sev politely asked Kotrol and Ukih not to wander too far, and Ori rolled her eyes good-naturedly.

"They won't listen, particularly Ukih."

"Yes, they will," Sev said, confidently, then wandered over to the water's edge, scooping the warm liquid into her palm. "Ooh, this is divine."

Ori took in the moment. The happiness on Sev's face, the way she shook her fingers to shower the ground with water, the way she slowly walked over to stand in Ori's space, so close, the way Ori's skin broke out in a million goosebumps.

"Feel like a swim?" Ori said, her voice catching. She couldn't wrench her gaze away. Sev held her transfixed, the pupils in those brown and gold eyes enlarging, darkening, and she couldn't have stopped, wouldn't have stopped, her hands reaching for Sev's face and bringing their lips together.

Their kiss was incendiary. Their bodies pressed tightly. Their hands roaming. Their tongues sliding together. Sev's lips were so soft and Ori clutched at her simply to hold her there for as long as possible. The kiss, the push and pull that asked and gave, sent waves of lust coursing through Ori's stomach.

Sev broke the kiss.

"Clothes off. Now."

Sev's command, delivered on a hoarse whisper, increased the warm, heavy slickness at the top of Ori's thighs, the liquid tickling intimately at her soft hair. She swallowed, thrilled by Sev's dominance, then stepped back, grabbing at the heel of each boot, yanking them off, and placing them to the side. Her pants were next, and Sev stared hungrily, her eyes roaming, as each item of clothing was divested.

Ori straightened. She knew her body was pleasing to look at, a fact confirmed by Sev's lustful gaze, her parted lips.

"Ori, you are magnificent," Sev gasped, raking her eyes across Ori's body.

Ori lifted an eyebrow.

"I'm going in. Care to join me?" Then she stepped backwards into the water, thoroughly enjoying the raw look on Sev's face.

Sev's response was to quickly remove her clothing, flinging each item onto a nearby rock, then stroll languidly, seductively, into the water. The surface slowly crept up Sev's gorgeous body—small breasts tipped with tight pink nipples, strong shoulders, wiry frame —until the depth meant that she was forced to tread water when she met Ori in the centre of the pond.

"Hi there," Ori murmured, her legs and arms undulating to keep her body afloat.

A slow smile grew on Sev's lips.

"Hi, yourself." She pushed forward and licked Ori's bottom lip.

Then, keeping fast eye contact, she dipped her hand below the surface. It took all of Ori's willpower and the threat of potential drowning to not reach for Sev's cheeks and bring her lips the short distance to her own. Kissing Sev was her most favourite activity, not even eclipsed by witnessing the woman, beautifully naked, slowly slinking, sliding, her lips parted, into the Giord. That image was now imprinted on her memory forever. Even a fleeting replay brought slickness to her sex. Her clit was already primed, ready for a single touch.

Just as she was about to run a finger over Sev's lips, risking a dunking, her nipples, tight with arousal, were lightly grazed by the back of Sev's hand.

"Oh!" Ori's eyes widened, her timing faltered, and she quickly stretched out her arm because she nearly sank just as she'd predicted. "Sev!"

Sev, her legs leisurely circling under her body, raised an eyebrow, and allowed a smirk to slide across her lips. Ori decided then and there that if she was going to die from drowning, she'd be thrilled to do so in Sev's smile, in Sev's hooded gaze, in the waters of the Juith River.

"Ori, do you know?" Sev tugged at her bottom lip with her teeth as she dragged her fingers across Ori's nipples and again Ori's timing faltered, forcing her hands to pick up their pace.

"Do I know what?" Ori's breath hitched. *What am I supposed to know?* All sorts of fabulous scenarios whisked through her mind. She definitely knew about those.

Sev grinned. "I was a state water polo player at high school, well…the period of high school when I could get to training." Something flashed in Sev's eyes but quickly vanished. "Do you know what that means?" she continued, maintaining intense eye contact as she ran a single finger down Ori's torso.

Ori's clit twitched.

Her abdominal muscles tightened.

Her breathing shallowed.

"What?" she managed.

"It means I can tread water for hours *and* multitask at the same time."

Sev did seem to be floating without exerting any energy at all, as if the water was supporting her, happy to assist with Sev's endeavours. Ori was at a distinct disadvantage, and yet could not have been more thrilled.

Then, Sev's hands disappeared underwater and she tweaked Ori's nipples, which produced a gasp-like moan; a sound which Ori was sure she'd never made in her life. This was torture. Exquisite torture and Ori couldn't believe how completely aroused she was, how slick she was, how much she was being reduced to a quivering mess by Sev's unshakable eye contact, and her seductive determination.

Submission. Ori realised that she'd do anything Sev commanded. Anything.

Meanwhile, she had to concentrate on staying afloat, because in so many other aspects, she was already drowning.

"Hours, hey?" she croaked.

"You have no idea of the things I want to do to you."

Ori kicked her legs faster. "Oh?" An idiotic response but excusable since Sev's fingers were now trailing down Ori's stomach and abdomen, outlining each muscle as if tracing a map.

"Mmhmm." Then Sev paused, brought her hands to the surface, and wiggled the tips of her fingers. "Are you ready?" she whispered.

Before Ori could respond, Sev, her hair wild and wet, her eyes flashing with intent and her mouth sporting a wicked grin, swung her hands into the water and quickly pressed one against Ori's clit, coating her fingers in the slick heavy liquid, and thumbed Ori's nipple with the other. She leaned forward to kiss away the gasp that fell out of Ori's mouth.

"Hold on," Sev whispered, clearly meaning that Ori should prepare herself for a wonderful ride, not to literally hold onto Sev's body even though Ori was beginning to think the latter option might be essential.

With a skill that spoke of years of experience keeping herself up in a body of water, and with Ori desperately attempting to hold herself up as well, Sev looked into Ori's eyes, circled the tight bundle of nerves at her sex and tweaked a very fortunate nipple. Ori's clit throbbed in time with her heart, and she groaned through ever-increasing panting, nearly taking in a mouthful of water.

"Sev, I don't think—"

"Yes, you can." Sev twisted the other nipple.

"Ah!" Ori was so close.

The warmth of the water wasn't helping. In fact, it seemed to have risen in temperature. Her body radiated heat. As did Sev's, if the steaming surface about her was any indication. Ori throbbed against Sev's hand and her pelvis rocked forward, chasing more pressure. Then, *then*, a wave of desire curled into her stomach, rising, rising, and a powerful orgasm ripped through her veins. Her head dropped back, and she shouted to the sky.

"Oh! Yes! Yes!"

Tremors wracked her body and distantly she felt Sev's arms wrap about her torso as she shook with pleasure.

How she ended up at the shallow edge of the pool, leaning back against Sev's chest and cradled in her arms, she had no idea. The orgasm seemed to have made her unconscious for a moment which had never happened in all her years of orgasm-having.

"Sev."

"Hi," Sev breathed into her ear, her chin resting on Ori's shoulder.

"That was...I'm lost for words." Ori gave a grunt of laughter. "No, I'm not. That was outstanding. I've never experienced an orgasm like that." She luxuriated in Sev's embrace for a number of minutes, relishing the feeling of Sev's breasts against her back, Sev's arms wrapped around her, Sev's soft breath in her ear. Perfect.

Finally, Ori turned, and pushed up on the soft moss that touched the water's edge, so that she was lying over Sev. She rested on her forearms, and her wet hair fell either side of Sev's head like a curtain.

They grinned at each other for a long time, and Ori's heart filled with the gold and brown of Sev's eyes, her slight smile that hinted at more than affection, the way her arms tightened around Ori's neck.

Then, without any signal, they brought their lips together to share a kiss that spoke of the intimacy they'd just shared, of the intimacy they had been sharing since the first time they'd ridden out into the plains. Sev's lips slid against Ori's, tongues tasting each other's mouths and Ori didn't think she'd ever been kissed so tenderly, so possessively.

She broke away and licked along Sev's jawline, eventually arriving at her earlobe, which she nibbled and nipped, and rejoiced at hearing her name pulled from Sev's throat in a guttural groan. The rush of adrenaline coursing through Ori's body was so intense it made her head spin.

She made her way back to Sev's mouth, kissing, pausing so that Sev's lips could capture her own.

"I want to make you come," Ori whispered, and thrilled in the shudder that ran through Sev's body. She shuffled down, kissing Sev's skin lightly until she reached Sev's nipples. "Do you like to be touched here?"

Sev gave a heavy swallow. "Very much," she murmured, and reached for Ori's hair, sliding her fingers through the tresses.

Ori stretched her hands, placing them over Sev's ribs, leaving her thumbs free to slowly skim Sev's rosy pink nipples. She watched, enjoying the way Sev's lips parted, the way her eyes darkened, the way she breathed a soft "Yes". Enjoying the flare of pure lust surging through Sev's gaze.

Ori bent her head to circle a nipple with her tongue, then increased the pace of her fingers, tweaking and twisting.

Sev hissed. "Jesus!"

Despite not understanding the desire-laden word, Ori grinned, and decided she wanted to hear more of the same. She shuffled down further.

"What else do you like?" she murmured, trailing her fingertips from knee to inner thigh.

"That."

"And more?"

"Y-yes."

"Do you want my fingers or my mouth?" Ori's fingers crept higher, lightly touching the curls at the juncture of Sev's thighs, her sex. She so wanted to put her mouth there.

"Ori. Oh, God." Sev was quickly unravelling.

"My fingers or my mouth?" Ori asked again, and continued to brush against Sev's sex. Just a whisper.

"Ori…oh, God." Sev brought her lust-laden gaze to Ori's. "Both," she breathed. "Fingers. Inside. Please"

Begging. Oh, yes. A deluge of desire crashed over Ori, and her clit throbbed back to life. She twisted her wrist and wet her fingers at Sev's entrance, teasing, as Sev groaned, her hands clutching at the spongy grass beside her. Then Ori eased two fingers inside, and bent her head to drag the flat of her tongue from where her fingers were slowly thrusting and up to the underside of Sev's clit.

"Yes! Oh! Oh, Ori. Oh, God." Sev's hands released the grass and scrabbled at Ori's hair, grasping, holding Ori in place. "Please. Please."

Sev's responsiveness was a spark and it lit Ori on fire. She circled her lips, and sucked, thrusting and curling her fingers, as her ears filled with the rising tone of Sev's cries. Suddenly Sev's body went rigid, and she held her breath, as her thighs trembled. A frozen moment. Then Sev shouted Ori's name.

Ori pressed the heel of her palm against Sev's clit as her shudders and aftershocks and panting eventually subsided and Sev brought her gaze back.

"Hi," Ori said, cheerily, a wide grin on her face.

"Oh, my God. Get up here." Ori complied and lay flush with Sev's body. "You are very smug, aren't you?" Sev gasped, her breath slowly returning to normal.

Ori's grin didn't fade. "Mmhm."

With a quick laugh, Sev kissed Ori hard, licking her lips when she pulled away. "How long do you think Ukih and Kotrol will tolerate being ignored?"

Ori raised an eyebrow. "Probably three more."

Sev laughed again, then Ori tucked into Sev's neck and pressed against her lean body. It felt completely wonderful. She trailed her fingertips aimlessly across Sev's skin, breathing deeply, a goofy grin on her face. Perfect.

Finally, after minutes and minutes of listening to each other's heartbeats, Sev's quiet voice rumbled in her ear. "I was thinking an extra four, actually, but if you can't handle that many orgasms, then we'll settle for—"

"Oh!" Ori jerked away and frowned in mock indignation. "Well, I was being conservative. I didn't want you to feel like you couldn't keep up."

Sev's playfulness elated her. How long had it been since someone had taken delight in teasing her, ignoring her status, seeing her as an equal, and a challenge, had fired her libido, made her laugh, and come to her with passion and intellect? Never. There'd been no-one. Until Sev.

Sev's aggrieved look at the aspersions being cast about her orgasm capabilities drew a laugh. Ori rose to her feet, and grabbed Sev's hand, hauling her up, then dragged her into the water, stopping when the surface reached their waists.

"I think we need to cool off and regain our energy so we can continue to ignore our horses."

Sev chuckled, then threw herself into the deeper water, and drifted into the middle of the pool. "Care to join me?" she asked seductively, repeating Ori's words from before.

Ori twisted her lips in thought, and Sev laughed quietly.

"I won't let you drown, Orilaevar Reysandoral Breula, princess of the realm."

Ori narrowed her eyes and returned Sev's grin. Then, in retaliation for the sass, skidded her hand across the water, splashing Sev who turned her head a second too late. Sev slowly flicked the water from her eyes, and lifted her chin.

"So that's how it's going to be, is it?" she said, with a wicked smile. "Okay. Back at you." Sev smacked the water, and Ori prepared herself for a similar soft spray.

But the water that lifted from the surface was not a soft spray. It was a wall that rose and rose and Ori's eye's widened, because the water paused, holding its form, its height, just for a moment, before dropping heavily onto Ori's head, forcing her under.

She came up spluttering, wiped her hands across her face, and stared at Sev.

Chapter Thirteen

Sev lifted her gaze from Ori's magnificent body, with those small breasts tipped with dark nipples, and fell into the most wide-eyed, shocked expression she'd ever seen on a person's face.

Ah, the Water element. Hello.

"How?" Ori exclaimed in a sort of whispered gasp, and slicked back her long hair.

Sev's shoulders dropped.

"I was hoping to explain rather than give you a spontaneous demonstration." She closed her eyes in resignation. "But apparently not."

Ori's eyes were shaped like saucers, and Sev thought a fleeting look of suspicion shimmered across her face. It was heartbreaking.

She exhaled, gathering more steam for the next collection of words. "Okay. So." *This is bloody difficult to explain.* "I possess all the elements. The ten." Ori hadn't moved, as if paralysed by the concept. Sev completely understood.

"When?" Ori had been reduced to single word questions. Again, completely understandable. Sev's responses had been similar each time a new element had appeared, albeit with a few swear words chucked in for effect.

"They started appearing properly a month and a half after I arrived in Breula, but actually I used the Air element in the assessment with Jihl and then I yelled at you and I shone with Light energy like some sort of angel and—"

"I remember that!" Ori exclaimed, gesturing for Sev to swim towards her. "The day you melted my sword."

"Yep."

Sev extended her hands, but Ori hesitated, looking at Sev's hands like she was wondering about the energy held inside. Then she nodded and slid her fingers between Sev's, her thumbs smoothing circles in the palms.

"So I've had a bit of a chat with Kotrol, and some trees." Sev nodded at Ori's expression. "Mmhmm. The first ride."

"The imbalance."

"Yeah, well, you're the one who made me chat to them."

"The Flora Elementals are right. They're adamant that there is an imbalance."

Sev waved. "Hi," she said with fake cheer, then grimaced as Ori frowned. "Sorry. Then I made a hole in a road, and, not an hour later, I created a layer of ice on the water barrel in the workshop. That one freaked me out." She jerked. "Oh! I think that's where I've seen that Councillor! She might have been the woman on the corner when I apologised to the dirt." She shook her head and gave a short, humourless laugh. "If I'd said something like that in Melbourne, they would have asked for the name of my dealer."

Ori frowned again, and Sev untangled her fingers to wave away the comment.

"This is unheard of," Ori murmured.

"Well, not anymore."

Ori drifted her gaze over Sev's body which created all sorts of poorly timed twists and tumbles of desire to drift through Sev's stomach.

Ori raised an eyebrow. "I'd like to put our clothes on to continue this discussion if you don't mind. I desperately want to find out what is happening and your nakedness is beautifully, yet entirely, distracting."

They shared a smile. The levity, the sensuality, diffused the tense moment, but Sev breathed deeply. There was still so much more to say.

After a slow kiss because of the still naked situation and because why not indulge in more sensual levity, Ori held out her hand, and led them to the mossy grass bank where their clothes were scattered. Getting dressed was closure on the afternoon's kissing and touching and orgasming and—butterflies swooped about in Sev's stomach and she bit her lip, stifling the groan of arousal. An intense conversation was about to occur so she packed away all the goosebumps and body memories and gallons of lust to concentrate on Ori's bewilderment.

They sat facing each other, cross-legged and knees touching. Ori's fingers ran softly across Sev's hands, knees, and her face as if Sev had suddenly become a fragile ornament.

"And when we had our very delicious make out session in the alley yesterday, I kind of." Sev squished up one cheek towards her eye as she continued in her retelling of Sev, the keeper of all and too much. "Made it dark." She inhaled deeply. "You didn't want to create too much interest so I asked the Dark a favour."

She shrugged as if it was completely normal to request assistance from an element. Her brain ached with the enormity.

"How are you doing this?"

Sev smacked Ori's knees. "I don't know."

"And just then…" Ori waved vaguely at the pond, and Sev sighed.

"I had nine and I've been waiting for the Water element to make itself known and I guess today was the day. So, happy Water day." She grimaced and finally, Ori gave a tiny flicker of a smile.

"You were very distracted at the beginning of our ride today. I thought it was because you were contemplating the potential of sex."

Sev laughed. "Yes, I was and yes, that was certainly distracting." They shared a grin.

"But it wasn't really that," Ori continued. "You were waiting."

"Mm."

Ori gasped, clutching at her own thighs, gripping the material. "You're the Guardian!"

"Oh, for Christ sake," Sev said, clenching her teeth. "I'm not, Ori." She paused. "I'm not. I can't be."

Ori stared, her expression thoughtful. "No, you might not be the Guardian." She flicked a finger at the orb at her throat. "You need permanency."

Sev shook her head. "No, I don't. Jino said so."

"Jino said?"

"Ah." *Shit.* "Yeah, Jino's…" She trailed off. Outing Jino as a seer was dangerous and while she trusted Ori, it wasn't her place to reveal that secret. "Jino's got a tonne of details about the prophecy."

Ori blinked, shook her head and a small smile slipped onto her lips. "Ten elements. Of course, they only last for a day then restore their energy overnight." She sounded hopeful.

"Okay, well, here's the cherry on top." Sev delivered finger guns at Ori's face. "That orb-permanency-business? Turns out I don't need an orb for my Metal element."

"Oh!" Ori's mouth dropped open.

"Yeah."

"No orb at all?"

"Not one."

All colour drained from Ori's face.

The only sound was the rushing water flowing over the rocks.

"Sev," Ori breathed, quickly untangled her legs, and pulled Sev into her chest, as if she knew all Sev's emotions were too much for one person to bear. Sev's eyes filled with tears. "It's the prophecy," Ori whispered.

"Yeah, nah. I'm pretty sure I'm just a person with odd elemental energy," Sev mumbled into Ori's shirt. She was jostled as Ori shook her head.

"I don't think so. It fits." Ori pushed on Sev's shoulders, holding her as she fixed Sev with a long look.

Sev rolled her eyes. "Ugh. This prophecy is following me everywhere."

"But there is always a reason for a prophecy as it is based on the images from an ancient seer. It is based on truth, on foresight."

The vague details of Jino's predictions drifted through Sev's mind. "Nope. There are bits missing."

Ori frowned and stared vacantly over Sev's shoulder, then brought her gaze back. "The Guardian arrives in Breula at a time of grave danger." Ori kept her frown as she continued. "The Guardian uses a great power to save Breula and ends up falling in l—" She stopped, and looked away, a soft blush colouring her cheeks. "Uh. So, Breula isn't in grave danger as far as I know."

Sev bit the inside of her cheek. Ori cutting away from that one detail said so much but nothing at all. Falling in love? Perhaps Ori was falling. Just like her.

Sev cleared her throat. "Well, I'm glad I'm not the Guardian," she said, deflecting like a champion. "I'm about as ferocious as this very comfortable grass. I'm a mouse, remember." She flicked a finger at Ori and gave a slightly sick smile.

Ori pulled her back into a hug. "Who else knows besides Jino and Askal?"

Sev wasn't surprised Ori had made that link. "Just them." After a tight squeeze, she released Ori and sat on her heels. "I'm worried for Jino because she seemed to be expecting the energy to arrive." That wasn't outing Jino. Not really. Sort of. Ori's narrowed eyes spoke otherwise. Damn.

"And Askal? Your concern is the same?"

"Sure. He's been, I don't know, kind of protecting me. I thought it was because I was his apprentice, but now I'm not so sure."

Ori spread her fingers and rested her hands on her own thighs. "I must tell my parents."

Sev clutched at Ori's hands. "You can't!"

"I have to. There will soon be danger for Breula."

"You don't know that."

"Sev, you can manipulate all the elements and—" Her eyes widened. "All at once or separately?"

Feeling suddenly like a science experiment, Sev leapt to her feet in agitation.

"I don't know!" she shouted, facing the waterfall so her words dissolved into the mist. She wasn't angry at Ori because Sev understood the curiosity. She'd experimented with the elements when each had arrived.

With a quick glance at Ori, she stepped to the water's edge, opened her hand so that the sun shone on her palm, then carefully crouched and laid her other hand on the surface of the pond. Nothing happened for a moment, then Sev remembered she needed to ask. Apologising for her lack of manners, she sent a thought to both elements requesting them to unbalance. The skin on her palm tingled and a glow expanded into a small dome of light cradled in her hand. A mini sun.

She felt rather than heard Ori's whispered, "No."

Holding the light carefully, she angled her head to check on the surface of the pool. Nothing. The water hadn't altered. *Well, that question's answered.*

She thanked the Light, which instantly shimmered and dissolved, then shook the water off her fingertips.

"That's astonishing," Ori said, softly.

Sev stared at the pond, then turned. "So, it looks like one element at a time." Pulling Ori to her feet, she held her hands between their bodies. She gazed into Ori's beautiful blue eyes. "You can't tell your parents."

"I—"

"If others found out, Jino and Askal will be harassed. I don't know—by Elementals or by the Guard."

Ori growled and her eyes turned to flint. "They'd have to get through me first."

Sev pushed up and kissed her, lingering for a moment. "You have to make sure that the idiotic census doesn't go ahead." She dropped back but held her gaze. "I'm positive those two Councillors know something and are using the census as a way to prove it." She shook their joined hands. "And now that you know about me and this skill, talent, energy, whatever, I'm worried for you as well." She untangled her hands and stroked Ori's cheek.

"I'm the Leader of the Guard, Sev." Ori's expression spoke of her belief that she could simply brandish her sword, and enemies would fall to the ground. That she could simply stand in her six foot goddess-like aura, her astonishing body, her gorgeous blonde hair, her wonderful blue eyes and oh, for Christ's sake.

Sev thinned her lips. "I don't care if you're bloody Superman. This collection in here," she poked herself in the chest, "is dangerous knowledge. Well, not the actual knowledge of it. More the consequences of knowing."

***

The ride back to the town was just like every other ride back to town, except for Ori's collection of random half sentences—"Oh, this is…"—stares—widest eyes ever—gestures—head shaking—and the long, scorching looks of desire and affection and something so much deeper. Those looks flipped Sev's stomach. Sharing theories about why her elemental energies existed meant that they arrived at the edge of town before they even realised.

"What are you going to do?" Ori asked, sliding her thumbs along Sev's cheekbones as they stood together outside Kotrol's stable once they'd settled the horses.

Sev leaned into Ori's hand. "Do?"

"Yes. With your elemental energies. With the myriad of skills from those elements."

Sev pulled Ori to her, enveloping her strong body in a hug. They fit together so well. In every way.

"I don't know," she mumbled into Ori's collarbone. "Keep it quiet, because what else can I do?" She pulled back. "Apply for the chief Elemental position if there is one?"

Ori rolled her eyes.

"I wouldn't want it anyway," Sev continued, and brushed her lips over Ori's.

"Let me think on it. Meanwhile, talk to Jino. Perhaps she has some guidance."

I bet she does. Sev stared into Ori's eyes and again decided that Ori probably knew about Jino. Her gaze was too knowing.

"I feel like I'm a bomb that hasn't exploded yet and everyone is just hovering, waiting for me to go off."

Ori's quizzical look was the last straw.

"Argh! This is…I'm sorry I nearly drowned you today. I'm sorry for…" She shrugged, completely at a loss, and leaned into Ori's chest, swallowing hard as tears threatened.

"It's okay," Ori whispered. "We'll think of something." She placed two fingers under Sev's chin and kissed her. "I'm not sorry about our time at the Giord."

Sev smiled, allowing the tingles of lust to gather. "Oh, I'm not either. At all. You did …you do things to me."

Ori pressed in again, running her tongue across Sev's top lip, causing all sorts of goosebumps and shivers to run up Sev's spine, through nerve endings, particularly those in between her thighs. She swept her hands across Ori's breasts.

"You are ridiculously sexy," she breathed, and Ori withdrew, grinning, then licked her lips as if tasting Sev's essence from their afternoon together. Her blue eyes were dark with desire. Talk about drowning in someone. Sev shivered.

"I think that title belongs to you, but I'll wear it if you insist." Ori tilted her head, like she was resigned to her fate, and Sev laughed.

"Well, thanks. I'll wear it, too, but believe me, you really are ridiculously sexy. I get flustered when I'm with you."

"Oh? You do?" Ori's slow smile only proved the point. Actually, flustered wasn't the word. Ori made her so aroused that a bazillion butterflies, chased by zaps of electricity, rampaged throughout her body.

"Yes. Because…" She waved her hand up and down in front of Ori's frame. Ori looked down at her chest, then back up. Her eyes glinted with mischief.

"You're flustered because of my physical attributes?"

Sev rolled her eyes and laughed as a warm glow of affection filled her heart. "Yes, Ori. You have astounding physical attributes."

Ori held her gaze. "I like flustering you."

All Sev could do was laugh again and grab Ori's face, pulling her down to plant a hard kiss on her lips.

"You're adorable."

"You've said that already," Ori mumbled against her mouth.

"And I stand by it." She ran her hands up and down Ori's arms, realising that she needed to go. "So, tomorrow. You've got that Council meeting or gathering or group project thing at midday and I really need to have a chat with Jino which will probably last all night and most of tomorrow morning." Ori gave a slow nod. "I'd like to see you tomorrow afternoon and…" Sev raised her eyebrows and delivered what she hoped was a sultry look. She'd never been fabulous at those, but from the way Ori's lips parted and her eyelids lowered to I-want-your-body-again, she assumed she'd been successful.

***

She and Jino spoke long into the night, picking up the conversation the next morning.

"Ori says not to say anything until she's sussed out the Council," Sev said, leaning over her hands at the table as she manipulated the lump of silver into another small animal. The sun's rays sliced through the window and bounced off the metal.

Creating the creatures without tools was a new development that had popped up that morning. Although, as she said to Jino, it hadn't really popped up that morning at all. She'd manipulated Metal in the bathroom in the arena, and when she'd whacked Ori's sword, and when she'd melted Ori's arm cuff. All of those moments had been non-tool occasions. Jino looked pointedly at her thumb ring, raising her eyebrows in a gesture of 'really?', and Sev hummed. The ring could be a tool. *I guess.* It didn't matter now. There she was; moulding metal like clay.

Manipulation by hand of the four tool-based elements was a skill she'd decided not to reveal to Ori. Not yet. Ori was already reeling.

Sev also hadn't shared with Ori that the problem with possessing great handfuls of elemental energy was the near constant ripples and tingles vibrating in her veins, which created an astounding compulsion to 'do things'.

Ever since the Ice element had shown up, she'd walked past and dipped her fingers into the water in the cooling barrels, sending fireworks of ice crystals across the surface, then on the way back, had flicked her finger on the ice, thawing it immediately. It made Askal a bit twitchy.

"Sevich, please do not do that," he implored. "Who knows what could happen!"

Sev smiled. "Nothing's going to happen, Askal."

He'd shaken his head in resignation.

But when she'd created an intricate metal frame that morning simply with her hands, it had caused Askal to lay his palm flat against the wall and gape for at least five minutes.

All Sev could do was shrug. The non-tool manipulation of Metal was always going to arrive sooner rather than later. The last three and a half months had been a rollercoaster ride of new knowledge, new people, new environment. And new super powers. It sucked that she hadn't been given photon blasters. *Who knows? Maybe next week.*

She missed Alex in these moments. He enjoyed fantastical thinking, and this wasn't a situation that would disappoint him, unlike the stolen identity business. No, this situation was inexplicable and Alex liked inexplicable. He'd say that she'd fallen into a novel where the lead character strode about with rippling muscles and strong shoulders and leather that covered various parts of her body and a sword and arrows and long blonde hair and lips just begging to—Sev widened her eyes in frustration. Not fantastical thinking at all.

The little turtle came to life in her fingers, almost without thought. Like a metal fidget spinner.

"I agree with Ori," Jino said, catching Sev's eye, who paused, trying to remember what she'd said.

"I feel like I'm not Sev anymore. I'm now the," she gently placed the turtle on the table to toss fingers into the air, "Keeper of the Elements." She dropped her hands. "I'm the potential Guardian of Breula which is *not* possible. I'm not an individual person now, I'm a title. It sucks. I didn't ask for this." Sev held the turtle in her palm and waved it about.

"I am not sure anyone would voluntarily request this."

"Exactly." Sev set the turtle down on the table again, stared at it, then visualised the child who would receive the gift tomorrow. Irmirn Solduz's youngest, Ralwi Solduz. As the son of a Water Arcanix, Ralwi would probably appreciate a turtle.

"You will need Askal's protection even more now." Jino looked contemplative.

"What do you mean? He's my mentor. That's all, right?"

"Yes, he is your mentor. He also feels it is his duty to protect you." The intensity of Jino's stare could have bored holes in the table top.

"Like family?" Sev warmed to the idea, but when Jino's gaze didn't alter, she swallowed heavily. "Um. Well, I'm flattered that he feels that way." The serious tone was odd. Jino made it sound like a switch had been activated when Sev had arrived in Breula causing Askal to launch into bodyguard mode. She chewed on her bottom lip. The older woman was probably concerned for everyone's safety, not just Sev's, and she ran her finger across the turtle's shell while that thought sank in.

"So, again," Jino continued, "we carry on as we have done. You are Sevich, the Metal Arcanix, who should not possess permanent Metal energy but does, who should not hold the other nine elements but does, and cannot manipulate Metal, Earth, Flora, and Fauna without tools but can."

Jino and Sev gazed at each other.

"It's ludicrous when you lay it all out like that, isn't it?"

Jino hummed and raised her eyebrows. "That is one way to describe it."

Their contemplation was interrupted by a knock at the door; hardly unusual for a regular morning. So when Sev rose, and opened it to Ori's beautiful face, she beamed. The smile wasn't returned; in fact, Ori looked faintly ill. Then Sev registered the two members of the Guard stationed either side of their leader; one she didn't recognise but one she did. Privana, who narrowed his eyes, a small smile tugging at the corners of his mouth.

Ori licked her lips and swallowed. "Sev, I am to escort you to the Council chambers for an extemporaneous Council meeting." She swallowed again and her eyes widened. "Please."

Sev gaped.

"I don't understand. You're going to the midday meeting. Why have they called it four hours earlier?"

"It's not the same one. This is…" Ori swallowed again, which was disconcerting. She was clearly in distress. "It's a meeting about you."

Sev gripped the door frame, absorbing it all.

A hiss issued through the doorway, and Sev glanced behind her to find Jino vibrating with fury.

"Orilaevar Reysandoral Breula! You have knowledge that should not be shared and yet here is a Council meeting which will allow—" Jino's words, harsh in delivery, caused Ori's shoulders to slump.

"I'm sorry, Jino Kirmiz." Ori shook her head, then looked imploringly at Sev. "Please," she whispered.

It was too much to take in. It felt overwhelmingly like Ori and the Guard members had arrived to take her away as if she were a prisoner. But she was not a coward, and if the Councillors wanted to inspect her as if she were a rare species—*which I am*—then so be it. She sent a look of livid fearlessness at both Guard members, adding extra venom for Privana. It had little effect, of course, but when Sev aimed the same look at Ori, the Leader of the Guard sagged under its weight.

Sev turned to Jino. "I'll be fine. This'll just be a chat and then I'll join the Councillors for a friendly cup of tea." She whipped her head back to Ori. "Right?"

Ori didn't respond.

Sev stepped onto the small path that led to the road, and into Ori's personal space.

"Let's go," she said, mainly for the benefit of the various onlookers who had stopped in curiosity. It probably wasn't every day that an Arcanix was escorted up to the mansion for a…a what? An interrogation? The word made her shiver. Sev kept pace with Ori as they walked up the road; the Guard members bringing up the rear. Sev flicked a glance over her shoulder. They were far enough away for her to deliver a harsh whisper at Ori.

"What the hell?"

Ori kept her eyes facing forward. "I'm sorry. My father called the meeting at the insistence of two Councillors. He and my mother felt it necessary."

Sev's mouth fell open. "You told them?"

"I had to."

"No, you didn't."

Ori's hands jerked like she wanted to clutch at Sev's wrist and bundle her into an embrace. "They're my parents first and foremost. But also they are the leaders of the realm. They had to know about you." She sounded miserable.

"Why?"

"Because!" she exclaimed, then lowered her voice. "Because you have power that many people will never comprehend."

"Bullshit."

"You do!"

"And now they've called a special Council meeting just to... what, Ori?" She shot Ori an irritated look. "Because the only that springs to mind is that you've gone and told the Councillors who now want to poke and prod to find out exactly what I'm hiding. Is that it?"

"I didn't tell anyone except my parents." Ori said, fiercely. Sev actually believed her, but remembered a comment she'd made a few months ago about Ori being a pawn in a bigger picture. This seemed like a pretty big picture.

"Then why?" Sev faced forward again.

"You're the anomaly."

Sev laughed bitterly. "We've established that. Why does that require a full Council meeting?"

"Because my parents agree that some people will be frightened of you because they don't understand how it is that you are able to..." Ori faded off and allowed her hand to twitch as if to indicate the remainder of the sentence. "You are a threat."

"Bullshit," Sev repeated, as little prickles of fear pulled saliva from her mouth and no amount of swallowing could replace it.

"*I* know you're not a threat, but you are powerful."

The mansion's enormous front doors came into view.

"I didn't ask for this, you know," Sev muttered through her teeth.

Ori's soft sigh hung between them. "I know."

They entered the foyer of the Council Chamber through a smaller set of doors.

And Sev came to a decision.

"I want to go back to Melbourne."

At the words, Ori paused, her steps faltering, then she came to a stop and faced Sev. Her mouth was downturned, and she looked like she was going to burst into tears. Sev's resolve wavered, but she held firm.

"I said I wanted to go back when we first met and you said you'd help. Ori, I know you were helping but I have the feeling that you hoped I'd forgotten. That I didn't want to go back home. But I never stopped wanting to leave."

The words were meant to hurt, because this meeting was Ori's fault, and Sev felt betrayed. But more than that, she now realised Ori's feelings for her, and in turn, her feelings for Ori. The stab in her heart hit hard because this was about Ori, and Jino, and Askal, and the townspeople. She should go back to Melbourne. If her elemental energy was such a threat that people felt scared, then she didn't belong here. The idea of putting these people in danger made her feel sick.

And Alex needed to know where she was. She'd seen those shows. Those press conferences, where distraught family members spoke directly to the cameras asking for witnesses to come forward because they'd never had closure after their special person went missing. She couldn't put Alex through that. He needed to know what happened. Probably not that she'd travelled through a magical portal, perhaps. She'd think of something.

Sev slid her gaze from Ori's distressed expression, and fell into the smug version on Privana's face. Shaking her head, she followed the Guard member at the door into the chamber.

***

Furious and frightened. *Both of those work.* Sev's heartbeat bounced in time with the dual emotions struggling for dominance until the two became a single word like those portmanteaus that people create for couples they ship. Frightious? Furitened?

"This is all simply a formality. You must not be concerned, young Sevich," Councillor Buwrec Robrong Breula stated from his seat; one of fifty that encircled the marble floor. He smiled unpleasantly.

Sev ground her teeth at the patronising tone, but Ori's voice echoed across the chamber before Sev could march across to the Councillor, grab a fistful of his shirt, yank him close and whisper threateningly about furnaces and water barrels.

"Her name is Sevich." Ori's voice was ice. Sev, standing in the middle of the floor, watched the magnificent warrior rise from her seat. Her heart clenched. "There is no need to add endearments or adjectives. We will maintain the integrity of this *meeting*." At that final hissed word, Sev gazed into Ori's eyes. They were ablaze with anger.

"Of course, of course," Councillor Dasoskach Vaern Breula chimed in, her high pitched tone cutting through the tension, yet adding more. "We have your best interests at heart. You must be very confused that we are discussing the implausible notion that you are able to manipulate multiple elements. Under advisement, King Rodlamar Reytoris Breula has called this extemporaneous meeting to discuss this hypothetical and unlikely situation."

The chamber filled with gasps, murmuring and expressions of disbelief.

Sev crossed her arms protectively, although it must have come across as defiance if the many narrowed eyes were any indication.

"I'm sure King Rodlamar Reytoris Breula did nothing of the sort." She flicked her gaze towards the royal seats. "I don't have any other elements except Metal." Sev was pleased with how steady and strong her voice sounded, not allowing the vibrations of fear that were festering in her stomach to intrude.

"Councillor Buwrec Robrong Breula," the King's voice silenced the mutterings. "You may put forward your claim." Sev slid her gaze to Ori's father. He was the epitome of what Sev had always thought of as royalty; a proud bearing, that regal presence, a beard. He resembled Gandalf but with more frequent visits to the hairdresser. However, it was his eyes, while not as blue as Ori's, that stood out the most. They were kind.

The Councillor rose from his seat. "King Rodlamar Reytoris Breula, I—we have reason to believe that Sevich possesses more than one element and has chosen to hide this anomaly, therefore creating an imbalance in our realm. It could threaten our way of life!"

"I feel you are mistaken." The calm voice of Queen Sermeh Reytoris Breula cut through the indistinct rumbling. Sev had been surprised by the Queen's presence. From what Ori had told her, the Queen didn't attend the Council meetings because they were "swollen with posturing, vacuous nonsense". Sev had laughed at Ori's imitation of her mother that day, both of them giggling as they'd rolled in the grass, wrestling, pinning the other, and smiling through kisses. She swallowed the memory before it sank under a weight of sadness.

The Queen continued, lightly touching Ori's arm as if to transfer some of her serenity to her daughter. "I very much doubt that the realm is in danger. I have met Sevich and found her to be sincere and trustworthy. Her intentions towards Breula and those who reside here are affectionate, and hardly a threat." She smiled down at Sev who knew, right then, that Queen Sermeh Reytoris Breula was not speaking about elemental energy at all.

Sev slid her gaze to Ori, and nearly burst into tears.

Councillor Buwrec Robrong Breula straightened. "Queen Sermeh Reytoris Breula and King Rodlamar Reytoris Breula, we have a witness who states that she saw Sevich, a Metal Arcanix, manipulate the Earth element." He'd clearly chosen to ignore the Queen's rather pointed statement.

There were more gasps.

Which gave Sev time to stare at Councillor Dasoskach Vaern Breula and realise, as a smile grew on the woman's lips, that she was the witness. A snippet of memory, the Elemental at the corner of the road, flashed through Sev's mind.

A Councillor behind Sev piped up. "If you did possess more than one element, then perhaps you have a desire to lead a great force from your realm and overthrow us, then use the orbs to conquer other realms?"

Sev spun around, unfolded her arms and thrust them sideways, staring in disbelief at the man with a green orb at his throat. His veins ran like milky blue lines under his almost translucent skin.

"No! Why would I?"

Another Councillor found their voice. "For land, or to gain more resources, or to claim power."

Another round of gasps greeted this statement.

"No! My realm has no need for more land. We have enough resources, and we do not need more power." She clenched her teeth at the lies. Her realm always wanted land, resources, and power. Usually all at once.

A third Councillor stood from her chair, fiddling with the buttons on her jacket. "It would benefit us if she possesses more than one element." There were mumbles of opposition and she scowled. "I simply mean that perhaps if your claim is true, Councillor Buwrec Robrong Breula, then her energy could be utilised. She could be useful."

"Goodness no!" Another Councillor stood, her arms sweeping about to focus the Council. "She might bring forces to overthrow us. I have heard of societies in other realms who have suffered an invasion and their people of importance, their decision-makers, their royalty have been banished!" She rolled her wrists so her palms faced upwards. "Royalty exiled to another portal where they are unable to return! That would be a disaster."

The babbling, and gasping, and oh-no-ing and goodness-me-ing was all too much. Sev tightened her fists at her chest.

"What is this questioning?" The King boomed, silencing the cacophony.

In the silence, Sev lifted her head and gazed at Ori, wanting to etch her lover's face on the inside of her eyelids.

"I'm sorry," Ori mouthed, and Sev nodded She was, too. So very sorry about all of it.

"Me, too," she mouthed in return, and they shared a moment which was interrupted by Councillor Dasoskach Vaern Breula, who had placed her hands on the low beautifully carved wooden railing and leaned forward, probably to ensure that she had everyone's attention.

"I say we test Arcanix Sevich to ensure that she does not possess more than one element."

Councillor Buwrec Robrong Breula, already standing, nodded. "Yes. If she does, then we must make a decision. Do we let her leave Breula with possible repercussions for our safety?"

Sev opened her mouth to protest. The accusation was ridiculous. Plus they were talking about her as if she were invisible. It pissed her off.

The Councillor continued. "Or does she stay here where she can be monitored and her energy contained?" He pressed his finger into the railing as if pressing the 'go' button for a nuclear launch.

The grumbles rolled like thunder through the room.

Sev had had enough.

"I'm right here, you know." She turned to Ori's father. "King Rodlamar Reytoris Breula, I have something to say." Then after receiving his nod of permission, and a slight smile of encouragement from the Queen, she spun in a slow circle, making sure that every Councillor heard her words.

"Does anyone care what I want?" She paused when she made eye contact with Councillor Dasoskach Vaern Breula. The smirk on the woman's face was troubling, but she moved on. "I want to go home to my realm." Sev was entirely grateful that her slow rotation meant that her back was to Ori when she said those words. "I don't have any extra elemental energy, and I really have no desire to live through another assessment. Look, vote to let me leave so I can get out of your hair."

Her rotation returned to her to where she'd started; facing the royal seats, and her heart sank at Ori's expression. Then she nearly burst into tears—again!—when she saw sadness drift across the Queen's face. Ori's mum knew. Not just about the elements. She knew how close Ori and Sev were to falling in love. So close.

It was just another reason to leave. Ori's parents would also be in danger if she stayed. There were Councillors talking right now about keeping her here to investigate her elemental energy. Like an experiment. It would create so much fear and doubt and gossip and perhaps the King, and the Queen, and Ori, and Jino, and Askal would try to save Sev from the scrutiny. Perhaps people would revolt.

Councillor Dasoskach Vaern Breula suddenly rose, and stepped down to the floor. She pointedly ignored Sev, and addressed the royal seats. "King Rodlamar Reytoris Breula, this will only take a small moment of the Council's time." She beckoned to Councillor Buwrec Robrong Breula, and eight other Councillors who quickly joined her in a curved line facing Sev. Each Councillor wore a different coloured orb, and Sev sucked in a quick breath. A sizzle of fear whisked up her spine.

Before the King, or Ori, or anyone else could react, the Councillors at each end of the line reached over the wall, retrieved two jugs of water, a length of metal chain, a lit candle in a small wooden boat, a mouse which squeaked in fear, and a vine in a pot. Sev quickly processed. Water and Ice Elementals; jugs of water. Metal chain; Metal Elemental. The Heat Elemental cradled the lit candle, the mouse cowered in the Fauna Elemental's palm, and the Flora Elemental grasped the potted vine.

Six.

Shit.

The plan to test Sev's elemental energy hadn't been a spontaneous idea. Councillors Dasoskach Vaern Breula, Buwrec Robrong Breula, and eight others, who they'd obviously persuaded with their arguments, had come prepared.

Her hands shook.

There are four more elements. Sev's brain froze. Her eyes flicked back and forth along the line, trying to match orb colours and elements and objects and suddenly lightheadedness threatened.

Then, amidst the uproar that had started to shake the chamber, all ten Councillors crouched, and then, as one, unbalanced the room.

Instantly, Sev felt the pain.

The elements had not been asked. They were being held hostage.

Water gushed from the two jugs, flowing much too quickly than was possible to the edges of the floor as if filling a swimming pool, Councillor Dasoskach Vaern Breula tapped the marble with what looked like a pointed dagger made of some type of crystal, and cracks appeared, spreading like veins through the stone. The mouse was released into the water, its sharp, high-pitched cries tugging at Sev's heart. Then, as she stood paralysed in horror, the chain unfurled and with a clang of a small hammer, the Metal Elemental sent the chain twisting through the rising water to curl around Sev's ankle as the vine, having wound its way out of the pot, snaked about the other. Clawing fingers of ice rose from the water and the little boat sailed closer, the flame expanding until Sev felt like she had walked into a sauna. A drifting shadow, like a soft grey veil that reached to the ceiling, somewhat obscured the view of the seated Councillors, while an incandescent glow hovered in front of Sev. She lifted her hand to shield her face, feeling the air near her head lazily swirling as if contemplating a cyclone.

It was breathtaking how quickly the elements had combined. How quickly they'd been manipulated. How quickly a split second passed by.

"You're unbalancing—just—what? Stop!" Ori's anguished yell cut through the darkness.

All the while, through the tumult of noise, through the shouts of dismay, Sev focused on one distinct sound. The little mouse, drowning, and drowning, and drowning. And Sev refused to leave them both to that fate.

She knew what she had to do.

"Thank you. I restore your balance," she murmured to the water, touching the swirling surface, with other hand raised, ready to rebalance the air next.

"Thank you. I restore your balance." Instantly the stiff breeze calmed. Sev didn't have time to fully appreciate each element's immediate response. She just knew they were listening.

Alternating hands, Sev crouched, laid her palm on the drying marble, sealing the cracks, urging the element to heal itself. The moment the earth was rebalanced, she yanked her hand away, dropping her other hand to the chain. Thanking it for its service, Sev held her breath as the metal released and fell to the floor, then she was in motion again, quickly stroking the stem of the vine, thanking it, watching it pull back, next pivoting to the large flame dwarfing its little vessel, and, with cupped hands, reducing its force.

The exertion required to rapidly channel energy with such precision was beginning to take its toll. Sev heaved in a breath and reached for the nearest spike of ice, its tip creeping closer.

"Thank you. I restore your balance."

Then exhaled as the ice melted in relief.

The mouse, sopping and terrified, barrelled into Sev's palms, where it hunched, shivering with fear.

"You're safe, and you can leave this space," Sev whispered, and nodded as the mouse paused, then scampered out of the little cave Sev had created with her hands, and dashed away.

Standing abruptly, even though her body wanted to crumple to the floor, Sev swiped her hand at the ball of light, sliding around the curve as she murmured the words of gratitude and rebalance. The ball dissolved into tiny sparks of white and drifted like dust motes to the ceiling to join the existing globes. Then she turned her attention to the final element; Dark.

Drawing on her last reserves, Sev danced her palms at the shadow, muttering the words for the last time. A bubble of hysterical laughter threatened to escape as she imagined she was channelling Mister Miyagi in the *Karate Kid*. Wax on, wax off.

The darkness cleared like smoke waved away from a campfire.

The entire rebalancing felt like it had spanned many minutes, but it was most likely a few seconds because when she cocked her head to listen properly, Sev could have sworn she heard the 'p' at the end of "Stop" from Ori's first cry of anguish.

It hadn't been long at all. She must have looked like Neo in the *Matrix*.

Sev's hands dropped, and she closed her eyes, as the cacophony of indistinct words speared directionless about the room.

Suddenly, she was bundled into an embrace, Ori's hand pressing into the back of Sev's head as if to shield her from the eyes of the Council.

"I'm so sorry. I had no idea they'd planned to do that. I'm so sorry," Ori whispered, clutching Sev to her body. "I'm so sorry." The apology hushed into her ear.

Sev focused on Ori's frantic heartbeat, but couldn't quite block out the tapestry of alarmed statements draping itself across her shoulders.

"—what she could do?"

"—at all those elements."

"—no tool needed for the Metal element!"

"—Earth by hand!"

"—too fast for any Breulan Elemental."

"—see it? Impossible!"

"— know how she can wield all of them?"

"—such an anomaly!"

"—if she is not? Perhaps a Guardian, like the—"

"—cannot be allowed to leave!"

"—must be made to leave!"

The waves crashed over and over, accusations and commentary and fear and the what if and the what now buffeting her mind and Sev pushed farther into Ori's chest.

"Enough!" King Rodlamar Reytoris Breula boomed, and yet the noise continued. "I said that is enough!"

Sev pulled away to take in the sight of the imposing ruler of Breula. He'd probably never seen anything like what had just transpired. He was standing, arms outstretched and an unexpected glow emanated from his orange Metal element orb. Her gaze slid to the ten Councillors standing at the other end of the floor, eyes wide, mouths agape, arms limp. The sight produced a fleeting moment of pride. She'd defeated—defeated? No, she'd rebalanced ten elements in quick succession. Two of them without tools. Rebalanced ten elements held by Elementals who could only manipulate one.

Suck on that, you arseholes.

She had to drag the insult through her brain to get any satisfaction from it.

"I am disgusted with what has transpired here today." The King's words chopped away at any further babble. "You have shown a complete disregard for the laws of our realm. We do not unbalance the elements in such a manner."

He was shaking, and Sev used his rage to bolster her strength, drawing away from Ori, turning them so they stood, hand in hand, facing Ori's father.

Then, Sev gazed at Queen Sermeh Reytoris Breula, and drew in a quick breath. Ori's mum should have been the one yelling at the Council, because, despite not uttering a word, her anger was a whole new level of terrifying. It looked dangerous; like it came from a place that combined fury at the Councillors and the fury from a mother whose daughter's lover had been subjected to pain and therefore, in turn, had created distress for her daughter. Sev had always wondered what a mother's protective instinct looked like. She swallowed.

Christ.

"What you have done is unacceptable." The King pointed at the straggly line of stunned Councillors.

Councillor Buwrec Robrong Breula, however, seemed to be made of stronger stuff or simply hadn't read the rcom, because he stepped forward from his place in the line. "King Rodlamar Reytoris Breula, surely you can understand how testing Sevich was necessary. Could you not see her energy with the elements? She is clearly powerful. Why, she could even manipulate tool-based elements with her hands!"

The murmuring restarted.

"It was most certainly not necessary." The King waved his finger again at the line of Councillors. "You will be dealt with because of this. Manipulating an element is about having a love for it, and you have not shown this today. You have created trauma for one of our Arcanix, and disrupted the balance within this chamber to a degree that we have never seen before."

Then Councillor Dasoskach Vaern Breula opened her mouth to speak, but Councillor Buwrec Robrong Breula clutched her shoulder, and they shared a swift glance.

"Of course," he continued. "You are correct, King Rodlamar Reytoris Breula. We are deeply apologetic for our actions, and will accept all consequences." He nodded slowly. "I implore you to allow us to reclaim our seats so that no further disruptions occur. Perhaps we could abstain from the vote as the first step towards our reparations."

Having delivered his impassioned plea, supported by the other nine Councillors all nodding at various speeds, the Councillor cupped his hands together behind his back, and lowered his head.

Eventually the King breathed deeply and gestured at their seats.

"You may."

Sev blinked.

What the hell?

Ori squeezed her hand. "My father will see that they are dealt with."

It didn't feel like it. Where were the members of the Guard marching in and turfing those ten out like they were unruly bar patrons?

"Sevich, despite the shameful series of events that have transpired today, it has unfortunately proven that you are indeed in control of all ten elements." The King tilted his head, almost in sorrow, as he sat heavily. The Queen reached across, wrapping her hand around his forearm.

"King Rodlamar Reytoris Breula!" Councillor Dasoskach Vaern Breula called from across the room.

God, she is not giving up.

Sev levelled a glare at the standing woman.

"Sevich should remain in Breula as her elemental energy reflects the details that have been foretold in the prophecy. Details about the Guardian," the Councillor said, her strident voice ringing out.

The storm of responses was loud and raucous.

"—but a fairytale!"

"—is the Guardian."

"—danger in the realm."

"—the seers foretold of the Guardian a century ago!"

"—is obvious."

"—must stay."

"—a danger so she must leave."

"You will be silent!" The King's powerful voice cut short the verbal pandemonium. Sev doubted that he'd ever had to control a Council meeting so forcefully. Every word he uttered was like a verbal smack on the back of each Councillor's head.

"You will be silent," he repeated, then contemplated Sev for a while as the silence settled. "What is it that you truly want to do?"

Ori's hand stiffened in hers, and out of the corner of her eye, Sev caught Ori's shoulders squaring as is preparing for the worst. Sev directed her gaze back to the King.

"I am not a threat, King Rodlamar Reytoris Breula. I am not the Guardian. I am not an experiment." She slipped her hand away. "I'm Sev, the Metal Arcanix in Breula, but I'm also Sev, the trespasser from Melbourne, and I'd like to go home."

A waterfall of tears threatened, and she grit her teeth.

The King nodded slowly.

"Sevich, you have experienced a traumatic incident today and, on behalf of this entire Council, you have my heartfelt apologies." He paused, then slowly raised himself from his chair. Sev held her breath because it seemed that when Kings stood to announce something, it was always monumentally life-changing.

"Based on each of your," he waved his hand at the fifty Councillors before him, "reactions to our discovery today, it is obvious that we will be unable to reach a consensus in the near future. The delay will create too much anxiety for Sevich if she is to return to her realm in a timely manner. Therefore," he paused, "for the first time in Breulan history, as ruler of this realm, I am announcing a verdict *without* the unanimous vote of the Council." The King drew his shoulders back. "By my decree, Sevich, Breulan Metal Arcanix, has been granted the right to free passage through the northern portal to return to her realm."

Sev's eyes widened.

Then she registered Ori's gasp. Her father had over-ruled the entire Council. Sev knew that Ori had been waiting for this moment, and finally, even though the King's break with tradition created a result that was painful for both of them, Ori's desire to see change had taken its first steps.

The Council started up again but a single glare was all the King needed to shut them down.

"To alleviate tension and hearsay, you should make plans to leave as soon as possible," he said, and Sev jerked.

"Um. Okay, I get that. Sure. Thank you for your decision, King Rodlamar Reytoris Breula. I appreciate it. I can definitely say that today's meeting has been unbelievably unpleasant, but I understand that you're all scared by what I can do. Believe me, your fear is nothing compared to mine every time my abilities arrived." There was a low hum.

Sev clasped her hands together. "I'd like to leave tomorrow. Noon?" The realm seemed to love that particular time of day. "I want to say goodbye to people first." Then she grabbed at Ori's hand, the action bringing their shoulders together.

The King studied them, then his mouth downturned, and Sev could have sworn that tears shone in his eyes. "Midday tomorrow, then," he said quietly.

"King Rodlamar Reytoris Breula," said Councillor Buwrec Robrong Breula. "I offer my services and…" He looked towards his fellow Councillor, who smiled toothily. "That of Councillor Dasoskach Vaern Breula to escort Sevich to her portal tomorrow. We have caused her great pain and giving her a calm journey will be a small step in gaining her forgiveness."

Ori yanked her hand away and pointed. "No." Her hand was trembling. "The Guard shall escort Sevich."

Sev knew that Ori would be that Guard. A Guard of one. It saddened her because Ori would be like those people who stood outside the departure hall at the airport, waving to their person for ages and ages, even when they couldn't see them any more. It broke her heart.

"This meeting is adjourned. However, I will now meet with those Councillors involved in this morning's *spectacle*," Ori's father stated, overly enunciating the last word. The amount of disgust he was able to inject into his sentence was masterly.

Ori turned to Sev. "Please come to my rooms. I need to talk to you, and—" Her voice broke, and she swallowed, those wonderful blue eyes filled with sadness.

Sev nodded. There were no words.

Ori clutched at Sev's hand, and spun them towards the exit. A member of the Guard drew himself upright as they approached the doors, but took one look at Ori's expression, and quickly moved aside. Sev, if she were a member of the Guard, wouldn't be arguing with her leader either, not unless she had a death wish.

As Ori closed the door to her rooms, Sev took in the utilitarian design of the sitting area. It was completely Ori; sensible, sleek, sparse.

"I'm so worried for you," Ori whispered from behind as her arms enveloped Sev's torso. Sev turned, and cradled Ori's cheeks, brushing her thumbs across the skin.

"I was about to say the same thing," she said, huffing a laugh that contained not a bit of humour.

Because none of this was amusing.

At all.

Chapter Fourteen

Ori tightened her embrace, and Sev tucked her forehead into Ori's neck.

"This is horrible," Ori whispered.

"Yeah." Sev's breath drifted across her skin and Ori shivered. Then Sev's next words were ice in her stomach.

"That test was dreadful." Sev pulled out of Ori's embrace, and moved away, wandering across to the enormous circular windows at the other side of the room. Ori's arms hung loosely. There was nothing to say. There was nothing to do. Except hold Sev so she wouldn't leave. *That would go down well.*

Ori had been taken completely by surprise with Sev's ability to manipulate the elements by hand. Either the skill had appeared right then or Sev had chosen not to reveal it yesterday. Most likely the latter which stung a little. They had a…thing, and Ori wanted to believe that sharing important information about themselves was part of that…thing. But Sev had her reasons and the Councillors had made enough of a spectacle that Ori chose not to mention the slight.

She crossed the floor, the bumpy covering familiar under her soft shoes, to stand next to Sev's shoulder.

"I'm so sorry they did that."

Sev continued to gaze at the view, running her finger along the metal band that framed the window. "You can see the whole town from here. Almost."

Ori nodded. "It's quite lovely in the late afternoon when the moons are sliding into view."

"Yeah." Sev sagged into Ori's shoulder, then curled around to rest her cheek against Ori's chest. "You know I have to leave."

Ori bounced the joints in her jaw. "Yes," she answered, the catch in her voice loud in the silent room.

Sev drew her head back. Her brown and gold eyes shimmered with tears. "That test. Those Councillors. I can't deal with that sort of scrutiny every day. That's the imbalance, Ori." She ducked her head again. "Not Sev the Arcanix who does all this amazing stuff. I'm not the imbalance. The reaction is the imbalance."

"And it's why you're leaving," Ori whispered.

Sev nodded and her cheek rubbed against the fabric of Ori's shirt, then she lifted her head, and kissed Ori. Hard. Desperately. Ori wanted to hold Sev and never let her go. It was overwhelming.

Sev looked just as desperate.

"That and because I…" She touched Ori's lips, lightly brushing her fingers across the skin. "It's better this way. I'm not the Guardian. And even in the unlikely situation that I am, Breula's not in danger and I don't know what I could do to save it anyway."

"But you have so many elemental skills. You *are* an Elemental." Ori felt claustrophobic in her pain. Everything hurt. She breathed deeply, subtly shifting Sev so that they were further apart.

"I'm going to miss you beyond reason," Ori murmured, and acknowledged the ache of sadness.

Sev grunted. "Do you know that I wasn't sure what to do until just before that meeting?"

Ori narrowed her eyes, her brow wrinkling. "What is it you weren't sure of?"

Sev clutched at Ori's hand and squeezed. "Us. You. I feel—I felt like I was being tugged in two different directions." Ori eased Sev around to gaze at her lips, her eyes, her confused, vulnerable expression. "Right now, in this very moment, I feel such a lot for you, Ori. But I feel a lot for Melbourne. For what Melbourne represents. It's so much."

"I feel," Ori cradled Sev's face in both hands, "so much for you as well." Then she leaned forward, and, with the lightest touch she could muster, kissed Sev. She wanted it to represent the way she felt. The feeling of so much. And from the way Sev placed her own hands on either side of Ori's head, Ori knew that Sev wanted the kiss to be everything and all of it and much more.

"Christ, I hate this," Sev whispered against Ori's lips. "We've spent such a short period together and—"

"Fifteen weeks, three days, and four hours," Ori murmured.

"Oh, Ori," Sev sighed and smoothed her hands down Ori's cheeks, then traced the patterns on her shirt. She tapped a line of stitching at Ori's sternum. "It would be irrational of me to consider staying here when my home is over there." She tilted her head towards the window. "Alex is there. Yes, I have these talents, but they are irrelevant in Melbourne, which is nice, and I know you think I'm part of a Breulan prophecy but that is a children's tale. I'm not that person."

Ori let the words sink in, eventually lowering her forehead gently to Sev's and simply breathed. "I'm sorry," she said again, then her entire body crumpled and she only made it to the lounge, collapsing onto the cushion. She sat with her elbows on her knees, and after a second Sev joined her, pressing her thigh against Ori's.

"I need to let all…" Sev began, and Ori turned at the pause. Sev waved vaguely at her body. "All this…whatever it is…go."

Ori stared down at the carpet. "I'm part of the whatever it is, aren't I?"

"Ori…" Sev swallowed. "You have to be, otherwise I'll be ripped in two."

"I could come with you." The desperate words fell from Ori's mouth, and she swept up Sev's hand in her own. "I mean, I could do something in your realm, although I fear I'd be a bit useless. I'd probably be that bomb you mentioned." Her lips arranged themselves into what she hoped looked like a smile.

Sev's smile looked just as sad. "No, you wouldn't. But you'd be where you shouldn't be. You'd be in exactly the same position as I am. Don't you see? This is the right thing to do."

Suddenly, Sev stood, clenched her hands, turned towards the door, turned back, looked at the ceiling, then dropped her gaze. She pulled Ori up to hold their bodies together which was just as well because Ori felt like disintegrating.

"Look after Jino. The census is soon and I fear for her safety."

Jino. Yes. Ori had an inkling that there was more to Jino Kirmiz than met the eye. It wouldn't surprise her if the woman was a seer or something else as wonderful.

"Of course." Then Ori's heart took control of her words. "Would you come back here tonight? To me? We could spend a night together before you leave tomorrow."

Sev held her gaze.

"I don't think that's a—"

Ori stared over Sev's shoulder at the beautiful mural that covered the entire wall leading to her bed chamber. "No, you're right. It's not. I'm sorry for suggesting it."

Sev held Ori's face. "Don't be sorry. It's a beautiful idea. But…"

There it was. The 'but'.

So Ori did the only thing left to do. She kissed Sev. It was a kiss that hinted of forever, of what they had, of what Sev meant to her, a kiss so deep that she felt Sev's nose pressed to her cheek. It was a kiss goodbye.

Ori slowly lifted her lips, and they stared at each other.

"I…" The words sat at the front of Ori's tongue but what a phrase to say to someone who was leaving. It wasn't fair to tell Sev that she, Orilaevar Reysandoral Breula, loved her. What a burden.

Sev took control of the conversation.

"I should go. I need to talk with Jino and Askal, because no doubt they will have heard. People spread rumours faster than the seeds in the fields."

Ori grunted a laugh.

Then with a final nod, Sev hurried across the room as if lingering would cause even more pain, opened the door, and with a final glance over her shoulder, allowed it to close softly behind her. Ori watched that spot, where Sev had stood, for a very long time. Enough time for her heart to break into tiny pieces.

***

Not an hour later, her mother and father perched on chairs they'd drawn close; patting her shoulder or rubbing her arm. Ori had thought it was Sev returning when there had been a soft knock on her door. Wishful, irrational thinking.

Her mother fixed her with an intense gaze. "And you will be her escort tomorrow?"

"Yes. Of course."

Her mother nodded. "Good. I think that there will be some who want to create disturbance for her."

Her father hummed in agreement. "I agree. There are many Councillors who dislike the idea of Sevich leaving the realm in light of her elemental energy and skills. They are beyond the reach of any of us and allowing her to leave Breula worries them."

He scoffed.

Pride filled Ori's heart. "She's amazing, isn't she?"

Her mother smiled indulgently. "Yes, darling, she is."

"I would not enjoy bearing the conflict she feels, but she is very strong. Not only in her manipulation of the elements," her father mused, a frown creasing his forehead.

"I was astonished to see her work by hand," her mother added.

"You and me both, Mother. That was unexpected." She swung their joined hands as she had when she was a child cocooned within the safety of her parents.

"You did not know?" Her father withdrew his hand to cross his arms.

"No." Ori hadn't known but she assumed it was because—

"I think she was protecting you by keeping the knowledge hidden," her mother said, again demonstrating her mind-reading abilities. *She should team up with Jino. They'd be a force.*

They sat in a tableau of sadness, and tears welled in Ori's eyes. She squeezed her mother's fingers.

"I love her."

Her mother delivered a slow nod.

"Did you tell her?" her father asked with a sympathetic half-smile.

"There is no point, Father. She's leaving and it would be unkind." Ori stared at the floor.

Her mother released her hand to lift Ori's chin. "I do not think you needed to say it aloud, my daughter. I have the distinct feeling that Sevich knows." Her mother smoothed her cheek. "Another example of not telling you something. She wants to protect you. Your heart, perhaps."

Ori felt her lips tremble.

"Darling, I think you fell under Sevich's spell from the first time you met." She looked thoughtful. "I feel that things have a way of working themselves out. You will mend your heart."

Ori grunted. "I don't think so. I always assumed that the woman I would fall completely in love with would have to come down from the sky because it seemed so unlikely that I'd ever find her here."

Her father tilted his head. "Sevich came down from the sky?"

Ori looked at her parents through a film of tears. "Yes, Sev came from the sky."

CHAPTER FIFTEEN

Sev paused halfway through the word. Then crossed it out. It wasn't right, and now there was a line on the thin parchment, which was basically paper but Breulans called it parchment because of course they did.

She'd made another instant decision as she'd walked back to Jino and Askal's home. Her home. Leaving tomorrow was only going to prolong the pain for everyone. It would give time for gossip to fester and while she didn't think that there'd be pitchforks and burning tiki torches when she left at midday, she didn't want to risk it. Leaving tonight was better. Somehow she'd find her portal. Kotrol would know. That idea formed the basis of her flimsy plan which was bound to blow over in a stiff breeze of logic. It worried her that she'd ride Kotrol to the portal, dismount, then send him on his way back to the stables. But wolves and god knows what roamed the plains and Kotrol would be vulnerable. Yeah. Shit plan.

Meanwhile the letters.

Sev traced her fingertip across the paper's surface, and paused at the word 'love'. It would be totally unfair to tell Ori that. What a burden.

"I'm leaving, Ori and guess what? I love you and I'll never see you again, so, bye," Sev whispered, then ground her palms into her eyes. As quietly as she could, she crumpled the paper, and restarted her letter.

Askal's and Jino's letters sat on her bed, neatly folded, their names printed on the front. Those letters had been just as difficult to write, although she'd had more content to work with after their discussion when she'd arrived back at the house.

***

"I'm so sorry," Sev mumbled into Askal's collar, then pulled back, her hands resting on his shoulders.

"I…" His eyes shimmered with tears, and he turned to his mother. Sev followed his gaze. Jino stood at the dining table, hand clutching the top of a chair, as if to brace her body in case it crumpled to the floor. She looked distraught.

"Ori's father made the call and so I'm heading back home tomorrow." Sev sighed deeply, wandered over to the table, and sank into a chair. "It's for the best." Sev was starting to have doubts about that idea but willed herself to be strong. Going back to Melbourne really was the best for everyone.

"I cannot imagine you not being here. You are part of," Askal flicked his gaze about, then sat next to Sev, "you are part of our family."

"Oh, Christ, Askal. Please don't say that." Sev's voice cracked.

"You are, and now that you are leaving, we have failed in our responsibility," Askal stared at the table top, as Jino sat opposite Sev.

"What responsibility?" Sev asked, swiping at her tears.

"Mine," Askal said, delivering a long look at his mother, who nodded. He faced Sev. "I am to protect the Guardian when they arrive in Breula. It was foreseen." He glanced at Jino. "And therefore I have failed as you are leaving our realm." He twisted his hands together.

Sev's eyes widened in comprehension. "The Guardian's protector? Why didn't you tell me earlier?"

"We—I needed to be sure," Jino said quietly.

Sev flipped her hands over, palms up. "Of what? That I am the actual Guardian?"

"Yes."

"But I'm not."

"Sevich, I am beginning to think you are. And now you are leaving." Jino shook her head sadly.

Sev reached across and grasped Jino's hands. "I'm really not the Guardian, you know. There's no danger present in the realm and just because I'm on a first name basis with ten elements doesn't make me Guardian Girl. But some powerful people think I am, so it's best that I leave. Life could get very uncomfortable for you both, and for Ori." Sev swallowed thickly. "And Alex has spent nearly four months wondering where the heck I am and is probably a basket case by now. He'll likely be on some true crime podcast, hoping to cast light on my disappearance." She withdrew her hands. "All of those are good reasons to leave."

"I have not fulfilled my role."

"Askal, come on. Having a role foreseen is different to having a life. A crystal ball moment isn't…" She winced at Jino. "That was flippant. Sorry." Then she inhaled deeply and returned her gaze to her mentor. "You can't have been waiting for—" Sev froze. "You have, haven't you? You've put your life on hold to wait for me, or the actual Guardian." This time, she clutched at Askal's hand, feeling the rough skin catch under her fingertips. "Have you not had a girlfriend or boyfriend? A long relationship?" She winced. "Sorry. Again."

Askal gave a small smile. "I cannot. My responsibility is to protect the Guardian. That role does not give time for a relationship, no matter how many suitors I have." He blushed, and Sev figured he was talking about Tuarn.

"And you really think I'm the Guardian."

Askal nodded. "Truly? Yes."

The fact that Askal had denied himself love because of her or the Guardian or whoever made her heart ache. Just another reason to leave. He could pursue love knowing he'd fulfilled his duties. Even if he believed he hadn't. It was all so messy and complicated.

Sev inhaled quickly. "But what if I'd never come, assuming I am the Guardian, which I'm not. I don't have protection in Melbourne." Jino made an odd squeak, and Sev gave her a quizzical glance. Then refocused on Askal. "What if I'd been killed there? You'd be waiting your whole life."

"Yes," he repeated.

"That's awful." Sev's eyes were still the size of dinner plates.

"No, it is not. Not really. While we," he looked at Jino who wore a strange expression on her face, "are not completely positive you are the Guardian, all I know is that you may be, and you are here, and it is my honour to protect you."

That did it. Tears, great waterfalls of them, cascaded down Sev's cheeks and she dropped her head; tiny puddles of water settling on the table.

***

Much like the tears that threatened now, as she folded Ori's letter.

"This is…" she whispered, and shook her head, unable to articulate the jumble of emotions in her heart. She collected the three letters, shouldered the leather carry bag—her original backpack lost in the first weeks—and crept along the hall to the kitchen. She'd decided to leave her tools behind. They were different from those used in Breulan workshops and Askal appreciated their uniqueness.

Letters deposited on the table, a small stoppered water jug tucked into her bag, she opened and closed the door behind her without making a sound. There wasn't a soul about—not at nine o'clock or thereabouts at night, so Sev walked down the middle of the vacant road towards the stables. She really couldn't think of any other plan and when she'd eventually say goodbye to Kotrol at the portal, she'd cross her fingers and toes that he'd be okay. That would be in a couple of hours. Who knew? She had no idea how far away the portal was. But two hours seemed like an optimistic number. Her heart shook.

The doors to the stables were open and Sev paused, her foot frozen in the air.

"Sevich."

The hushed voice came from her left and Sev leapt a mile.

"Shit!" She spun around to peer into the shadows of the building. "Christ, who's that?"

Two people stepped out onto the road. Privana and Councillor Buwrec Robrong Breula, their tall, thin bodies casting anaemic shadows in the light of the moons. The Councillor smiled.

"I am so sorry that we frightened you. That was not our intention."

Sev breathed deeply, attempting to calm her quickly beating heart. What the hell were they doing here?

"We felt that you would leave earlier than instructed. You seem to regard rules, both those applied in nature and those given by governing bodies, as somewhat flexible," Privana sneered.

"Privana Trissandoral Breula, that was unnecessary," The Councillor admonished, not taking his eyes away from Sev. "I apologise for my Guard member's attitude. He tells me that he is a last minute replacement for the Guard member I had chosen. Perhaps your sleep has been interrupted." The last comment, directed at Privana, carried a frown, a shake of his head, and pursed lips. The whole package.

"What are you doing here?" Sev found her voice.

Councillor Buwrec Robrong Breula stepped forward, his hands hanging loosely by his side, which seemed more threatening than if they were raised.

"My assumption was correct. You will be taking the horse that you have borrowed during your time in Breula."

"Kotrol."

He waved his hand dismissively. "However, perhaps this is ill-advised. If you wish to reach the portal before people." He narrowed his eyes, and Sev knew that he meant Ori. "Are aware of your absence, then taking the horse is not wise." He raised his hand as if an idea had just occurred to him. "We could offer you assistance to reach your portal. You could ride with one of us, and so alleviate detection. Your horse would be safe here and not in danger during a return journey."

That sounded remarkably like a threat. A threat that spoke of something awful happening to Kotrol as he returned to the town. Sev ground her teeth. As much as she hated to admit it, the Councillor was right. She weighed up her options. Privana seemed the least offensive. She'd be likely to slide off the Councillor's horse from all the sleazy slime he exuded. Privana was simply prickly. And grumpy. And Mr Frowny McFrowny, which didn't matter because she wouldn't be seeing his face.

"Okay. That seems reasonable." She flicked a finger at Privana. "Is your horse happy to carry two people?"

Privana scowled. "Why not ask her yourself?"

"The Fauna element doesn't work at night for me, so get off your high horse, Privana."

He frowned. Nothing new. "My horse is strong but she is not high."

Sev rolled her eyes. "Come on. This chat is wasting time."

Privana's horse, Ceas, *was* strong, barely flinching at the weight of an extra body. The unusual, intricately worked double saddle was incredibly comfortable and Sev felt that the estimated two hours would go by in a flash. She'd have to be careful not to fall asleep against Privana's back.

Which she did only a half hour into their journey. Privana had been droning on about how inappropriate it was for an Elemental, a royal Elemental at that, to be involved with an Arcanix, and Sev had immediately ignored him, because it didn't matter anymore. She was leaving, and she and the daughter of the King would no longer be involved. Sleep seemed like a great solution to blocking out his whinging.

Suddenly Privana jerked, waking Sev, who blinked, taking in her surroundings. Trees. Lots and lots of trees, which was fine because that's where she'd landed after falling into Breula just shy of four months ago.

"Awesome. Thanks so much." She wriggled, ready to dismount, but Privana's hand gripped her knee, and stilled her action.

"Councillor Buwrec Robrong Breula," Privana said, carefully. The Councillor brought his horse around and walked it closer.

"Yes?"

"It has just now occurred to me that you will be missed at the morning meeting if you do not return immediately."

The Councillor furrowed his brow. "I have much time."

"There may be delays on your return journey. The other Council members might question your absence, particularly as the King has insisted on your attendance at today's meeting. Is he not discussing the assessment of Sevich with the Council?" Privana's voice was measured as if speaking to a dangerous animal.

Sev tried not to breathe loudly.

"Councillor Buwrec Robrong Breula," Privana continued. "I am able to escort Sevich the remainder of the journey. The portal is only a short distance over those small hills." Then he inhaled as if preparing to deliver an important sentence. "I have an understanding of your plan and the expected outcome of this journey tonight."

"What pl—?" Sev's knee was squeezed again, and she snapped her mouth shut, gritting her teeth instead.

The Councillor flicked his gaze from Privana to Sev who'd angled her head to see around Privana's wide shoulders.

"Councillor Dasoskach Vaern Breula has spoken to you," he said. It was almost a question but not quite.

"Yes." Privana hesitated. "She has."

After a moment of contemplation, and a hard stare, Councillor Buwrec Robrong Breula nodded and twitched the reins in his hands. "Then I will heed your advice. It is logical and I thank you for your foresight."

With a final look at Privana and Sev, he pushed his horse into a trot, then a full canter and he disappeared over the rise into the plains.

"What the hell?" Sev whispered.

Privana released Sev's knee, and pointed to the edge of the forest faintly visible in the distance. "Do you know what portal is over those small hills? The ones I indicated to Councillor Buwrec Robrong Breula?"

"No, of course I bloody don't."

"It is the portal to Bianuwruh," he answered.

"That's…" Sev gasped. "That's not the Northern portal!"

"No, it is not."

"How the hell could you not know where we were heading? You're a member of the Guard, for Christ's sake!" She thumped his shoulder.

"I was distracted."

"What?" Sev spoke to the heavy material on Privana's back. "Too busy being a jealous dickhead and lecturing me about tradition and rules because you're holding great handfuls of unrequited love and a bloody candle for Ori which is driving you bonkers."

Privana encouraged Ceas into a canter. "I do not completely understand your sentence, but yes, that is why I was distracted."

It hadn't been lost on Sev that Privana had just saved her from a disastrous fate, because if she'd been shoved into Bianuwruh, there was no telling what or who was waiting for her there. It also meant that she would never have been able to return to Breula, if for some reason she wanted or needed to. Like if she was the Guardian.

"Oh my God."

"You are welcome," Privana said sarcastically.

"God, sorry. Thanks." She took a hand from the small bracing bar on the saddle and this time patted Privana's shoulder. "He, the Councillor, and it sounds like the other Councillor as well, that was their plan, wasn't it?"

"Yes, it seems so."

They cleared the forest and made for the next collection of trees in the distance.

"They think I'm the Guardian."

"Perhaps. They certainly wanted to make sure that if you are, then you would have no opportunity to defend Breula."

"Do you think I'm the Guardian?"

Privana scoffed and Sev could visualise his expression of 'yeah, right'.

"No."

There was a silence as Ceas's hooves thudded into the ground.

"Well, possibly," he corrected.

Sev grinned, despite the tension of the moment. The tension of the whole night.

"I'm not, you know."

"I agree. I am certain that you are not."

"Would it kill you to use a contraction?"

"I would feel close to death."

Sev laughed, then the sound quickly fell away. They rocked back and forth in time with Ceas's gait.

"How did you know that was their plan?"

"I did not. Not until I saw our direction."

"Why didn't you…?"

"Why did I not accept their plan and submit to Councillor Buwrec Robrong Breula's authority?" he responded, then hissed. "I will not engage in such a heinous act. I do not like you, but I will not kill you and tonight could very well have resulted in your death. The trespassers from Bianuwruh are always frightened and tell of a society that abhors elemental energy. The rulers choose to view elemental energy as a power source, not to be manipulated by mere citizens, and it is said that they are creating technology that is powered by something akin to our orbs."

"Sounds like my realm."

Privana stiffened. "You were trespassing to attain an orb for your realm?"

"No!" Sev shook her head emphatically, which nearly threw her off Ceas as the horse cantered through the entrance to the next forest.

"You switched with the member of the Guard at the last minute. I think I know why," Sev said quietly, as Privana brought Ceas to a trot. The silence of the trees hushed her voice.

He didn't respond.

"You wanted to make sure I went home. I mean, you wanted to see me actually go through the portal."

Ceas increased her stride as they exited the forest.

"Yes," he answered finally.

"It's okay to love her, you know."

Privana straightened his spine again. "I know!"

"She loves you like a brother."

"That is not how I love her." He sounded so sad.

"Have you told her?"

"That is not your con—"

"Privana, you're never going to see me again, so you could literally tell me your life story and it wouldn't matter. Have you told her?"

"No," he ground out, then jerked on Ceas's reins. "We are here." He waited until Sev dismounted then jumped down lightly from the saddle, and turned to face her. Sev adjusted her bag, then held Privana's stormy gaze.

"Even though you're grumpy, and mean, I'm grateful that you brought me to the correct portal."

"I did not do it for you. I did it for Orilaevar."

Sev delivered a one shoulder shrug. "Okay. Well, thanks any—"

"Orilaevar will soon understand that you are not a good match for her, and she will be glad that you have come to your senses, Arcanix Sevich." He kept his gaze firmly on her. "She will be disappointed but it is for the best. Exposing the heinous plan which was to be enacted by Councillors Buwrec Robrong Breula and Dasoskach Vaern Breula will give her a more important issue to focus upon."

Sev swallowed. Privana's words cut, which he'd no doubt intended. *Ori will be glad I've come to my senses?* Sev nearly burst into tears. That wasn't what she wanted Ori to think at all.

The very thought paralysed her and it was only when Privana thrust out his arm to point that Sev could move. She turned. A large person-sized circle shimmered in the air, a few centimetres above the ground.

"Your portal. Even at this time when you are conflicted, it calls to you. You must return. Even if you are the Guardian, it is irrelevant as there is no danger in Breula. Therefore, you are not needed. You must be cast out."

The words were like a punch to her chest, forcing an abrupt exhalation. She turned back to Privana and caught a shimmer of remorse or regret or something other than disdain flash across his face.

"Sevich," he said quietly, the moons casting bright light between them. "It is for the best."

Words were too difficult, so she rubbed at her chest, then nodded. Turning back to the glowing portal, she narrowed her eyes in indecision. *Do I ask it to open?*

The thought must have been the key, because the exit door became more defined, a large sticker plastered on the glass informing anyone interested that trespassers would be prosecuted. She almost laughed out loud at the irony.

They shared a long look, then Sev gave Privana a singular nod, and stepped towards the door. She pulled on the handle, surprised that it opened. Clearly trespassers were welcome to liberate large industrial appliances before their prosecution.

She stepped over the threshold, the door slamming behind her, and the glow lighting up the interior of the shop was snuffed out. Without turning around to check, Sev knew the portal had closed.

She stood in the middle of the aisle between the dryers and washing machines and the folding tables and the coin machine and the powder dispenser and stared blankly at the front door. Her mind was too busy, her heart so bruised, the room beyond silent, yet she forced her feet forward because through that door was her dearest friend.

The locks, one at the top and one at the bottom, flicked open when Sev pushed at them, and she slipped out to stand on the footpath. The door needed to be locked. It wasn't the laundromat owner's fault that a portal existed at their back door. She contemplated the door. The lock was built into the push bar, so she wrapped two fingers over the bar, touching the lock with the other three.

"Thank you for your service. I restore the balance," she whispered, then nodded as the locks clicked back into place. Still an Elemental even in her own realm. Fancy that.

Then she breathed in the Melbourne air. This is where her journey had begun. The place, the sounds, the smells felt so foreign. She grunted humourlessly, checked her bag, then took her first step towards Alex's flat.

Perhaps it was midnight. Probably later. Who knew? The city's not-quite-quiet hushed as the noise in her mind cleared, and she discovered how loud it was when a heart breaks into tiny pieces.

Chapter Sixteen

"What do you mean she's gone?"

Ori clutched at the doorframe and stared down at Jino's distraught expression. Surely this was an error. It had to be.

"Sevich departed during the night. There were letters waiting for us this morning." Jino's eyes filled with tears, then she shook her head, and stepped to the side, indicating that Ori should enter. Askal, who'd stood in the meantime, gestured to the chair opposite him at the table, then reclaimed his seat.

"There is a letter for you also, Orilaevar Reysandoral Breula," Askal said quietly, and pointed at the folded parchment in the middle of the table.

Ori sat heavily, and gazed at it. That piece of parchment would contain words of departure and distress and she was loathe to open it.

"Orilaevar," Ori muttered abstractedly.

"Pardon?" Jino asked, frowning.

Ori sighed, then delivered a small smile. "Please call me Orilaevar. The rest of it is unnecessary grandeur and besides, I think of you as Sev's family." She huffed a laugh. "Sev told me that having to say my full name brought on the potential of being struck by a bus vehicle." She shrugged in time with Askal and Jino. "I wish to avoid that fate."

Jino tilted her head, mirroring Ori's smile, and Askal hummed, clearly not comfortable with the sudden casual nature of addressing an Elemental. A royal one at that. He'd work it out, Ori thought to herself.

She slowly rubbed her palms together, then linked her fingers.

"I'll read that later," she said, tipping her chin at the letter. "Tell me what you know, please."

***

"I thought so," Ori stated much later, and Jino's eyebrows lifted significantly.

"Perhaps I am not masking my gift as well as I should," Jino said, contemplatively, giving Ori a long look.

Ori smiled. "Sev gave away more than she realised." Then her smile dropped. "The census will expose you as a seer."

"I am aware of that. My thoughts and visions bring discomfort when my mind touches upon this event. There is a concealed conflict, and I cannot see details. The census feels almost like a subterfuge. A dangerous one."

Ori hummed softly. Councillors Buwrec Robrong Breula and Dasoskach Vaern Breula had insisted on Ori's help with the census. If it was simply a facade for something else, then she needed to investigate. The fact that at least half the Guard had been requested by the Councillors and her father, and then begrudgingly redirected by Ori, to visit each home to gather information was concerning. Particularly if some sort of conflict was to coincide with the census.

"I can stop it. The census," Ori stated emphatically. "I can stop it happening."

Jino studied her. "Can you?"

The number of people she'd have to convince to ensure the census was cancelled suddenly overwhelmed her. The counting and cataloguing of townspeople was a boulder falling down the side of Mount Proneuth. She had as much chance of stopping it as she did of finding Sev in Melbourne.

"No, I can't." Ori sighed. "But I can ensure that certain members of the Guard are assigned to streets where seers reside."

Jino inclined her head in gratitude. Then it was like a thunderstorm crossed her face. "Sevich described the events of the Council meeting when she returned to the house yesterday."

Ori clenched her jaw.

"I'm so sorry. That display yesterday was unpleasant and as a member of the Council I feel much guilt."

"It was not your fault," Askal said, then added hesitantly, "Orilaevar."

"I know, however I feel guilt for allowing it to continue, despite how brief the actual event was. It was over within a minute." Ori swivelled her gaze to take in both mother and son. "Did she tell you?"

"Yes. She described her powers and manipulation so clearly that it was as if we were in the room," Askal said.

"I'm sorry," Ori repeated, and stared at the letter. "My father requested that the Councillors responsible attend an early morning meeting today to discuss their actions." She looked up and caught Askal's gaze. "Being forcibly exposed like that may have pushed Sev into her decision to leave so quickly."

"I feel you are correct," he replied.

"I'd rather be correct about other things, Askal." She paused deliberately, giving Askal time to acknowledge her request to change the way she addressed him.

Askal nodded, a smile lifting his lips. "Yes."

They sat in silence for a moment.

Then Jino broke the quiet moment. "I am sorry that your love has left."

Ori jerked slightly, taking in Jino's sympathetic expression, and swallowed, her throat thick with sudden tears. Jino hesitated for a moment, then laid her hand over Ori's.

"I am, too," Ori said quietly.

"Sevich scoffed at the idea that your love for each other was part of the Guardian's prophecy."

Ori's brain screeched to a halt, and her heart flipped over.

"Sev loves me?"

Jino tilted her head. "Forgive me, Orilaevar, but you are both as oblivious as each other." Her expression was very much like the one that Queen Sermeh Reytoris Breula had worn when a teenaged Ori thought it an excellent idea to install enormous candles in her bedroom to practice her Light enhancing skills.

Ori felt the smile, unbidden and probably inappropriate for the moment, arrive on her lips, then the crash of sadness. She held Jino's gaze.

"She loves me."

"Yes." Jino withdrew her hand. "And in my letter it is one of the reasons she gives for why she needed to leave. I imagine it is written in your letter as well."

Ori looked at the ceiling, the beautiful blonde wood joined seamlessly by love, gratitude, and kindness for the element.

"If she loves me," the sad smile flashed across her lips, "and has such a vast amount of energy, and there are Elementals who were so concerned about her energy that they wanted her to leave, then all that's missing is the great danger facing Breula." Ori pursed her lips, then dropped her head, eyes landing straight into Askal's knowing gaze. She flattened her hands on the table, her gasp filling the silence in the room. "The conflict. The one that is hidden under the census. That's the danger, which means Sev is—"

"The Guardian," Askal said. "Yes, she is."

Ori's mouth opened and closed. "And…she went home." It was the softest whisper, a breath. Then she snapped her head around to Jino.

"You must have foreseen it! Why didn't you tell her?"

"I was going to tell her this morning. I foresaw it yesterday after the assessment."

"But you could have told her before all of that even if you weren't sure."

"It would have been irresponsible to tell Sevich that she is the Guardian when it was also possible that she is not. As it turns out she is, and if we are discussing guilt then I feel a great deal because I have made a grave error in judgement. I did not trust my vision. It played tricks on my mind, and I dallied. It is true that the gift of seeing can become impaired when what you seek is hidden, and because of that delay, Sevich has returned to Melbourne."

Ori contemplated Jino's distress. "Sev had many reasons to return to her realm. Finding out that she is the Guardian was going to be another item on her shopping list of burdens." A little voice niggled. If Sev had known she was the Guardian, then maybe she would have stayed. The voice niggled again. Sev didn't stay for Ori, so why would she stay on the off-chance that she was the Guardian? Ori banished the little voice. She completely understood Sev's logic, which was awful. Her heart hurt.

Jino reached for Ori's hand. "I feel she knows who she is even if her mind will not accept it."

Ori clenched her teeth, and Jino patted Ori's hand as she pulled away.

"I foresaw Askal's role," Jino continued, looking at her son with fondness and affection. Ori followed her gaze.

"What role?"

Askal chewed on his lip. "My role is to protect the Guardian while they are in Breula. Not to protect their strength. That would be impossible. My role is to protect their heart, their balance, their sense of place." His eyes filled with tears. "My role is to ensure that the Guardian will always find their way home." A single tear fell. "And I failed because Breula's Guardian has left so I cannot help her find her way home. She is not protected in her realm."

None of them spoke. Askal whisked away the tears, and Ori tried desperately not to cry for Jino, and for Askal, and for Sev. For herself.

Jino smoothed her palm over the table, staring at the back of her hand. Then she looked over to her son.

"Not exactly."

The statement was so vague that Askal and Ori simply blinked.

"She has protection in Melbourne, and I hope that the protection still exists as she has been absent for quite a while."

Askal spoke first. "She does?"

This time Jino reached across, and held Askal's hand. "It is how we still know about the prophecy. Askal, you protect the Guardian. But there are Breulans, seers like me, who protect the prophecy, and quietly share it with the people, the Arcanix, who then ensure that the Elementals hear about the prophecy as well."

Ori nodded, lifting a shoulder to indicate that she had heard the prophecy when she was young.

"The seers ensure that the Breulan who is foreseen to be a protector is able to fulfil that role. They ensure that this person is kept secret in case the Guardian is not welcomed; a situation which could place the protector in danger. And so I have fulfilled my role." She looked at her son. "As you have done."

Askal opened his mouth to respond, most likely with the argument that he hadn't fulfilled his role at all, but Jino shook her head.

"You did fulfil your role. Sevich found her home here. She found her balance, and despite all of her elemental energy, you were able to bring stability to the turmoil in her heart."

Askal lightly squeezed his mother's fingers. "Thank you. But I do not understand how Sevich is protected in Melbourne." Ori shifted in her chair, leaning into the back. This was suddenly an intensely intimate moment; one that she didn't need to interrupt.

"Again, I have made a grave error and I wish that days, years, may be lived again so that I could have told you this sooner." She squeezed Askal's fingers until her knuckles turned white.

Askal's face paled, probably from Jino's impending news and her grip of death.

"Sevich is protected in Melbourne by a Breulan named Alex."

Forget the idea of not interrupting.

"I'm sorry, but what?"

"What?" Askal said simultaneously, pulling his hand away.

Jino resumed staring at the table, and her shoulders dropped. She looked frail and vulnerable.

"I have a sister."

Askal gasped, and Ori wasn't far behind.

"My sister, Nowa, is also a seer. We are twins, and she has a son. Alex." She stopped as if that was the end of the revelation, and Ori wanted to reach across the table, pat Jino's hand to let her know that a lot of information was missing, and could she keep going, please.

"So, I have a cousin," Askal said, his voice flat and emotionless. "And an aunt." He folded his arms. "You have lied to me for my entire life."

Ori slipped her hands onto her knees, and gripped the fabric. The situation was tense enough without her banging the table or something else as equally attention-seeking. So she squeezed her knee caps and flicked her gaze between mother and son.

"Yes." Jino looked beseechingly at Askal. "I am so very sorry that I have never told you."

"Why?" The word drifted into the room.

"I—it would have burdened you."

Ori pulled her hands up and crossed her arms. There was an awful lot of burdening going on lately, along with assumptions about people's abilities to deal with those burdens. She was guilty of it as well. Lying by omission was just the start of—

"I lied by omission," Jino said, and Ori blinked. Add mind-reading to a seer's skill set.

"It would not have burdened me."

Jino's face dropped. "Of course it would have. What if my sister and her son had never found Sevich? If you had known of their existence, who knows what would have happened to your heart if Sevich had never arrived in Breula? Who knows what would have happened to your heart if Sevich did arrive in Breula but told us Alex had not lived? Fortunately, we know that Alex has survived. Yet I delayed telling you the truth." A brief, sharp sob fell from her mouth. "Perhaps I was protecting my heart. I do not know of Nowa's fate, and it saddens me to think that she has passed away outside this realm."

She turned her gaze to Ori, tears appearing in her eyes. "We are all destined for something. Something of importance. Such as you, Orilaevar. Perhaps you do not know it yet, but something important is in your future. And my importance, my destiny, was to ensure that Askal was ready for the Guardian's arrival, as was Nowa's importance with her son. Clearly, Alex found Sevich and has protected her since." She shook her head. "Although, he will be distressed at Sevich's disappearance." Her hand, rolling slowly over her wrist, was aimed at Askal. "It is the mirror to your distress about Sevich leaving."

Askal held Jino's gaze.

"I am shocked by this news, Mother, however even through my heartbreak, I see your logic."

Jino flicked away her tears. "My logic is flawed. As I said, I have made an error that impacts many people. I delayed sharing my knowledge, my history," she pointed at Askal again, "*your* history, and that is negligent, and I beg your forgiveness."

Askal chewed his lip, clearly absorbing the idea of an extended family, so Ori jumped into the silence.

"When did Nowa leave Breula?"

"When Alex was one year old."

"That's…" Ori paused. She didn't know Askal's age, and it felt rude to ask.

"I am thirty-six years old."

Ori blinked at him, then swung her gaze to Jino. "You haven't seen your sister for thirty-five years?" Such a huge amount of time.

Jino shook her head sadly.

"No."

And with that she burst into tears, twisting her fingers together in agitation. Ori leapt up, rounded the table then stopped abruptly because Askal had lifted his mother from her chair and enveloped her in an embrace, murmuring "I forgive you," over and over as she sobbed in his arms.

***

Breula could be in danger from an unknown force. It was absolutely the reason why Ori insisted on the intensive training schedules for the Guard. For situations like this.

"For situations where members of a Guard of some sort might invade any time in the future from an unknown portal in numbers that can't be predicted," she muttered, two days after Jino's revelation. Checking in with the Guard at the Orb Lagoon had been her morning activity, and now Ukih snorted in happiness as he galloped across the plains towards town.

Throwing herself into training and mentoring and riding out to the Orb Lagoon made her feel useful and in charge, like she knew things. Which she didn't.

Askal was probably feeling the same way. Maybe. Finding out that his cousin was also a protector had knocked him sideways, and he'd instantly expressed a concern about whether Alex knew who Sev was. Perhaps Alex had spent years ignorant of the fact that he harboured the Breulan Guardian. Sev had said that she didn't exhibit any elemental energy in Melbourne so it was most likely that Alex had no idea.

A small figure waved frantically at her from the middle of the bridge that spanned the Juith river.

Jino.

Ori tugged lightly on Ukih's reins, and she leapt down as he slowed to a walk, his hooves clicking on the wood.

"Orilaevar!" Jino clutched at Ori's wrist. Eyes wide.

"Jino. Is everything alright?"

"I needed to find you. I have seen the danger." She tightened her grip on Ori's wrist. "The conflict. It is not the census which began just this morning in the south. I saw a vast amount of people from another realm." Her breathing was rapid, so Ori guided her to the bench seat that ran the length of the bridge. She held Jino's hands.

"An invasion?"

"I do not know, but our people are in danger, and the orbs are threatened. It was essential to find you to prepare the Guard."

Ori rubbed the woman's cold hands. Her shaking hands. "When? Through which portal?"

Jino made a small noise of distress. "I do not know! I see the people as indistinct figures so I cannot tell you which portal. The vision did not reveal to me when this event would occur." She stared into Ori's eyes. "I am sorry."

Ori released Jino's hands to wrap an arm about her shoulders. The woman was so tiny, her confidence and sass having disappeared entirely.

"You shouldn't be sorry, Jino. It isn't your fault at all. You see what your skill allows you to see. You are not responsible for its clouds." She pulled her arm back, slapped at her knees, and stood. "I'll put a stop to the census, recall the Guard and prepare for the realisation of your vision." Ori set her mouth in a straight line, and looked down at Jino. "I know exactly who I'm going to speak to first."

***

"But you must!" Ori threw her hands out in frustration and paced about her father's reception room.

"The census will progress because the Council made a decision to implement it. The results will be valuable." King Rodlamar Reytoris Breula frowned at his daughter, exhaling loudly through his nose. He leaned over his hands which were pressed firmly on the desk.

Ori spun around. "Father! You have overruled the Council once before. Why not now?"

Her father shook his head, then gestured for Ori to follow him as he moved to a pair of intricately carved chairs arranged about a matching table. Two mugs of tea sat on top, steam curling into the room. Ori stared hard at him, his body relaxed in the seat, a small smile on his mouth, as if he were indulging a petulant teenager who needed to see reason. She clenched her teeth. Arguing with her father was awful but this was too important to worry about familial hierarchy. Therefore, she remained standing; a stance much more effective when making a point.

"I do not understand why you are opposed to such a useful exercise," her father said, the confused frown infuriating Ori. She threw out her hands again.

"Because it's a ploy to divert our attention!" She examined the ceiling for a moment, purely to find composure, then dropped her head. "There is danger coming!"

Consulting the ceiling hadn't helped at all.

"Of course, there is not," the King scoffed. "That is a children's tale." He smiled indulgently. "I think you have spent too long preparing for danger that now you find it difficult to contemplate peace."

Ori inhaled sharply. "Father, it is not a children's tale, and it is short-sighted of you to make that judgement."

"Orilaevar, you forget yourself." His eyes narrowed and both father and daughter glared at each other.

Anger churned in Ori's stomach. "I haven't forgotten myself, Father. I know exactly who I am," she said. "I am Orilaevar Reysandoral Breula, Leader of the Guard, and daughter of the King of this realm, and I will not have my Guard redirected from their duties to assist with a pointless exercise." She took a deep breath, staring at her father's astonished face. "Not when it has been foretold that a great danger will threaten Breula." They held their gaze, and King Rodlamar Reytoris Breula slowly lifted himself from the chair.

"It is a—"

"No, it's not!" Ori said loudly. "It was told to me today!" She clenched her fists.

Her father jerked, and his head tipped to the side in query. "Today? By whom?"

"Jino Kirmiz. She is a seer. Breula has protected the seers for generations because their role is to ensure that the prophecy is passed on. They ensure that we don't forget its message, and now, because we've cast out our Guardian, we—"

"Sevich? Hardly cast out. She asked to leave," King Rodlamar Reytoris Breula said.

Ori blinked. "You knew that Sev is the Guardian?"

Her father's shoulders dropped. "I came to that conclusion."

Ori flung out her hands again. "Then *why* did you allow her to leave? We need the Guardian to join us in our fight!" It did not escape Ori's notice that she was referring to Sev as the Guardian more and more as if blending the two. As if erasing Sev.

She was vibrating with frustration at her father, at the Council, at herself.

"This battle may not happen," her father said, and that was the last straw.

"Father! I won't argue about this any more!" She pointed, and held her nerve when his eyes narrowed. "Even if you insist on allowing the census to proceed, I am overruling your decision to utilise the Guard." She breathed heavily like she'd run a great distance. Maybe she had. Maybe the need to run a great distance was the meaning behind Jino's prediction. That Ori was destined for something important. Certainly Breula was of importance. She loved her realm and the people and if Jino said that they were in danger, then they were.

"Orilaevar!"

"No, father. We need change and I am determined to enact that change. If change means that I overrule decisions, if you overrule the Council, if Arcanix are not harassed by a pointless census, then so be it. And now the census will stall because assistance from the Guard will not be available." She swallowed heavily as she took in her father's expression. Anger, disbelief, sadness.

"Father." Ori exhaled, and opened her hands. "I know I have spoken harshly but you did not raise a daughter to cower behind others. I speak my truth, and I believe in Jino's visions."

With a final glance, she turned on her heel and marched through the exit. It was the first time she'd ever spoken to her father in that manner, and striding to the stables to inform her Guard to abandon the census was an excellent method to dispel the astonishment she felt at her actions.

She needed to find Privana to help communicate the order even though she hadn't seen him for two days. It felt like he'd been avoiding her which was a ridiculous thought. Perhaps he was involved with the census. Ori scowled. Exactly.

***

Ori eventually found Privana in his quarters on the outer edge of the township. He answered the door at her knock.

"Privana!" Ori sighed with relief, and stepped into the main room. The beautiful masculinity—it was really the only description—of the space always surprised her. Dark furniture, sleek lines. Privana had commissioned a couple of Flora Arcanix to create wood panelling which bent in unusual waves, creating a wall of potential movement. It was quite lovely.

She turned, then stopped short. Her friend stood at attention in the middle of room, his gaze flitting about. Ori squinted, as he eventually met her eyes.

If she didn't know better, she could have sworn that Privana was guilty. Of what, she had no idea. Perhaps it was her imagination.

She folded her arms.

"We are withdrawing the Guard from participating in the census."

Privana jerked, and parted his lips. "We are? But we have over two-hundred members deployed to assist. It will take at least half the day to hand over the results they have gathered to the Elementals." Then his face closed, and he stared blankly ahead.

Ori studied him. "I know that, and we will deal with that issue efficiently. I have made this decision based on information I was given this morning." Something told her not to share Jino's gift or her vision. "We need the entire Guard within the township and at the Orb Lagoon, not wandering the streets counting Arcanix."

The muscles in Privana's jaw bounced, but he nodded quickly.

Ori let the silence grow. They'd been friends for twenty years, they knew each other well, and so small nuances were very obvious. Something was off, and she didn't think it was the withdrawal of the Guard.

She relaxed her stance. "Have you been avoiding me?"

Privana let his gaze slide away, and, although it seemed impossible, became even more rigid.

"No, of course not."

They shared another moment of silence. Ori tipped her head and squinted again. Privana was hiding something. Time to cast some light on what that 'something' was, because even though she normally wouldn't pry, it felt like the 'something' involved Sev.

"Sev departed two nights ago."

Privana's eyes flashed and he brought his gaze back. "I heard."

He was too quick to respond.

"She may return," Ori said, hopefully.

The skin over Privana's knuckles whitened, and he fixed Ori with a harsh stare.

"I sincerely hope she stays in her realm," he snarled and Ori inhaled slowly. *Ah. The 'something'.* "In fact, I know she will stay there because she did not hesitate at the portal when she left. Her departure is for the best, and beyond that, she wanted to leave."

Ori hummed at the animosity in his response.

"I am concerned for her safety," she said slowly.

Privana shook his head, possibly in frustration, and unglued his feet from the floor to pace a few steps, only to return, and level an intense gaze at Ori. It was the look she'd seen on her Deputy when he was furious with a member of the Guard who was taking too long to learn a new skill. A look she had spoken to him about. New recruits in a permanent state of anxiety were reluctant and unsure; neither of which were useful qualities.

His gaze hadn't wavered, and seemed laced with challenge. "Why be concerned? She is back in her own realm. She knows how that realm is structured. She has lived in it."

The moment felt like a cross in the road in their friendship. She reflected on Privana's behaviour towards Sev over the last four months. His comments. His suspicions. *Oh, Privana. What have you done?*

Ori's lips flattened to a straight line. "I love her, my friend. She is my Light." She let that news land, and based on the clouds that flitted across Privana's expression, he didn't enjoy hearing it.

"It is impossible that she is your Light. She has returned to her realm," he said, grunting at the end of his sentence. "So now you will find a new person to love." He grit his teeth, white against his tanned skin, and delivered a single thump against his chest. "You could have anyone in Breula."

His emotions were riding high on waves of vulnerability.

"I don't want anyone in Breula," Ori said, carefully.

Privana growled, pacing about the room as if he were an unsettled wild beast. The agitated meandering brought him closer. Close enough for Ori to see tears shimmering in his eyes.

"I have waited and waited in the background, Orilaevar. Through your dalliances with the sons and daughters of Council members, then your relationship with Hruti, to this affair with Sevich." He widened his eyes beseechingly. "Through all that you never saw me." His breathing had shallowed, quickened. "You never saw that I love you."

Ori gaped.

Privana looked as if he was relieved to finally get all of that off his chest, because the air seemed to leave his lungs and he dropped his head.

Ori reached out and rested her hand on his shoulder. "Of course I see you. You're my best friend, but, Privana?" He lifted his head. "I love you as a brother. I did not realise your—" Ori gasped, dropped her hand and stepped back, her mind instantly erasing Privana's declaration. A much more pressing issue now occupied her thoughts

"How do you know Sev didn't hesitate at her portal?"

Taking a step back as well, Privana flicked his gaze away, and this time Ori didn't imagine his guilty expression. He refused to look at her, and remained silent.

Ori stretched to her full height. "Privara Trissandoral Breula, answer me."

Privana jerked his head up, and angrily swiped at the last of his tears. "Fine. I carried her on Ceas to the Northern portal."

Ori blinked. "You...why?"

Privana inhaled deeply. "I had heard that Councillor Buwrec Robrong Breula intended to wait at the stables that night. He believed that Sevich would attempt to leave early. It seems he was correct, because Sevich did arrive at the stables with the idea that she would ride Kotrol to the portal."

"But she didn't know how to get to her portal!"

"Yes, she made that clear." Privana quickly shook his head. "Councillor Buwrec Robrong Breula offered to escort Sevich to the portal with an accompanying member of the Guard."

Ori hissed. "You?"

He shook his head.

"You will tell me this member's name when you have finished your explanation," Ori said, authoritatively.

Privana nodded briefly, then gathered more oxygen in a long, deep breath almost as if he were buying time. "I overheard that member of the Guard talking to another." He closed his eyes briefly, and flicked his finger at Ori. "Yes, one more name for you. So, I changed places with that member of the Guard, and Ceas carried me and Sevich to the—" He snapped his mouth shut, and took another step back.

Ori widened her eyes. "What?"

Privana looked for all the world like he wished to be invisible.

"Finish your sentence, Privana." It was like pulling teeth. Very fraught and somewhat volatile teeth.

"The Councillor rode in front of me and I was distracted by," he looked briefly at the ceiling, "it is not important. We arrived near the portal to Bianuwruh."

Ori took one stride forward, and clutched at Privana's shoulder again. This time not in sympathy. Privana grimaced in pain.

"Why," she growled, "were the three of you at the Bianuwruh portal?"

Waves of nausea roiled inside Ori's stomach, rising into her throat. Privana had said he'd seen Sev pass through her portal, and while he was not fond of Sev, he'd never send her through another realm's portal. Particularly to Bianuwruh. Would he? No. Ori was certain he wouldn't.

She pulled away, recrossed her arms, then glanced down at Privana's nervous tell; the one where he quickly tapped his fingertips together. He'd revealed so much in a short amount of time and now Ori was pushing for more. It was little wonder he was jittery.

"Councillor Buwrec Robrong Breula explained to Sevich," Privana flicked his finger at his chest, "and myself, that trespassers escaped to Breula because they were seeking refuge, which is true but he said the refuge offered by Breula could really be offered by other realms."

"Oh!" Realisation dawned, and an ice cold trickle of fear rolled down Ori's spine.

"He told us that if a trespasser was looking for a new life, then travelling through a portal that was not their own would achieve that goal. They would be permanently welcomed, settled and free. Breula would simply act as a sort of holding centre."

Ori stared at Privana as his face paled.

"You didn't know this, did you?" she whispered.

"No! I swear." His hands had clenched again.

Agitation rippled through Ori's body. Flapping her hands to shake out the tension, she paced blindly about the large room, her shoes softly scuffing when she changed direction. Her thoughts buzzed.

"Why wasn't Sev put through the Bianuwruh portal if that was Councillor Buwrec Robrong Breula's plan?" She stared out the window, and heard Privana's loud exhalation.

"I made sure he did not. I convinced him to ride back to the township, then I took Sevich to the correct portal."

The idea that trespassers—people—were being used as test subjects in a social experiment was reprehensible. Ori spun around. "When were you going to tell me?" Her voice held barely contained anger.

For a moment it looked like Privana was going to refuse to answer this question as well, then he grimaced.

"I delayed because I thought you would be upset with me for helping Sevich leave early."

"You…" Ori was rooted to the spot. "You thought I'd be upset?"

He nodded.

"Let me understand this conversation." Her voice lowered and fury underlined every word. "You knew that Councillor Buwrec Robrong Breula was waiting for Sev, you swapped places with the Guard member to," she pointed aggressively at Privana, "ensure that Sev went home because you are blinded by jealousy, but then you demonstrated honour by rescuing Sev from a fate worse than death because some Councillors are intent on using trespassers as toys for a sadistic game; the point of which is unknown. But." Ori narrowed her eyes, then strode across the room into Privana's space. He flinched. "You kept that little gem to yourself because you thought I'd be upset about Sev riding with you to her portal *a half day earlier than expected*."

"This is also my understanding of the conversation," Privana murmured.

"I am very close to striking something and I do not want it to be you." Ori turned on her heel and marched over to the window.

"Orilaevar, I—"

"No." Ori sliced her hand away from her body. "Logically, I should be grateful to you for rescuing Sev but my gratitude is tarnished by your cowardice." She placed her hand on the window sill, ran her palm along its beautiful surface, then turned to face her friend.

Privana rolled his palms out in placation. "I have a thought which I would like to share if it is appropriate, Orilaevar."

"It needs to be. This conversation is already full."

Privana nodded quickly. "While I was returning to the township that night," he averted his eyes, then brought his gaze back, "I wondered if trespassers were the only people to involuntarily journey through incorrect portals."

Ori cocked her head. "The trespassers are the only—" She gasped. "The census! It's not to count people. It's to find Arcanix who don't have an element, who are deemed dangerous to who knows whom, then sent through the portals." A tight band constricted her lungs. Jino.

"No!" she breathed.

She clutched at the hilt of her sword. "If people are sent through alternate portals, what's to stop people from those realms coming into Breula, particularly if the portal is held open."

Privana stepped forward. "That would take an enormous amount of energy to hold the portal open for so long!"

"Not if two Councillors held the portal open for the regular duration. You know the portal can be held open for short bursts of time, so that the inspection can be conducted. Then the Elementals rest briefly, then they open it again. It is how the trespassers are able to slip through." Her grip tightened, the leather strapping biting into her palm. "But an entire Guard is not a trespasser attempting to evade detection. If the Guard was invited, then large numbers could quickly cross over each time the portal was opened." They held eye contact. "A Guard of immense size could assemble within a few hours."

"An invasion?" Privana swallowed. "No realm has ever attempted this. They exist within their own land. Breula has never heard of something so horrifying."

"No, we haven't, but Breula possesses something valuable that other realms might now want. Orbs. We know that not all realms think this way, but one realm in particular might have changed their minds. Bianuwruh." Ori paused so her jumbled thoughts could settle on the disturbing truth. "Bianuwruhan trespassers have expressed fear because of the recent unseating of their government. What if the only way for Bianuwruh to take our orbs was to stage an invasion and perhaps a coup at the same time?"

Privana's fingers trembled. "King Rodlamar Reytoris Breula…"

Another wave of nausea struck. "My parents. Me." Her hand twitched, wanting to unsheathe her sword simply to feel the strength. Its solidity. "Perhaps there are Elementals here who wish to govern Breula, perhaps with the assistance of another realm's Guard."

Privana gaped. "That is not possible!"

Ori moved away from the window. "The anomaly was never Sev. It's this." She gestured behind her. "The census. The potential of invasion. The potential of capture." She pointed at Privana. "You will be responsible for the Guard at the Orb Lagoon. Prepare them for an attack from an unknown force. And," she glared, "We have not finished our conversation."

Then, just as Privana nodded in acquiescence, an arrow, merely a sliver of light, cut through the air and thudded into the seat next to Ori, the fletching shuddering with the impact.

"Down!" Ori yelled, dropping to the floor, then stared into Privana's wide eyes only a short distance away. She waited for a moment in case more arrows sliced through the window, then she stretched out her hand, and quickly shook the arrow's shaft to release it from the chair leg.

She held it close. The tip was rounded as if a ball of metal had been welded to the end of the hardened wood. The arrow itself was shorter than those used by the Guard, but the fletching worried her most of all. The fins were metal.

The arrow was menacing. It was frightening. It was deadly.

Ori looked quickly at her Deputy. "Orb Lagoon," she hissed. "Gather as many members as you can right now, and take the fastest horses available." She widened her eyes, increasing the intensity of her instructions. "Your Element is Ice. Use it at the lagoon."

Privana nodded, his eyes just as wide.

Then, clutching the strange arrow, Ori pushed up, and sprinted to the door.

Chapter Seventeen

When Alex's slightly hysterical voice, shaky with tension, drifted under the front door, it created a pang in Sev's heart, and highlighted just how much she had missed him.

"I have a gun!"

She would have laughed if she wasn't so anxious.

"No, you don't, Alex. It's Melbourne. Open the door."

The door was yanked open and Alex's wide eyes filled the space.

"Oh my God! You're here! Where have you been?"

He grabbed her hand, then dragged her inside, and slammed the door.

Everything was the same. The flat, with its somewhat threadbare carpet, the mismatched furniture, the little kitchen with the slightly off centre cupboard doors. All the same after four months. Tears filled her eyes.

Alex spun her around, and gasped.

"Rhi, you're crying! Are you hurt? I've missed you so much! Where have you been?"

"Sev," she automatically corrected. Her old name felt so foreign that she almost looked around to find the extra person in the room.

"What?"

Sev shook her head. "Long story. I've missed you so much as well, mate. I'm just really tired. But I'm fine." She wasn't fine, then the everything of the everything became too much and she fell into Alex, hugging her best friend as more tears tracked down her face, leaking onto his floral pyjama top. She was homesick for Breula, happy to be back in Melbourne, overjoyed to see Alex, and heartsick at leaving Askal and Jino and the townspeople who'd become friends. And Ori who'd become so much more.

More tears.

"Oh, sweetie." Alex rubbed circles over her back. "You've been gone eight weeks. It's such a long time. No wonder you're upset."

Sev jerked away. "What?"

Alex looked at her quizzically. "You've been gone eight weeks?" Then he growled. "If you've been in hospital with amnesia and they didn't ring me as your emergency contact, I swear I'm going—"

"Two months," Sev whispered, then turned away, and walked as if in a daze over to the green velvet armchair. She yanked the throw cushion off, and sat heavily. "Eight weeks. That's impossible."

Alex's head, followed by the rest of his body gradually appeared in her line of sight, and he stared at her like she was a loaded bazooka. "Rhi?"

Hygt had said that time was a social construct. Sev hadn't really been paying attention to him at that moment, what with everyone at the Facility totally confused by her accidental trespassing excuse.

But Sev had lived in Breula for sixteen weeks but in Melbourne, she'd only been absent for eight.

"This is…I can't comprehend this," she said, looking up into Alex's wary expression.

"That would make two of us. I can't believe you're here." He plonked down onto the sofa seat closest to Sev, shuffled his slipper-clad feet and clasped his hands together, staring at her as if she were an unknown specimen.

Eight weeks. Sev knew what she'd experienced, but what had Alex experienced in that time?

"Oh!" She gasped. "The thugs. The…poker woman," she flapped her hand, "What's-her-name…Madison. Did they hassle you?"

Alex's eyebrows shot to his hairline, and his lips looked frozen into their 'O'. Then he jumped up, and paced about the room, clearly trying to comprehend Rhiannon's absence, Rhiannon's stolen identity, then Rhiannon's return. It was a lot.

"Yes. Two guys turned up here." He paced some more. "Maybe two weeks after you disappeared, and they threatened to do all sorts of horrible." He turned abruptly, and poked his chest. "Things to me, if I didn't say where you were, but I had no idea where you were. By the way," he pointed his finger, "I have been interrogated by the police, harassed by thugs, hassled by debt collectors, and then the last straw!" He pointed his finger skyward. "I had to force myself to watch commercial television in case you were mentioned." His attempt at a scowl was undermined by the utter relief plastered over his face.

Sev held her hands over her chest. "I'm so sorry, Alex." She gripped the fabric of her shirt. "What did you tell them? Those thugs?"

Alex circled back and threw himself onto the sofa. "I managed to convince them that you were backpacking around South Australia."

Sev spluttered. "South Australia?"

"It was all I could think of, Rhi! I don't know!" He wrinkled his forehead. "They have vineyards in South Australia."

A bubble of laughter rose up, and Sev dropped her head. "This is crazy. I'm so sorry. I really am. I've missed you terribly and this has been so hard."

"Look, Rhi," Alex started, and Sev looked up. "Don't worry about any of that. Madison was arrested at the end of last month, and I know about the stolen identity business." He frowned again. "Why you didn't tell me, I'll never know, but moving on." He grumbled. "Your stolen identity was all fixed and the debt collectors buggered off because all the outstanding debts were wiped." Alex pretended to brush his hands together. "I'm more interested in what happened to you. So…" He let the word drag out. "Where have—hang on, what on earth are you wearing?"

He furrowed his brow at her clothing almost as if she were rematerialising on the transporter of the *Starship Enterprise* and all her sparkly bits of matter hadn't sorted themselves out yet.

Sev knew the time had come.

Deep breath.

Check.

Shoulders relaxed.

Check.

"My name isn't Rhiannon anymore. It's Sevich. Sev, for short, which confuses the heck out of everyone there, particularly the Elementals. Apparently, they can't abbreviate any—"

"No!" Alex whispered, and his face lost all colour. "You've been to Breula."

Sev gaped. "I—what? How? I haven't told you anything. You know about Breula?"

They stared at each other in astonishment.

"I...I do, but you are definitely telling your story first," Alex said, finding the words. "I'll tell you what I know after you tell me what you know." Then he jumped up. "We need hot chocolate for this." He rushed off as fast as someone in fuzzy panda slippers can rush, and the familiar sounds of mugs landing on kitchen bench tops, and the burbling of the jug boiling water washed over her.

Alex's frantic muttering filled the space. He was probably reeling. He'd had one and a half extraordinary sentences pitched into his ears, and that sort of thing should come with a prior warning.

Like the prior warning she should have received for the extraordinary fact that Alex knew about Breula. How? Sev gazed unseeing at the coffee table, and it took a moment to register the two mugs of hot chocolate that Alex had placed in front of her.

She looked sideways to find her friend sitting with his knees pressed together, hands clasped, as if waiting for the best story in the world. Or the worst.

It was probably both.

"I've been in Breula for sixteen weeks, and I only went there because I fell through a portal at the back of a laundromat."

Sev sat back in her chair, rested her palms on her thighs, and released a long breath.

Alex blinked. And blinked again. "Right." He nodded slowly, then circled his finger at her. "I'm going to need a lot more information."

It took the first mug of hot chocolate, and half of the next one, to retell the events of the last four months, and that was just the highlights reel. Alex didn't get through even one mug because his mouth kept falling open or he'd interrupt with a question or an exclamation.

"—it shimmer?"

"I don't know! I was being chased by two large blokes. I wasn't looking for fairy sparkles around a laundromat door."

"—and there are different realms?"

"Yes. Breula, and a bunch of others all with portals."

"—demonstrate your skill with metal."

"It was more like a test, and I'm glad I held the element of the month."

"—them around their necks?"

"Yep. Each element has a different colour."

"—like a mentor?"

"Basically. I got to work in Askal's studio which was wonderful. He and Jino looked after me." Sev drew the line at mentioning Askal's role to protect the Guardian. It was irrelevant and besides, Alex's head looked like it was about to explode.

He stared, shaking his head in amazement. "This is incredible. I can't believe this. I can't believe you're here."

Sev huffed a laugh. "I know. Insane, right? A different realm. A different time construct. At least the language is the same, although thank Christ you can use contractions."

Alex squinted. "Um…"

Sev laughed, then smacked his shoulder, nearly causing a hot chocolate disaster.

"Okay. I've given you my story. Well, enough of it to be getting on with." She pointed. "Your turn. How do you know about Breula?"

Alex tipped his mug up, drained the last of his drink, and set the mug down. He leaned into the back of the sofa, and flicked his gaze to the ceiling. Then he dropped it, and gave Sev a long look.

"I've told you that my mother died when I was twenty," he said, quietly.

Sev hadn't expected that. She reached for Alex's hand and squeezed his fingers.

"Yes. The car accident."

They shared a slow nod.

"I know about Breula because of her and because," he swallowed, "I'm Breulan."

Paralysis of the mind had to be a real thing because Sev was convinced that her mind was frozen, incapable of absorbing her friend's words.

"You're Breulan," Sev confirmed. "But why don't you know a lot about Breula?"

Alex disentangled his hand, and rubbed his palms together. "We left when I was a year old."

Sev inhaled quickly. "Oh, Alex." She stood and stepped around the edge of the coffee table to sit beside him, then leant into his shoulder. "So you've been absent for thirty five years." She stared at the side of his face until he turned his head and nodded.

"It's funny, you know?" he said, his face showing not a bit of humour. "For about six months, I've been accidentally dropping Breulan-type words into our conversations. Element and energy, etcetera. I didn't mean to but it's like I couldn't help it. Perhaps it's your influence." He laughed the sad, quiet laugh that people do when reliving a particularly painful memory.

They sat in silence for a moment. Shoulder to shoulder, and contemplating at the far wall. Then the realisation crashed into Sev's mind.

"You're a Heat Elemental!" She twisted her body, and grasped Alex's forearm. "No, not an Elemental because you'd be doing it right now, but you possess the element of Heat." She flipped her hands in the air. "It explains everything. God, I'm so dense."

Alex smiled. "You weren't to know."

Tapping her fingertips together, Sev studied Alex. "Sure, but I've been sitting here, rambling on about Breula this, and Breula that, and then you tell me you're Breulan, and all the while I'm forgetting that all Breulans have an element." She pointed. "Extra warmth on weekends in winter."

Alex blushed. "I like to make our home comfortable."

"Oh my God, you're amazing." Sev wrapped her arms about his shoulders, and squeezed. Then questions, just as rapid as Alex's, filled her mind.

"Why haven't I possessed my Metal element for my whole life? I'm not Breulan, so why do I even have an element? Were my parents Breulan?" Hugging Alex felt like protection from the potential answers, so she ducked her head into his shoulder, and waited.

"I don't know," Alex said.

So much for answers arriving.

"Maybe it's an accident that I have an element," Sev mumbled into his pyjama top.

"I don't think so," Alex responded, curling his hands over Sev's forearm that embraced his chest. "I think it's because you crossed *to* Breula from Melbourne, whereas I crossed *from* Breula to Melbourne. I was born into the element. You possess it organically. It called to you." He leaned the side of his head onto Sev's. "Your parents had nothing to do with it. Just like they had nothing to do with how astonishing you are."

Quiet tears tracked down Sev's face, and exhaustion crept into her bones. Sneaking away from Breula, nearly being shovelled through the wrong portal, Privana's overt jealousy, reuniting with Alex, sharing her experiences—with a lot omitted—had suddenly joined together, and the nausea that extreme fatigue can induce filled her stomach.

"I need a shower."

"You do, and you need to sleep. You look like you've been awake for a couple of days."

She had.

"R—Sev, it's five in the morning. We can talk more in a while, but right now, you go have a quick sleep. I put fresh sheets on the bed." He patted her arm. "Must have known."

Sev laughed, squeezed his shoulders again, then pulled away. "You must have." She stood, and swayed. "Oh wow. Okay. Shower and sleep. Got it."

Alex lifted himself from the sofa. "You okay to get to the bathroom?"

"Mate, I can walk twenty steps by myself." Sev quirked a smile, then staggered off, turning into the small hallway that led to the bathroom. And promptly crashed into the wall. Clearly right-hand turns were tricky when sleep deprived.

"You okay?" Alex's question rolled in from the lounge.

Sev clutched the wall, and walked her hands across the flat surface to reach the doorknob.

"All good."

***

A quick sleep turned into nearly seven hours of unconsciousness. Sev, dressed in her favourite flannel pjs and Ugg boots, wandered into the kitchen, drawn by the aromas of a cooked lunch. Basil pesto and fettuccine.

She collapsed onto a kitchen stool. "That smells amazing. I've missed your cooking."

"My cooking? That's what you've missed?" Alex waved the pronged utensil that stirred the fettuccine.

Sev grinned. "Fine. I missed you as well. Actually, Jino cooked amazing meals, too." Again, the stab of inexplicable homesickness.

Alex smiled sympathetically. Sev's face must have worn all that homesickness like a giant poster.

"Talk to me while I'm cooking. Why did you leave Breula?"

Sev's mouth feel open. "Because of you! I wasn't going to stay there while you were here worrying like crazy."

Alex looked over his shoulder. "I'm really glad you did, but I know you and there's more."

Sev spluttered. "Worrying about you should be the only reason."

"Perhaps." Alex went back to stirring the sauce with the wooden spoon. "I love that you're here. I'm relieved that you're here. You're my family." He placed the spoon on a side plate, and came over to the bench. "Because you're you, I know that returning to me was probably the number one reason." He cocked his head. "But it's not the only one."

He held her gaze, and finally Sev looked away. "You're right. It's not."

"Thought so, hon."

"I—I had to leave because of what I can do." Sev couldn't bring herself to meet his eyes.

"What can you do?"

Sev ran her fingers through her hair, and eventually looked at Alex's face. Concern and worry.

"My element isn't just metal. I possess all ten." Her voice lifted at the end. She wondered how many beats it would take for Alex to freak out.

"All ten? What the hell?"

Three beats, apparently.

Sev rested her hands on the bench top. "Oh, you have no idea. I said that very phrase and others every time a new element turned up." She rubbed her palms over the formica. "About a month into my time there, I gained a few elements, then the rest seemed to arrive all at once. So, Metal, Heat, Ice, Dark, Light, Earth, Fauna, Flora, Water, Air." She tapped the bench top with her finger at each element. "The fettuccine is boiling over."

Alex whipped around, twiddled with knobs, and moved the saucepan to a new location on the stove. Then he spun back. "Ten?"

"Yeah."

"That's impossible."

"I've been told."

"How?"

"I have no idea. I just seemed to attract them. They felt like they belonged in me." She shrugged, then paused as something registered.

"Alex." She stared him down. "How do you know there are ten elements? You freaked out at me possessing ten elements, but not the fact that there *are* ten elements."

Guilt took over Alex's features, and he twisted around to turn off the burner under the pan of pesto sauce.

Then he came back and studied the counter.

"Alex, why are you in Melbourne?" Sev asked softly. Something told her that she already knew the answer. "Alex?"

He lifted his head, and swallowed hard. "To protect the Guardian."

Sev blinked.

"You're kidding."

"I'm not. My mother was a seer, and told me that my role was to protect the Guardian until they were ready to defend Breula." He inhaled, then let out a very long breath.

An army of goosebumps paraded along Sev's skin.

"Alex, did your mum have a sister?" She held her breath.

He shook his head, and frowned. "I'm fairly sure—no, I'm sure. Mum never mentioned one."

Sev's chest constricted in shock. There had to be a connection, but apparently not. Alex was definite. But Askal and his Guardian-protecting? Jino and her seer-skills? The idea of a connection had taken up residence in her mind, and she knew it would be difficult to dislodge. It was all too much of a coincidence.

At the pause in the conversation, Alex quickly rescued lunch, and, indicating with a tip of his chin at the lounge, they made their way to the sofa, balancing their bowls of food on their laps.

After a couple of bites, Sev settled her fork, and placed the bowl on the table.

"I reckon you've come to the same conclusion that everyone in Breula came to."

"What's that?" Alex said, carefully, not taking his eyes off Sev's face.

"That I'm the Guardian."

"Mm. Yeah, I kinda have."

"Why?"

"Your energy called to me. It's how I found you at Queer Drop-in." He smiled, then after another bite of food, placed his bowl next to Sev's. "You have a lot of Elemental energy."

"And because of that you think I'm the Guardian." Sev squinted, and Alex nodded.

"Well, that, and the ten elements. The prophecy states that the Guardian will hold powerful elemental energy."

"The prophecy," Sev said, in resignation.

"Yes. My mother's role as a seer was to protect the prophecy, and to ensure that I was able to fulfil my role, and I believe you are the Guardian who I have been foretold to protect."

Sev stared at him. "My disappearance distressed you more than you let on, didn't it?" She held his hand, and after a beat, his face crumpled.

"Oh God, I was so, so worried. You're the Guardian and I feared for your safety. I've been beside myself contemplating all sorts of horrible scenarios."

His eyes filled with tears and with his free hand, he plucked randomly at the threads on his jeans. "For two months, I couldn't protect you. I couldn't fulfil my role."

"But now I'm back, and because you think I'm the Guardian, you can pick up where you left off." Sev raised an eyebrow. Alex jerked his hand away, and glared.

"You *are* the Guardian. I know it." He clapped his hands once, then clenched them together, and gazed fervently into Sev's eyes. "Listen."

Sev tightened various muscles because she just knew that Alex was going to retell the—.

"The prophecy states," he began, and Sev's shoulders dropped. "That a Guardian will arrive in Breula to rescue the realm from great danger. It is told that there is one," he pointed to his chest, "who is tasked with protecting the Guardian until they are ready." He raised an eyebrow, and rolled his hands over his wrists as if to say, 'see?'

"That's not all of it," Sev said, and wanted to bite off her tongue. They didn't need to rehash the entire prophecy because then they'd reach the part about Ori.

"No, you're right." Alex frowned as if recalling the rest. "The Guardian is able to wield all ten elements with more power than any Elemental." He shot finger guns at Sev. "But the Elementals become worried about the Guardian's energy so some conspire to capture the Guardian and cast them out of the realm." He raised his eyebrows in question.

Sev pursed her lips to the side. "Yeah, that happened."

Alex gasped. "It did?"

"Mmhmm. I had to undergo an interrogation of sorts. They chucked a heap of unbalanced elements at me, and I rebalanced them in about a second. It would have been awesome if I wasn't so frightened."

"That's appalling!" Alex's eyes were round.

"Pretty much. It's another reason I chose to go, rather than be cast out. It was easier." Sev's mouth downturned.

This time, Alex held Sev's hand, and they leaned into each other's shoulders.

"I'm sorry. Your heart must feel like those awful kettle balls they make me carry around at the gym."

Sev laughed. "My heart's fairly heavy, yes." She pulled away, and closed her eyes. "Okay, finish the rest of prophecy."

"You sure? You look like you really don't—"

"Alex, finish it, please."

"Well, after the Guardian is cast out." He grimaced. "Or decides to leave voluntarily because an awful test that is mean, and very much like a clickbait gotcha moment, makes them feel unwanted, the Guardian goes back to Breula, avenges the danger and—"

"Avenges?" Sev looked at him with raised eyebrows.

"I'm updating it. It's more sexy. Not so much the 'old fogies sitting around the campfire a thousand years ago' version." He flicked his long hair dramatically over his shoulder.

Sev giggled. "I can handle avenging. Do I get spandex?"

"Blue?"

"Always." Sev circled her finger to indicate that Alex should continue.

"You know this. The Guardian's energy diminishes—"

Sev rested her elbows on her knees, and cupped her chin. "Dead Duracell."

"Apt."

She caught Alex's nod, then he continued. "Then the Elementals allow you—sorry, allow the Guardian to stay in Breula because the Guardian saves the realm and all, but also the Guardian has fallen in love and…" Alex trailed off, and Sev knew that, because he'd gathered enough information for the time being, and because he'd known Sev for over a decade, he would be able to read Sev's face like a book. Any moment he'd lean forward, tilt his head so he could look into her eyes.

"Don't look at me like that."

"How am I looking at you?" Alex sat back, and Sev lifted her head, then fell into the back of the sofa.

"Like you know something."

"Who is she?"

Sev growled softly in response.

"Not an answer, Sev," Alex said, and she wanted to hug him for using her new name. It must have been a mind-trip to swap after twelve years of Rhiannon. They held their gaze, Sev absorbing the waves of sympathy in his brown eyes. The brown eyes of her protector. Because that's what he was. Because she was the Guardian, and she'd fallen love.

"Her name's Ori."

"Ori."

Sev couldn't help the watery smile lifting her lips.

"Ori. Her full name is Orilaevar Reysandoral Breula."

Alex blinked. "Heck of a name." He shifted so he was square on. "And Ori is?"

The breath she took sucked in all available oxygen. "Ori is the daughter of the King of Breula."

Alex rolled his lips together. "You fell for the daughter of the King."

"Mm."

Alex's lips curved into a slow smile, a sparkle in his eyes.

"Of course you did."

A matching smile drifted onto Sev's mouth.

"Smart arse," she said, then the smile fell away. "I miss her terribly."

"You need a clone." Alex nodded with authority, and Sev grunted.

"I said that when I was leaving." Then she pointed to the cooling fettuccine. "There's enough warmth in the flat. Want to harness it and heat these for us?"

"I'm not going to demonstrate—"

Sev smirked. "Serves you right for sassing me about Ori." Then she hummed. "You know I shouldn't be in love with her."

Alex jerked his head back into his neck. "What? Why not?"

Their lunch was doomed, but channelling optimism, Sev picked up the bowl, and twirled her fork into the pasta, then ate the mouthful, slowly chewing as she created an answer to Alex's question.

"The prophecy says that the Guardian falls in love, and in some versions the Guardian falls in love with the princess and that…" Sev shoved another mouth full in.

"What?" Alex paused as he reached for his bowl.

"It scares me senseless, Alex."

"Because then the whole prophecy is true?" His hand paused in mid-air.

The pasta had become rubbery and she plonked the bowl on the table, tossing her fork beside it.

"Yes. The rest of it is, so why not that part? If I deny that I'm in love with her, then I'm not the Guardian, and I can get on with my life." It was the most ridiculous amount of gibberish in the world.

Sev sighed.

"So…" Alex picked up his bowl, looked at his congealed lunch, and put it down. "You love her because a prophecy says you have to." He tipped his head and frowned in confusion.

Sev clenched her hands, then flicked the fingers away from body. "No. Yes. No. Oh my God, this is so hard."

"No, it's not. Say it."

Sev shook her head hoping the action would toss the words into sentences.

"I don't love her because the prophecy says I will. I love her because…I love her."

It felt good to say it out loud.

"You can't help who you fall in love with no matter what a bunch of old fogies sitting around the campfire a thousand years ago said." He nodded with authority, and Sev cracked up.

"There you go," she laughed.

Then she nodded. "So, that means I'm the Guardian."

"Yes." Alex tucked his hand into her elbow. "It does, which is very cool. I've been harbouring the Guardian for years like Wakanda hides an infinity stone."

"Alex, I'm not a comic." She wrinkled her forehead at her friend.

"But that'd be awesome, right?" Then he sobered. "You have to go back, you know."

"I don't, you know," she replied, sharply.

Agitation sizzled in her bones, and she sprang up to pace about the lounge. "I don't. It's not my job to save any realm, let alone Breula." She tucked her hands into her armpits. The flannel rubbed against her palms, and suddenly her Ugg boots felt too hot for her feet. She kicked them away, and rolled her toes into the threadbare rug.

"I know it's not your job."

"Good. I'm glad we—"

"It's your calling." Alex gave Sev a long look.

"Really?" she challenged, sarcasm dripping from the word. "My calling. Why?"

Alex crossed his arms. "Because you're Breulan."

"Oh, for the love of…" The rest of the sentence faded away, and her hands fell to her sides. The realisation—another one—hit her. She'd told Alex that all Breulans possessed elemental energy. All Breulans. The truth had been staring her in the face since the moment in the arena's bathroom when she'd turned her sword into a pretzel.

"And…there we are," Alex hummed.

"Oh, Christ."

"So, as the Guardian you have a calling, and you have a prophecy that needs fulfilling, and you have love to nurture. Your love for Ori, and your love for the people of Breula."

Sev rocked on her feet, side to side. "Jino said that the realm will protect me because to possess and manipulate an element is about love."

"Jino knows what she's talking about."

Alex crossed his legs, and bobbed his head as if to indicate just how wise Askal's mother was, then he jerked, unwound his legs, and sat forward.

"Can you do anything else that's not mentioned in the prophecy?" He sounded curious and worried and uneasy at the same time. Just like Askal had. The similarities between the two men were eerie.

"Lucky it's you and not an audience of Councillors who should have known better." She darted her eyes about the room, eventually stopping at the fork next to her bowl. It seemed the most likely item to turn into abstract art. She knelt down at the table, and dragged the fork towards her.

"Hang on, don't you need a tool or something for whatever it is you're about to do?" Alex frowned.

"You'd think."

Running her fingertip softly over the handle, she whispered. "I request your service. I will return your balance." Then she smoothed the handle, stretched it, twisted it until the handle was shaped into a heart with the three tines standing upright at the top like the stalk on an apple. Sev paused for a moment, then looked up, and fell into the same stunned expression that Ori had worn when engulfed by the Giord tsunami.

"Oh my God," Alex whispered, then flicked his fingers at himself indicating for Sev to pass the fork to him.

He turned it over in his hands. "This is incredible."

Sev chewed her lip. "It's…" She hunted for the word. "It's nice. I feel more connected to the metal than I ever have."

Alex passed it back. "So, now we have affectionate cutlery?"

Sev rolled her eyes, then held the heart in her palm. "Thank you. I restore your balance," she murmured, and quickly, as if a rubber band had snapped, the metal straightened, flattened, and settled into its original shape.

Alex blinked again, and looked askance at the fork. He was clearly waiting for it to become sentient and dance across the coffee table. Sev chuckled.

"I can also manipulate Earth, Flora, and Fauna by hand."

"That's not in the prophecy." Alex's eyebrows were lost in his hairline.

"Thought I'd go for an A plus." She grinned widely; the first time she'd done so since leaving Breula. Perhaps accepting that she was truly the Guardian made it less of a burden.

Sev rested her elbows on the table, sitting back on her heels. "Ready for another one?"

Alex's eyes widened. "There's more?'

"Yeah. I have Metal element permanency. No orb," she said, then laughed at Alex's gape.

"That's incredible," he repeated, then grinned. "Any photon blasters?"

"Unfortunately not but I'm still hopeful.'

With another careful glance at the fork, Alex sat back in the sofa and crossed his legs.

"Okay. You really need to go back to Breula. The shit's going to hit the fan in that realm, and you need to be there."

Sev sighed. "It's not my home, Alex."

He held her gaze, turning it into a long, considered look.

"There's a very old Breulan song that my mother sang to me for years about how the realm will always bring her people home." He continued to gaze at Sev, and Sev averted her eyes. Alex's mother had told Alex about his role as the Guardian's protector, but she had also shared Breulan knowledge. Very old traditions passed on sounded really nice. It sounded familial. She'd missed out on that experience, and her heart hurt.

Jino was the closest that she'd got to it. And Ori had sung to Sev in the ancient language. It had been a beautiful experience. Perhaps it was the same song that Alex's mother had sung. Sev hunted about in her memories for Ori's words from the festival.

"A ekaver a je Breula," she sang, and cringed at her tone-deaf version.

Alex stared at her for what felt like a full minute, and it soon became uncomfortable. Was her singing that appalling?

"Now we absolutely have to go back," he whispered, eventually.

"Because..?" Sev said, her eyes wide.

Alex dropped to his knees so he could reach across the coffee table and clutch Sev's hands.

"You're being called home, Sev."

They held hands for a moment, then Sev frowned.

"Hang on. You said 'we'." Sev gripped his fingers. "Alex, if I go back to Breula, you can't—"

"Of course I'm coming with you!" Alex squeezed her fingers in return. "You're not the only one going home." He gave a final squeeze, then released her hands. "Lots to talk about. Come on. Let's get lunch tidied up, so we can plan our return." He stood, and smiled. "Should I get out marker pens and a large piece of paper?"

Sev stayed where she was, and studied her friend. Alex's remark was overly flippant.

"Alex, Melbourne is all you've ever known. Do you actually want to go to Breula? You'll be giving up so much."

He shrugged, his hands flicking sideways with the movement. "But I'll be gaining so much more. I've fulfilled my role. I've protected the Guardian." He pointed emphatically at Sev. "It's time to go back."

***

According to Alex, and with complete agreement from Sev, five-thirty on Monday morning was a perfectly good time to walk calmly and innocently through the back door of a laundromat.

"It really is," Sev repeated, tipping her chin towards Alex's chart paper. He hadn't been joking about the marker pens, either.

Alex tapped the list of 'things to get done in twelve hours' which was growing at an alarming rate.

"I'll send my boss a text."

Sev gaped. "That's your resignation?"

"Why not? It's a shitty job with a shitty boss." He reached for his phone, and tapped out a message, dictating as he went. "Hi Helen. I'm just heading off to another realm for the rest of my life. By the way, one of the wheels on my office chair is wonky." Alex pressed send, then beamed, and Sev laughed.

"Don't worry," he continued. "It's not like Helen's going to think my text is weird. She thinks I'm weird all ready."

The list also contained questions such as what to do with the flat

—"Mike next door can have it. The landlord's a good guy and won't mind, and Mike could do with a change. He and I hung out a bit and he told me he's sick of his flatmate, Sarah, chanting in the middle of the night at the turn of each moon phase."

"And this has happened in the last two months?"

"I had to keep busy, you know." He grinned. "I'll tell him I'm going overseas indefinitely."

"What about..?" Sev gestured at the furniture.

"He can have that, too, and my clothes, although he's a string bean and I'm a human teardrop." He circled his finger at Sev. "Your clothes?"

"Um…" Sev began. "I guess they can stay here. I really don't need them. I have my Breulan clothes that I came back to Melbourne in, but I think I'll wear jeans on the way…" She couldn't say it.

"You can say it," Alex said quietly.

"On the way home." Sev exhaled carefully. Saying the word felt like one more step towards Ori, and her heart expanded.

Then she gasped. "What about my studio?"

Alex pursed his lips, then grimaced. "Please don't hate me."

"What?" Sev clenched muscles in various locations. Asking someone not to hate them just before delivering news was never good.

"It sounds like you've been creating beautiful art with beautiful tools in a beautiful workshop in Breula and I reckon," he paused, "I'm sorry, Sev, but I think you can let the Melbourne gear go." He ducked his head into his neck as if preparing for a reaction with dire consequences.

But he wasn't going to get one.

"You know? I can do that." Sev smiled as Alex raised his head like a turtle coming out of its shell. "Askal has my special tools, and I get to manipulate my element openly there. Can you imagine if someone wandered in to my Melbourne studio and saw me twisting about a blob of melted steel like I was making toffee?"

Alex stared over her shoulder for a beat, then fell about laughing. "It's almost worth staying here an extra day just to see that happen."

***

Leaving her life behind felt bizarre. Like being wiped off the face of the earth. Yet not. Definitely not as cataclysmic because Sev realised that there was a whole life waiting for her, where she existed, and lived, and loved.

After a few hours of horizontal eyelid closing, and after Alex had finished packing a couple of necessary items into his own satchel bag—"I don't have anything as luxe as your leather bag"—very early the next morning, they stood looking at each other at the front door.

Sev pointed to Alex's non-luxe bag. "Please tell me you didn't pack your Medicare card."

Alex pouted. "It's the only form of identification I have. How will they know who I am?"

Sev blinked. "Alex, Breula doesn't do plastic. It's against the law."

"It is?" Alex's eyes widened.

Sev chuckled. "No. But they don't know it. Everything is natural, so toss all your plastic, mate."

Alex frowned, then flicked out all of his cards; credit, bank, Medicare, Woolworths points, FlyBuys rewards, and let them fall to the floor.

Then he reached into the small broom closet, shoved aside the vacuum cleaner, and tugged on a large, tied-up plastic bag.

Incredible. Clearly he hadn't got the message.

"Alex, I just—"

Alex pointed aggressively at the bag. "Clothes. We're undercover." He shook his head. "Sort of. But we need a reason to be turning up at the laundromat at five-thirty in the morning. We can't very well open the door, and ask the attendant if we can pop to the back of their establishment for a spot of portalling."

Sev laughed loudly. "Fair enough." Then she waved her hands in front of her torso. "Undercover enough for you?"

His top-to-toe scan was more thorough than an airport x-ray machine.

"Yep. Black leather boots, black jeans, black skivvy, black jumper." He chewed his top lip, then let his wrist become loose so he could wave it at her jeans. "It needs a splash of..." He couldn't finish his sentence because he'd broken into a fit of giggles.

Sev smiled at his silliness, but caught the anxiety threaded into his laughter, and she held his shoulders.

"It's going to be okay. You can still back out, you know."

Alex nodded as if his head didn't know any other movement. Those bobble-heads on car dashboards.

"Alex!" Sev said, loudly.

After a large exhalation, Alex blinked, and settled his gaze on Sev's face. "I'm okay." He licked his lips as if they'd dried up like dead leaves.

Sev pulled him into a hug, holding the back of his head, his long black hair sliding against her fingertips.

"You are the bravest person I know. Not only have you protected me for twelve years, but you're giving up your world, everything you know, to start all over again." She felt Alex's quick breath.

"I'm not giving up anything important. I promise. Something important is waiting over there," he mumbled into her jumper.

They held each other for another minute, then Alex pulled away. They nodded at the same time, then turned to gaze into the room.

"Bye Alex's old life," Alex said decisively, and Sev reached for his hand. Then she stared at the far wall with the two small windows proudly displaying their view of next door's exterior brickwork. The dawn nibbled at the shadows on the glass.

"See you."

Sev smiled at her words. Words of goodbye, and irony. She wouldn't be seeing this life again.

What an amazing concept.

***

Alex was fully immersed in his role as an undercover agent. He peered around the electricity pole outside the laundromat, and Sev crossed her arms.

"I can see you, you know. The black Santa sack, your boots, your —"

"Fine." Alex stomped out from behind the pole, stood in the middle of the footpath, and dropped the bag on the ground. "I'm a thirty-six-year-old nerd." He puffed out his chest. "And proud of it."

Sev punched him lightly in the arm. "You're wonderful. Now, let's get this show on the road. Ready?"

Alex cleared his throat. "Not really." He peered into Sev's face. "Does it hurt?"

"What?" Sev's imagination ran riot. Breula contained all manner of things that could hurt. Hard to narrow it down to one in particular.

"Going through the portal." He twisted his fingers together.

"I...no?" Sev tried to remember the two times she'd gone through. If there was any pain involved, it was psychological. But that wasn't pain.

Rubbish. So much pain.

She stilled his fingers. "There's no pain. But there are pretty golden edges that glow."

"You're joking!"

"No, this time I'm serious. I'll pay more attention this time." She hefted Alex's bag of clothes. The attendant appeared at the glass in the top half of the door, his face obscured by flyers advertising local markets, and sign-up days for karate classes. He flipped over the 'closed' sign, jerked the locks up, then made eye contact with Sev, and gave her a thumbs up.

She puffed out a breath. "Here we go."

She grabbed the handle and pushed, holding the door open for Alex.

Who had lost all colour from his face.

"It's okay," Sev murmured, then she smiled at the attendant. "Hi. Just doing some washing," she said inanely.

The attendant shrugged as if to say, "Yeah, you're in a laundromat so that's an obvious and unnecessary statement."

Sev smiled again, all teeth, which probably looked slightly manic but she needed to get to the washing machines at the back so they could dump the clothes, and so she could calm Alex down. She could hear his veins vibrating with stress.

She set down the bag near the back exit. "Hey, Alex?"

Alex grunted, his eyes darting about.

"What'll happen to the clothes in this bag?" She held his elbow and turned him towards the door.

"Uh. Um." His eyes refocused as he remembered the details. "Any clothes left at a laundromat get donated to charity."

"Good. Someone will be thrilled to receive your paisley jacket," she snarked. Alex turned his head, and his aggrieved expression was worth the distraction.

She nearly forget the words.

Then she didn't.

"I am the Guardian and I will restore the balance," she whispered, and a slow smile grew as the promised gold glow shimmered to life around the door frame. Alex didn't have time to reacquaint himself with his stress because Sev pushed open the door and shoved Alex through. Then she quickly followed, and heard the door snap closed behind her.

The sounds, the smells, the colours, the everything that was Breula filled her heart. How could she have ever doubted? She dropped her head back, and gazed up at the pink and white sky.

Right. Sometime in the day.

Sev quickly calculated. She'd been in Melbourne for around thirty hours, so if those calculations were correct, it was approximately sixty hours since she'd stepped back through the portal. Two-and-a-half days. She was loathe to think what had happened in that time.

Alex wandered over to one of the trees in the large grove. He patted its trunk.

"Wanna say hi?"

Sev narrowed her eyes. "You're not funny." She beckoned him over. "Come on, the township is this way, and who knows how long it'll take on foot."

Alex fell into step. "Pink and white, hey?" He gestured towards the sky. Of course. Baby Alex would not have known any of that.

"Mmhmm."

"What's the night sky like?"

"Purple and two moons."

Alex's steps faltered, and he quickly readjusted his stride to catch up. "Two moons?"

Sev ran her fingers through her hair, and smiled. "Yeah, they're overachievers."

"Trespassers, you have entered Breula illegally." The authoritative voice cut through their conversation. Alex squeaked, as Sev stopped, then sighed. She turned to face the group of Guard members fanned out in a tight semi-circle.

Sev rolled her hands to the side. "Okay." Her tone must have indicated that she was not tolerating any rubbish, and Alex's second squeak clearly indicated that tolerating any and all rubbish from people with arrows and swords was fine. His gaze ping-ponged between the Guard members and Sev.

Sev closed her eyes briefly. "We've had this discussion before. I'm not entering illegally. I've already been to the Facility. I've recently had my assessment." She held up two fingers. "Twice. So I'd like to get to the town, please. Apparently, you're in for some great danger, and while I'm not sure what that will consist of, I—"

"I have not heard of any great danger."

"I'm not up to date with the details either. Perhaps you've been galloping about the borders, and the danger might have come from a whole different direction. Maybe the sky," Sev said, with not a small amount of sarcasm.

Something told her not to announce to the Guard members, or anyone else in the vicinity, that she was the Guardian. She was chucked out of Breula for that very reason.

Then she recognised one of them. "I know you!"

The Guard member looked around, then pointed to her chest. "Me?"

"Yeah. You performed one of the sword dances at the festival." Sev pursed her lips, and squished them to the side. "The Flora element. It was excellent."

As one, the Guard members gasped. "You are Orilaevar Reysandoral Breula's…"

Sev almost laughed at how they were twisting themselves into knots trying to work out how to address the lover of the princess of the realm. She put them out of their misery.

"Yep, that's me. Can we get a lift, please? I'd really appreciate it, and I know Ori would as well." That was manipulative, but Sev had no problem playing that card. They needed to return to the township, and something told her that it should be soon.

"What about your companion?" said the Guard member who'd spoken first, his deep voice resonating in the trees. "He is a trespasser."

Sev waggled her finger. "Oh no. Nope. Alex is vitally important, and I can vouch for his presence. He isn't a trespasser. He's the ring-bearer and must find the bridge over the river."

Alex lowered his voice. "What?"

"The bridge across the Juith river?" the Guard member said, his brow furrowed.

"That'll do. Perfect. Let's go there."

Sev looked pointedly at Alex, and tipped her chin at the horses.

"Ring-bearer? Bridge?" Alex threw Sev an askance look, then the same look at the horses, then at the Guard members—two of which were adjusting their saddles for Sev and Alex.

"I'm messing with them. They take themselves so bloody seriously."

Chapter Eighteen

Hair streaming out behind her, Ori sprinted along the roads, and as she flew past, commanded townspeople to either remain inside their homes or gather at the mansion's forecourt ready to defend the town. It was hardly surprising that hundreds, with a love for Breula burning in their veins, hurried along in her wake as she leaned into corners and shot up the main road. She covered the eight thousand paces from Privana's rooms in little under twenty minutes, and a disconnected section of her brain recognised that her time would have been faster than that of last year's winner at the Guard championships.

She turned onto the small access bridge that led up to the mansion, the soft soles of her boots gripping the rough yet smooth surface, and the enormous forecourt in front of the grand doors came into view.

The slight incline and the low walls flanking the bridge hid the archer until the last minute.

It took all of a second for Ori to process the crouched stance—one knee on the ground, one bent—the double-handed grip on a weapon, and the direction that the archer was aiming; directly at the first window on the mansion. Her mother's room.

Anger licked through her. Without pausing for breath, without breaking her stride, without altering her focus, Ori unsheathed her sword, pushed off, and in mid-air, plunged the blade into the archer's shoulder.

Instantly, he gave a guttural cry, the weapon fell from his hands, and he rolled into the wall as Ori withdrew her sword. She stood over him, turned her hand, and using the sun's rays, created a globe of light in her palm. She held her hand near his face, and as she'd expected, he quickly shut his eyes.

"Who are you? Where are you from?"

Ori almost didn't recognise her voice. Animalistic, laced with fury. She probably looked like an avenging being from the sun, a storm of rage, towering over the crouched figure. How *dare* these people? She kicked the weapon and the quiver further up the road, so the arrows scattered, the metal fins screeching on the ground.

Ori could also be accused of violently unbalancing the realm by shoving a sword through the flesh of a person within the realm's borders, but it hadn't occurred to her at the time. She'd analyse that thought later.

"Thank you for the Light," she whispered, then waited while the member of the foreign Guard blinked frantically. Finally, clutching his shoulder with the blood seeping through his fingers, the man looked about, noticed the absence of his weapons, and slumped back into the wall.

"Where are you from?" Ori repeated, adjusting her hand on the sword's hilt; a completely unnecessary gesture but the man took the small movement as a threat.

"Bianuwruh," he hissed, saliva following the word as it left his mouth.

Ori gasped. "Bianuwruh! And you are an advance Guard member?"

The man grunted, and with his uninjured hand, quickly withdrew a dagger from the outside pocket of his trousers, and leaned forward to stab at Ori's thigh.

With natural skill and speed, Ori darted to the side, reignited her globe, thrust it at the man's face, then sliced at the dagger with her sword, sending the weapon flying. She waited another moment before extinguishing the light.

"You're an advance Guard member," she repeated.

The man blinked again, shaking his head as if to dismiss the green dots in his vision. "You are the princess. You were supposed to be incapacitated by another scout."

"It seems your weapons are inaccurate. Your scout missed."

"There will be others." He sneered. "I am not as immobilised as you think. Our weapons can be fired by either hand."

Ori growled, drew her sword and pressed it against his injured shoulder. The man yelled through gritted teeth, and attempted to dislodge the tip from his wound.

"No, they can't," Ori hissed. "That shoulder under my blade cushioned the base of your weapon, your hand manipulated the triggering mechanism, and the other hand aimed the arrow. You favour one side of your body when shooting."

The archer glared, breathing shallowly through his teeth.

Ori nodded. "Do not underestimate me. We may not know of your technology, but we are skilled and perceptive. So, now I know that you're a scout; most likely one of a few scattered to cover more ground. I also know that your arrows don't fly true, which means that my Guard will know all this as well." Then she looked up to find a small group of townspeople, some of the many who had answered Ori's call, at the base of the bridge.

"I require two with the Flora element!"

Without hesitation, as if it were their honour to assist the Leader of the Guard, two young women rushed forwards. Ori recognised them; Likovu and Tonn Finjuk, sisters from the eastern border of the town. She gave a brief nod, then with a final flick at the scout's shoulder, waved the tip of her sword at the vine that was climbing the wall and creeping across the top.

"Please use this to bind him. You won't be unbalancing the element. It will answer your call."

Then Ori sheathed her sword, and crouched in front of the man, his knuckles white as he gripped his shoulder.

"Those with the Fauna element will attend to you soon, and you will heal, then you will be held in a contained space while I protect my realm. I don't know why you're here and you probably won't tell me. But I will find out." She leaned closer and murmured. "Our arrows may not be as strong, nor as powerful, but my archers are very, very accurate."

Ori collected the scout's equipment, watched the two women whispering to the plant, bending the stem across small wooden tools plucked from their belts, so that the ivy quickly strengthened and wrapped itself around the hapless man.

Then she wheeled around to race up the last section of the road, across the forecourt, and crash through the small door to the side of the enormous entrance.

***

Having called for them throughout the ground floor—Elementals and Arcanix leaping aside as she flew past—Ori found her parents standing in the centre of a small meeting room attached to the Council chambers.

"It was my suggestion to come here," her mother said anxiously as soon as Ori closed the door, then turned to Ori's father. "I know you wanted to face whoever is out there, but I wanted you to be safe. Orilaevar and the Guard are more than capable." A long look was directed at Ori. "Yes?"

"Yes. Very capable." She returned the long look, and crossed her arms. "The Guard members who attend to both of you. Why aren't they here?"

Her mother inhaled loudly, like she always did when preparing to have the last word.

Ori knew exactly what her mother was doing. She was the Queen protecting the King, just like in the game the members of the Guard played. And, really, if she were being completely honest, the Guard members who protected her parents were needed elsewhere.

So, Ori shook her head, and directed them to a group of seats around a low table. She addressed her father, the King.

"The invading Guard are from Bianuwruh." She dropped the weapons on the ornate table; the metal scratching the beautiful wood, and both parents leaned away from, almost in horror, from the vicious equipment. "The portal must have been held open for there to be a complete Guard."

"Are there many?"

"I don't know exactly, but there must be because they have scouts, which tells me that more are due to arrive." She opened her arms to take in both parents. "Mother had the correct thought even if it is misguided." She absorbed the glare. "I must get you to safety. I feel like this invading Guard has an agenda that involves more than the orbs." She growled. "Stealing the orbs is devastating enough, because they will be used without regard for balance. Without an understanding of the delicate strength of the elements." Ori stood quickly. "I need to talk to the townspeople."

A statement which propelled the King and Queen to their feet.

"Yes. Let me join you at the forecourt. I assume that is where you will be speaking," King Rodlamar Reytoris Breula said decisively, and Ori gently rested her hand on his shoulder.

"No, father. Let me do this. I'm organising the defence of the town, and as Leader of the Guard, it is my duty to deliver news of strategies that are best for the people and the realm." She gestured for them to follow her from the room, speaking quickly as they strode through the halls. "Wait inside the access door, and after I've finished speaking to everyone, I'll take you to the Guard's quarters. It's the most secure location in the realm. Breula's mansion is not. Not at the moment."

***

It worried her that it was only three hours until dusk, knowing it would impact on the townspeople's ability to utilise their elements. Ori flicked a glance at the faint purple blush dusting the western sky, then clenched her teeth in determination.

The crowd, in its hundreds, filled the mansion's vast forecourt, shifting nervously, murmurs of distress rising into the air. Ori nodded to twenty of the fifty Guard members and pointed to the three roads and bridges that led to the mansion. Hopefully they could hold off any further scouts until after she'd delivered her message.

She beckoned to a townsperson near the steps.

"Nusaed Taah, would you call on your element, please? I need your assistance."

The young woman, her eyes wide, nodded, and circled her fingers above her palm. Then she slowly moved her hand away from her body as if showing off an attraction to a new citizen in Breula. A memory of Sev joking that she was on a tour stabbed at Ori's heart.

"Breulans!" Her words travelled along Nusaed Taah's enhanced current even to those at the far bridge.

"The Guard from Bianuwruh has entered Breula, and as you no doubt know, they are intent on injuring, perhaps killing, the people of our realm."

Gasps, and shouts rose from the crowd, and Ori lifted her hands in supplication.

"I tell you this because I need you to call upon your element to restore the balance in the remaining light of the day. It will be dangerous as we are dealing with a new type of weapon. An arrow without a point which is faster and more sturdy than the arrows of the Guard. Their bows are flat and powerful."

A ripple of concern washed through the gathering, so Ori quickly delivered the remainder of her plea.

"Please! Those with Metal, Water, and Fauna elements! Work together as small groups of three. You are the medical teams. Extract the metal, staunch the blood, and seal the wounds, because saving the lives of every Guard member *no matter their realm* will rebalance Breula."

There was not a single note of dissension at the emphasised words, and Ori felt her heart fill with love for these people.

"Those with the remaining elements are just as vit—."

Movement from the side door paused her instructions. Her parents were engaged in a conversation with four Councillors; two of them Councillors Buwrec Robrong Breula and Dasoskach Vaern Breula, and while the interaction looked amicable, a warning tingle fizzed under Ori's skin. Then her father glanced over, nodded once, and indicated that the group would be reentering the mansion. She let out a breath. If her father, and, more to the point her mother— given her intolerance of the Councillors—felt safer inside with the four than standing out in the open with Ori, then that was fine. She would reunite with them after her address.

"Use your element to defend, not to maim or deprive anyone of existence. To do so will unbalance us even further. We have three hours of sunlight. Create large globes that temporarily blind the Bianuwruh Guard. Turn the roads into rivers." She pointed to an Ice Arcanix. "Combine with the Water element to make the roads difficult to traverse. We need shadows in alleys, we need roots and leaves, we need currents that redirect arrows, we need Earth to rise, we must diffuse fires."

Ori swallowed her emotion, and collected her fingers in her palms.

"Breula needs you."

There was a moment of silence, then those holding the Light element fashioned small globes in their palms and raised them high. Ori felt tears prick at her eyes. Her element. The townspeople didn't need to yell a battle cry. Their elemental love was stronger than any combination of voices.

"May I thank the air, Orilaevar Reysonadol Breula?" Nusaed Taah asked. Ori brought her gaze to the Arcanix, and delivered a warm smile.

"Yes, of course. Thank you, Nusaed Taah. I appreciate your assistance."

She smiled, whispered her gratitude, then looked out over the crowd. And gasped.

"It is the Guardian!"

Ori's head snapped up. In the distance, where the main road began its rise to the mansion, strode a figure in black, an aura of light about their body. The figure was accompanied by another, although when the figure in black gestured, the companion broke away and disappeared down a nearby alley.

Ori knew it was Sev. She knew that walk. That bearing. That… everything. It was Sev.

Her desire to rush to the woman—the glowing woman— competed with her need to disperse the enormous crowd of Breulans so that they could call upon their elements in their section of the town.

Dedication to her realm won.

This time, her voice rang out with little need for Nusaed Taah's help.

"Please hurry. We are in danger, so working together is our only hope."

There were no yells of vengeance, no shouts of retribution. Just a calm determination from people quickly withdrawing and flowing down the roads and bridges. No doubt some would come across Sev, and stop dead in their tracks. A woman wearing the sun tended to have that effect on a person.

Ori sprinted down the steps as the last townspeople exited the forecourt and the members of the Guard, rejoined by the twenty deployed earlier, took up stations at the wall.

Then she pulled up short. Sev appeared at the edge of the smooth surface of the forecourt, dressed in fitted black trousers, some sort of black knitted long-sleeved garment, and black laced boots. She was breathtaking.

They stepped forward at the same time.

"Hi," Ori said gently.

Sev's glow shimmered, then disappeared. "Hi, yourself." Her lips ticked up at the sides as if holding a grin at bay.

Ori circled her finger at Sev's torso. "Quite the entrance," she commented dryly, smothering her own grin. Oh, she'd missed this flirting. Ori was almost tempted to delay the inevitable kiss to let the conversation play out.

"I have to show off a bit being the Guardian and all," Sev said, deadpan.

And with that, Ori took the last step and bundled Sev into her arms, holding the back of her head, murmuring the words she'd needed to say since she'd seen Sev striding into Breula.

"I missed you so much. You have no idea."

"Actually, I have a pretty good idea."

"It's been days."

Sev pulled away. "Yeah. Not so much. I'll fill you in later. Meanwhile...oh."

Holding the sides of Sev's head, Ori kissed her with such passion that she was positive she'd suddenly been gifted the element of Heat.

She pulled back, and rested her forehead against Sev's, her thumbs sliding across Sev's cheekbones.

The faint hum of pleasure drifted into Ori's ears.

"I've missed your lips specifically. Maybe other parts," Sev murmured, and Ori laughed, drawing away to smile into Sev's beautiful eyes.

"I wanted to kiss you before we—"

"Put some cranky Bianuwruh dudes with crossbows, who are behaving like toddlers, in the naughty corner?"

Ori blinked. Some of that, no, all of that sentence was incomprehensible. And she adored the discombobulation.

"I don't have a clue what you just said, but I agree that cranky... dudes." The word felt strange in her mouth. "Is rather apt." Then a thought occurred to her. "Who was your companion?"

Sev stepped back, and held Ori's hands. "Alex."

Ori's eyes widened. "Your Alex?"

"Yes. Turns out he's Breulan."

Ori nodded. Now this was something she did know. Sev gave her a puzzled look, then continued.

"I directed him to Askal and Jino's house. They've got a lot to catch up on." Sev pointed. "Something else to add to the filling-in-Ori situation."

Ori wrinkled her forehead. It was almost too much to take in. Then she indicated to the low wall, and Sev turned. The noise, the turbulence in the air, rose over them; the whoosh of enhanced air currents, rushing water, yells of Bianuwruh Guard members sliding on roads of ice down to the boundaries of the township.

"Sounds like Breula doesn't need my help," Sev said, staring down into the township, and Ori tightened her grip on Sev's hand, not wanting to ever let Sev leave again.

Then she saw it. The arrow, aimed at their chests, streaking through the air, metal fins glinting, But before she could react, before she could shove Sev to the side and let the projectile strike herself instead, Sev's shout, filled with fear, anger, and outrage, reverberated around the forecourt.

"No!"

Sev flung her arm across Ori's chest, and splayed her fingers at the arrow now only centimetres from her palm. As if struck by an invisible force, the shaft shivered, and the arrow clattered to the ground.

The gasps from the fifty Guard members was louder than the elemental energy rising from below.

"You…?" Ori stuttered, mouth agape.

Sev was staring at her hand, then looked up.

"Huh. Apparently, I can cast my element." She nodded slowly. "Good to know."

Realising that other arrows could be following the one immobilised on the ground, Ori fell to her knees, pulling Sev down beside her.

"You can manipulate Metal from afar?"

"Got the memo just then." Sev said, her eyes wide with shock. Then she grimaced. "Horrible way to find out. Are you okay?" Ori leaned into the caress that Sev ran across her cheek.

"I'm fine. Thank you for doing that. It's…you're remarkable." Then, with little regard for any potential danger, and because she desperately needed to say it, Ori cradled Sev's chin, and kissed her softly

"I love you," she murmured, then kissed Sev again, peppering her lips, her cheeks, her nose, her forehead with soft kisses that carried the words every time they landed on Sev's skin. Eventually, she moved back so she could take in Sev's reaction.

Ori fell into a smile that reignited the glow that had encompassed Sev's body on her journey into Breula.

"Oh," Sev said, almost a sigh, and reigned in her Light, so it sat, woven into the fabric, at Sev's chest. Ori held her breath. It would be devastating if her love drifted away without finding its home, not that she expected Sev to echo the words simply to balance the conversation. But, how she wanted those words to—

"I love you, too." Sev looked almost shy; an expression which lasted for the smallest moment before confidence took over.

Ori blinked, then huffed out the air from her body through a smile that grew until it matched Sev's.

Sev touched her fingertip against Ori's sternum, snaking it down the leather ties, all the while holding Ori's gaze. "You're glowing."

Ori hummed with happiness. "Between you and me, we've been creating a giant target, but…"

Ori lips were pressed hard, her hair clutched between fingers, her body held firmly, flush against Sev's. Their knees balanced them against the ground.

"We should reduce our Light," Ori mumbled, mindful that they were kissing passionately which was most likely distracting her Guard when distraction was not ideal.

"Great idea," Sev murmured in reply.

Ori sat back on her heels. "I need to find my parents. They returned to the mansion with Councillors Buwrec Robrong Breula and Dasoskach Vaern Breula and I'm not comfortable with that development."

"I wouldn't be, either. Those two, particularly Councillor Buwrec Robrong Breula, may have decided to overthrow the government," she tipped her chin at the mansion, "and send your parents God knows where."

Ori blinked, horrified.

"Then they must have opened the portal for the Bianuwruh Guard. We know from the trespassers of that realm that the Bianuwruh leadership desire to utilise the orbs' energy in vast, unchecked quantities. Bu they've never indicated that an invasion was a likely plan." She stared at Sev. "Perhaps the Councillors want the leadership for themselves, and this invasion is a decoy?"

"I reckon you're right."

Ori shook her head. She had to leave.

Sev nodded as if Ori had spoken. "Go. Go find your parents."

Ori flicked her gaze at the ground, the arrow, then back to Sev's brown and amber eyes. "You need to go as well. Do Guardian things."

"Guardian things…" Sev said, raising her eyebrows.

Ori nodded, and hauled Sev upright. "Guardian things. I don't know what you can do, Sev. How vast your elemental energy is. But the realm needs you, and the prophecy says that you will protect Breula."

Sev stared into Ori's eyes, and Ori felt like she was seeing into Sev's soul. She wanted to cherish that soul forever.

"Then that's what I'll do." The determination in Sev's voice was inspiring and wonderful, and despite a desperate desire to protect her from everything, which was irrational as Sev had more elemental energy than anyone in the realm, Ori knew that Sev would go forth and be amazing.

Ori kissed her again. Quickly. Her lips sharing those three words that had now found their home. Then, she held Sev's shoulders.

"Be safe. I'm rather fond of you."

Sev quirked a smile. "I'm rather fond of you, too."

Then they stepped back, and Sev flicked her finger at the mansion.

"You go find your parents, and those two Councillor shits." Ori watched Sev's face harden. "This is my realm now, so I'm off to avenge this travesty." With a nod, she mouthed "I love you", and spun away.

Ori was instantly alarmed by Sev's potential conflict with the balance.

"No! No avenging!" Ori called, and watched as her lover raced to the other end of the forecourt, seemingly intent on launching herself at any and all comers.

"And we're avenging," she sighed in resignation, then sprinted to the access door.

***

Figuring that shouting for her parents throughout the mansion wasn't a particularly good plan, Ori moved along the corridors in a quick, light jog, listening at closed doors. Every Elemental and Arcanix seemed to have found sanctuary somewhere else as the mansion was completely empty. It was quite eerie. Disturbing. Foreboding, as if the building was holding its breath, darting its wide eyes about, its walls tense, and ready to flee.

There were only a few corridors left to investigate; those that housed the Council antechambers. Ori's hopes of finding her parents were dropping, which produced a terrifying combination of rage and fear. Her mouth dried.

She pressed her ear to a closed door at the beginning of the corridor. Empty. Both in sound and presence, because even through the beautifully carved wood, she could sense a lack of elemental energy vibrating inside.

It was the second last door that caused her to jerk, blink, centre her breathing, then slowly rest her ear against the flat surface.

The voices were not friendly, more polite if anything; the forced politeness of people circling each other while trapped in a whirlpool of wariness.

Hardly surprising given the situation outside the mansion with invading Bianuwruh battling against her Guard, and a glowing Guardian, although none of the people inside knew about Sev.

Ori decided that the room only held four people, because she recognised her mother's voice, her father's. Then, nearer the door, Councillors Buwrec Robrong Breula and Dasoskach Vaern Breula, whose words were more discernible.

"Orilaevar Reysandoral Breula has suggested that we escort you out of the township towards the northern forests," Councillor Dasoskach Vaern Breula, her high pitched voice rolling from high to low on the final word, as if talking to children.

Ori coiled, ready to crash through the doors.

"Why would she say that?" her mother asked.

Pausing, Ori allowed the answer to decide her next step.

"The Bianuwruh Guard came from the west. It is wise to head north to keep you safe."

"It does sound sensible," her father said, and Ori breathed softly through her nose. That was not a sentence of agreement. It was a sentence of appeasement.

Her father continued. "As your King, you know that I value your thoughts about various matters that affect the realm. It interests me how you know the motivations of the Bianuwruh."

Ori almost nodded against the door. It interested her as well.

"Our thoughts are merely conjecture, King Rodlamar Reytoris Breula," Councillor Dasoskach Vaern Breula said lightly.

"But you seemed so definite about their interest in the orbs. Why do they want the orbs if they have no interest in the orb's energy?" Her mother's voice was sweet and deadly.

"Well." Ori could visualise Councillor Dasoskach Vaern Breula's dismissive wave that probably accompanied the word. The woman had used it in many Council meetings. "They might use the orbs to power technology. Advancements that—"

Councillor Buwrec Robrong Breula interjected. "King Rodlamar Reytoris Breula, imagine if we controlled the supply of the orbs. We could control the technological advancements from any realm around us."

Ori heard the vehemence in his voice.

"I do not think that control is wise. It will create an imb—"

"But it will not! We would be wealthy in resources we could only dream of. Increase our own technology."

This time, she visualised Councillor Buwrec Robrong Breula pointing. He was well-known for that particular gesture. She let the conversation play out, because it wasn't time for her presence.

Councillor Dasoskach Vaern Breula's voice carried more clearly through the door. "Breula would advance more quickly. The orbs are ready to be traded for knowledge. Breula would become a better, more progressive society."

That sentence was a break-the-doors-in-two type of sentence. Breula was already a wonderful society. How dare she? *It's time to join this lovely chat.* Ori smiled thinly. That thought was dripping with Sev's sarcasm.

Without making a sound, Ori slowly cracked open the door and eased through the gap. Her father, with years of experience at keeping a closed expression even when events prompted involuntary gasps, such as his daughter stealthily entering a room and unsheathing her small dagger, took a small step towards the Councillors. The movement held their attention.

"You are placing new ideas in my mind. Breula could be the richest realm, particularly if we convinced the other realms of the orb's rarity," he said earnestly.

Clearly, Queen Sermeh Reytoris Breula hadn't seen Ori, because her appalled reaction to her husband's conjecture was entirely expected.

"Rodlamar! You are not considering this notion!"

Ori understood the emotion completely, as she stepped closer to the Councillors, catching the intense gaze her father aimed at his wife.

"It bears thinking on, Queen Sermeh Reytoris Breula. Even Orilaevar, *our dearest daughter,* would agree with their proposal." He gestured at Councillors Buwrec Robrong Breula and Dasoskach Vaern Breula.

That was Ori's cue. She slid behind Councillor Dasoskach Vaern Breula, and pressed the tip of the dagger to her neck. The Councillor gave a high pitched squeal.

"No, Orilaevar would not agree with your proposal," Ori said, her voice flat, yet filled with rage. Catching movement from the other Councillor, she wriggled the point of the blade, eliciting another alarmed gasp.

"Despite the imbalance I would cause, I'm not worried about incapacitating both of you," she said, menacingly.

Then, with the same speed and skill she'd used when disarming the scout, Ori whipped around the woman, sheathed her dagger, and drew her sword. It would have looked like one motion.

"Don't move!" she growled, touching the tip of her sword to the threads on Councillor Buwrec Robrong Breula's elaborate vest. He swallowed heavily.

Then, without taking her eyes off the Councillors, Ori spoke over her shoulder. "Are you both fine?"

"Yes. We have had an enlightening conversation. Apparently, Councillors Buwrec Robrong Breula and Dasoskach Vaern Breula are interested in becoming leaders of Breula, trading our orbs for knowledge, and increasing our technology at an alarming rate." Her father's sneer dripped into the flooring.

"I gained the distinct impression that we were to be escorted through a portal," her mother added. "The Bianuwruh portal, perhaps."

Councillor Buwrec Robrong Breula narrowed his eyes.

"Your Guard will not succeed," he hissed. "Those weapons." He tipped his chin at the bow, arrows, and dagger which Ori had left in the room. "Will triumph."

"Yes, they are stronger, and more powerful. I've had first hand experience. However, we have our elemental energy."

"It is nightfall, Orilaevar Reysandoral Breula," Councillor Dasoskach Vaern Breula laughed. "The Guard and the Elementals alone cannot win against so many Bianuwruh."

Despite Ori's sword hovering dangerously, the Councillor smirked.

Which wasn't a good choice as the glow about Ori's blade grew in direct correlation with her anger.

"You have little clue of the events unfolding outside this mansion. The townspeople have provided a defensive base for the Guard to work with. The Orb Lagoon is safe." Ori bluffed, hoping—knowing —that Privana's coordination, and defensive skills were up to the challenge, even if his emotional intelligence left a lot to be desired. The two Councillors seemed to sag at the statement. "The Elementals who believe in Breula, who love Breula, will assist as best they can." She paused, completely unnecessarily but if she was going to wave a sword about while listing defensive successes, then pausing dramatically was allowed. "And the Guardian has returned."

It was a wonder that any oxygen was left in the room. The four gasps ranged in pitch, but all contained a similar volume of disbelief.

"Sevich is here?" The question, asked simultaneously by both the King and Queen, almost caused Ori to turn around just so she could nod enthusiastically and beam with joy.

"Yes." She needed to get things moving. "I'd like to secure these two. Father, would you choose some metal from which to request its assistance?" Ori didn't enjoy pitting one element against another, but this moment called for rule-breaking. She figured that her father's Metal energy would successfully bind Earth and Dark.

Her father appeared beside her.

"I have the Bianuwruh dagger, however I require a much more substantial piece of metal to create the ribbons that will complete the task."

Ori blinked.

"Would you hold your dagger in your weapon hand, and your sword in the other, please?"

The light of understanding flicked on. *Really? Another one?* She swapped the weapons over, then her father smacked the Bianuwruh dagger against her sword, and murmured gratefully to the metal to bind the two Councillors together. Strings of steel flowed from the ever decreasing blade, and wrapped about the Councillor's torsos.

Ori sighed. At this rate, she'd need a a secret stash of swords in her closet if people were going to continue liquifying her weapons.

With both Councillors detained, Ori escorted her parents from the room, and they made their way towards the front entrance. A Guard member, busily checking each corridor, was redirected to the small Council antechamber to take the two Councillors to a more secure location.

"Please stay just inside the door," Ori pleaded as they stood together at the small entrance. "I'll be back when I know what's happening with the Guard and with...and with Sev."

Her mother's eyes twinkled. Even though there was a battle going on, her mother was not averse to—

"Sevich has returned," the Queen said, nodding slowly. "Excellent. Finally my daughter has found a woman to wife up."

Uh huh.

Ori might be Leader of the Guard, and dealing with an invasion, but her mother was able to sneak a tease into any situation.

"Really not the time, Mother," Ori ground out, and stalked through the doorway.

***

Not a smudge of pink and white remained in the sky. The purple reigned, and dots of light were winking out across the township.

Ori's heart sank. The townspeople's energy was depleting, but they couldn't retire to their homes to restore it. It was too dangerous.

Annoyingly, the two Councillors had actually made sense when they'd suggested the northern forests as a temporary safe haven. The Bianuwruh had arrived from the west, so moving north seemed logical.

However, seeing their way to the northern forests would challenge the townspeople. None of them, even if they held that element, would be able to create Light.

She stepped further onto the far edge of the wide portico, glanced to her right, and paused at the sight of the enormous front doors stripped of at least half their metal panels. Then looked across the forecourt, barely visible, at the members of her Guard defending the forecourt and mansion. Each member was tucked behind a shield. A shield which looked remarkably like one of the metal panels from the massive front doors.

Sev.

Ori had no idea how Sev had ripped off fifty panels from the doors but that was neither here nor there. Her Guard were protected against a projectile that would kill instantly, even when her archers were not shooting to kill in return. She knew that they would understand the imbalance, and would use their astonishing accuracy to send three arrows into the front of the flat bow, intent on puncturing the wood, disrupting the draw so that the Bianuwruh Guard member had to stop to extract each arrow.

Acknowledging that their training and their dedication were working beautifully, Ori focused on her goal: the bridge at the far side of the forecourt.

Ori crouched, running over to the large span across the Juith river tributary. Dozens of Arcanix, their arms bent over their heads in fear, huddled in the centre.

"Who here carries the element of Light?" She pointed to several who raised their hands. "I need you to guide the townspeople to the northern forests."

Joskado Yol spoke up. Ori recognised her because of her enthusiasm for the lanterns at the festival each year.

"Orilaevar Reysandoral Breula! Our energy has depleted. We have no light to guide anyone," she said frantically.

Even though the noise from Elementals manipulating their element, the noise of arrows streaking the air, the noise of injured people shouting with anger and anxiety filled the air about them, Ori paused, and regarded Joskado Yol.

"Yes, you do have energy."

She reached behind her neck, unclasped the band that held her orb, and cradled it in her palms.

"You do have energy," she repeated, pushing the necklace forward.

Joskado Yol, fingers trembling, carefully took the orb, and looped it around her neck. She gazed at Ori, her eyes filling with tears.

"But I am a trespasser, Orilaevar Reysandoral Breula."

"No, Joskado Yol." She held the young woman's forearm. "You're a Light Arcanix, a townsperson I know well. You are a Breulan, and right now, you are an Elemental."

Then, she lifted her gaze. "There are approximately fifteen Light Elemental Guard members on the forecourt. It is dangerous to go up there, but if you are willing, I would like to ensure that you have enough light to help guide people to reach the forest."

With another nod at Joskado Yol, whose palm now held a globe of light, gathered from the flaming torch secured in a hole on top of the bridge wall, Ori beckoned to the group.

"Stay close to me!"

Hoping that the small group would keep up, she raced towards the first Guard member who bore Light energy. She knew each Guard member's element, but even in the impossible event that she'd forgotten, it would have been obvious from the arrows.

The Guard members, all utilising their Guardian-created shields, were skilfully firing three arrows each draw, their fingers weaving through the strong, thin wood. The arrows shimmered with the energy of each member's element; dark arrows invisible in the night, arrows tipped with heat, or ice, or rock, or sap from the ivy that grew on the wall in front of the shields. All aimed at the front of the crossbows.

It was the element of Light which was irrelevant. A glowing arrow was hardly stealthy, or subtle. It was a beacon advertising the Guard member's location. All Guard members were well-practised in archery, so the Light Elementals called on that skill alone.

Ori stopped behind each Light Elemental Guard member, who paused their defence, and listened carefully to Ori's request. She did not command. Giving an orb to another was a serious, and symbolic decision for its wearer, and it was not her place to demand compliance. When each of the fifteen Light Elemental Guard members removed their neck bands, nodded to the townsperson beside Ori, and quietly delivered their orbs. Ori couldn't hold back the tears that burned in her eyes. Tears of pride. Of love for her people.

Swallowing hard, and with a hasty, "Take care," to the new Light bearers, Ori ran past the line of archers, ducking out of the way as each arm drew back, the elbow cocked. She reached the final Guard member. The thick smoke, rising as her Guard used litres of water requested from the river to douse the fires set by the Bianuwruh Guard, forced a series of hacking coughs from Ori's throat.

She shouted a one word question at the Guard member's non-draw side.

"Shields?"

And received a one word answer. "Guardian."

Of course.

Ori squinted through the shifting, swirling air, the dark attempting to smother the sporadic light from the moons.

There.

Near the small entrance to the mansion, a figure squatted on her heels, fingertips touching the ground as if they were the only things supporting her body, and stopping her falling forward.

Ori, with a quick glance at the main road where it spilled onto the forecourt, and judging her run to be fifty paces of open space, took off towards the crouched figure.

She skidded to her knees, caring little for any damage to her pants, and held Sev's face.

"Are you okay? What's happened?"

CHAPTER NINETEEN

Sev hoped that sending Ori into the mansion to find her parents, then announcing that she was avenging, then running assertively across the forecourt, looked and sounded commanding, like she knew what she was doing, like she knew where to be. Neither of which she did. Not at all.

Sev had no idea how to be the Guardian. Yes, she could stop arrows dead in their flight. That was a fortunate and necessary talent. And she could manipulate the other elements by hand, but not from a distance which would have been nice.

How to combine those multi-faceted elements was her dilemma. What good was a Guardian who stood there, announcing how Guardian-y they were, all glowing and what-not, if that was the extent of the performance?

Sev paused behind the brave Guard member at the end of the line of the other brave Guard members defending the mansion with its beautiful hammered metal doors. No matter how incredibly accurate the members were, they looked far too vulnerable, with just their bows and arrows, against the bullet-like ferocity of a bolt from a crossbow. It wasn't much, but she decided to spend a minute or two behind each archer, thrusting her hand past their chest, and deflecting the battery of projectiles aimed at them. Then move onto the next in line.

She felt incredibly impotent.

"Sevich!"

Sev whipped her head around at the cry to find Privana sprinting towards her, skidding to a stop behind the archer.

"Privana. Long time, no see." She rolled her eyes at him, then started to turn away.

"I must speak to Orilaevar. The Orb Lagoon has been contained. Do you know where she is?"

Orb Lagoon? It sounded like something you'd find at a tropical resort. Sev had a feeling she knew what the Orb Lagoon was, but needed her theory confirmed. She called on the poker face that Alex said she didn't possess.

"Orb Lagoon. Good to know. How did you…contain it?"

Privana cocked his head. "I was able to manipulate the element of Ice in combination with the other Ice Elemental Guard members to create an impenetrable layer on the surface of the lagoon. We captured quite a few Bianuwruh Guard members, and placed them in the arena. We did drive away more, but I will return when I have assisted here, and I have delivered my news to Orilaevar."

The formality.

"I can do that, if you want to head back…" Sev faded off. Where? Head back north? South? She had no idea where the Orb Lagoon was located.

"No. I must give my report." He frowned aggressively.

"Okay! Gees." Frowny McFrowny was back.

"Also," Privana lifted his chin, "I had heard of the Guardian's arrival in Breula."

Sev folded her arms. "I'm a novelty, am I?"

"No, you are…" Folding his arms in reply, Privana straightened his shoulders. "I am sorry for doubting your worth."

Sev cocked her head. "So." She drew out the word. "Now that you know I'm the Guardian, I'm worthy, but before you knew that, I was unworthy."

Privana growled. "No!" He undid his arms, and stretched his fingers taught in frustration. "I am apologising for my rudeness!"

Sev rocked back on her heels. "That's a backhanded apology, but better than nothing. We'll sit down with a beer later and catch up. Meanwhile, I'm still working on—"

"Look out!"

The shout came from the end of the line. Privana and Sev spun around to take in the frightening sight of a Bianuwruh Guard member crouching on the far bridge, and nocking a bolt into the channel running down the centre of his bow. The Breulan Guard member curled their body around to attend to the rogue archer.

Who had loosed his arrow.

Straight at Privana.

Sev yelled. "No. He apologised!"

With a speed that surprised herself, Sev flicked her hand back, then forward as if pitching for the winning team in an international softball tournament.

The pressed metal rectangle, one of the many panels attached to the doors that towered over the forecourt, shivered, then wrenched itself from its wooden frame. It whipped through the air, deflecting the arrow as it travelled across the endless expanse of marble, then crashed into the archer, tumbling away to reveal their body flattened on the ground.

Sev gasped—apparently she could fling metal about—then not heeding Privana's warning, raced over to the prone man.

He wasn't moving.

"Oh, shit. I've killed him." Sev wrung her hands. "That's going to unbalance—Christ, I've killed him!"

She pressed her fingers to her lips, held her breath, then exhaled with a whoosh as the man groaned in pain.

Sev pressed her stomach. "Oh! Yes. I didn't kill him!" She turned around to Privana. "I didn't kill—" Her mouth gaped.

Privana had drawn his bow, hand steady, and Sev's lungs constricted. Then he sent the arrow on its way. It whistled past Sev's ear, and a scream of pain filled the air behind her. Spinning around, she was confronted with the sight of the Bianuwruh Guard member with his hand impaled against the wall by the arrow, a small dagger falling from his grip.

Sev turned back to Privana, who relaxed his hold on the bow so that it hung lightly from his fingers.

"I also did not kill him."

Sev blinked, then shook her head. "You...this."

Her attempt at a complete sentence was disrupted when a mounted Guard member, horse breathing heavily, halted in the middle of the forecourt.

Participating in a battle generally meant that you could flout all rules, because Sev knew that horses weren't really appreciated right outside the mansion. Particularly on the marble. It was like wearing shoes, and walking on Grandma Maude's good rug in the front sitting room.

They ran to meet the mounted Guard member.

"Deputy Leader Privana Trissandoral Breula, I have information —"

The Guard member slid her gaze from Privana to Sev, then back to Privana who pointed to Sev, and nodded. It was as if Privana was directing the Guard member to report to Sev.

"Sevich Guardian, I…"

Sev blinked. Privana *had* redirected the report. *Wow.* She tuned in.

"I have information that two hundred Bianuwruh Guard members are making a final assault on the mansion to capture the King and Queen." She paused, then narrowed her eyes. "And Orilaevar Reysandoral Breula." Sev knew, without a shadow of a doubt, that this woman, and the entire Guard, would lay down their lives for Ori. It was breathtaking.

"They desire to capture the family with the help of two Council members, then send them through a portal so that they cannot return. They talk of many Council members receiving the same fate. Once all obstacles are removed, the Bianuwruh will access the Orb Lagoon!"

She sagged in the saddle, shoulders slumped under the weight of her devastating news.

Sev's brain absorbed key words. Two hundred. Capture Ori's parents. Capture Ori. Portal.

She grit her teeth.

"Nope. Not happening. Not while I'm doing Guardian things." She pointed up at the Guard member. "You get back to the Orb Lagoon. Grab some more Ice Elementals as you go. Maybe some Elementals on horses. They're handy. I'll look after the imminent shitstorm featuring two hundred very focused Bianuwruh."

The Guard member nodded seriously, as if she understood the command, which she probably didn't, but most of it was comprehensible. Then pushed her horse into a gallop, and disappeared across the far road that ran at an angle to the mansion.

"May I assist with your...Guardian things?" Privana said, his eyebrows raised.

Sev scowled at him. "If you're being helpful because you want Ori to know how nice you are, I will turf you over that." As if to indicate the location, she waved her hand at the forecourt front wall a hundred metres away.

"I am not being disingenuous, Sevich."

After another long look, Sev nodded. "Right. Well, catch this." She pointed her hand, palm up, at another metal panel attached to the door, next to the space that had been occupied by the one responsible for the Bianuwruh archer's concussion. Neatness counted when wrenching her element off exteriors.

"This is yours, Privana. Heads up." She yanked her hand back, rolling her fingers into her palm, and the panel burst forth, and flew towards Privana's chest. His eyes were huge and his wrists locked to soften the impact of catching a person-sized sheet of metal.

He looked sideways. "I have great admiration for you."

"Terrific." She tipped her head at the line of archers. "We'll do them in groups of five, okay?"

Clutching his shield, which Sev curved as they ran, they stopped short of the archers' elbows. Distantly, Sev wondered about the continuous, almost unlimited, supply of arrows. A quick glance, something she'd missed in her arrow deflecting, revealed the Metal, and Flora Elemental Guard members standing side by side, bending every so often to create metal-tipped wooden arrows from large blocks of wood, and lumps of metal. Small tools lay beside the material.

Resourceful, and clever.

"Privana."

Orilaevar's Deputy squared his shoulders, and he nodded once, knowing exactly what Sev required. As Ori had explained to Sev months ago, the Guard had been trained for the potential of actual combat. And here was actual combat, and here they were, realising that potential with a bit of help from giant metal serving trays.

"Guard members! Turn to me five at a time. Now!" Privana yelled over the noise.

The first five spun, and crouched in a fluid motion, then stared up at Sev, who gestured with both hands at the mansion doors.

"I'm sending you a shield! It'll be moving like an out of control tr —" she blinked. "It'll be moving at a rapid rate, so I need you to catch it like this." She pointed to Privana who held his away from his body like he was demonstrating a product on the shopping channel.

Then repeating her pitching gesture, she yanked off five panels in quick succession, curving them as each Guard member held the edges. Then clutching their new piece of armour as if they'd wielded one since birth, the members spun back to the wall, and settled the shield, removing their hands when they realised it could stand independently.

"The bolts will still penetrate," Privana observed.

"You're right. Okay." Sev reached under the arm of the archer, held her hand to the metal, and felt the sheet thicken. "That should do it."

As darkness descended, they moved to the next five, and repeated the process, then the next, until all fifty Guard members crouched behind a wall of reinforced metal.

Sev inhaled, and shook out her hands as if she were attempting to scale the intermediate wall at the South Melbourne Indoor Rock Climbing Centre. Another Guardian thing done. Now what?

"Hey, Privana. Didn't you need to report to Ori? She's in the mansion. I think."

There. That was helpful. A Guardian-like instruction.

Then she looked askance at the night sky. Half of Breula was now powerless, and so two hundred Bianuwruh Guard members were going to just stroll onto the forecourt, and plant a flag. Or whatever invading realms did.

Sev didn't even notice Privana leave, and a sudden exhaustion smacked at her muscles. She dropped onto her heels, and crouched over her fingertips, pressing them into the ground, as if to brace her body in the hope of avoiding potential concussion from the marble.

All of sudden, Ori was right there, holding her face.

"Are you okay? What's happened?"

Sev lifted her head and focused on those beautiful blue eyes.

"Hey! Hi. Did you find your mum and dad?" Her body swayed slightly, rolling on the heels of her boots, like she'd had a few too many drinks at the local pub. Ori gently smoothed her hands over Sev's shoulders, kissing her forehead, her nose, her mouth, each cheek, as if to check that Sev was solid.

"I did. What happened here?" Ori took a hand away to wave it vaguely in the direction of the line of Guard members.

"Shields." Sev smiled at Ori's bewildered expression, then tipped her head towards the mansion. "Sorry about your doors." With what little energy she had left, Sev grinned as Ori's eyebrows disappeared into her hairline.

"Well, I'm grateful that the Guard members are protected against those arrows."

"Me too." Sev swallowed. "Ori, I don't know what to do. I mean, I made shields from the door panels and chucked one at a Bianuwruh Guard member, although Privana shot him when the guy tried to stab me."

"Privana is here?"

"Yeah. He wanted to deliver a message." Sev swayed again. Utter exhaustion felt a lot like tequila.

"Why isn't Privana at the Orb Lagoon?"

"He reckons that the lagoon—" Sev pointed. "Let's go visit that place after all this is finished."

Ori nodded, eyes wide, and Sev continued. "He said that he and the Breulan Guard members drove off a bunch of Bianuwruh Guard members, but captured a few of them, and shoved them into the arena."

She leaned away, and glared. "*That's* what you use an arena for, by the way."

Ori rolled her lips in, and Sev stared at that beautiful face, until another wave of tiredness hit her, and she tipped onto her knees, leaning into Ori's chest.

"I can feel the elements inside me, but I'm hampered by the darkness. They feel thin. My Metal element as well." Sev sighed into the leather jerkin. "What good is a Guardian who can only save people for twelve hours?"

Ori's hands caressed the back of Sev's head. Over the noise of crossbow bolts thudding into reinforced metal, and the deadly hiss of the fletching on Breulan arrows, Ori's heartbeat settled her soul, arranged her thoughts.

"What good is a Guardian?" Ori murmured. "You possess more love for this realm than any citizen. You are magnificent, and worthy, and smart, and resourceful, and my mouse."

Sev smiled, then lifted her head, tugging on Ori's hands so that she could hold them to her chest.

"You're good for a Guardian's ego." Then she stared at the base of Ori's throat, and gasped. "Where's your orb?" She flicked her gaze back.

"I gave it to Joskado Yol so she could lead a group of townspeople to the northern forest." Ori wrinkled her forehead. "They needed to see their way to safety."

"You gave your orb away." Sev's gape lifted into a smile of wonder. "You gave…you are incredible."

Ori shrugged, self-deprecation lifting her shoulders. "Light was needed elsewhere." She smiled. "It doesn't matter who bears the Light, because there is still the same amount. It has simply moved, because every element—

Sev jerked. "Every element is of equal value. Every element has its place." Cogs whirred in her brain, and an idea gathered steam.

"Yes." Ori smiled again. "That is the balance. Elements shift, rebalance, combine, exist on the same plane. Equally."

Suddenly energised, Sev disentangled her fingers. "That's genius," she breathed, gazing at Ori, who looked perplexed. It was hardly a stroke of genius to express what was a commonly known fact, but that wasn't the idea that Sev's brain cogs were massaging into being.

"The balance is genius?"

"Yes!" The zaps of electricity in her veins felt too large to crouch over, so she sprang up, hauling on Ori's hand so that they stood together. Sev held Ori's shoulders. "The elements combine, shift, move, all of that. It's the balance." She gently smacked the leather covering Ori's upper arms. "I'm the balance. I can combine, shift, and move. I need…" Sev stepped away, as her brain cogs chewed on their final thought, and spat out the first draft of a plan. It would have to do.

"How can I help?" Ori's hand fluttered at the hilt of her sword, and a wave of affection filled Sev's heart.

"Come with me. I think I know what to do now, and you gave me the idea." Sev held Ori's gaze, then huffed a smile. "Do you know how astonishing you are, you gorgeous, wonderful, genetically-blessed woman?" She stepped forward, grasped the sides of Ori's head, and kissed her soundly on the lips. "I love you."

Then she spun around and strode off towards the top of the main road, knowing but not knowing what to do. But mostly knowing.

She argued with her brain as she halted at the juncture of the road and the forecourt. Manipulating all ten elements at once wasn't supposed to happen. The prophecy didn't mention any extra elemental carry-on. But potential elemental carrying-on fizzed through her nerves.

But it was stuck.

Like unopened lemonade.

There was a pause in the arrow-exchanging, and sword-clanging as if the Guard on each side was daring the other to make the next move, and the stillness gave her brain cogs time to restart.

How to metaphorically unstopper the recyclable plastic bottle of potential. She would need an orb from each element, and wear them about her neck like grandmother's pearls.

She'd probably blow herself to smithereens.

"I need the energy of an orb but not the orb itself," she said to the darkened road. "I need an Elemental."

"You need us."

Sev squeaked, staggered back, and turned to take in nine Elementals, who huddled in a tight group behind her, their eyes darting about in apprehension.

Yet their mouths were set in straight lines.

"You need us," the solidly-built woman repeated, the white orb at her throat shining in the moonlight. "We are not Councillors, nor members of the Guard. We are simply Elementals, born into our position, with a love for Breula. It is our honour to bring you energy."

Sev blinked. Jino had said that Breula would protect the Guardian, and here was that protection. That love. Well, not love for her as such. Love for the realm, and that was good enough because didn't she represent the realm?

Tears pricked at her eyes. Her unopened lemonade was about to explode all over the forecourt.

"Okay, then," she said, nodding at the group, then continued nodding hoping the action would rattle her tiny idea into a snowball of a plan. A visual of the V-shaped flight formation that flocks of geese created, which bird-studying folk reckoned improved energy efficiency, shimmered into her mind.

Yes.

"Each of you. We're making a shape like an arrow. Hold the shoulder of the one in front. Then on my call..." Sev faded off. She'd be at the front with a nuclear bomb of energy coursing through her heart. She needed to know what to do with it before that happened.

"Sevich Guardian." The Ice Elemental spoke again. "You will need protection."

"Hmm. That just occurred to me as well." Sev looked about, taking in the Elementals in their tense V—good, taking in her distinct lack of protection—not good, then spotted the final panel gripping the mansion doors—really good.

She thrust out her arm, and aimed it at the metal rectangle.

"Everyone! Drop!" Ori's commanding tone cut through the air, and created all sorts of delicious dips, and swirls low in Sev's stomach. It seemed Ori could read Sev's thoughts, which would make for interesting multitasking later, but right then it had the desired effect of eliminating potential concussion as Sev chucked about more art deco.

With the duly strengthened metal panel in hand, Sev peered over the top of her new shield, then flicked a glance over each shoulder.

Still with no real idea of what she was doing, but hoping to have a quick chat with the elements as they landed in her heart, Sev asked quietly;

"Everyone ready?"

Murmurs of affirmation enveloped her, and she smiled grimly.

"Awesome. Hit me with it."

Somehow all nine Elementals understood the instruction, even though, for a moment, Sev worried that they'd take her literally.

Even still, it was like a lightning strike. No. It was like those fireworks that run along fuse lines during Chinese New Year.

The energy burst into her body, filling every crevice, and valley, and mountain of her soul.

"Ah. Jesus Christ!"

The elements, the energy, the colours were jostling, fighting for the exits. They had their passports, and they'd boarded their plane.

Sev grit her teeth.

She needed to…what? Her jaw ached.

Oh!

She needed to combine the elements, and direct their journey.

Straightening her arms, and resting the side of her hands, palms out, against her legs, Sev closed her eyes.

Suddenly, a map of Breula blinked into life on the inside of her eyelids. Roads, and alleys, and houses, and people, and the arena. The arena!

Sev's eyes flew open, and she hummed in determination.

Okay, everyone. Let's go.

There was no pain, but her skin felt as if it was being peeled off her bones. Light shot out from her pores through the fabric of her clothes, and into the air. It would have been awesome to check out the whole effect, but apparently bending her neck to peer down at herself wasn't an option.

Then, as if a memo had been circulated, all the elements congregated in her hands, and with a final instruction from her heart, burst forth as a discordant rainbow, lighting the sky.

"Work together, you lot," she hissed.

With her brow furrowed in concentration, the Guardian reigned in the elements, and directed them, binding them into a river which coursed through the town, into the alleys, onto the roads, into the houses, and swept past the people. The Guardian floated on the river, swam in its colours, directed the ten elements, and watched as weapons were tossed to the side, or wrested from hands which covered eyes only to peek through gaps between fingers. The Guardian rode the waves of energy from afar, and close by. Onwards, and forth. Elsewhere, and known.

The Guardian knew when the Bianuwruh Guard were overwhelmed. The Air told her. The Light, and the Dark, and the Ice, and the Water spoke of tributaries of luminous shadows. Of driving the Guard to an arena now manipulated by Earth, and convinced of its altered purpose. Metal whispered of arrows, and fletching, and bows, and daggers contorted in surrender. The Guardian knew when the riderless horses in the fields and the wolves in the valleys shepherded the Bianuwruh Guard towards their assessment. Heat murmured of sliding behind the tributaries, and melting their duty. Finally, the Guardian, breathing in the love of her realm, lowered her eyelids, and studied the map, a small smile on her lips as the vines, thick and strong, sealed the arena's doors.

As quickly as they had burst forth, the elements, the colours, withdrew, vacuumed into the Guardian's body. There was silence, and the Elementals released each others shoulders, breathed deeply, and stepped back.

The smoke cleared, whisked away by Air as it returned to its home, and the twin moons shone on the lone figure at the top of the road.

Sev curled her fingers into her palms and brought her fists to her chest, holding her heart inside her skin. Every particle was shaking.

The speed of it all. She remembered her trial in the Council Chambers. The speed of it all. The speed.

She swayed.

Then arms, strong arms tight with love, enveloped her torso, and she leaned into "You're amazing," and "Thank you," and so much love.

"Ori," Sev croaked. Even her throat hurt.

"I'm here."

"How does a Guardian save an entire realm with five minutes and a rainbow?"

Ori's laughter, full of relief, and a realm of love, filled Sev's chest, and again she leaned back, basking in the sound.

"I don't know, my love, but it was utterly breathtaking." Ori turned Sev around, which brought on another bout of drunken swaying.

"Woah." Tequila exhaustion.

Sev fell into the kisses. The soft, light kisses that landed on her face, her lips, and her smile grew.

"Hey," she said, and Ori leaned away. "You've got a bunch of very pissed off, slightly stunned Bianuwrth in the arena. You might want to deal with that soon. I doubt you want them to stay in your realm."

She enjoyed Ori's long look. The love, the adoration. The disbelief. *What?*

"Your realm, Sev," Ori said, a half smile lifting her lips.

Sev hummed, then mirrored the smile. She brought her hands to Ori's cheeks, and nodded.

"My realm."

CHAPTER TWENTY

Sev assessed the situation. She was naked. A light sheet lay across her body. Her head rested upon a very luxurious pillow if softness was the criteria. And, when she rolled her head to the side, her gaze fell on an equally naked Ori stretched out beside her, head cradled in her palm, a tender smile playing on her lips.

A similar smile lifted Sev's.

"Hi," she said.

"Hi, yourself."

"I'm naked." Sev's eyebrow rose.

"So am I. I thought it only fair," Ori said, her serious expression ruined by a barely contained grin. She leaned down, and pressed her lips to Sev's.

Sev sighed, and sank into the kiss, relishing the taste of her lover. Then visions of the previous night crashed into her mind, and she pulled away, her thoughts jumbled.

"Sorry. I'm still processing," she whispered, bringing her hands up to her face, pressing her eyelids as if to scrub away the too much, and the too large.

Ori sifted her fingers through Sev's hair. "It's okay. Yesterday was extraordinary. You were extraordinary."

Sev pulled her hands away. "I feel like a fraud."

Ori paused, then rolled onto her stomach, and perched over her elbows.

"Why?" Her eyebrows were diagonal, aimed down her nose, and her forehead wrinkled.

Yes. Why?

"Because I chucked together some elements." Sev tossed off the sheet, pivoted, then got out of bed, and looked around for a robe. She pulled on a blue shirt that was draped over a chair, and turned to Ori. The sheet had drifted down, and her breasts were visible in the morning light currently peeking through the sheer drapes in Ori's bedroom. So distracting.

"Exactly," Ori said, clearly not understanding. "You...chucked together elements." The unfamiliar word produced a smile on their faces, then Sev sobered, and came to sit on the side of the bed.

"It's more than that. It's the speed."

Ori cocked her head.

Sev continued. "It's the speed in which I was able to fix everything. You know, rescue Breula from the *great danger.*" She tossed her fingers up to air quote the last two words.

"But that's a good thing?"

"No. Yes. I don't know." Sev glared at the ceiling, then brought her head down to meet Ori's quizzical gaze. "I did what I did last night so quickly. Yet the prophecy has been nurtured for hundreds of years. It feels wrong that I solved everything in five minutes with a giant rainbow. There's no balance."

Ori hummed. "I can't imagine how you must feel, Sev. All I know is that you, the Guardian, were courageous, and clever, and thoughtful, and you saved the realm from an invading Guard who would have wreaked havoc on Breula, devastating it forever. We would not have recovered." Ori shifted over, hung her legs over the side of the bed, and held Sev's hands. "You saved the realm for the future."

***

Ori's words didn't reassure her. Maybe it was the disappearance of the nine elements that she wasn't supposed to possess. Maybe it was the disappearance of Metal permanency. Maybe it was the disappearance of hand manipulation of the four tool-based elements that provided that reassurance.

Or maybe she'd needed to feel the loss of all of it. The thought rolled around in her head as she walked with Ori down to the arena, by way of Jino and Askal's house.

"Speaking of loss," Sev mumbled.

"What?" Ori leaned into her shoulder.

"Oh, Jino and Askal. And Alex, for that matter. They probably haven't had a wink of sleep what with a bunch of Bianuwruh invading, and Alex turning up out of the blue, and I imagine they've heard about Alex's mum by now." Sev exhaled slowly as she returned the shoulder bump. She could lay money on all three not moving for twenty-four hours from the dining chairs as they filled each other in with their individual stories.

Ori slipped her hand into Sev's. "Be with your family. I'll be at the arena if you need me."

Sev tugged her to a stop, turned square on, and delivered a quick kiss, followed by a smile. "I know. You're wonderful, and I adore you."

Ori beamed, then pointed at the arena in the distance. "I must be going. I need to—"

"Go. Go do Leader of the Guard things."

The eye contact spoke of love, promised years, and hinted at possibilities for later in the day.

"Will you come to find me?"

"Always."

Sev stared after Ori, admiring her bearing, her body, and thrilled at how much her heart felt at home.

Then she opened the small gate to Jino and Askal's house. Her house.

***

Jino opened the door, and Sev was instantly enveloped in a hug.

"You did it," Jino said, as she pulled back. "You did it." Her eyes filled with tears.

"I guess. I still feel like I'm—"

"A fraud?" Alex's voice emanated from the kitchen, and Sev disentangled herself, then held Jino's hand as she led her inside.

Alex strode over, and threw his arms around her, squeezing her hard. "You're not a fraud, but nobody's going to convince you otherwise. But you're not, you know."

Sev pushed on his shoulders, scanning his face. He looked wan, pale, but relieved as if the weight of two realms had been lifted.

"You okay?" She didn't release his shoulders until he nodded.

"Yeah. It's a lot."

"I can imagine." Sev looked up, and spotted Askal hovering behind his cousin. Seeing the two together highlighted their physical similarities. All of her vague ideas and gut feelings had been proven correct. Sidestepping around Alex, she delivered another tight embrace to her mentor. He was no longer her protector. Neither was Alex. They were her relatives. Her brothers. And it felt wonderful.

Tears gathered in her eyes, they had a meeting, then they fell over the edge to course down her cheeks.

"This is a joy, and a sadness," Jino said quietly, and Sev turned to her...what was Jino? A mother figure? Not quite. Jino was Jino, who was waving at the chairs, taking the one nearest for herself, and sitting with a loud sigh.

"Queen Sermeh Reytoris Breula suggested," Jino continued, "during her quick visit this morning that I act as an advisor for the King, but I declined. I did not feel comfortable taking on that role. I would like to mentor the new seer. Openly. So that she may protect a new prophecy, then welcome the protection of the townspeople, and of the realm."

"There's a new seer?" Sev blinked at the announcement, and at Askal and Alex's subsequent nods. Clearly they'd done some intense catching up.

"I feel her presence, Sevich. I doubt she knows who she is yet. Many people do not know who they are. We grow into ourselves when we search inside, and our discoveries are tools to develop what is shown to others. She will see herself when she searches."

Sev contemplated Jino's words for a moment.

"Does the Queen know about Nowa?" Sev swiped at her wet cheeks, then tucked her knuckles under her chin, and leaned on her elbow. Tears gathered in Jino's eyes.

"Yes. I delivered that information. She suggested a ceremony of sorts. Not really the ceremony of the dead. More a ceremony of mourning." Jino nodded once. "It is a lovely gesture." She pondered Sev. "Does Orilaevar know?"

"I told her last night." Sev bobbed her head. "I needed to fill her in on so much." Then her mouth turned down, and her lips wobbled slightly. "The ceremony sounds really nice." More tears burned.

"I asked to coordinate it," Alex said softly. "I need to grieve as well."

Sev reached across the table, and curled her fingers over his hand. "Yeah. Yeah, you do, mate." They shared a watery smile, and all four sat in a silence that spoke of sorrow, yet with each breath, it spoke of serenity. Then Sev straightened.

"Where are you staying, Alex?"

Askal replied first. "He is staying here. I will find accomodation in the workshop."

Sev's mouth fell open. "Absolutely not. You'll be a mess of black, and metal shavings, and Jino will chuck a mental at the dirt."

Everyone blinked, then Jino laughed. "Oh, Sevich. It is wonderful to laugh in the depths of our grief. You keep spirits high. We will miss you but I expect many visits, please."

Sev frowned, adding a one-shoulder shrug to demonstrate her confusion.

"Where am I going?"

"I assumed you would be accommodated in the mansion," Jino said as if that was the most logical thing in the world.

A bark of laughter came from the other end of the table. "U-Hauling already? How very lesbian." Alex, familiar with Sev's narrowed eyes, simply smirked, enjoying the effect his comment had produced.

Sev growled, and flicked a finger at Askal. "How did that," she tipped her chin at Alex, "smart-arse find you?"

Askal flipped his hands in a sort of 'well, actually' gesture.

"I found him. We knew of Alex, and apparently you had told him some of our joined history. Alex knew our names. So, over the shouting of both realm's Guard, I could hear someone calling our first names only, which of course is unusual. I went to investigate, and found Alex lost inside the smoke. Besides his usage of our first names, he also exclaimed that he should have stayed in the realm of Melbourne as his only danger there was being eaten by mozzies."

He cocked his head at Alex. "What are mozzies?"

**

Sev departed after making a commitment that she'd return the next day to help Askal start the art piece for Nowa, which would be placed at the foot of the bridge over the Juith river after the ceremony. It would be a bittersweet session in the workshop. She loved working with Askal, and with her element. But the reason for the piece? So sad.

She knew the metal would understand.

The walk to the arena was a series of stops and starts as townspeople's eyes widened, their steps stuttering, as their hands flew to their chests in deference to the Guardian of the realm. It made Sev distinctly uncomfortable. *I hope the novelty wears off soon.*

The children held no such hesitation, running over, and hugging Sev about her hips, beaming up with smiles that warmed her heart. Many of them wanted precise details of the Guardian's defeat of the Bianuwruh.

"I didn't defeat anyone, kiddo," she said quietly to a girl; the daughter of a Light Arcanix whose name she couldn't place. "I balanced things. It's different."

"But their Guard was captured!"

"Of course. They need to return to Bianuwruh. This is not their realm. If they stay here, then there remains an imbalance."

Another voice piped up. "Do you still have all the elements?"

Sev ruffled his hair. "Nope. Just the one."

He shook his head sadly, clearly disappointed at her careless misplacement of such essential superpowers. Sev laughed. Not moments after the Guardian's rainbow nuclear explosion, her energy had dissipated. It had surprised her how much she really didn't miss the other elements.

"I reckon it's great just to have one. Imagine trying to ride ten horses at once." Sev grinned at the looks of horror, then nodded. "Yeah. Pretty difficult, hey?"

The group of kids huddled around her legs nodded wisely in that way kids do when an adult they respect says something that they need to analyse later but it sounds good right then.

Remembering too late that kids were masters in blackmail, Sev was wheedled into promising a veritable menagerie of silver animals for each child before being allowed to continue on her journey.

The arena's entrance came into view, and Sev spotted Ori standing outside speaking to two members of the Guard. She paused to rake her gaze over her lover, and hummed with happiness.

As soon as the Guard members left, Sev stepped up behind Ori, and snaked her arms about her waist. Ori turned, and smiled affectionately.

"Everything okay?"

Sev pulled her into a hug. "It's such a delayed grief." She leaned away, and looked into Ori's face, which filled with sympathy. "There's going to be a ceremony."

Ori nodded. "Good."

"Alex is organising it, and Askal's creating a beautiful piece of art. And Jino is off to find the new seer."

"There's a new seer?"

"Apparently, but she's hoping everyone leaves them alone to get on with their seer business."

Ori narrowed her eyes, and touched the hilt of her sword, just as she'd done last night. Sev's heart exploded with love.

"So, what Leader-ish things were you up to?"

Ori poked her in the ribs, and she dissolved into a fit of giggles.

"I'm approving leave for any Guard member who requests it." Ori ran her hands down Sev's arms. "Many feel unbalanced from yesterday so if they need to speak with the trees, then they should."

Sev stared. "Mental health, and meditation," she said, and decided that Ori couldn't be any more perfect.

"Yes. My mother also suggested that any Flora Elemental willing to accompany an Arcanix or townsperson in the evening so they, too, could talk to the trees, should do so. The Arcanix, and the townspeople may also feel unbalanced."

Privana chose that moment to appear from a nearby tunnel, and spotted Sev and Ori. He made his way over, and waited until both women faced him.

"The Bianuwruh Guard members will be ready to leave later this afternoon." His glance at Sev meant that she'd been included in the report. Incredible.

"Did anyone..? Did anyone die?" Sev asked, dreading the answer. She looked at Ori.

"No, fortunately. It is quite remarkable. We have Breulan and Bianuwruh Guard members recovering from injuries. We received damage to many buildings and the natural environment but that is the extent of our suffering."

Privana spoke up. "There are just over two hundred well-fed and healed Bianuwruh Guard members in the arena. Relieved of their weapons and motivation, many of the Guard have revealed themselves to be friendly and amenable, chatting to our Elementals and townspeople." He looked over Sev's shoulder, then brought his gaze back. "It is interesting to witness a person become acquainted with another person when their animosity is eradicated and they choose to understand," he mused.

Sev stared. "Um…"

Privana cocked his head. "Um?" His furrowed brow added to Sev's incredulity.

"Privana, you know that you and I could be these guys. Eradicating animosity, and all that."

"I do not feel we carried the extent of animosity as witnessed here," he said, frowning, and nodding simultaneously.

"Sure." She turned to Ori, and winked. "Ori, have you decided on a suitable consequence regarding the sending-Sev-through-the-portal jealousy thing?"

Ori adopted a serious expression, flattening her eyebrows. "I haven't, actually." She regarded Privana, whose face lost all colour. "Privana Trissandoral Breula, you saved Sev's life twice, and assisted in her role as Guardian, and while this is admirable, I agree with Sev that you should receive a consequence. Sev should decide."

Ori's eyes twinkled with mischief.

"Right-o." Sev delivered a top to toe scan of Ori's Deputy, who seemed to tense every muscle in worried anticipation. "Privana, you're going to spend a whole day with me learning how to use contractions."

Privana blinked, then his mouth fell open. "I do not—"

"Nope." Sev made a buzzing sound. "Try again."

Ori was vibrating with poorly contained laughter.

Privana glared. "I…" He swallowed. "I don't feel that this is—"

Sev punched him in the shoulder. "See? You're a natural."

***

The day didn't get any easier. Ori's dad called for an urgent Council meeting which Sev thought very sensible, particularly after the behaviour of Councillors Buwrec Robrong Breula and Dasoskach Vaern Breula.

She wondered if he'd be as incandescent as he was in the Let's-See-If-Sev's-The-Guardian Assessment. Probably.

She was able to judge the incandescent level herself because King Rodlamar Reytoris Breula insisted on Sev's attendance.

"Me?"

"Yes, Sevich. You are an important member of our society." He paused. "Everyone is an important member of our society. You just happen to be rather current."

Sev grinned. "Makes me sound like a viral TikTok."

Absolutely everyone within hearing range paused, and Sev hummed. "Not even explaining that." She nodded at the King. "I'll be there."

So, there she was, seated between Ori and the Queen, feeling somewhat like a fish out of water. The strained debate tumbled about the chamber.

"We must seal the Bianuwruh portal!" The shout came from a Metal Elemental directly across from Sev. She leaned into Ori's shoulder.

"Can you do that?" she whispered.

"Yes. It's an extreme measure, and has only been done once in our history."

Sev fidgeted in discomfort at the thought of the realm having to make such a monumental decision. The idea that they would do it again didn't sit well.

"Sevich, you are welcome to participate in the debates."

Sev whipped her head around to stare wide-eyed at Queen Sermeh Reytoris Breula.

"I really don't think—"

"Much of what we are deciding today impacts directly on the entire realm. You saved us last night, but beyond that, as a Breulan, you have every right to add your thoughts." The Queen gave a slight smile of encouragement.

Sev nodded, took a deep breath, and another, then stood on shaky legs.

"I...I have something to say." By the time she sent out the final word, her voice sounded impressively strong. Even if she wasn't feeling the same inside. After reminding herself that last night she threw an entire door's worth of metal panels across one-hundred metres of marble, so holding court to a handful of Councillors was a walk in the park, Sev repeated her statement.

"I have something to say."

All conversation ceased, and heads turned to regard her. A range of expressions met Sev's sudden intrusion into the meeting. Mostly interested. Some were of the 'who-does-she-think-she-is?' variety.

I'm the Guardian, you patronising arseholes.

Technically, she wasn't. Not anymore. But the words felt confident. Courageous. And her heart settled.

"I don't think you should close the portal to Bianuwruh."

Mumbles met her statement.

"Why should we leave it open when we were invaded by their Guard?" The same Metal Elemental stood abruptly.

"Look, I get your point, but..." Sev shook her hands out in front of her body. "Look, imagine you're in a realm that sucks. The government is a dictatorship. They hate your kind, whatever that kind is. So they chase you, and stick you in jail or whatever incarceration there looks like. Your life is not a life. It's an existence. So you need to escape." She gestured hopefully at the Elemental, then scanned the room. "We can't close the portal because we don't know if there are other portals for the Bianuwruh people to go through. What if we're the only realm that is even vaguely friendly? If you were one of those people, you'd need to know that there was a way to escape. Even if it's simply a hope."

Sev exhaled loudly. Right. She'd said what her brain, and heart were desperate to share. Then she caught the nods. The smiles. The interest on the faces of more than half of the Councillors.

"But the trespassers sometimes are not—"

"Who they say they are?" Ori quickly stood beside Sev, who swallowed thickly. She wanted to slide her hand along Ori's palm, clutch her fingers, and rest her head on Ori's shoulder.

Sev caught the slight chin lift of the proud leader, the fearless woman, and breathed in the goodness that was everything about her lover.

"I know some trespassers will not be as they claim, but most are people who the Bianuwruh leadership despise," Ori said, her voice ringing out over the marble, up the steps into the two rows of seats, and climbing the walls to drift into the arched beams at the ceiling.

"Who are we to close a portal based on information we do not have. We can only act with the information we do have."

"How will we monitor this portal? We will need to increase our patrols," a Flora Councillor stated, very logically if Ori's nods were any indication.

"Yes. I will begin by assigning a group of Guard members exclusively to that portal as of this afternoon when the Bianuwruh Guard have been escorted back to their realm." Ori crossed her arms, and cast her gaze about the room. Nobody was going to argue with her. Not with all those muscles, and straight eyebrows. Sev's lips quirked involuntarily. The stance reminded her of their first interaction months ago in the Facility.

"Of course, those trespassers will still need to be held in the Facility." A Dark Elemental, seated only a few places past the King, struggled to his feet, and grasped the walking stick leaning against the small table attached to the arm of his chair.

Sev had many, many opinions about the Facility, and the arena for that matter.

Which Ori knew.

"Go for it," she whispered, and sat, giving Sev the metaphorical stage. Another wave of love washed through Sev's heart.

"Okay. So, I agree with you." She peered around King Rodlamar Reytoris Breula, and pointed at the elderly Councillor. "Speaking as someone who's been a trespasser who was held in the Facility, and then made to participate in the assessment, I can categorically say that I think the idea of the Facility is actually fine. The trespassers get food, and somewhere to sleep, and medical aid, and…it's good. Breula cares for these people." She swallowed down tears.

"But I truly believe." Her voice wobbled. "If you insist on having trespassers demonstrate their elements by engaging in combat" She thrust out her hand, and touched a finger. "By pitting one element against another, even though you're not supposed to because it unbalances the realm." She tapped another finger. "By making trespassers do it because you say that trespassers aren't Breulan yet, so they don't unbalance the realm when they fight." Sev took a breath. "Then you're just as awful as the realm that the trespassers have run away from in the first place."

Sev's heart was shaking, and she breathed quietly through her teeth.

"How will we know who is truly a potential Arcanix, and who is a trespasser?" The Councillor, sitting in the first row in front of Sev, turned, and shook her head in puzzlement. She seemed genuinely perplexed. Sev couldn't answer the question. Not only because she had no idea how to answer it in the first place, but also it wasn't her position to answer it. She sank into her seat, and glanced at the King. Her hand twitched because she really wanted to deliver a five-finger point, as if to say, "All yours."

The King must have read Sev's mind, because he stood, patting the air so that the Councillor in front sat down, then addressed the chamber.

"We will ask them."

An uproar of voices met this simple statement.

"They will not tell the truth!"

"We must assess them properly!"

"How do we know if they deserve to be in Breula?"

That last sentence seemed to be the spark that lit the King's anger.

"Deserve?" he thundered. His eyes had narrowed, and his hand, used to elaborate his words, curled into a fist.

"You want to know how we should determine if a trespasser deserves to remain in Breula? It should not be with elemental combat. I agree with Sevich."

Sev's eyebrows shot up, and she gaped at Ori's father.

"This word. *Deserve.*" The word fell out of his mouth as if it was too sour to remain on his tongue. "It is laden with judgement." He gestured at the Metal Elemental over the other side of the circular seating. "Councillor Xuh Vel Breula. Do you deserve the position of Councillor?"

The man spluttered. "Of course. It is my right as an Elemental!"

The King smiled thinly. "But how do we know you are up to the task?"

"I am an Elemental, and a Councillor," he said loudly, as if that answered King Rodlamar Reytoris Breula's question. Which it didn't.

The King wasn't done.

"So you say."

His voice grew quiet. Not the good quiet. More the quiet of someone about to rip another person to shreds.

"Currently being held in the Guard quarters are two Councillors not worthy of their role. Perhaps Councillors should undergo an assessment with arbitrary criteria before taking up their position?"

Three Councillors immediately stood in protest. "We do not need to be assessed to prove our worth!"

Sev felt movement beside her. Queen Sermeh Reytoris Breula didn't need to stand. She had command of the entire space with a raised eyebrow and four words.

"Oh? That is interesting."

As one, like children caught out in a lie, the three Councillors registered the verbal trap they'd walked into, and flushed. The Queen didn't tolerate fools, and when presented with three at once, clearly chose to expend the least amount of energy dismissing their blustering antics. Sev smiled to herself. Getting to know Ori's mum was going to be awesome.

"As you can see, assessments must have relevance, and be delivered with care." The King sighed, and stretched out his arms placatingly. "I know these are not easy concepts to dwell upon. We will not solve these issues today, or in the near future. But one thing has been demonstrated over the last few months. It is the idea that our traditions can change while maintaining their significance, so let us focus on that thought during our meetings."

Sev heard Ori's grunt. "Good."

"I would like to share another view that occupied my mind until yesterday." The Council seemed to hold their breath. "Months ago, I was discussing with an Elemental, an exceptional person whom I respect highly, the supposed hypothetical event of a Guard invading our realm."

Sev felt Ori straighten. Taking a glance sideways, Sev caught Ori's quick swallow, then another, her eyes glistening with tears.

"This Elemental and I shared our thoughts about who would defend Breula against such a calamity. I stated categorically that Elementals would do so." He shook his head, and gestured at the Council. "But I was wrong, because yesterday we were saved by Arcanix, townspeople, and Elementals. And because of this, we rebalanced the realm not just with the elements coursing through the Guardian." He nodded at Sev. "But with an understanding that a separation of people due to an archaic societal organisation becomes irrelevant when presented with an event that affects all." He inclined his head regally, the first of such gestures that Sev had seen in the entire meeting.

"As I mentioned previously, traditions *can* change while maintaining their significance. We must hold this thought as the conduit through which to pass any future discussions."

This was the epiphany, the change, that Ori had wanted to see in Breula, and Sev slid her hand across to quickly squeeze Ori's fingers in acknowledgement.

Then Ori cleared her throat, flicked her fingers against her eyelids, and stood. With a long look at her father, which ended in a mutual smile, she marched down the steps into the centre of the chamber. She glared at the Councillors, almost challenging them to dismiss her presence. None turned away.

"The consequences for Councillors Dasoskach Vaern Breula, and Buwrec Robrong Breula must be decided today. The Guard should not hold them indefinitely."

Silence expanded inside the room, and glances met other glances. Sev rolled her eyes. Forty-eight people obviously wanted Ori to solve this by herself.

Ori shook her head briefly, and Sev knew that she'd reached the same conclusion.

"I assume you all agree that these two Councillors do not deserve to occupy the position." Ori's commanding voice rang out, and Sev gazed at her. Inappropriately, given the moment, she mentally divested Ori of every article of clothing. Then blushed as she remembered that Ori's mum sat one chair to her right, and, according to Ori, could read minds.

Time to focus.

"I needn't point out that they unbalanced our realm almost to the point of no return. They cast aside their love of the elements. They choked the energy from their orb." Ori turned slowly to make eye contact with the entire chamber..

"Therefore, I put forward the motion that they are stripped of their orbs."

General muttering of agreement followed this statement. Disagreement wasn't ever going to be likely. It would have been a brave, or foolish, soul that thought those particular Councillors could parade about with their jewellery after the last few months of planning. Ori's motion meant that Councillors Dasoskach Vaern Breula, and Buwrec Robrong Breula would no longer be Councillors.

They'd no longer be Elementals.

Sev winced.

The Councillors seemed to think that dispossessing an Elemental of their orb was such a severe consequence that they couldn't possibly contemplate something more devastating. But there were a few thousand townspeople who would have a strong opinion about that. They didn't possess orbs, and for the Councillors to gasp about relinquishing theirs meant that, to them, becoming a townsperson was the most awful thing in the world.

Sev was reminded strongly of a movie she'd seen where the upper class referred to the townspeople as the 'unwashed masses'. But she knew many Elementals regarded townspeople as equals. Many Elementals could, and would relinquish their orbs without hesitation, because yesterday Ori and fifteen Light Elemental Guard members had given their orbs freely, so—

Sev leaned into Queen Sermeh Reytoris Breula's space. "Why can't townspeople be on the Council?"

The Queen blinked. "I...do not know. It has only ever been Elementals." Her lips parted in realisation, and she held Sev's gaze. "The orbs are the energy source that denotes an Elemental. If an Elemental were to surrender their orb, then they are only able to access their energy in daylight."

"What if Councillors were chosen from the whole population? Elementals, and townspeople. The townspeople would have to be given an orb so that they could continue their Council tasks at night, but perhaps this is a way to respect those who do not possess an orb normally. Maybe make it an honour to wear one. Much like the honour of possessing an element. Sixteen Arcanix and townspeople wore an orb yesterday. Proudly, respectfully, using the orb's permanency to lead people to safety. It can be done."

Sev blinked, stunned that she'd basically told the Queen how to reorganise the government of Breula.

A warm hand covered her own, and she looked up into kindhearted eyes.

"Sevich, your idea will need time to come to fruition. As my husband said; traditions take time to change, but can do so if people are reassured that the traditions remain significant." Ori's mum smiled. "I am very pleased that you felt comfortable to share your thoughts with me." She patted Sev's hand. "Perhaps we should take notice of the meeting. My daughter does not look impressed at our inattention."

Sev snapped her head around. Ori was staring up at her mother, then she shifted her gaze to Sev, and furrowed her brow.

Sev waved her hand quickly, and mouthed, "All good."

It was.

***

It was Ori's idea to wander in the fields beyond the mansion, explaining that the Council meeting had created a jumble of thoughts that cluttered their minds, and so needed tossing into the breeze to float amongst the wind wolves.

It was an excellent idea.

Sev held Ori's hand, running her thumb over the soft skin. "More," she murmured, and smiled at Ori's mock sigh as they stopped to face each other.

"More kissing? It's just as well we have no destination because with so many stops, we—"

Sev pulled Ori's head down, and delivered a kiss filled with such passion that they moaned simultaneously. She slid her hands onto Ori's cheeks, broke the kiss, and sighed happily.

"I love you."

Ori pushed out a slow breath. "Those three words are exquisite. Exquisite to hear, and to say." She smiled softly. "I love you." Then she cocked her head. "It hasn't escaped me that you are here only because two Councillors invited a foreign Guard into Breula."

Sev shook her head. "Ori, that's not why I'm here." She threaded her fingers through Ori's. "That prophecy is a thousand years old which means it could have changed over time. In Melbourne, in fact all over the world, there's a game where one person whispers a sentence to the next person, and each person must pass on that sentence in line." Sev kissed Ori's knuckles. "Sometimes some people in the line don't hear the sentence correctly, which means that by the time it reaches the end, the sentence has changed so much that it's lost its original meaning. Replace the people in the game with chunks of time, and you can see my analogy." She kissed Ori's knuckles on her other hand.

"Many children's games are reflections of the vagaries of society." Ori guided Sev's arm around her back, and draped hers across Sev's shoulders. The wandering in the fields restarted.

Sev bumped against Ori's side. "Exactly. So the current version of the prophecy says that the Guardian arrives to rescue the realm from great danger." Sev waited for Ori's nod. "But, what if the original prophecy said that the Guardian arrives in Breula to *remind* the realm of great danger. A great danger such as forgetting about balance like Buwrec Robrong and Dasoskach Vaern did. Such as forgetting that love for the elements and from the elements is essential. Such as the danger of forgetting about love. Maybe the Guardian arrived in Breula to rescue herself. To find herself." Sev turned square on to Ori. "To find you."

Ori gazed over Sev's shoulder for a while, then returned it, crinkling the skin around her eyes as she smiled.

"Like I found you."

"Yes."

"You should inform Jino of the potential for prophecy misinterpretation."

Sev laughed. "I reckon she knows." Then she relished the sight of Ori's blue eyes darkening as desire whisked through them. Ori had said that Sev's laugh aroused her. Also Sev's smile. Her hair. Her sarcasm. There was a list. Sev grinned, and dropped her gaze to Ori's lips, then dragged it back up.

"More?" Ori asked.

"Always."

And with that, Ori gently held Sev's chin between her thumb and forefinger, and leaned close, her lips not quite touching Sev's.

"I'm glad you fell through the portal at the back of your laundromat," Ori whispered, then covered Sev's smile with a kiss.

Sev luxuriated in the shower, her body still vibrating from the orgasm Ori had given her not five minutes ago. She'd been instructed not to enter the bedroom as Ori had a surprise, and arriving early would spoil it.

The anticipation made her light-headed.

Ducking under the hot water, she wondered if Ori would dance the Valwith for her at the next festival. The very important question she was going to ask Ori when she finished the intricate ring next week would compliment the dance beautifully. Her heart filled with love, and longing, and of her joy in their life. Their union.

Deciding that she'd delayed long enough, Sev shut off the shower, and wrapped one of the ubiquitous textured towels around her body.

Then froze.

Her palm sizzled, and she stared at the skin, unable to see a reason for the odd sensation. It was like a toy taser had touched down briefly, then disappeared.

Suddenly, a light, neon blue, crackled to life in her hand, and miniature sparks hovered above the veins.

Sev gaped, and stretched out her arm, squinting at the tiny electrical storm cradled by her palm.

Then, after a long moment, a grin slowly slid onto her lips.

"Hello, little blue light. What do you do?"

The End

I sincerely hope you enjoyed reading 'Outcast'. If you did, I would greatly appreciate a review on your favourite book website such as Goodreads or Amazon. Maybe a tweet. Or even a recommendation in your favourite Facebook sapphic fiction group. Reviews and recommendations are crucial for any author, and even just a line or two can make a huge difference. Thanks!

Coming Home
GCLS Goldie Award finalist
LesFic Bard Award finalist

Kick Back
GCLS Goldie Award finalist

An Unexpected Gift: Christmas in Australia: Five Short Stories

Art of Magic
GCLS Goldie Award finalist (cover design)
LesFic Bard Award finalist (cover design)
Lesfic Bard Award winner (romance)
Silver Medalist eLit Award

Change of Plans
GCLS Goldie Award finalist

Ignis
GCLS Goldie Award winner (Romantic Blend)

The Forever and The Now

Kjauthor.com

Printed in Great Britain
by Amazon

49482578R00188